The Garden of Eva

The Garden of Eva

Ana Waterman

The Garden of Eva

Ana Waterman

Names, characters, places, and incidents are either the product of the author's imagination or are used fictitiously.
Any resemblance to actual persons, living or dead, locations, or events is entirely coincidental.

ISBN   978-0-9729824-6-7   (digital)
ISBN   978-0-9729824-8-1   (paperback)

Printed in the United States of America.

To Ralph

My best friend and the love of my life.

Every girl deserves a man such as Ralph.

Acknowledgment

The Mighty Majestic Mildred
(aka Triple Trumpet plant)

The Mighty Majestic Mildred's message is this:

Make a magnificent difference in your world, and in the
lives of the ones you love.
Never back down on what you know to be right and
good.

Acknowledgment continued

This book might not have come to fruition had it not been for the constant encouragement of my dear friend, mentor, and a Southern author, Mildred Nelson Holmes.

Mildred is one of the most amazing ladies I have ever had the privilege of knowing and loving. Everyone needs and deserves a friend, such as Mildred! Her bold personality brings out the best in everyone around her. Her tell-it-like-it-is-tongue will never lie or candy-coat-it when a person asks her what she thinks of a particular situation. When her advice is taken, the results will always be for the betterment of all concerned. She's long-headed like that.

Love

Love, like friendship, is something you cannot wish for, hope for, or even pray for. You cannot make it happen. It comes to you slowly, just as surely as night turns into day.

Mildred Nelson Holmes

Love

Love is a decision made in the heart.
Ana Waterman

Love and Happiness

Al Green sings lyrics
written by Allen Georgio

Love and happiness
Make you do right; Love'll make you do wrong
Make you come home early   Make you stay out all
night long
The power of love

The Garden of Eva

These 69 chapters are titled by the names of the
flowers in Eva's garden.
Each flower's meaning and symbolism are revealed
after the title.
Each meaning is interwoven into the story.

Table of Contents

Preface

Whether you believe it to be a scientific theory, Biblical fact, or a fairy tale, most people would agree that at the beginning of civilization on earth, two people were the original Mother and Father of all human beings. Their names were Adam and Eve.

The story is that in the beginning, they had no sin, or should I say, they made no mistakes in their paradise of a simple life on earth. Because Eve was new in the area, she did not know who was who. One day, Eve started talking to a good-looking, silver-tongued, slim guy called Sly. He was bad company, but Eve took his lousy advice. To put it simply, after she took his terrible advice, all hell broke loose!

Suddenly, Adam looked at Eve and saw that she was naked and beautiful. He suddenly had the urge to do something. Although Adam did not know what it was that he wanted to do, he did it anyway, and he was glad that he did it. Eve was not so happy. Shortly after he did what he had done, his wife, Eve, started to get fat and fatter as the days went by. Then she was unhappy with her appearance. Moodiness overtook her, then she started bitching at Adam. Poor Adam, he did not know what he had done to upset his new wife.

Within nine months, Eve was having labor pains! She was screaming in agony from labor pains and suffering the tortures of regret from ever speaking to that damn-ole-lying-slimy-Sly! She wondered, *what the hell is this little slippery-pudgy-thing that's painfully sliding out of me that looks strangely like a small Adam's apple*? The little thing just worked it is way out of her with what appeared to be a vine attached. She picked up the red blob of slim and rushed to show it to Adam. On the way, she tripped over a bush, and the vine got tangled, severing the vine in half and the blob fell to the ground with a thud. Suddenly the blob started making an animal-like screeching sound. Eve picked up the screeching-screaming-bloody-blob once again. When she did, the blob latched itself onto her breast and started sucking. She was from then on known as Mother Eve.

When Eve showed the new creature to Adam, she said, "You are man, you name all the creatures of the earth. What will you call this new creature?"

Adam said, "I am tired of naming creatures; I *cain* think of a name." So, they called it *Cain*.

Another creature followed shortly after that. Adam said, "I'm not *able* to think of another name." So they called the next creature *Able*.

Thus, Eve had delivered the second generation of sinners: Cain and Able.

If we could talk to Mother Eve today, what advice would she give us girls concerning the mistakes she made?

Mother Eve's advice would be simple, for she lived in a simple world. I think she would say:

- ***Be wary when talking to strangers.***
- ***Be cautious of the company you keep, and with whom you take your advice.***
- ***Do not make the same mistake twice.***

It would be impossible to talk with Mother Eve today. There is, however, another well-experienced and savvy lady who can help navigate us through the mysteries of life and explain how to enjoy living in our *Garden of Paradise* in the new world in which we live today.

Eva Adams tells her life story through

The Garden of Eva.

Enjoy and learn!

From the Author

This lascivious romance novel was intended to share a beautiful love story about two people who desperately wanted to share their lives together.

Somehow, while writing, I found myself revealing details of my own personal life and lessons learned along the way. I realized I knew a great deal about love, life, and sex. I felt compelled to share that information with you, my readers.

This information on sexology is the interaction of the sexes. It also has to do with our sexual life, sexual behavior, sexual attitude, and our knowledge of sex education. All this added together, has to do with our relationships when dealing with the opposite sex.

When we know and better understand our own sexuality, we can better control, predict, and enjoy our sexual events.

The lessons expressed in this book are merely those of an experienced, seasoned lady. Feel free to use them at your discretion, or not.

Your friend,

Ana

Foreword

Assuming the reader would want to put faces to the characters in this story, let us cut to the chase and do so right off.

The protagonist of the story is young Eva. Think of her as the young, beautiful YOU. The younger Eva is naïve and inexperienced to the world but has a unique way of covering it up by acting as if she knows more than she does.

The <u>real heroine</u> is the older Eva, the one who is sharing her story retrospectively from her more seasoned point of view. From her, you will learn more than you ever thought was possible from one little book on life, love, and sex. You can imagine a gruff-tell-it-like-it-is type of gal, leading you through her past love life and giving advice on how to better live your life and encouraging you not to make the same mistakes she has made. She knows a little bit about a lot of things and a lot of things about a few things. But if you were to ask her about something, she would just bullshit-ya-about-everything! She's just savvy like that.

Last but not least, the hero and prince charming of the story would look like whoever-your-dream-boat-guy would look like. The tall-dark-and-handsome, tough guy that you love-to-hate-at-first, but you love-to-make-love-to-all-the-time. Can he ever be tamed into the man that will respect you and love you for the lady that you are? Who the hell knows?

Let us take that sultry journey, learn, and enjoy.

xvii

Introduction

Consider the rose. For many, it is thought to be the most beautiful of all the flowers in the garden. From a distance, its vibrant colors are captivating, drawing you closer for more of its sweet fragrance, ever closer for more of its pleasantries. There you are, wanting more of that rose. You must touch it, and you must have it. The petals are soft and smooth to touch. Once you have it within your grasp, you realize the rose has thorns that will prick you and hurt you when you are close. You must handle the rose with extreme care if you are to enjoy it to its fullest.

So, there he was; I had found my rose, who would be the love of my life and my biggest challenge. He was so utterly beautiful, so soft and tender. He was exponentially pleasurable intimately, but every rose has its thorns. He could cause so much pain in so many other ways; I needed to learn how to handle this rose if I was going to enjoy him to the fullest. It would take many sultry, tumultuous years for this rose to go from a bud to full blossom. It was a sweet yet thorny growing experience. It was worth the wait for me to tame my rose.

"It is harder to fight against pleasure than against anger." Aristotle

Chapter 1 Behold the Rose!

The rose represents the birth flower of June.

No matter what the color may be, the rose always symbolizes *Love.*

I had always heard the phrase 'Tall, Dark and Handsome.' On the other hand, I had never met such a man; I had only seen those men in the movies. It was by happenstance that I met Mr. Tall, Dark, and Handsome, or better yet said, Mr. 'Wonderful–make–you–cream–your–panties-wonderful!'

It happened this way:

It was in the spring of the year 1984. I was thirty-two years of age with an eleven-year-old little boy whom I adored; his name was Nathan. I had been married for a little over thirteen years in an unhappy marriage. I knew it was going to fail from the very first year after I had endured his raging screams and fits of anger.

In spite of that, I was determined to stay in the marriage for the sake of Nathan; I did not want him to be a child from a broken family. I realize now that was a mistake; a good divorce is better than a bad marriage. A bad marriage can do more harm than good to a child's mental stability. But I will talk more about that later.

My husband and I had recently moved our family from Birmingham to a small southern town called New Fort, which was a ritzy, cosmopolitan old town, run mostly by the upper crust of society. New Fort was located on the sunny, warm Gulf Coast of Alabama, and was known as the *bedroom community* for the people residing in New Fort yet working in Mobile. The quaint little sailing, fishing, and golfing retirement town was known throughout the nation as one of the safest places to live, work, and play. The downtown streets were immaculately groomed daily with freshly planted flowers on almost every corner. The 100-year-old buildings were always under renovation to keep up the nostalgia from the town's history.

The town square was remarkably old-fashioned with more luscious flowers, and park benches under a gazebo on which to sit and feed the birds or have a picnic. In the center of the town square was a big round wading pool with a large fountain of cool water in the middle flowing and spurting high into the air. Well-wishers threw their pennies into the pool regularly to make-a-wish. The children splashed around in the pool daily during the hot summer days to cool themselves.

Then there was the pride of the town; that tall, black-wrought-iron, 80-year-old clock, which stood on the corner of Main and North Street. The town founders donated the clock in 1904. It was loved by all who passed by it, residents and tourist alike. Although the clock had been broken for several years, it always read 2:15. But that was okay, we figured the time was correct at least twice a day.

Because New Fort was located on Mobile Bay, boating, swimming, fishing, and sailing were merely a way of life for the rich and poor alike. Anyone living in New Fort lived a good life.

We brought our small family pool business with us when we moved down and reopened it in New Fort. My husband, Cody and I managed it together. On this crisp, sunshiny, spring morning, I needed to have a key made.

I walked into the local hardware store that was located across the street from my new business. Being new in town, I did not know many people, nor who was who. As I walked in the front door, which was propped open by a wooden wedge, no sound was heard. No one was around, only him. There he was, sitting on a tall stool, wearing khaki pants and a stiffly starched, white shirt with sleeves he had rolled up to just above his Rolex. His shoes were highly polished. A slight sinful smile was just below his thick, black mustache as he asked, "may I help you?" I could feel my heart rate spike when I made eye contact with him.

This gorgeous man did not fit the type of person that would be working in a hardware store. *Where were all the other employees*? I wondered. I was embarrassed! He was the best-looking man that I had ever laid eyes on! He truly fits the bill of 'Tall, Dark, and Handsome' in real life!

What a handsome devil! I thought. I could almost feel his brown bedroom eyes penetrating through me as he narrowed them in curiosity while observing me, waiting for my response.

"I need to have a key made," I said in a voice that was nervously two octaves above normal. I felt my voice lilt uncontrollably at the end of the sentence. I handed the original key to Mr. 'Tall, Dark and Handsome.' He softly and slowly took it out of my hand, stroking my palm with his index finger while looking me in the eye. That 'stroke-in-the-palm-thing' meant something, and we both knew it. It felt like the beginning of a spark in a fire that would never be put out.

"Okay, I can help you with that," his voice was warm and seductive as he walked toward the key-making machine; I followed him. He stood over six feet tall and smelled of expensive aftershave lotion that I had never smelled. It was not overwhelming, just clean, and mildly manly. His salt and pepper hair looked distinguished. As he leaned in to find the right key form, I could see his chest hair slightly above his unbuttoned first button. He was fumbling to find the proper key form, and I could tell he might not have known what he was doing.

In his smooth, baritone voice, he said softly to himself, "let me see, no that one doesn't match either." Then he looked at me and said, "this must be a Russian key." I thought, *Oh hell! Is a Russian key a bad thing, cheap thing or what?* I was embarrassed. Then he asked, "what does this key go to?" I replied, "to a U- Store-It." I wondered if he had noticed that I had slightly slobbered as my lips were quivering with my response to him. Hope not!

I should have responded with something bright, like, "The key goes to my apartment, would you like a copy?" But I didn't say that; it wouldn't have been a brilliant idea, not at that time anyway. I could tell that handsome Devil was interested in me and I didn't know how to respond to him. No man that beautiful had ever paid that kind of attention to me in my entire life. But I could get used to it, and I could learn how to better respond to him in the way he wants a woman to respond.

Get it out of your head, Eva; you'll never see him again, my good-girl-subconscious scolded me for those lustful thoughts that I was enjoying.

There isn't a woman alive who doesn't love to know that a man finds her physically attractive.

He told me to come back tomorrow when the other employees would be back at work. They were all in the warehouse that day taking inventory. They would know more about how to find the proper key form and would be able to help me. I could feel his breath on my face as he leaned a little closer when he spoke; it was lovely. *I knew* he didn't look like the usual man working in a hardware store. So, who was he, and why was he there?

I told my good-girl-subconscious to, *shut-up! You were wrong. See, I will get to see him again!*

He introduced himself as Alexander Rosenberg, one of the owners of the store. He said I could call him Alex. He laughed as he jokingly said, "Some folks call me Alex Rottenberg." I would later learn why. But for this day it was a delightful surprise to make the acquaintance of Alex Rosenberg. I told him my name was Eva, Eva Adams.

We managed to make a little more conversation, mostly small talk, about the wheelbarrows they had on sale and how they were a good buy, should someone need one. We both knew that neither of us was interested in talking about those wheelbarrows. Had anyone in the store been noticing, they would have known full well that we were chemically charged and enjoying one another's company. Not having any experience with a man of his caliber, I knew if I stayed too long, I would show my ignorance. The time had come for me to depart. I thanked him for his politeness and his out of the ordinary assistance. With that said, I glanced down to check for a wedding band, none. Hmm! Good!

I then headed out his door and back across the street to my own little family business, knowing full well that he was watching my every move. Remembering my past modeling training: walk slowly, tuck your butt, shoulders back, and chin up. Standing straight and trying to act as confidently as possible, I started walking across the street and thinking, *Oh God! Please don't let me turn my ankle, or trip over a rock, or frog, or anything else for that matter while I wasn't looking down---with my nose in the air.* Then I thought, *Oh hell! Why did I have to wear these old faded blue jeans and tennis shoes today?*

Reaching the other side of the street, I turned around to see if he was watching me. That handsome devil was standing outside of the building, with one foot propped against the wall, smoking a cigarette, watching my every move! (Yes, men *can* see better than you think they can!) To say it mildly, I creamed my panties! Hmm! Giving him one final smile, I coyly lowered my head, turned, and walked into my small business.

When comfortably inside, my face was hot and flushed, and my heart was about to pound out of my chest. I was breathlessly thinking, *what are the chances that a little ole vanilla girl like me would catch the attention of a man like that? And who would have ever thought that the Devil wore a Rolex?*

Deep thoughts came to me as I was reminded that nothing *just happens*; it is the Law of Cause and Effect.

<u>The Universal Law of Cause and Effect</u> states that for every **effect,** there is a precise **cause**, also for every **cause**, there is a determined **effect**. Your every thought, and every action create special **effects** that personify your life as you know it. If you are unhappy with the **effects** you have made, then you must change the **causes**

that created them in the first place. Change your way of doing things, and you can change your life. Transform your way of thinking, and you will change your future.
https://www.blog.igmatrix.com/law-of-cause-effect
As I was further thinking, I remembered the wise words from a former mentor:

"If there is anything in life you want, go and get it, don't wait for someone to give it to you."

Was Alex Rosenberg one of those things in life that I should 'go and get' if I wanted him?

Could Alex Rosenberg be the real man I had been waiting and searching for all along? He was everything all in one, as far as I could see that day. I knew some things needed to be changed in my life if I were to win this man over permanently. Likewise, he had some behavioral tweaking that needed to be done (but I would see to that later when he was unaware.)

Mr. Rosenberg, what a spellbinding rose he was! He looked good, he smelled good. I just knew he would feel good, should I have the unique opportunity to get closer. What I did not know at that time was how painful that feeling could be--coming from that thorny rose.

That is why they make a rose trellis, you know; so you can train a rose to grow in the direction in which you desire.

It would be a long, painful, growing experience. . . to bend my rose and get him ready for me. It would be especially painful for me at times. But it would prove to be worth the wait and having to put up with those damn rose thorns along the way.

Chapter 2 The Lovely Little Violet

Violets represent loyalty, devotion, and faithfulness.

I, Eva, had lived a somewhat sheltered life with little exposure to the more beautiful things of the world, or to the elite world of which I had a great desire to be a part of.

I was married to a controlling man at the early age of nineteen. Cody would rather rant and rave to get his way than consider the feelings of his wife and child. It has been said that *failure is an event, not a person.* I tried to

9

remind myself that the many failed events leading up to my failed marriage were not all my fault, although I certainly had been assigned the blame. I thought of my marriage as a big rock, with every unfortunate event that occurred taking a chip off that rock. One small chip at a time, my foundation of marriage was chipped away almost to a tiny pebble after thirteen years of his verbal abuse. He beat me one time. I told myself I deserved it, and I put up with it and stayed. I vowed it would never happen again. I had seen that type of abuse as a child while growing up in a violent family environment. I was determined not to live in violence again. Except, for some reason, I felt trapped with this verbally abusive and overbearing man. I should have known better. Well, getting married at the age of nineteen, what did I know about men or life for that matter? I had only a few dates in high school.

I met Cody while attending modeling school in Birmingham, Alabama, when I was eighteen. He was ten years older than I and handsome. He had a steady job and a beautiful new car; I was impressed. I should have taken my first clue when I heard him yell at his mother, but I didn't. I thought she deserved that too. I learned later:

The way a man treats his mother is the way he will treat his wife.

Cody was always jealous of my modeling career. He was suspicious that men were watching me and trying to flirt with me. It was no wonder my career never got off the ground, with a ball and chain like him holding me down. I could not realize my hopes and dreams of becoming a successful model with him lurking and criticizing every job I went on. Then there was my employment as an executive secretary for a large corporation. The job paid very well, and I loved it. He hated it. He demanded that I quit that fantastic job and stay home, so I did. I was his bird in a cage. It was soon that I found myself pregnant with my pride and joy, Nathan.

Nathan was born in 1973. He was a beautiful and precocious child. He brought sunshine to every room that he entered. Nathan was like his mother, headstrong. He brought joy and happiness wherever he went. He was unlike his father, who was happy to be unhappy. Nathan's trait of joy came in handy when times were loathsome around the house. He hated confrontations. He avoided them at all cost. Our mother-son team had to stick together to make the best of things from time-to-time. We could always cheer one another up when yelling and screaming would erupt, and it did quite often.

Nevertheless, a bad marriage or not, I was determined to make the best of it. I did not want Nathan to be a child from a broken home. I learned after 28 years of torture that a good divorce is better than a bad marriage, at least as far as the children are concerned.

Cody was continually finding fault with me for one reason or another. I should be helping Nathan with his homework more. The house was not clean enough to please him. The laundry should have been done more often. I could not cook as well as my sister-in-law. I was never going to be his perfect wife. Then there were his expectations in bed, which were far less than what I would call a pleasant experience. Therefore, I will not speak of it *at this time.*

I was slowly slipping deeply into insecurity about myself. It is hard for a little flower to grow when someone is trampling it into the ground every time it sprouts new growth. A little violet does not grow too large anyway. I wasn't asking for much. So, where do you go for self-esteem and ego building when you do not get it at home? If you cannot pull it out from within, it is hard to find it elsewhere. Nathan and I lived in a pesky world in which no one else knew. Keeping up a good image in public was what we were doing well, and we did it very well. No one ever knew what went on in our home, and we were not talking. It would have been too embarrassing for anyone to know the truth.

This little violet had to decide whether to continue to be trampled down or to spread her roots on to better soil, where she could grow and mature into the beautiful flower that she was meant to be.

Remembering the Law of Cause and Effect, I decided it was time to grow, I didn't know how I was going to do it, but I would find a way. I had to set a new course if I was to change my destiny.

There was not a day that went by that I did not think of Alex Rosenberg. I would look out my store window to see if I could spot Mr. Rosenberg or shall I say Mr. Wonderful? Sometimes I would see him getting out of his car and walking into his hardware store. But where was he going? I never saw him inside the store again, although I visited there often in hopes of seeing him. One day as he was getting out of his car, he glanced ever so casually over my way. He caught me looking at him; I was embarrassed that he saw me, for I knew that he knew I was looking for him. He looked gorgeous that day. He was standing tall in his black pants and white shirt, his jacket was thrown over his left shoulder, as he was walking toward his hardware store. He looked stimulating in black and white, as it complimented his salt and pepper black hair. I wondered why he did not have on a wedding band the day I met him. A lot of men are married, but they do not wear their wedding bands. Was he one of those men?

Yeah! He is probably married, with four kids and one in the oven. He probably has a tall, beautiful, well-educated, and sophisticated wife who meets him at the door each night with a cocktail in hand. She probably has dinner ready and the table set, complete with candles. I bet she uses her best china, crystals, and silver at each meal, just for him. They probably have a conversation about whatever he wants to talk about, business or pleasure trips while sitting in an elegant dining room. I imagine after dinner and cocktails each night they make mad, passionate love, while she wears the sexiest of lingerie – for his eyes only! Then I thought,

I could be that type of wife if I were married to a man like that. If only I had that chance!

Chapter 3 The Goldenrod

The goldenrod represents encouragement.

It was the beginning of fall that year, but not many trees in the deep south had started to turn their captivating yellows, orange, and red. The northern part of Alabama had barely begun to welcome fall, but not yet for the lower part of our state. We were continuing to enjoy warm days and cool evenings. It was the perfect time of year to walk along the beach barefoot and watch the golden sunset as the seagulls and pelicans fished for their dinner.

My aunt Patty, who lived in Mobile, told me that the Glee Girls were taking auditions for a few vacancies. I did not think I would be selected for this fantastic chorus, but Aunt Patty persuaded me to try out for it anyway. The Glee Girls were well-known as a show chorus that entertained with their song and dance. Songs were sung in A cappella, four-part harmony. I had always wanted to sing and show off as a little girl, so this could be my outlet to spread my wings and grow. I finally had the encouragement to step up and step out. So, I wanted to audition to join the group. Cody did not like it! He pitched a temper-tantrum and tried to bully me into not joining the group. I tried to ignore him. Whenever I would ignore him, he usually kicked his anger-fits up a notch. It didn't matter to me. I was tired of being controlled by him. It was now my time to do something just for me. (Remember that change-and-destiny-thing?)

I attended one of the Glee Girl's delightful meetings along with my aunt Patty, who was already a member of the seventy-strong member show chorus. I was given sheet music and a cassette tape with my voice part. I was to audition the next week. The song was, *On Broadway.* I listened to that song all week and practiced my part until I had it perfect. The following week I was nervous. I did not think I would be able to sing and hold my part with the three other girls. I did not know the other girls who would be singing with me during my audition. Therefore, we did not have the opportunity to practice together. I could only practice with the tape.

It was my time to go into the private audition room. The director was very kind and smiled at me to make me feel at ease. Aunt Patty had told the director about me, so she felt as if she already knew me and treated me as such. That made it easier for me. She said, "Hello, Eva. I have heard many good things about you from Patty. What song have you chosen to sing for me tonight?"

I told her, "*On Broadway*."

"Okay, let's hear it."

The pitch pipe was blown, I took the pitch in my head, and then I began, "They say the neon lights are bright on Broadway. . ." I lifted my voice and raised my eyes and brows with a smile on my face as if to say, "Broadway, here I am!" I was giving it all I had; that was my only chance! Then the other three remarkable voices joined in with mine in harmony. I don't think I made any mistakes; although my upper lip was quivering!

The audition was over before I knew it and the director was thanking me. Then I was out of the room, and the next girl was up for her audition. All I could do from there was hope and pray that I made the chorus. Aunt Patty was confident that I had.

A week after auditions, my answer came; I had made the chorus! I was ecstatic! Elated! Cody was infuriated, but I didn't care. By that time in my life, I had outgrown his barbaric, brutal ways and had decided it was time for me to fly out of his cage, and fly I did---just a little at a time, I might add.

The Glee Girls was the outlet for which I had been waiting. It was a breath of fresh air, a night away from my oppressive, obnoxious, husband who only wanted me to serve him and do as I was instructed. Over time I had lost myself, but I knew I was still in there---somewhere.

I did not mind being a loyal wife, for I knew that was expected. If only he had been a little more understanding of my needs, I would not have resented him later in our relationship.

I had now grown callous to his demands. His little–bird–in–a–cage was growing into a songbird, and she had a new song to sing;

"I'll fly away, oh glory! I'll fly away!"

Chapter 4 The Carnation

The carnation represents the birth flower of January.

The white carnation means "sweet and lovely." The pink means "I will never forget you." The two-toned version means "I cannot be with you."

The Glee Girls met once a week on Monday nights for a strenuous rehearsal. It was a challenge for me to get every note right to every song, along with the choreography. But, if I was to stay in the chorus, it had to be done. I felt as if I had made it to my own 'Broadway.'

The name of the show that we were preparing for in a few months was titled "On Broadway." It was a compilation of famous Broadway tunes from years past, all brought together in one show. Our costumes were flashy and beautiful. The chorus had three costume changes. I had four changes because I was chosen to sing in a double quartet.

Our double quartet song was, "If my friends could see me now." *How appropriate that song was*, I thought! As a little girl, I had always wanted to be a star. Look at me now! I was going to perform in a "Broadway" show of my very own. But, before the show could go on, there was a great deal of preparation still ahead.

Costumes had to be made, stage sets had to be built, and tickets needed to be sold. Also required were advertising sales to go in the program; the ad sales would offset the cost of the show. The chorus had a contest to see who could sell the most ads. Since I was new to the group, I set out to sell the most ads.

I dressed as business-like, yet pretty and feminine as I could that day. A pale blue sundress was my choice for the day. My long blonde hair was worn softly down on my shoulders. My blue eyes were accented with cream and gray eyeshadow; pale pink lipstick topped off my little bird lips.

With my sample program in hand, advertising contract and ball-point pen, and a picture of our fantastic group, I was ready to sell ads. I was excited and fearless! Cody was furious and raving. I didn't care; it was my day off from work.

I immediately sold five ads to other small local businesspeople who were fond of our group; this gave me the confidence to keep up the good work. After all, I was on a mission. I passed by Mr. Wonderful's hardware store. He was standing outside, talking to a man about repaving his parking lot. I bravely and confidently walked right up to him and said, "You're just the man I wanted to see." He was about to finish his conversation with the paving contractor, so he bid the man goodbye. He turned to me with a slight lustful smile, lowered his sunglasses, and said, "Where did you come from?" I was embarrassed; did he remember me or not? I said, "I work across the street."

He asked, "Why haven't I seen you in the local dens of iniquities?"

"Because I don't hang out in those local dens of iniquities," I responded promptly and probably a little pious.

Mr. Wonderful just looked at me with his brown bedroom eyes. I was melting right there in the presence of this spectacular specimen of a man! I had to take a deep breath if I were to appear confident enough to continue. I did.

I told him that I sang with the Glee Girls and that we were having a show in a few weeks. I was selling ads for the program; then I handed him the program for his scrutiny. He took the program from my hand ever so slowly, never looking down at it, and never taking his eyes off me. I was melting, but I continued with my selling job. He still did not say a word, he just continued to look me straight in my eyes. I couldn't stand it any longer; I lowered my eyes and had to turn my head away from his piercing brown eyes that seem to be saying, *I want to know you better with that long blonde hair spread out on my bed.*

Then with quick thinking, I remembered to close my ad sales pitch with, "Oh yes! And if you buy an ad today, you'll get two free tickets to the show." He responded without hesitation, "I don't think my heart could stand it." Oh my! He *did* have a way with words! Buying that ad was not what he wanted to do. His eyes were saying, "I want you in my bedroom." I knew it, I could feel it! He knew if we were to continue, he had to buy that ad, so he signed on the dotted line. I watched as he scribbled his name: Alexander S. Rosenberg. Then he told me that I would need to come back later to pick up the check as his secretary was not at work that day. That was fine with me. It gave me another opportunity to further grow this whatever-it-was-thing that we had developing.

As I was watching him sign his name, I was blissfully thinking, *Eva Rosenberg. Humm, how nice that sounded.* I wondered what it would be like to be married to a man like him. The chemistry was strong between us. That was something I had not felt in many years. I longed for a handsome, romantic, strong, and intelligent man like him. Then I came to my senses. *I can't think about things like that; I am a married woman!* No, I could never be married to Mr. Wonderful, because at least one of us is married. I knew I was; I did not know for sure about him. Although I could never be with him, I knew I would never be able to forget about the most handsome, macho man that I had ever met. And he seemed to be interested in this average little girl!

Chapter 5 The Chamomile

The chamomile signified "energy in adversity."

I did not have to wait very long to see Mr. Wonderful again. He did his research and found that my husband and I owned and operated the swimming pool business across the street from his hardware store. It was less than a month when he decided to visit me. I was late coming to work that day. As I entered the store, Cody was in his usual abhorrent state when he said, "some man came here looking for you. He said that you sold him an ad in that silly ole program of yours. You told him that he would receive free tickets to the show. He has not received the tickets yet. Here's his number, call him." I was feeling guilty, for I knew who that man might be. I simply said, "I will call him when the tickets are printed and ready. Anyway, he is impatient for expecting them so soon. The show is still a month away!" Secretly, I thought it was Mr. Wonderful who had stopped in to see me, but I wasn't for sure. I bet he was surprised to find Cody there instead of me. That makes it even more embarrassing. I would hate for Mr. Wonderful to know that I was married to such a jerk! But I was, so what could I do about it now? He would know sooner or later, I guess.

I hated that I always had to cover up for Cody's bad manners and crude ways. I didn't want Mr. Wonderful to know just how obnoxious Cody could be. I couldn't hide it all the time. My only hope was that Cody was kind to Mr. Wonderful on that day. I was beginning to wonder, *why did I marry him in the first place?*

A few weeks passed, and the programs and tickets were printed. I was now ready to distribute the free tickets to my advertisers. I knew I would be going to see Mr. Wonderful, so I dressed as best I could that day, a short cream skirt and matching knit top that may have been cut a little too low for my small breasts, off-white pantyhose, and off-white heels. I wore my blonde hair in the usual way, down, softly on my shoulders. I wore extra makeup that day to look pretty, just for him. Gold hoop earrings topped it off. I was now set to make my deliveries.

One last glance in the mirror, I kept telling myself, "This is only a delivery. . . this is only a delivery!" Then I sprayed myself with an extra mist of perfume for added success, just in case.

When I arrived at his hardware store, I asked to see Mr. Rosenberg. "He is in his office." A polite young male employee said as he led the way to a red door, which I had seen many times, but paid no attention. "Let's go up to the stairs, and his secretary will help you," he said. "May I say who is calling?" I told him my name was Eva Adams.

Wow! Up we went through a red door that led to a hidden stairway, then up farther to more double hand-carved mahogany doors, which led into the offices. I had no idea these offices existed! As we approached these ultra-luxurious, spacious offices that took up the whole second floor of the hardware store, I was beginning to feel a little out-of-place. With fancy offices like that, it appeared more than a one-horse-town hardware store operation! Glass windows were all around so every employee in each office could see out all over the town as they worked. I estimated there were fifty or more employees; who would have ever guessed?

In the middle of this centrifuge-type setting, a gorgeous lady was sitting behind a desk with fancy carvings. She was immaculately groomed, wearing a dark grey business suit. Her gold-rimmed glasses made her look intelligent, she most likely was.

"Ms. Adams is here to see Mr. Rosenberg," the polite young man said to the secretary. Then he turned to me and said, "I hope you have a good day," as he headed back downstairs to his usual duties.

"Do you have an appointment with Mr. Rosenberg?" the secretary asked.

"No, I did not know that I would need an appointment, until now," I said with extreme intimidation. I thought to myself, *what is a plain-ole-vanilla-girl like me doing in a place like this?*

The beautiful lady said, "That's okay, I don't think you will have a problem today. Let me check with Mr. Rosenberg. Once again, whom may I say is calling?"

"Eva Adams . . . err, just tell him the girl who sold him the ad in the Glee Girl show program. He'll know. I have his program and tickets." I tried not to sound nervous, but I was, and my words were not coming out with an ease that I had hoped.

"One moment, please. Just have a seat over there in the sitting room. May I get you something to drink, water, or coffee?" Ms. Prim-n-Proper asked.

"No, thank you," I responded, as I made my way over to the French provincial couch. I tried to sit up as straight as possible while waiting for him. My palms were sweaty, and I was fidgety.

How did you ever talk yourself into doing a thing like this? Eva! You are definitely out of your league! I told my good-girl conscience to "shut-up!"

The bad girl in my panties said, *"that's right, you heard her! Shut up!"*

With a courteous soft voice, Ms. Prim-n-Proper returned and said, "Mr. Rosenberg will see you now." Nervous, yet trying to appear confident, I entered his office. There he was sitting behind his shiny black mahogany desk. The most captivating man I had ever laid eyes on got up from behind his desk and met me.

"Eva, it's good to see you again." With that being said, he took my hand and softly kissed it, then brushed it with his mustache. Heat rose up in my spine, and every muscle in my lower abdomen seem to stir deeply with excitement. Oh my! No one had ever kissed my hand before! What a perfect gentleman he was! OMG! Can this be true? His eyes were penetrating deeply into mine, checking for my response. It was apparent there as intense energy between us. I was like putty in the master's hands. I knew what would happen if I were ever alone with him. And there I was, alone with him. . . hot and soft as putty in his hands.

Take a deep breath, Eva, I told myself.

"I think you have been expecting these?" Never taking his blazing eyes off me, he took the program and tickets from me and laid them on the desk on which he was leaning.

"I've been waiting for you," he said brazenly.

"What do you mean by that?" I asked.

"I think you know what I mean; didn't your husband tell you I came by your business looking for you?"

"Yes, but I thought you were just anxious for the tickets that I had promised you."

"I couldn't get my mind off you. I have wanted you since the day I laid eyes on you," he said.

"Does it matter to you that I am married?" I was feeling intimidated by his direct manner and explicit attention. No man had ever spoken to me so uncensored before, and I did not know how to handle it.

"No." he said, "I know what I like and what I want."

"Do you always get what you want?" I asked as my breath grew shallow.

"Well, no." He said with a shy smile then slightly turned away.

It was time to get back onto the subject of those tickets. After all, that was the reason for making the trip to see him. Right?

"The show will be next Saturday night; I hope to see you there."

With a smile, he said, "I'll probably give the tickets to my mother, she loves things like that."

Disappointed with his last statement, I decided the visit should come to an end. As I was standing to leave, my skirt clung a little too tightly to my thighs. I was trying to pull it down, without him noticing, when he leaned in and put one arm around me and put his other hand on my knee. Drawing me in, he kissed me with a passionate French kiss that set my upper thighs and lower abdomen on fire! His erection was against my hips; Little Eva was about to explode with desire for that erection!. His kiss was wet, and sweltry; I could hardly breathe. His lips and mustache seemed to engulf my thin little lips. The electricity between us was sparking and filling the air with static.

OMG! I'm going to frigging orgasm right here, and now, I thought! If his hand goes any higher up my leg, I <u>will</u> orgasm! My heart was beating so fast, I could hear it pounding in my ears. We probably would have made love right there on his desk, had I not worn those damned old pantyhose! Besides, there were so many other employees right outside his door, how could we? We just couldn't. Not right then.

One of my legs was wrapped around his waist, while I was enjoying every in and out of his tongue into my mouth. We were rocking tantalizingly back and forth with one another as if we were making love without taking off our clothes. I was hunching to massage my clit against his throbbing bulge through his pants. I wanted to embrace that bulge unashamedly flesh to flesh. But I only caressed his thick black hair and neck, while we were reclining on his desk and mischievously stimulating one another, knowing this fire would not be quickly extinguished. I longed to find out what that bulge in his pants was all about. But at that moment, my good-girl-subconscious was scolding me. *Are you going to let this man's horniness sexploit you?*

"I must go before we get into trouble. By the way, I can tell you were a jock." I couldn't believe those words came out of my mouth! I was referring to his anxious, wet, passionate kiss.

"What do you mean?" He asked. I had to think fast. I couldn't tell him I thought he kissed me too anxiously, too soon. I prefer kisses slowly and tender at first, then hot and passionately a little later. I looked around his office then quickly responded, "You have a lot of Georgia Tech memorabilia."

"Yeah, I played football there while I was in college. Good luck with your performance." He said as he stood up, straightened his tie and smoothed his hair. I did the same straightening act before exiting his office. I looked back at him once with a smile of shameless, thrilling satisfaction of what had just transpired.

He winked and smiled back at me.

Passing Ms. Prim-n-Proper, I thanked her for her kind assistance. She nodded and smiled back to me as a courtesy.

Later that night, while lying in my bed, and replaying those spicy moments in my mind, over and over, I wondered, *could Alex Rosenberg be the right man for me?* How could such chemistry and energy feel so right, yet be so wrong? Why did a man like that pay attention to a little oh vanilla girl like me? I did not know, but the bad-girl-in-my-panties liked it, and I had never felt like that before. It felt good. I had a deep longing for more of his hypnotic eyes and his sensual touches.

Then I came to my senses. My good-girl-subconscious plagued me. *He's probably just a player. He probably talks and acts like that to all his ladies, to get what he wants.* What a silly fool I must be to fall for a cad like that. Well! It won't happen again! Good girls don't do things like that! I certainly did not want to be just another one of his conquests!

Chapter 6 Enter, the Iris

The iris symbolizes royalty and respect.

The Glee Girl's *Broadway* show was performed, and a success. I looked for Alex in the audience, but he was not there. I wondered if one of the many old blue-haired ladies in the audience might have been his mother.

30

I tried not to think about Alex (Mr. Wonderful), but I could not get him out of my mind. I thought about him, and that day of hot, romantic, passionate kisses in his beautiful, spacious office. Was that just a chance happening, or would I ever see Mr. Wonderful again?

Then one night at the local theater for amateurs, I saw him across the theater. He was with a strikingly, beautiful, tall blonde in the "Angel Section." The Angel Section was that part of the theater where the significant contributors to the theater had seasonal tickets and box seats with the best view. Wine and cheese were served to these special guests before the performance and during intermission. My heart sank when I saw him with her. Yes, this indeed must be Mrs. Rosenberg. She certainly looked the part, tall, beautiful, and sophisticated. She stood at least 5' 9" or more, wearing black stiletto heels. Her thick, long blonde hair was healthy and shiny. I could tell she had a professional hair stylist. Her make-up looked as if she were a movie star. He helped her out of her mink coat. What a gentleman he was to his wife! Under her full-length mink was a low-cut, black, silk cocktail dress. Her stockings had a black seam running up the back of her legs. *How damned sexy is that?* I thought. What a lovely couple they made. They were the perfect couple, or so it seemed.

During the intermission, the "Angels" were recognized. Much to my surprise, it was not Mrs. Rosenberg, who was introduced! It was Ms. Phillips! As in--*Phillips Petroleum Company*! She was not his wife, after all! She was heir to one of the largest oil companies in America. Or should I say---the world? She was Mr. Wonderful's girlfriend! Now I felt really intimidated! I certainly could not compete with her! She was classy; I was so plain—just vanilla Eva. I had little sophistication and no real experience with the finer things of life.

Ms. Phillips was recently divorced and had moved to New Fort to make a new life of her own. She had reclaimed her original family name of Phillips. I guess she knew it would garner respect. It did. She was well respected around the town, mostly because she was a philanthropist. Money <u>does</u> talk! She was gorgeous to go along with that money; having the arm of the best-looking man in the town was indeed advantageous. Throughout the town, Alex was also known and respected. He was president of the Chamber of Commerce, as well as a member of other elite social clubs such as the New Fort Yacht Club, to name one. That's not to forget he was a blue-blood from "Old Mobile" money and high society. Remarkably, his family made their money the old-fashioned way; they worked for it!

I knew on this very night, as I watched the happy couple, if I had any hopes and dreams of ever being with this hunk of a man, I was only fooling myself! It would never come to pass; I just knew it in my heart. I watched with envy as he gave her his full attention, only occasionally glancing over to me.

When the play was over, I tried as discreetly as I could, to slip on my London Fog, (without any help from Cody,) and get the hell out of there! As we were leaving, the lovely couple entered the lobby at the same time as Cody and I! Alex politely nodded, winked his eye, and smiled at me without Ms. Phillips knowing. Then he spoke to me as we were exiting, "that was a comical play, wouldn't you say Eva?"

"Yes, it was, not bad for a few people who act just for the fun of it," I responded to him quite shyly. Then Ms. Phillips turned to see with whom he was speaking. We both made full eye contact with one another. I was sizing her up, and she was sizing me up too, for future reference. She won.

She was the "Iris," tall, beautiful, and regal. She had the respect of everyone in the room and the town alike. I was just the lowly little violet. A violet cannot compete with an Iris, for they are not even in the same class! While they are both beautiful in their special way, they are very different. An Iris appears suddenly on the scene, wows everyone, then in a flash, she is gone for another season.

A little violet is more down to earth; she hangs around much longer, for she is more devoted to those she loves.

Chapter 7 The Verbena

These delicate flowers mean, "pray for me."

Cody, Nathan and I had been living in New Fort less than two years when Cody's mother fell and broke her hip. She was living alone at the time with no one to care for her when she came home from the hospital. I agreed that she could stay with us, and I would care for her until she recovered. Her other son was living in Texas and could not, or would not, take her into his home and care for her.

She had not liked me from the first day we met. I was eighteen years old at the time and was an aspiring model, before Cody and I married. I tried to dress the part and act the role of a model on and off the runway. She said I wore my skirts too short and wore too much makeup, which I probably did. At the time, I thought I looked great. Oh well! Too bad! I did not care for her, either!

Cody's sister-in-law did not care for me either. Her problem was, she was jealous of me because she thought I was prettier than she. I never felt so. The harder I tried to make these two women like me, the more they both seemed to hate me. It was useless, I learned that lesson too late. Cody's sister-in-law was well-educated. I did not have a degree, but I wanted one. A couple of years of college was all I obtained. So, I do not know why she had reason to be jealous. I always went out of my way to make her feel comfortable around me; nothing ever worked. Insecure people are just like that.

Now here is the issue of Mrs. Adams. The Old Bat hated me, but I was stuck with her, and she was stuck with me. After being married for 13 years and spending the past ten years raising Cody's son from a previous marriage, (while in Birmingham), I knew not to pray for God to give me patience. God does not give patients. He teaches it very slowly. When we moved to New Fort, my stepson stayed in Birmingham with his mother. Now that he was grown, his mother wanted him to come back and live with her. I was more than happy!

Now Cody's mother was going to come to live with us! So how do I pray in this new situation? I certainly was not going to pray for patience again! It didn't work the first time, so maybe I should pray (this time) that God would give me compassion---compassion for this Old Bat who hated me!

The day came for her to stay with us. Cody and I moved out of our master bedroom with its adjoining bathroom; it would now belong to her. The hospital bed arrived the day before her arrival. The next day, the ambulance delivered our semi-invalid, cranky, Old Bat.

I had gone to her apartment a few days prior and retrieved nightgowns and toiletries, thinking that would be all she would need. Wrong! The very first day, she needed her bedside lamp. The next day she needed her magnifying glass. The next day she needed her puzzle books. Her demanding and wanting various small items went on and on. I was the one to fetch them for her, with no thanks I might add.

Three meals per day were served to her in bed. The bedpan was brought in when needed. Then sponge baths were given daily. Her medicine was administered regularly and on time. The newspaper was brought for her in the mornings, not to mention picking up a television remote control when she dropped it several times a day. She would ring her little bell when she wanted me to come and do something for her. I would humbly come running. All these things were just a few of the chores that were required of me to do for my old-bat-mother-in-law because I was the daughter-in-law, and it was all dumped on me! So yes! Dear God! Give me compassion, right now!

Not only did the Old Bat not like me, but she also did not like children. She liked small babies, but when they got big enough to get into her belongings, she had no use for them. So, babysitting was out of the question. When the children got big enough to do things for her, she started back liking them again, if they would pander to her. By this time, Nathan was twelve years old. He could tell that the Old Bat had no use for him. He usually stayed out of her way, to ensure that she did not complain to Cody about anything that he might have done wrong that day.

Mrs. Adams slowly got better. Physical therapists came to the home and worked with her twice a week. She went from a wheelchair to a walker in about six months. By this time, I thought it was time for her to move back into her apartment. Wrong! She was now accustomed to me taking care of her and had decided to stay permanently. Cody agreed, without consulting me. I was the live-in nursemaid for the Old Bat! I had agreed to care for her until she recuperated, but not for the rest of her life! It was no use!

I had just finished taking care of a stepson for the past ten years of my life, and now here I am taking care of Cody's mother for the next best ten years of my life. . . best or not. Like I said, she did not like me, and I did not like her! But I would learn to cope with her, especially when she decided to pay me for my services. It certainly wasn't much, but it did sweeten the pot.

Cody's brother got word that I was taking his mother's money. He said, "It is horrible that you are charging my mother to live with you!" All I could say was, "come get her and let her live with you if you think we are doing her wrong." That ended that talk!

The sponge baths turned into tub baths. Every week I shampooed and set the Old Bat's hair to save on salon charges. Besides, I could fix her hair better to suit her than the salon could.

The Old Bat soon found out what a dingbat son she had produced. One night, during one of our many knock-down-and-drag-out-fights, she decided to hobble into the living room with her walker and referee the fuss. "Now, stop it right now! Stop it! You're going to kill one another!" We were screaming but not hitting. I said, "Grandmama, go back to your room."

She said, "No, I'm, not! Not until you settle down." I said more firmly, "Grandmama, I told you to go back to your room; we will talk this out." Cody just sat there, saying nothing. He was watching me confront his mother. I was surprised by his complacency.

"No, I'm not!" She shouted.

"Grandmama, if you don't go back to your room. I'm going to take you back to your room!"

"No, you won't!" She exclaimed.

She should not have said that. I got up and picked up her eighty-five pounds of bones and toted her back to her room. She sprawled out both arms and legs in the doorway, like an "X" wedging herself so we could go no farther. That was her big mistake. I was stronger than she was. We made it through the door, and I sat her on her bed. I gently said, "Now Grandmama you stay in here. We will be all right without your help. I know you mean well, and I appreciate it. But this is something that your son and I will have to work out between ourselves. Thank you for offering your help."

I closed the door and went back to the living room. We did not see her or hear from her the rest of the night. I can say that she <u>did</u> end our fight that night because we forgot what we were fussing about after all that was over. From that night on, when Cody and I would fuss and argue, she would close her door and ignore us.

The next day, she had bruises on her frail little arms. (You know how easily old people bruise.) I felt terrible about having done that. The next weekend, her other son was coming to visit. I wondered if she might show her bruises to him and complain. She didn't. I guess she was afraid he might take her to live with him. The Old Bat didn't want to live with him. She disliked the other daughter-in-law more than she disliked me!

All I can say about taking in relatives is this: you had better think long and hard about it before you do it. It causes a lot of stress on the family, having an added person in the house, especially if that person is a burden and an old sourpuss! It is bad enough in the best of circumstances.

She lived with us for ten *very long years*. I cared for her every day until she fell and broke her other hip at the age of eighty-three. At that time, hospice came in to care for her. She contacted the flu from one of her nurses and passed away shortly thereafter.

The last two weeks of her life were the worst of all, trying to care for her and remain kind. She was in a great deal of pain and suffering. She passed that pain on to all those around her, mostly me.

My prayers asking God for compassion for her was all that got me through those ten long years while caring for her.

God rest her soul. . . the Old Bat!

Chapter 8 The Forget-Me-Nots

Forget-me-nots ask that you *forget-me-not*.

The colder months had come and gone, and spring was here. I had been swamped taking care of Mrs. Adams and seeing to it that, my son Nathan was keeping up with his studies, especially on his band lessons. He was now playing the saxophone in middle school and doing very well. His band teacher said he was a natural musician. Nathan had a beautiful voice and could sing on pitch. Therefore, he was active in the church youth choir. He loved it, or maybe he just loved being away from the house. Whatever it was, I understood his desire for outside activities.

I too, was busy with the Glee Girls every Monday night. I practiced every day to make sure I was prepared for the next week's rehearsal. I had to keep my mind occupied, or I would have gone crazy—from having to take care of the Old Bat and my demanding husband! I never complained, or Cody would have made me quit the Glee Girls. He would have said that I was too busy with my home responsibilities to take on an outside activity. What he did not realize was that this other activity was keeping me sane and giving me a reason for living. Other than Nathan, I had no incentive to get up and get going each day.

It was a beautiful spring day, and Cody had a job installing a new swimming pool for a customer. He and his crew would be working all week on the project. I was glad to have him out of the office. I did not mind running the office alone. I was delighted for peace; it was a nice change.

I had not seen Mr. Wonderful in some time, other than looking out my window and adoring him as he walked in and out of his hardware store. One day, I saw him get out of his car with a young boy about the age of Nathan. They both went into his store. I wondered who this child might be. He had black hair as did Alex. But who could he be? I never saw that child come out so I thought he must be an employee's child.

Anyway, there was never a day that went by that I did not think about that handsome man and the hot, passionate kisses we exchanged that day in his office. I would never forget that day until I died! I longed for more of those times to be with him. Would they ever come again?

I was alone that day in my pool business, helping customers with pool supplies. I wasn't dressed very well, just faded blue jeans with my hair pulled back, sloppily in a ponytail. I guess I had given up on ever having a chance with him again, especially after seeing him with his beautiful girlfriend that night at the theater. What was the use of ever trying to look good for him again? I didn't care anymore, or so I told myself.

The business seemed to slow down around 11:45, when who do you think came walking in the door? Mr. Wonderful himself! I couldn't believe my eyes! *What the hell does he want now?* I wondered. He was dating the most gorgeous and richest woman in town, so why is he here?

OMG! Did he ever look good! No. . . . fabulous! His black-salt-n-pepper hair was still wet from being recently shampooed. Maybe it was his hair gel, I could not tell, but it smelled nice! His shaving lotion was the same fragrance that I had smelled that day in his office, manly, yet not overwhelming. . . sexy and romantic. His black jeans were slightly creased; his shirt was untucked. I could see his chest hair peeking out from above his first button as if to say, "Come hither, let's play!" He had on deck shoes but no socks. How cool is that? I thought.

I was embarrassed for him to see me in faded blue jeans and no makeup. But I made up for it acting professional and courteous, with my fake confidence.

"Good morning, Mr. Rosenberg," I said in my most friendly voice.

"Please call me Alex, remember?"

"Alex, yes. . . Alex"

"Would you please test this swimming pool water sample to see if it is out of balance? Do you think I need to add some chemicals?" he asked.

"Why, of course!" I answered with a smile as I flashed my eyelashes at him. I was secretly hoping he would not notice that I did not have on makeup.

I took the pool water sample to the back of the room and ran the usual pH test as Alex looked around the store.

"Looks like your pH is in perfect balance, Mr. Rosenberg."

He corrected me. "Alex."

I repeated back to him. "Alex."

"Really? The pool man said something was not in balance, and I needed to have the water checked."

"Who takes care of your pool?"

"Clarence Jones."

"Clarence? He comes in every month, same time with a sample, and buys the chemicals needed, to keep your pool in balance. I do not know why you would be having a problem. He was just in last week." Then it occurred to me; he did not have a pool water problem. He was visiting the store for another reason. He came in to see me! (Or so I hoped!)

"Well, I just..." stroking his chin, Mr. Wonderful stammered to find a logical reason for his pool problem, which he did not have.

"Well, I am sure you know your business. It appears I have nothing to worry about it. It looks like you and Clarence are doing a good job with my pool."

I knew how he felt. . . uneasy. I had felt the same way when I was in his hardware store—looking for something to say when there was nothing to say and no logical reason to be there.

Then he just blurted out, "I was about to go and have lunch at the Magnolia Bar and Grill, would you like to come with me?" The true meaning of his visit was apparent.

As quickly as he asked, I responded just as quickly, "no, thank you. I can't. When I close the store, I have to go to Mobile to visit my aunt, Patty. She has cancer and has just come home from the hospital. I need to help her get settled in."

"Not even for a quick drink?" Now his persuading, bedroom eyes were talking to me again!

"I can't; I just can't!"

Taking a long heavy breath, I lowered my eyes and looked away from him. Oh, how I wanted to go with him!

"That's okay, I understand. Maybe next time." He then took my hand, kissed it, and brushed it with his soft mustache. Man! I loved it when he did that! It just thrilled the hell out of me and my panties!

He walked toward the front door, looking back once with a wink, he said, "Are you sure?"

Then he was gone once again out of my life. Yes, he was gone, not forgotten.

Chapter 9 The Forsythia

The forsythia represents anticipation.

After that day in my store when I received an unexpected visit from Mr. Wonderful, I decided I would never look frumpy again in public, never knowing when I might see him. He made it once again evident to me that for some reason, he was still interested in me. Why?

I did not know! But he was, and I liked it! So, from that day on, I always tried to look my best when I left my home, in anticipation of running into the best-looking man I had ever met.

You see, men don't have to try and look their best, they either look good, or they don't. Girls must fix their hair and wear makeup to look their best. I do not look good or feel good about myself without makeup. I do not care what anyone tells me! I have a mirror! I can tell you that I look better when I wear makeup, and I look like hell when I don't! I decided I would always try and look beautiful for Mr. Wonderful-make-you-cream-your-panties-Wonderful from then on. And I did!

Cody did not like it. "Why are you getting so dressed up? Who are you trying to impress?" He asked with a condescending attitude. My only response was, "I am dressing for myself." And I was, it gave me the confidence to look good. I found that when I looked good, I smiled more at people and they smiled back at me. When I smiled, I made more friends. Everyone should try it!

Cody had just left the store to go on a service call when Mr. Wonderful showed up at my front door,

'Looking better than a body had a right to' . . . or so the song goes.

He just came moseying in the front door, smiling sinfully--like a fox. What he did not know was that he was in my henhouse! So, there we were once again, playing cat and mouse with one another. We both knew what we were doing, and we liked it. Electricity and sparks were obviously between us. Slight little touches to my hand as he leaned across the counter and his eyes never leaving mine! Oh! How he could penetrate me with those brown bedroom eyes! My panties were getting wet again, and I could feel it. My heart was racing, and my face was flush. It was hard for me to carry on a conversation with a man who was so much more intelligent than I. What did we have to talk about anyway? Pool business? Hardware stuff? Hell no! The only thing we were interested in was one another, and we did not know enough about one another to talk.

So, what now? Let's get to know each other! Yeah! That's a great idea! But how? The only thing I knew was that we had great chemistry together. But I didn't know a damn thing about chemistry; I didn't even take chemistry in high school! So that subject was out! Okay, so let's not talk.

It was apparent he had only one thing on his highly sexed mind, and my mind was right there with his. The only problem was, my good-girl-subconscious was talking louder than the bad girl inside of my panties! Oh hell! Decisions, decisions! I will deal with those decisions later after he is gone, or maybe tomorrow . . . as Ms. Scarlett O'Hara would say. But for that moment, I was enjoying his presence. I was alone with Mr. Wonderful once again, flirting and teasing and yearning to comment sexpionage with him.

Kissing started. This time I instigated it the way I wanted it to go, with slow kisses, softly with my tongue surrounding his mouth and mustache. Then inside his mouth, in and out, he reciprocated with his tongue, softly and romantically. His hand moved slowly up my leg and touched my panties. OMG! My panties were soaked! He knew I wanted him. I *did* want him! I wanted to make love to him then and there like I had never made love before. But I couldn't! I just couldn't. I knew if I did, it would all be over.

<u>You know, it's like a little deer running & the hunter</u>.

If the little deer is running, the hunter continues the chase. When that little deer stops running, the hunter has no reason to continue the pursuit. . . it is all over. I had to continue to run for him to keep the quest. I did not want to be one of his many conquests. I had to play hard to get if I was to win him over.

Our little romantic kissy-kissy, cream-your-panties, and something-big-n-hard-n-his-pants caressing session went on for several minutes. When it was clear to Alex that we were going no farther, he began to get frustrated. Then he said, "I am 40 years old! I'm too old to be playing these games . . .you little prick tease!"

I was embarrassed. I didn't know what to say, except, "you know that I am married."

"So?" He responded quickly.

"So, you know this can never go anywhere." I sadly said.

"Why not?" He asked.

"I will never do anything to mess up my marriage. I have a young son, and I don't want him to be a child from a broken home. It's not a good nor happy marriage, but I'm staying in it for the sake of my son."

With all my babbling, the hot romance cooled off. That formidable big bulge in his pants disappeared. "I understand; that's noble of you." Was his only comment.

After throwing cold water on our little romantic session, there was nothing left for him to say except, "Well, I just stepped over to get a haircut next door, and I thought I'd drop in to speak with you, so I guess I'd better be going." He turned and was gone once again.

Hell's bells! He's gone again! I just stuck my big foot in my mouth once more. Why did I have to go and say all that?

Little deer running stuff, huh! Hell! I wanted to have red-hot sex with him as much as he wanted to have sex with me. What a damn fool I was! I guess I scared him off for good.

Or did I?

Chapter 10 The Candytuft

The candytuft signifies indifference.

While being married to Nathan's father for twenty-eight years and believing it not prudent to speak ill of Cody in the presence of my son, I never did. Never while married to him, during the divorce, or afterward did I ever speak negatively of him in Nathan's presence. After all, I was the one who got a divorce from him, not my son.

51

Nathan witnessed the events that unfolded in our home and lived through them and was fully capable of forming his own opinions of right and wrong. I will say this about Nathan. He will go to great links today to avoid controversy if possible; he is a peacemaker. When a child lives in unrest, he learns a coping mechanism. Most of the time, while growing up, Nathan would go to his room, shut the door, turn on his stereo, and try to pretend everything was okay. He knew it was not. It's sad to say he was living in a dysfunctional family. At the time, I thought I was doing what was best for him by keeping the family together. I did not want Nathan to be a child from a broken home. In retrospect, I realize that a good divorce is better than a bad marriage. Especially as far as the children are concerned.

The first year of our marriage, I realized that I had chosen the wrong man. We were like oil and vinegar. We simply did not mix! Occasionally, we got along just fine. If we could be mixed and blended well, then the oil and vinegar together made it as one team. You know, like oil and vinegar make a tasty salad dressing. But when left to settle, it goes back into two separate things: oil and vinegar. That's how we were. Two very different people, occasionally getting along. That was not my idea of how a marriage should be.

I have always thought marriage should be a team where the two have mutual respect. Not where the man is the ruler over the wife and where his demands invariably come first.

*Wives submit yourselves unto your own husbands, as
unto the Lord. (Eph. 5:22)*
I cannot tell you how many times I heard that
Scripture. One time, after having problems in our
marriage, we called for our preacher to come to our
home and council with us. Cody told the humble
preacher that I was not in submission to him. The
preacher asked Cody in what ways was I not?

"I can't even get her to sew a button on for me!" He
blurted out.

"Well, Cody, I can't get my wife to sew a button on
for me either; but that doesn't mean she isn't
submissive," the preacher said. That ended that.

After that first year of marriage, I realized my
mistake; I knew the marriage was bound to be a failure.
I had to keep reminding myself:

Failure is an event, not a person.

It was not all my fault that this marriage was not
going to make it; although I had indeed been blamed for
most, if not all, of the problems.

After two years of marriage, I found myself
accidentally pregnant. I missed one of my birth control
pills; it only takes one! Now I was stuck! But I was happy
that I would be having a baby. In February 1973, Nathan
was born prematurely. Weighing only five pounds and
two ounces at birth and struggling, he barely made it. He
looked like a skinned rabbit; I didn't care. I dressed him
up and took him to church. All the ladies said, "Oh, isn't

he precious!" I knew then, and there I had an ugly baby! Otherwise, they would have said he was beautiful like they often said to other mothers. I didn't care; he was beautiful to me. He just needed to gain some weight and fill out some of that loose, saggy red skin. Eventually, he did. Today he is a very handsome man.

In May 1973, Cody's son by another marriage had failed the second grade. He was living with his mother. Cody insisted that he come to live with us for the summer. He told his previous wife that I would tutor this child all summer, then he could be retested in August to see if he could be placed into third grade. She agreed. The only problem was this: he never asked me if I would be willing to do such a thing. After all, I had just had a baby in February. I was busy taking care of my baby. How was I to care for and tutor a 7-year-old child? I had no voice in the matter. I did as I was told.

My sister-in-law was a schoolteacher. Each week, she would test him. At the end of the summer, he was prepared to take the final test for placement into third grade. He passed with flying colors! That was great, except for one problem; Cody now decided that his son should live with us permanently. The child's mother agreed, all of which was decided without consulting me.

I now had two children to care for without having any voice in the matter, and I secretly resented it! I resented it primarily because this child resented me also. It was a mutual feeling between us. No words were spoken; they did not have to be. Actions speak louder than words, as they say. That child did more harm to the marriage than

I could have imagined possible! He lived with us for ten years, until he graduated from high school.

My only advice to anyone who might be considering taking in a stepchild is this: if you want to put stress on your marriage, do it. But you had better have a mighty healthy marriage if your marriage is going to survive it.

Nathan was 18 months old when I had taken enough of all this. I decided it was time for me to get the hell out of this marriage before it was too late. I packed all my clothes, along with Nathan's and drove to Mobile, Alabama, where my aunt Patty lived. I had decided I would get a divorce and go to work for the same corporation that I had worked for when I was an executive secretary in Birmingham. The corporation had locations all over the nation; I knew my previous boss would give me a good recommendation. Aunt Patty and Uncle Arty welcomed me with open arms. They both knew the circumstances in which I was living. They never said it, but I could tell they did not care for Cody either.

After three days, Cody finally called and asked if I was with them. Uncle Arty said yes, I was and handed the phone to me. Cody was sweet and charming; he was sorry for whatever it was that had upset me and promised to be a better husband. I was young and naïve. I should have known that a person cannot change. And not wanting Nathan to be raised without his father, I went back and gave Cody another chance. I should have stayed in Mobile and applied for a job with that corporation.

What I did not know at that time was this: Mr. Wonderful was working at that same corporation at that very same time in 1973! But it wasn't our time yet. God knew his perfect timing, and that time was not it. Our time was a very long time away. We both had a great deal of maturing to do before Mr. Wonderful, and I would be ready for one another.

Cody and I stayed married for a few more years. Then, Cody was ready for retirement from the city of Birmingham, after twenty years of service. For many years we had been going on vacations to Gulf Shore, Alabama. We loved it there, and we decided somewhere near Gulf Shores was where we wanted to spend the rest of our lives. We found New Fort and moved there in 1983. Cody's son decided to stay in Birmingham and go back to live with his mother after his high school graduation; I was elated.

Having only my son and Cody in the house, I thought perhaps things would cool down a bit and maybe. . . just maybe, our marriage would make it. But I was wrong. The rantings and ravings had now zeroed in more closely on me. Some people may think I was only unhappy because of a lackluster marriage. That was wrong also. Too much water had gone under the bridge. Too much hurt had taken place, and too many unresolved conflicts had chipped away our relationship. By now, I felt no love for Cody. There was only indifference. I was merely coexisting with a man who was the father of my son. I was putting up a front for others to see and think of us as a happy family. We were not at all what we seemed to be.

Let's make one thing clear; this story is not about Cody. True, things were not good at my home. Otherwise, I would have never been interested in another man. The details are not significant about the things Cody did or said. The decision to divorce was mine and mine alone. Writing about what happened between Cody and me does not justify me or my reasons why. Besides, it would not be fair to Cody, or Nathan, because Cody is still his father. As previously stated, I will speak no evil of him. There were plenty of reasons. I will later express the *Coupe De Grace* in this story as my reason for divorce, but not now.

I hope the world will not think of me as an immoral person, just a person in a bad situation. Knowing eventually, I was going to find a way out of that very uncomfortable situation, but not knowing how or when. My preference was for it to be after Nathan was grown. I did not want him to have a stepfather, knowing what it was like having a stepchild and what stress it can put on a marriage. I did not desire Nathan or myself to go through that pain again.

I will tell you this profoundly! After finding my rose, a herd of wild elephants could not pull me away from him or turn my head to look at another man; he was the manly man for me! I was not a bad girl, just a good girl looking for the right man. My rose was the right man; although he did have a few thorns that needed pruning. I guess I did too.

Chapter 11 The Nasturtium

The nasturtium symbolizes conquest.

It was another Monday night; I was all dolled up and ready to go to Glee Girls rehearsal. I was happy for my girl's night out. I had practiced each note of every song, and I had my choreography down perfectly. It was time for our monthly auditions. We were to turn in our cassette tapes to our section leader for approval. The audition tape would prove that we knew how to sing our part in every song. I had my tape ready. My confidence was soaring. I had made several good friends within the chorus, and I had learned a new way of dressing. These girls knew how to look good on and off the stage, their confidence was contagious, and now I had a new attitude.

On that night, I wore a simple mid-calf, straight skirt, a solid pink silk blouse with a scarf that tied around my waist, nothing sexy, just classy. Pantyhose and flats were also worn. Flats were worn because of our rigorous workout. The Glee Girls met in the next county over, and it took about 45 minutes to get there. As I was leaving the town square, I glanced over in the next lane, and there he was, staring at me. He rolled down his passenger window and said, "where are you going looking so pretty?" His words were like honey dripping from a honeycomb. I felt my face getting hot and flush once again. The hair on the back of my neck started to stand up with arousal.

"I'm on my way to Glee Girls practice in Mobile," I responded when the light suddenly changed.

"Pull over there for a moment, will you?" He gestured toward a gas station. I smiled back at him as I pulled over.

"How long will your meeting last?" He sounded inquisitive, yet I knew he was leading up to something.

"The rehearsal is from 6 o'clock until 10 o'clock," I told him. "Why do you ask?"

"I was wondering if you might squeeze in a little time for us to have a private drink. Maybe we could get to know one another better. The truth is, I want to see you again." My vagina started to get sexed up when I heard those words. Yes, I wanted to get to know him better too! I wanted to know him inside and out! Mostly my vagina wanted to know him inside of me at that moment. My breathing started to grow shallow.

"I am not allowed to miss practice if I am to stay in good standing with the chorus; I'll see if I can slip out a little early. But only for one drink because I will have to get home on time." I could not risk sending out any red flags that would make Cody suspicious. Coming home later than usual could make Cody start asking questions. I did not want that.

With a slight sigh, Mr. Wonderful gave me explicit directions to a house located in the Waterfront subdivision near the Grand Hotel. Waterfront was a beautiful gated subdivision. He also gave me the code to get past the front gate. I wrote it all down, in case I got nervous and forgot something.

"When you get there, pull your car around to the back of the house and park next to my car so that no one will see your car." I thought that was nice that he was concerned about my privacy because I was married.

"If you get lost, call me."

"Oh, I won't get lost. . . I might chicken out!" I responded.

"Don't do that; I'll be waiting for you."

As I was driving off, I glanced in my rearview mirror at him; damn, he was so good-looking! While driving to rehearsal, I was nervous as hell! What was I doing; what was I thinking? I couldn't meet with this man! But what could be wrong with one little drink? All we wanted to do was talk and get to know one another better, right? I guess I would never know the answer to that question unless I gave it a try. Right? I was willing to risk it and give it a try. That burning fire inside of me wanted to know him much, much better!

With very mixed emotions, I approached my section leader and handed her my audition tape before the meeting. I told her I was sorry, but I was having family problems, and I needed to get back home. I asked what I needed to know and do to make up for missing the rehearsal that night. She said she would let me know after listening to my tape. She assured me everything would be okay for me to go home and take care of my family business.

That was not like me, to miss out on a night of fun with the girls. But everyone has family problems from time to time, and everyone can relate to them, right? So hopefully, she could understand the situation that I was lying about. Nervously I drove back to New Fort.

The good girl inside of me was asking, *where in the hell are you going, Eva? What are you getting yourself into?* The bad girl inside my panties was saying, *Shut up! Let her have some fun for a change! She deserves it, after all, look what all she has to put up with!* I decided to listen to the bad girl inside my panties, for she was screaming at me to take a chance for once in my life!

In no time at all, I was at the subdivision gates. My heart was pounding with excitement, or maybe it was fear. . . fear of getting caught. I punched in the code with great care, and the large iron gates opened automatically without making a sound in the still night air. I drove into the subdivision very cautiously. I had not been inside this swanky subdivision before; it was lovely. Every home was a mansion, or so it seemed to me. I followed his directions two streets down on the right, then one road over to the left. The first house on the corner, house number 1257 was engraved on the cornerstone. There was a name also on the cornerstone, but I did not take time to read it. I drove in as quickly as I could, then around to the back where his car was parked. He was waiting there for me.

He greeted me with a soft kiss on my hand as he opened my car door and assisted me out. I could smell the sweet fragrance of the roses on the lawn in the hot summer night as I exited my car. He leaned in and smelled behind my left ear. "Humm, nice perfume," was his only comment. He put this arm around me, and we walked through the decorative, stained-glass, double doors that led into the den area of this beautiful colossal home, closing the doors behind us cautiously after we had entered.

He had already showered, shaved, and changed into casual evening clothing. Black silk lounging pants and matching silk shirt was worn along with his house slippers. The slippers had a sheep logo on the top. I couldn't tell what that symbol stood for, because I had never seen that brand before. I am sure they must have been purchased in some fancy men's store; that's why I didn't recognize the brand.

Looking out the back wall of glass windows was a lovely view of the golf course which was adjacent to the exquisitely landscaped backyard. A sizeable kidney-shaped swimming pool was just outside the double doors.

A long bar ran along another wall of the den. Behind the bar was a mirrored wall that was lined with shelves of beautiful crystal glass and stemware. Liquors of all sorts were stocked at the bar for anyone who should desire any libation. I was overwhelmed, but I tried not to show it.

Throughout the house intercom system Stevie Wonder was singing:

> *Isn't she lovely,*
> *Isn't she wonderful,*
> *Isn't she precious. . .?*

"I love that song," he said as he joined in singing with Stevie Wonder. I was embarrassed as he continued to sing, *"Isn't she pretty."* He was staring straight at me, looking me straight in the eyes. My heart was about to come out of my throat! Man! And he can sing too! He could tell that he was embarrassing me by his singing to me, so he stopped.

I was relieved when he stopped singing, although I liked it and thought it was romantic. No man had ever sung to me before.

He changed the subject by asking, "Did you have any trouble getting away from your rehearsal?"

"No, but I wonder if my section leader might have been suspicious. Or maybe I was feeling guilty." I told him.

"What can I make for you to drink?" He asked.

"Something sweet and bubbly, I'll leave it up to you." I did not know the names of any fancy drinks.

"Alright, how about a wine spritzer?"

"Sounds good to me."

I was sitting at the bar as I watched him make my drink, then he made an Old Fashion for himself. When he handed my cocktail to me, he tapped his glass to mine and said, "To a pretty lady." Then he sat down beside me. *Yeah! That silver-tongued devil! He sure knows how to talk to ladies*, I thought.

Okay, so there I was, alone with Mr. Wonderful *supposedly* for the sole purpose of getting to know one another better. We both knew there was more to the visit than that. So, what now? How much small talk can we conjure up? He was as nervous as I was, I could tell, but I didn't exactly understand why. Of course, I was nervous because I was a married woman doing the unthinkable. Or should I say *the unallowable*? He was not married and could do whatever he wanted to do, and probably did so all of the time! That was obvious.

We had a small amount of conversation about my son, but when it came to his son, he cut the conversation short. It was clear to me for some reason, he did not want to go any farther into the conversation about his son. I didn't press the issue. Some people are private like that, I guess. Besides, we needed to stay focused on one another. And focused we did for the rest of the visit!

"Would you mind if we moved to the back of the house so that we can have more privacy?" he asked. I agreed because I was uncomfortable sitting in front of the full glassed wall of windows for the rest of the world to see me there, where I should not be.

He gently took me by the hand and led me down the hall, which was lined with unique paintings from all over the world, or so it appeared. At the end of the long hallway, we entered the bedroom. Why was I not surprised? Can you spell *overwhelmed*? I was standing in the most beautifully decorated bedroom I had ever been in; the size was enormous. The decor was in black and gold. The room was spacious and tastefully laid out. There were custom-made draperies with heavy tassels that matched the bedspread. In the center of the comforter was a large monogrammed letter. The letter was so scrolly I couldn't make out what the letter was. I guessed it was an "R" for Rosenberg? A large oriental rug accented the rest of the décor. Two wing-backed chairs were placed beside the king-size poster bed. Beautiful paintings were hanging on two walls. Other artworks from all over the world were on various pieces of massive furniture.

I asked to use the restroom. Alex motioned to the adjoining room, which was another great surprise! This room was more significant than the bedroom! Mirrors were along one wall; the floors were marble. The shower was completely open, with no enclosures. The four-sink vanity and makeup area took up another wall, complemented by a crystal chandelier and lighted mirrors. A Jacuzzi was in the corner of the bathroom with a mural behind it. A lovely tub set close by with gold trimmed faucets in the shape of swans. A large statue of an Italian Goddess stood in the middle of the room with a fountain of water flowing from her vase.

Then there was the biggest surprise of all! There were two commodes, open and exposed for all to see a person do their business! I don't think I could use that restroom should another person be in there at the same time. I later found out the other facility was a bidet. Having never seen a bidet before, I was intrigued.

After I got over my wide-eyed-wonder at the beauty of the bathroom, I went about taking care of the business of why I went in that gorgeous room in the first place. I then refreshed myself, just in case events got to where I expected (and hoped) they would go. I immediately took off those damned ole pantyhose and stuffed them into my purse.

When I came out, Mr. Wonderful was once again waiting for me. He handed my drink to me. I thought he might be sitting in one of those beautiful winged-back chairs, but no, he was reclined on the bed. He had taken off his shirt and had on only his silk lounging pants. God! He looked fabulous without his shirt! He had a full chest of black hair, which was the sexiest, manliest thing I had ever seen!

I have always loved hair on my chest (just not growing there.)

I thought, *how did a plain ole vanilla girl like me, get here with a man like him?*

He patted on the bed for me to come to lie with him. Reluctantly, I sat in the chair beside the bed. He reached over and took my hand gently and kissed it. I melted, set my drink on a nearby table, and slid into bed beside him. (He was such a smooth talker.)

Without another word, slow kisses started. I longed for Alex's slow, hot kisses. I responded with my tongue, in and out of his mouth. Over and over, we played cat and mouse with one another. Slowly his hand slid up my leg, then back down; he took off my left shoe and dropped it onto the floor. Then back up my leg, and down; he was teasing me, kissing me and titillating me with his slow hands. He changed legs, up, then down; he took off my right shoe, glanced at it only momentarily, then dropped it to the floor.

He started massaging my feet gently, more firmly around the toes, then he moved on to my arches. Hmmm! His manipulations, rubbing, stroking, and kneading were fabulous! It sent waves of desire throughout my body. I felt my solar plexus flexing and releasing. Then my uterus began to tighten and contract. I wanted to have him inside me; I was sex-starved for a man like him!

He tenderly helped me out of my blouse, and I slid out of my skirt, leaving just my little lace bra and bikinis exposed for his visual enjoyment as I laid on the bed. His eyes dilated as we continued with our sexual fore-playtime.

His teasing hands did not move up to my panties, not just yet. The bad girl in my panties was begging him to get there. She desperately wanted him to feel those silk bikinis and take them off. But he didn't, he loved to touch and play with my long, naked legs; he was a leg man. I loved it. That way, I would not be embarrassed because I had small breasts. Large breasts were not a big deal to him. He loved long, slender legs that led him up to the Promised Land.

I was going crazy with arousal, I couldn't take much more of his teasing, and he knew I was ready. He reached up and carefully pulled off my panties. They were wet, as was that pretty little fun spot. He took a quick sneak peek at my dainty white bikinis as he dropped them onto the floor. Then he put the palm of his hand and completely covered my clitoris. He started to massage it with his warm palm, and with gentle pressure, he was driving me out of my mind! My clitoris was already engorged and throbbing, and his massaging was almost more than I could stand. He continued to deep kiss me as I spread my legs farther, wanting and waiting for his penetration.

He slid out of his silk lounging pants and out sprang his Big Boy like a Jack-in-the-Box that stood at attention! Damn! It was big, hard, and throbbing. How was I to handle that big thing? I didn't know, but I knew it would be fabulous when it happened. My wet hot spot got even wetter and ready for him when I saw it, knowing it was big and hard because he wanted me too. As I looked at him, his eyes were dilated. I knew this was lust in his eyes. . . a desire for me. I loved it. My breasts nipples started to get hard and sensitive as I was ready to share myself with him. I could feel myself arching my neck and back as I was preparing myself to receive him, but he didn't give it to me yet. He only watched me. . . watched me wanting him and waiting for him to enter me. I **_did_** want him! I wanted to enjoy hot, forbidden sex with him long and hard like a wild-ass animal in heat! I felt like a she-animal, searching and aching for her mate to soothe that spot that was itching to be scratched.

"Oh! Alex, please." I moaned as I reached up and kissed him deeply. I tilted my pretty little fun spot up toward him; I spread my labia, giving him a clear view of my Garden of Pleasure, letting him smell my emitting sex scent, and letting him know I was ready to receive him. He wet the tip of his penis with the honey dripping from my honeypot. After wetting his penis, he flexed it up and down on my clit. His penis pounding hard on my already swollen clit was something I had never experienced. OMG! It made me anxious! My Garden of Paradise was ready to take us both on a sextravaganza of a lifetime! Ahhh! There it was! He entered me, slowly, sliding slowly in, only a very little. He stopped and looked me in the eyes. "Are you okay?" He asked. He knew his penis was more abundant than usual; he was concerned I would not be able to handle all of him.

"Oh, yes!" Not being able to hold back any longer, I hunched toward him to get more of him inside me. More of that Big Boy felt good the deeper it went. Yes, he was more substantial than anything I had ever had or imagined! But it was *better* than anything I had ever imagined or experienced, the deeper he slowly worked himself into me. He was the manliest man I had ever met much less ever had sex with!

Then! There it was! OMG! He just touched a place that I did not know was inside of me! OMG! It was my G-Spot, and he has found it! I had heard of it before, but never thought I would ever find mine, much less know it could feel so heavenly to be stroked! It was like losing my virginity, in a totally different fantastic way.

He was sexfully stroking my G-Spot each time he entered me as if he were a sexpert! I wanted the night to never end. We started our hunching rhythm back and forth. He was pumping me slowly and deeply while he was stroking my clitoris with his fingertips. My clitoris was engorged, and his every touch was like heaven. His Big Boy was touching my G-Spot—the place that had never been touched before. Up and down, in and out, every stroke was hitting me just right. He was going where no man had ever gone. I could not believe what I was feeling. The excitement of being with this handsome man added to my pleasure exponentially. We kept kissing and sucking on one another until I had all I thought I could stand. Without warning, Alex stopped, looked at me, and smiled in a dreamy sort of way; then he started again with his mind-blowing sextraganza.

The hunching started again just like brand-new. Alex knew what he was doing—driving me crazy! I was reaching higher and higher for his penis to go deeper inside me! Deeper inside of me to feel him stroke that spot again and again. Ohhhh. Then! There it was! I began to breathlessly have an orgasm like never before! He kept watching me, his eyes were focused on my eyes. His eyes were locked on mine, but I did not care. I continued to moan and release the pleasure of a lifetime. It made him more excited to see that I was fully satisfied. His penis got harder; he drove it into me faster and deeper than before! He began his release. With a loud groan of unashamed ecstasy, he had a great climax, shooting his seeds of hot sperm into me, filling me and overflowing. I continued to squeeze tightly on his penis, so I could feel it deep inside of me a little longer. Then he fell on me, and we collapsed together. I was worn out and breathless from the pleasure of it all. I was sweaty all over. My pretty little fun spot was soaked with hot semen, as well as the bed. My clitoris was still throbbing, engorged, and sensitive.

I can genuinely say I had been well *sassy-fied*. We laid there with Alex still inside me. I continued to flex and tighten my vagina muscles to enjoy a few more final pleasures for both of us. I didn't want him to come out of me; I wanted him to stay inside me forever.

What a fabulous, *sex-sational* experience it was that night! I wanted more of this man for the rest of my life! I would do anything to get and keep him! He truly was *sex-sational!*

Chapter 12 The Periwinkle

The periwinkle evokes feelings of:
- Blossoming friendship that is still in its first stages.
- Reminiscing about pleasant memories shared with a friend.
- Reaching your full potential and achieving your dreams.

- Existence throughout eternity and extending your time with what you love.
- Everlasting love.

After we made love that first night, he kissed me briefly, then he put back on his lounging pants, but not his shirt. His hairy chest looked so sexy! He went to the bathroom for a few moments, and when he returned, he sat in a nearby chair. I felt a little awkward, so I went to the bathroom and refreshed myself too. I was a total mess, and I knew I had to get back to looking normal before going home.

A very wise person once told me:

"Always pay close attention to the way a man treats you <u>after</u> he has had sex with you, and you will be able to know how he truly feels about you."

Those thoughts were going through my mind as I entered the bathroom.

When I re-entered the bedroom, he was sitting in a chair beside the bed petting a beautiful Springer Spaniel. I asked what his or her name was. He told me her name was Abby. She was magnificent! I could see he was enthralled with this dog, and for a good reason. I petted her only briefly. I had never had an inside dog before. But this dog was something else! She was a superior show dog. I could see why he loved her so. It was obvious this man had a big heart and could show love because of the way he was doting over his dog. Most of the time, he kept his affections closely guarded.

It was shortly afterward that he told me, "I guess you had better be going, so you won't get into trouble." I thought to myself, *I'm the timekeeper here, why did he say that?* Again, I remembered those wise old words from that wise friend from my past:

"Pay close attention to the way a man treats you <u>after</u> he has had sex with you, and you will know how he truly feels about you."

There was my answer. I felt used as though he only wanted me for one thing. He got it, and now he was finished with me. He had made his conquest, it was over, and he was ready to move on. So, I moved on too.

I moved on--out of his door as quickly as possible and drove myself home, crying.

Upon arrival at my home, it was a relief to see that all the lights were out, and everyone was asleep. I slipped out of my clothes, got into bed next to Cody, and continued to cry silently.

I stayed awake for a long time that night. There I was at the beginning of a new relationship with this handsome man with whom I had fallen in love. It was truly *love at first sight*, but it was not reciprocal.

Beautiful thoughts and reminisces of the night and our lovemaking kept running through my mind. Those deep hot kisses and his warm touches made up the most pleasant moments of my life thus far. For the rest of my life, I would never forget that night with him. I would take that night into eternity with me. I would always remember Alex's loving touches and him going to places that no one had ever gone before. My only hope was that I could make him feel for me what I was feeling for him.

Then horror struck my heart! Oh hell! What if I have gotten pregnant, or what if he has given me a venereal disease? He *is* a man about the town, you know! He could have any woman in two counties, and probably already has! Then I thought about HIV. It sometimes can take up to seven years for those symptoms to occur! Oh hell! Eva! What the hell have you done?

The next day I hurried to my doctor's office and confessed what I had done while begging for an injection of penicillin as a precautionary measure. I would not tell the doctor who the man was, but he gave me the injection anyway. He thought it was funny that I was so concerned and scared. I did not think it was so damn funny at all!

I vowed never to do it again!

Chapter 13 The Snapdragons

The snapdragons message is this: things are not always what they appear to be. Be careful where you stick your nose because magic is in the air.

A month or more had ped, and I had not seen nor heard from Mr. Wonderful. I was depressed and was sure that my predictions of post-lovemaking actions were valid. He had conquered me, and now he had no further use for me. Then one day, out of the blue, he popped into my store. My vows to 'never-do- it-again' were forgotten then and there!

I was lucky; Cody was not there. Neither Alex nor I mentioned that first night. It was as if it never happened. "I've been in Chicago, setting up and working a trade show for the past two weeks. I'm so glad to be back home in paradise! How have you been?" he asked.

What the hell! I thought. *It's been over a month, and I have not heard from him.* Well if that was the best excuse he could come up with, I would accept it. After all, there I was again, like a damn fool, looking into his brown bedroom eyes, about to cream my panties! I was crazy about this man that I called Mr. Wonderful.

"How was Chicago?" I asked. "It was still there when I left it." was his quick response. I thought *he's so damn cool and witty; I could get along with a guy like that.*

"What are you doing later this afternoon?" He asked. "Why?" I replied.

"I have to go to Mobile to check on a few things, and I was wondering if you would like to ride over with me?"

"I can't ride over with you, but I might meet you over there, and then we can ride together."

"That'll work," he said.

"Can you meet me at University Boulevard and Azalea Street around 4 o'clock? There is a barbecue restaurant on the corner."

"Okay, I will try, but if anything comes up and I can't make it, how can I get in touch with you to let you know?"

"Here's my beeper number, page me if anything happens. Otherwise, I'll be waiting for you."

I agreed, and once again, we were back into making sparks and electricity. The bad girl in my panties was feeling sorta vampy, I could feel her smiling.

I told Cody I needed to go to Mobile and help Aunt Patty that afternoon because she was not feeling well. She had cancer, and it was progressing. He was somewhat understanding; but he did not like it that I was going to Mobile.

I took the time to run home and freshen up before driving over. This time I did not wear pantyhose! To keep from sending out a red flag, I simply wore pants and a button-down blouse. Had I worn a skirt or anything sexy, Cody would have gotten suspicious. I did wear perfume and sexy lace matching underwear that I had purchased from Victoria's Secret earlier, for his eyes only. I kept them hidden from Cody in the bottom of my lingerie drawer.

I arrived early, so I stopped by a little card shop and purchased a card for him. It simply read:

"You charm the pants off me."

Then I drove across the street where he was waiting in the parking lot. He motioned for me to come over to his Mercedes, and he got out and opened the door for me.

Wow! I thought. *Cody has never opened the door for me! What a gentleman, this man is!* I loved every moment with him. As I sat down in his car, I noticed the music on his stereo was Bob Marley. When he got into the car, I handed him the card; without reading it, he just put it over his visor. I was disappointed because I wanted to see his reaction when it was read. Oh well! He seemed to be a private sort of guy anyway. I simply had to assume he wanted to read it and digest it in private.

His car was a mess. Business papers were strewn all over the floor and backseat. Chocolate milk cartons and cookie wrappers were scattered everywhere. The ashtray was full and getting more so. I didn't mind that he smoked. I smoked when I was younger and liked it. I would still smoke cigarettes if Cody let me. I liked the way Alex tasted when he smoked. He reminded me of the Marlboro Man, (only in a business suit.) I couldn't wait to taste him again that day, knowing I would be doing so very soon.

I asked him where we were going, and he said he had to check on a house that he owned in West Mobile. I wondered about that but didn't go any farther with my questioning. I didn't know if it was a rental house or what. I figured it was none of my business and certainly did not want him to tell me it was none of my business, assuming I would find out soon enough.

When we arrived at the house, it was apparent he was getting agitated. The house was vacant, the doors were open, and the grass had not been cut in a long while. When we went into the house, he became even more frustrated upon seeing the condition of the inside. The house was empty, and the tenants had moved out, leaving it in ill repair. I walked around the house with him as he searched each room and investigated each closet. I said nothing but felt uneasy under the circumstances. I did not understand why he was so upset. He finally told me that this house belonged to him, and he had allowed his ex-wife and her new husband to live there. The house was furnished with his furnishings, and they were to leave them when they left. Not keeping their end of the bargain, they took all his furnishings when they moved. In addition to leaving without notice, they went with unpaid rent. The only thing he could find during his search was his Air Force flak jacket, which he took with him as we left. While feeling bad for him, this incident did tell me one thing; he had a slight temper that could be displayed when he was riled. But it was nothing compared to that of Cody, who was a maniac when he got upset. Mr. Wonderful was a gentleman when he was mad, mostly keeping his anger to himself and under control. Rather stoic, one might say.

When he had finished his exploratory efforts, he decided to settle down and pay attention to me. I was glad. It wasn't the best of circumstances, nor the most romantic of settings, especially the beautiful place we were on our first date. I did not care. I felt that I was with the most exciting man in the world! For some reason, he asked me to go with him to this location. But why? Was he comfortable enough with me to take me here? I bet he would never take Ms. Phillips here. By-the-way, where was she anyway? (You remember her---the wealthy, regal iris from chapter 6.) I had not seen them together around town in quite a while. What's up with that? I was not about to ask any questions about her, being merely happy to be with him for the moment.

Alex found a clean set of sheets in the hall closet and spread them on the master bedroom floor. We sat there, leaning against the wall and talked about his problems concerning his house and his ex-wife while he smoked a cigarette. Not much information was shared, but it was apparent he had a great deal of resentment built up toward his ex, due to past events. Some of the trouble had to do with her influencing their son to feel indifferent toward him. It was as if he needed someone to talk to about it. He was still very hesitant about sharing too much information. His feelings were closely guarded. I knew it would be difficult for him to open up to me, so I didn't push the issue. I felt sad for his pain. How could anyone cause such pain to this wonderful man? He seemed successful, kind-hearted, and I knew he had a lot of love that he could share, but I would have to break down those barriers. Someone had hurt him badly, and he had built a fence around himself to protect his feelings against any future pain. That lady was a fool, in my opinion, to mistreat a man like him! I would give anything to have a man like him!

I leaned in and kissed him gently to let him know that I cared. Slowly he seemed to forget his problems. After a short while of kissing, we went from sitting, to reclining, to lying on the floor. He was beside me, slightly hovering over me, just looking at me. He began to kiss me again, only this time more passionately. He unbuttoned my blouse, and I helped him take it off. There he found my pink lace push-up bra that made my small breasts appear larger than they were. He was kissing my mouth, then he moved down my neck, then lower to my breasts. He kissed and rolled my nipples with his tongue and tickled them with his mustache while still in my bra. Arching my back gave him more access to suck on. Oh hell! It felt so damn good! It was sending feel-good-rolling-messages down to my vagina. My pretty-little-fun-spot was getting ready to enjoy him. I could feel my uterus contracting tighter and tighter.

I pulled him back up to my face so I could kiss his mouth more deeply and suck on his tongue as it was going in and out. He took off his shirt, exposing his big hairy chest that turned me on even more. I moved down and sucked on his left nipple, he groaned slightly and bit his lower lip. When he started to unzip his pants, his Big Boy sprang out before he could get out of his pants. Oh God! I wanted to hump it right then and there!

He finished undressing me down to my pink lace bikinis, that I had purchased for his eyes only. I hoped he liked what he was seeing. He must have because he immediately started fellatio my pretty-little-fun-spot through my panties. Looking up only once to say, "I adore your body!" He kissed his way back up from my stomach to my breasts, going from one to another. His Big Boy was getting bigger and harder by the second. Big Boy would flex from time to time like a bucking bronco waiting for the ride! I was ready to be ridden. He kissed and rolled his tongue from my breasts, back down to my belly button, and there he stuck his tongue in and sucked, then further down he went. I was about to explode with a hot passion for getting Big Boy inside me, but it didn't happen just yet. He pulled my bikinis to the side and put his whole mouth around my clitoris and sucked the hell out of it! He sucked hard and long, as I nearly died from pleasure! His mustache was tickling, his tongue was circling, and his sucking was almost more than I could stand when--he slowly put his index finger into my vagina and commenced to masterfully massage my G-Spot. I was out of my mind when I climaxed before I could stop myself! My clitoris was throbbing, and my belly was rolling and flexing inside and outside. I felt myself curling up almost into a fetal position with the best pleasurable sensation that I could ever imagine, and it was still going on and on! He was a master lover, and he knew how to make a woman climax out of her mind! He certainly knew where the Grafenberg Spot (G-Spot) was located and how to massage it like a pro!

After what seemed to be a long time, I settled down and relaxed. I was embarrassed because Alex had not participated in the climax. He just smiled at me and said, "Was that fun?" All I could breathlessly say was, "Uh, huh!" He let me rest for a while as he playfully stroked my arm. He breathed and blew his breath on the back of my neck only nano-inches away, without actually touching me, making the hair on my back and neck stand up; I quivered from the delight of it all.

When Alex knew I was ready for my postfuck, he began his magic once again. He took me tenderly by my hips and rolled me over onto my stomach, then he pulled me up onto my knees. My ass was fully exposed in the air as he was softly rubbing it before slowly and carefully inserting Big Boy into my vagina from behind. Oh! He was BIG! He was big, hard, and full! Concerned, he asked, "Is that okay?" He knew it might be hurting me; he wanted to be sure before proceeding. I could tell he was sex-starved for a good playful sexercise and he needed a good sexual release; Big Boy was about to burst at the seams. I told him I was "just fine." He grabbed my shoulders as he proceeded to thrust into me more deeply, filling me from wall to wall, with flesh to flesh.

He anxiously drove more deeply into me. With one hand, he started caressing my breast, then both hands. Deeper, then side to side with each thrust. He rolled his hips in a circular-type-motion like a fine-tuned instrument. Gently he took hold of my hips as he pulled me back toward him, then we got into a rocking rhythm. There we were, a couple of wild bucking broncos! It didn't take long, and he climaxed long and hard with a loud groan of contentment, over and over he released and released again. "Oh, Baby! Oh, Baby!" I could tell it was good for him; I wanted it to be good---No! I wanted it to be great for him! This highly sexed man needed a spicy, little gal like me who could return his masculine needs like a real woman!

We both fell to the floor, onto the sheets, and caught our breath. Then Alex found his shirt, reached into the shirt pocket, and took out a cigarette. He lit one and inhaled. A relaxed, contented look came over his face. I was lying there, smiling at him. Out of nowhere, he said, "You must be some sort of magician."

I was mystified at his words. "What do you mean by that?"

"Because you sure can make a man's problems disappear!"

I responded, "When you stuck your nose in my panties, you sure worked magic there! So, now who's the magician?"

P.S.

Girls, if you have never had a Grafenberg orgasm, you are missing out! Learn how to locate your G-Spot and teach your man how to pleasure you there. The best way to find your G-Spot is usually right after you are aroused (or during masturbation.) Insert your middle finger (because it is the longest) into your vagina. Push upward toward your pelvis bone, around that area is the soft spot to massage. You will know when you are there. A penis need not go in very far to hit the spot. Usually, the mushroom shape of the penis head can gently massage the spot if your lover takes his time when stroking in and out, he will send you into orbit!

Don't be bashful about telling your lover what you need and desire during sex. Lovemaking is a two-way game; don't be left out of the fun and pleasure. If you let your lover have all the pleasure, you will eventually resent it!

You should not allow yourself to be used as the vehicle that takes him to his destination.

Do you know what I mean?

Chapter 14 The Crown Imperial

The crown imperial represents powerfulness and mightiness.

Girls, you may not know this, but you are in possession of the most powerful gift on earth! Actually, you own two mighty gifts, if used properly. One is your brain. You can have your man eating out of your hands if you handle him with special care. Only you know your man. You know what will make him happy and what will upset him. You know how to avoid those unfortunate situations. You know how to make him feel like the king of the hill. So, use your brain without him knowing it, to your advantage.

If you love your man and want to keep him, be careful of the things you do unconsciously. If he is the jealous type, make it a point not to be flirty. It makes him feel less of a man when his lady is showing attention to other men. It appears he is not taking care of business at home. Therefore, his position as 'king of the hill' is threatened. Fireworks will always erupt.

You should not speak negatively of your man to others. You may be mad at him today, but tomorrow you will be over your anger. Meanwhile, the foxes will be ready to move in to help you out of your problems. There are plenty of other lady foxes who need and want your man; don't think they don't.

It is not a good idea to advertise to your friends how good your man is in bed. They will try to steal him every time!

Do not argue in public with your man. It makes you both look bad, and it embarrasses everyone in the room. Use your brain to outsmart the uncomfortable situation. What-ever-it-is can wait until you get home, then discuss it in private. Yes, sometimes there will be hurt feelings. But remember this:

**"The smartest person (the peacemaker)
apologizes first."**

I did not say you have to take the blame for what-ever-it-was. A simple statement such as, "I am sorry we had that misunderstanding," will suffice. Do not, under any circumstance, add the word "BUT. . ." If you do, it negates everything.

Sometimes to keep the peace, we must have hard conversations. I'm not talking about avoiding conflict for *artificial harmony*. I'm talking about you initiating the conversation, taking the first step, to engage one another toward a peaceful way to settle the conflict for loving harmony. Remember:

Hurting people---hurt other people.

Having talked about one gift, your brain, let's move on to the other most powerful gift known to humanity. If this powerful treasure is used with precision, you will almost always get what you want from your man.

<u>Always think twice before giving this treasure away the first time. Once it is given away, there no longer remains any mystery.</u> Remember the "little-deer-running" thing?

Your most powerful gift is your *Garden of Pleasure*, or whatever pet name you may choose to use. I use "Little Eva" along with my "Garden of Pleasure."

Your Garden of Pleasure is beautiful, lush, and pleasant to all who enter. You are the garden keeper, and you are in complete control over this paradise. Your Little Eva is adorned with the most beautiful, most expensive fur known to man. Her coat is soft, just enough to add that fluffy comfort needed for her lover. It smells of clean, sweet perfume.

Little Eva wears her crown proudly on top of her clitoris, which is where the fun usually begins.

Extending downward from her crown on the inside and each side are the two Labia minor of Little Eva. They are the welcoming, smooth lips that warmly caress her lover while he is visiting her Garden of Pleasure. When her tender, soft lips are kissed by her lover, the taste of milk and honey drip from her Garden of Pleasure (which is also referred to as her vagina.) Only special invited lovers are allowed entry into her Garden of Pleasure. It is always a unique sensation when the penis of her lover first enters her vagina for it is swollen and moist. All her body is aching to be filled with his full-length penis to come inside and move in concert with her. Many times, she has experienced this sensation, but there is always something unique about the first penile probing into her Garden of Pleasure. The warm feeling of stretching as the head of her lover's penis enters the garden and the solid sense of pleasure, she is sure they will be sharing. She has exercised her vaginal muscles in order to squeeze and flex tightly around the penis of her lover to give him greater pleasure. In doing so, it heightens her pleasure to orgasm.

Yes, your Garden of Pleasure is truly a prized possession. Many a man has fought and died for her. You own her. You must take outstanding care of her for your own health's sake as well as others. Use her wisely, and you too will be treated like a queen! Be strong and always show yourself as a lady so you may prosper in all that you do and wherever you go. Remember, you are in charge of your Garden of Pleasure; whom you invite to enter therein is critical! Sometimes you must make the all-important decision to disinvite a consistently destructive lover from your Garden of Pleasure. Only you can make that decision, and it is up to you to be strong and in charge.

It has been said that women are in charge of 80% of the world's money and 100% of the sex. Is that surprising?

If you haven't taken the time to acquaint yourself with your Garden of Pleasure, I strongly suggest you do so. Get a hand mirror and look at what your lover enjoys viewing. Do not be bashful. Your Garden of Pleasure is a potent attraction when used correctly. Now, make sure yours is always just that. . . a clean, sweet-smelling little garden. A pretty little fun spot for your man and you to enjoy.

Your Garden of Pleasure is a powerful gift when used with precision. If you are not comfortable with having and enjoying sex, hopefully by the end of this book, you will have learned some pointers. <u>Men love a confident woman in bed</u>. If you are not confident, you can learn to be. *I am not talking about faking an orgasm*. I'm talking about getting what you want in bed from your man. If you do not tell him what you want and need him to do, he will not know. He will continue to do the same old things he has always done, his way, to please himself. You must train him to do what you want him to do to please you, i.e., slow down, speed up, harder, etc. I'm not talking about speaking bossy to him during sex. Just tell him in your sexiest voice what you need him to do, show him suggestively with your hands. Let him know when he is doing something that is pleasing you, even with unspoken words. He will work harder to bring you to orgasm the more you enjoy it.

Sex is not "erection to ejaculation." That is such a penis thing. It is about two people enjoying one another's company and each other's bodies in mutual consent. Don't do anything you are uncomfortable doing. Your lover should understand. But, don't be embarrassed to show your lover what you want. You might be surprised at the results!

A very wise lady once told me:

A man wants his lady to be two in one:

"He wants a whore in his bedroom and a lady in the living room."

Another word of advice: Never use your gift against your man. I'm talking about withholding sex from him as a punishment for something. That is like cutting off your nose to spite your face. Work out your problems, whatever they may be, in other ways. If you love your man and want to keep him, do not let that problem go on for long periods. I realize some issues may be unsolvable. If you keep it right in the bedroom, that loving relationship will head off a lot of problems!

A lady can use her gifts for her good, or to her detriment. When misused, she may end up a lonely old woman. But when she spends her gifts wisely, her wealth doubles.

Chapter 15 The Pansy

The pansy represents the birth flower of February.

The pansy means three things: be of good cheer, a clear mind, and a calm spirit.

Once again, a long time passed, and I had not heard from Mr. Wonderful. I always hoped he would call me, but he seldom did. There was not a day that passed that I did not think about him; I was indeed in love with Mr.

Rosenberg. Sometimes, most of the time, I felt like a fool for being in love with a man who had no thoughts or feelings for me. I could not help that I had strong feelings for him. Those thoughts and feelings would not go away; I tried to no avail.

One night after returning from Glee Girls rehearsal, I drove into his gated community to investigate things. I had no idea what I might find. Probably nothing, because it was late at night. But I went in any way out of curiosity. I drove around and right up to the house. I noticed the cornerstone that I could not read the name that first night when I was there, but I read it this time. It did not read "Rosenberg." It read "Phillips." *What the hell?* It wasn't his house! What was he doing in her home that first night without her there; and why did he invite me to her house? It was getting very confusing to me; I hurried away so I would not be caught spying on her home.

Questions, questions! I then remembered that fancy, scrolly monogram in the center of the beautiful bedspread. It was not a beautiful scrolly "R" . . . for Rosenberg. It was a beautiful, scrolly "P" for Phillips!

My mind went back to that night. He wanted me to pull my car around to the back of the house so that no one could see my car. I thought he wanted to preserve my privacy. Then, when we were sitting in the den, and he wanted us to move out of the den area because there were glass windows all along the back of the wall where we were exposed to the world for everyone to see us sitting there. Again, I thought he had my privacy in mind because I was married. And lastly, when he told me, "it's time you should be going before you get into trouble at your house." All these things I thought were because he had my safety in mind, now I realize it was for his safety. He did not want anyone to know he had another woman at his girlfriend's home!

I wondered if he might be living there with her. I guess I would not know for now. If she was so great, why in the hell was he occasionally interested in plain old me, a married woman? He could have any lady in this city and two counties over. Why me? I wanted desperately to get this damn man out of my mind and heart forever! But I couldn't. I was always thinking of him and remembering the times we spent together. I loved every minute of those times, and I longed for more times to be with him. I never knew when the next time would be. But in the meantime, when I wasn't with him, I was mad at him. Mad because he would not call me. But when he did call, it was all over, my madness disappeared. I melted again. Could this be love or just lust?

It was now February 1986. I was at a service station getting gas before going to work. Alex pulled in behind me. It started all over. I couldn't help but be glad. My heart began to race at the sight of him. He walked up and put out his cigarette, then said, "Hey pretty lady. What are you up to today?"

"Just getting ready to go to work," I responded.

"What time do you have to be there?"

I didn't have to be at work until noon, so I was early. I had a little time to spare before going in.

"What do you have in mind?" I asked. We toyed with one another like a cat and mouse, which was our style before our escapades. It was as if he had to talk me into it. (He <u>was</u> such a smooth talker!)

He said, "I have to go to Pensacola to work in our store for the afternoon and train our employees on a new product. Would you care to ride over with me?" Of course, I could not be gone for the entire afternoon. I told him I couldn't go that far, but how about we rendezvous in the next town over for a little while? He agreed.

I followed him to the next town, which seemed to take forever. *Where in the hell was he taking me,* I wondered? Then he pulled in behind a little obscure church, which appeared to be abandoned, but it wasn't, because there were picnic tables behind it and the grass was cut. We pulled behind the church and parked. I felt sleazy about meeting at a place like that, but I was happy to be with this wonderful man with whom I was enthralled.

Alex drove around the building and got out of his car first. He stood beside his car, pulled off his navy blazer, then slid his necktie out of his stiffly starched, white shirt, laying them both neatly across the back seat. Alex casually walked over to my car, and opened the door, took me by the hand to help me out. Before we could go any farther, he kissed me, passionately. No time was wasted on small talk. We both knew why we were there. We were both adults who liked sex. And we were damn good at pleasing one another. We loved it together, and we couldn't get enough of it. Time was wasting. We had traveled a long distance already, and it would take a long time for me to get back to my workplace. Yes, I knew we were going to have sex that day, but not before we had a little talk. He had some explaining to do.

The day was beautiful; it was warm, and the sun was shining brightly. There wasn't a cloud in the sky. The daffodils were blooming, and the bees were buzzing around them. The red birds were singing and mating. Watching those birds mating was like an aphrodisiac. And there I was, with the right man to enjoy it with!

We walked over to an old picnic table that was located under a pavilion and sat down. "Do you mind if I ask you a question?" I asked. "No. Certainly not. Shoot!" He said, seemingly assured of himself.

"That night at Waterfront. . ." I hesitated. "Yes? What about it?" He asked.

"Whose house was that?"

"A friend's house. I was house sitting." He said.

"House sitting?" I said with a questionable look on my face.

"Yes. You know the lady you saw me with at the theater a few months ago? It's her house. She asked me to stay in her house while she was away for a month in the drunk tank."

"Drunk tank? I have never heard of a drunk tank." I almost laughed, but I didn't.

I guess he knew I was curious about this mysterious lady, so he felt compelled to explain the relationship between them. I was glad I didn't have to probe any farther for more answers. He continued with his story.

"I met her last March at the St. Patrick's Friends of Folly party downtown. We hit it off right away and started dating. It did not take long for me to know I was not in her league. She has more money than God, and she does not know what to do with it. She has a full-time maid, so she has nothing to do all day. Therefore, she takes to drinking. And drinking she does. . . all day long. Wednesday is the only day she has something to do, and that is to play golf with her friends. Other than that, beauty salons, nail parlors, and the bottle are her best friends. After she and I became close friends, we would have our friends over to her house and I would cook for the dinner parties. It wasn't long before she asked me to stay over for the night, then eventually, it lasted longer until I moved in with her. Her drinking was a real problem because she did not know when to quit. She would get sloppy drunk, and that would embarrass me!"

"One time, we were in New Orleans at Commander's Palace with some business partners. We were ready to go to dinner when I drove the car around to pick everyone up at the front door. When I got there, she was sitting in the middle of the floor like a three-year-old child playing with some other children; that got off with me! I just took her back up to the room and left her for the night."

I was enjoying hearing the not-so-good-news about the "Iris" of whom I was jealous. I listened as he continued with his side of the story as to why they were not together any longer.

"I gotta tell you; she was a *dead fish* in bed too!" He chuckled as he said it. I was glad to hear that extra bit of information!

"While she was in the drunk tank, I had already made up my mind, I was going to move out as soon as she returned, and I did. On the day she returned, I told Kate, the maid, what I was doing. I said goodbye to Kate, and Kate only, also it had been a pleasure knowing her."

"You mean, you never told her why you were moving out?" I asked.

"Nope. I never spoke to her again. That was that."

I can't say that his simple explanation disappointed me in the least! I was elated!

When all the heavy conversation was out of the way, it was as if we could both take a deep breath and start over. And start over we did!

So, there we were sitting on a picnic table, under the pavilion, on that beautiful warm morning, listening to the birds mating, when Alex said, "Today is my birthday."

"Is it? Well, let me see. What can I give you as a birthday present?" I said sexily and suggestively, as I lowered my head and slowly looked up at him through squinting eyes.

"You could start with. . ." he said, with a wicked smile as he began unzipping his pants.

I thought, *Hell yes! I can give him what every man wants!* I reached over and put my hands on his hands as if I were helping him unzip his pants. Except, I did it slower; he seemed to be rushing. I knew if I moved slower, Big Boy would get bigger and harder. I unbuckled his nice leather belt, then unbuttoned his trousers. I was constantly keeping my eyes focused on his blazing-brown-bedroom-eyes when I moved lower and sat on the bench. My mouth was now near Big Boy. His eyes were full of lust, and I could feel his desire for me down to my panties. My vagina was flexing with want and desire to have him inside of me too. I continued my slow moves with tender hands---slowly-----slowly until his zipper was down. I could now put my hand inside his boxer underwear and find Big Boy! He wasn't hard to find, but when I found him, he **was hard!**

I gently and meticulously took him out, stroking him with both hands. The head of Big Boy was perky, purple, full and ready as I pulled back his foreskin more tightly and stroked it with my fingers, tickling it---down the backside vein, then back up. Mr. Wonderful flinched with pleasure; then he closed his eyes as he leaned his head back to relax further and enjoy his birthday gift, which was only beginning.

I was stroking Big Boy up and down, making sure the backside vein was caressed firmly, then back to the head of this beautiful penis. I wanted to give him a full-blown, mouth-to-head sucky-sucky, kissy-dicky, playful blow job. But I couldn't make myself do it; I didn't know him that well, not yet anyway. I blew my hot, steamy breath provocatively close, and all-around Big Boy, without actually touching. He flinched, wanting to give it all to my mouth. But the bad girl in my panties wanted that big hard playful penis all to herself! She was now obsessed with having a *real man* to torridly give her what she had been missing-out-on for years---deep penetrative sex!

"Where am I going to take you and finish giving you your birthday gift?" I asked with a sinful lust in my eyes. He looked up and around, then he responded, "have you ever done it in the back seat of a Cadillac?" I smiled, and without another word spoken, he buckled his belt, we took one another's hands and walked toward my car.

He got in first and sat down, unbuckling his belt once again as we proceeded with our lovemaking. Big Boy was standing at attention like a guard at the queen's palace. I climbed in and straddled his lap. We started kissing and teasing one another with our tongues once again. I was hunching back and forth on Big Boy with my clit through my panties. I could feel him pumping back to me. It was getting hot in that backseat, so we left the door open. He unbuttoned my blouse with my help. I kept my blouse on, and open, just in case someone walked up I could re-dress quickly.

My breasts were exposed and pushed high out of my bra cup, into his face for him to suck on my nipples. They were hard and standing at attention like little toy soldiers. My half shell, push-up, and wireless bra made my small breasts appear larger than they actually were. He nibbled and sucked and rolled my nipples; they were getting raw with pleasure. Then he slightly bit one. It was a hurt-good, do-that-again, sensation; I loved it! That sensation made my pretty little fun spot get wet and ready for him; he kept nibbling and kissing on my nipples; it was driving me crazy! Those feel-good vibrations rolled from my breasts, down the center of my belly, and on to my pretty little fun spot. The bad girl inside my panties helped me rush out of my bikinis. Alex watched as I pulled them off. He took a few moments to look at my body, then he said, "you sure have got a perfectly beautiful body. I wish I could have it every time I think of you."

Hearing his words were intoxicating! I was feeling frisky, rowdy, and ready to ride his penis whimsically to the end! I raised up; he slid his penis into me like a sexpert. With slow hands, holding his penis just right, he pulled back the small amount of foreskin for better sensation and guided his full, throbbing penis into me. Because I was already wet with desire, his penis slid in smoothly, profoundly and ever so fine! Ohhhh! I sighed when I felt all of him inside of me. I started pumping him up and down. He was slowly rocking back and forth.

His talented fingers were massaging the crown of my smooth, throbbing clitoris, as we kissed and sucked on one another's tongues and lips. My clit was getting larger and erect; it was like a small penis with all the sensations of one. But it wasn't a penis; it was the tiny little crown covering my clit of my little Eva in my Garden of Pleasure. OMG! His massaging my clitoris tickled so damn fine! I could hardly stand it; I could not get enough! I kept pumping and hunching for more of his Big Boy to fill that longing spot in my Garden of Pleasure that was begging for Alex and him alone! He was sending me into euphoria. He was sending me into places like never before. It was a heavenly sensation that I had never felt.

The head of Big Boy was touching my G-Spot on every long, slow stroke as he entered little Eva's welcoming Garden of Pleasure that was aching for more of his passionate pumping. His hard pumping lifted me, causing my head to hit the roof of the car. He continued massaging my clit with his thumb; it was the best rhythm and harmony I had ever heard or felt in my life!

"How nice is this?" I asked. He licked his lips and responded, "Do you know what effect you have on me?"

"Mmmm" I responded as my head was lolling from side to side. My lower abdomen was about to combust!! I spread my legs farther to take in all Big Boy that I could; I knew the climax was near. I didn't want it to happen, not just yet. I wanted this loving to last all day because it was feeling too damn luscious for it to end. But the storm was about to explode. I couldn't stop myself! I locked my arms around his head, my breasts cupped his nose, and I held on tightly! I let it all out! My vagina was throbbing as the orgasm onset and spasmed with sensations that were out of this world! Then he started his release; his penis grew harder as he climaxed. He closed his eyes tightly; his lips were in a straight, tight line. His deep throated groan was music to my ears. I felt his hot semen release into my garden as he ejaculated; then he arched his neck back and released more hot semen into me a second time with another final moan of pleasure.

How in the hell did I ever get here with a man like this? I wondered. I didn't know, but I knew I was never going to let him go. My pretty little Eva and his Big Boy were a match made in paradise! We both knew what one another wanted and needed. We both knew how to give it to the other. We knew we would be lovers for a very long time.

I loved giving my rose the perfect birthday gift, or *maybe* it was a gift to me.

Chapter 16 The Protea

What the protea flower means depends on the circumstances and the relationship between the giver and receiver, but there are some commonly agreed upon meanings: diversity, daring, transformation, and courage.

I had not seen, nor heard from Alex in a long time. One morning in the summer of 1986, I saw him at the Mayor's Prayer Breakfast at the Grand Hotel. As president of the Chamber of Commerce, he oversaw the meeting and had to give a speech. When he came forward, we made eye contact. I was sitting with Cody and two of our employees. I did not expect to see him there, nor did he expect to see me. It was as if seeing me was a reminder that maybe he should get in touch with me. I waited for his call, but he didn't.

I have no idea what he did or where he went during those times that I did not see him. I wondered if he was with someone else. I only knew that I thought of him every day of my life from the very first day we met. I wish I could tell you it wasn't so. It caused me a great deal of pain and sorrow, hoping he would call, or drop by, or just anything! It seemed like an eternity of not seeing him; I was living in limbo.

I tried to keep myself busy and tried not to think of Alex, so I would not get depressed. I had a business to run, which was doing quite well. I had a son to raise who was also doing well in his endeavors. Nathan was in the band and playing the saxophone proficiently. His musical future appeared promising. We were hoping he would receive a college scholarship for all his hard work. In addition to everything else, I was still busy caring for the Old Bat. I had to hop-to-it whenever she would ring that damned old bell!

The Old Bat seemed to be in good health, but she enjoyed being treated like a baby. I didn't mind coddling her, if she continued to pay me. The money I received was all mine, to do with as I pleased. I liked that. Now I would not feel guilty about taking money from the family budget to spend on myself, because I received my slave money from the Old Bat. I deserved every penny of it! I bought fine jewelry and pretty sexy lingerie that Cody never saw. The lingerie was for Mr. Wonderful's eyes only.

Other than Nathan and Mr. Wonderful, the Glee Girls were the only bright spot in my life. I loved the weekly rehearsals and singing engagements with the chorus. On occasions, we went out of town for competition or other events. The *slave money* that I earned from the Old Bat paid for these special events. Cody did not like it one little bit, but I did not care. I had to do something for myself, or I would have lost my mind!

One night in the fall of 1986, after a full night of rigorous rehearsing at Glee Girls, my carpool of four girls returned late to our side of New Fort. My car was parked outside my place of business. The carpool let me out, then they drove away. As I approached my car, I noticed a soggy note left on the windshield of my car. Because of the night dew, the writing on the note was almost too wet to read. I finally made it out, "Meet me at the yacht club. I will wait for you until 2:00." I knew who wrote that note.

Since we were late returning from Glee Girls rehearsal, I worried that Cody would be expecting me any minute. Sometimes he would be waiting up for me, sometimes not. I never knew which it would be. It was then 11:00 p.m., and usually it took me fifteen minutes more to get home from my store's location. I had to decide; I was already in trouble for being a little late. Do I risk it and hope Cody had gotten drunk and fallen asleep? I desperately wanted to see this man whom I loved so passionately!

How many Monday nights had he seen my car parked at this location and not written me a note? He knew on Monday nights I was out with the Glee Girls, and it would be the opportune time for us to get together. He had never taken advantage of the situation on other Monday nights---not until that night. I thought about it for about two seconds, then I drove directly to the yacht club, which was just down the street, less than a mile. I guess he must have been watching me from a distance somewhere because Alex pulled into the parking lot behind me precisely at the same time.

He walked over to my car and took me by the hand. "I didn't think you would come. I'm glad you did." He said in a low voice.

What could I say? You haven't called . . .you haven't written. . .? No, I did not mention any of those things. I said nothing. I let him do all the talking. After all, it was his party, and I was the guest. I always felt inhibited around him!

"I want to show you something." He whispered as he led me around to the back of the grounds of the yacht club and onto the island, where the boats were docked. It was dark and eerily quiet, not another soul was around, just the two of us.

As we were approaching the dock, he said, "Now count one, two, three boat slips. This is my boat. Remember where it is located." He helped me onto his sailing vessel. It was my first time aboard a sailing yacht. I was once again overwhelmed. When we went aboard, he helped me step below where I was astonished at the size of the interior. It was as spacious below as most people's homes. Sometimes he did live aboard his boat quite comfortably.

He tried to make me feel at ease by offering a glass of wine; but it wasn't working, I was nervous because I knew I had to get home very soon.

The clock was ticking . . .

I was afraid Cody might be waiting for me. I was wondering, *why in the hell did he ask me here?* Shortly after that, Alex got right to the point. He had finally gotten up the courage to express his feelings openly to me. I guess drinking alcoholic beverages does have its advantages; at least it did that night.

"I have been avoiding you for a long time. I've had these feelings, and I don't know how to deal with them. I am now ready to make a commitment." When he said those words, I melted once again! I walked over closer to him, and we hugged. I could not believe what I had just heard!

Time was ticking away. . .

We continued to hug, then kissing started. I knew I had to get home, or else I would catch hell from Cody! I told him I had to leave, but he would not let me. He continued to kiss me even more passionately. He was desperate to keep me with him. He led me into the galley; he was getting a little pushy. He genuinely wanted to have sex with me then and there. I resisted, trying to get out of his hold. The harder I tried, the harder he held on to me. I finally said, "are you going to rape me, Alex?"

Hearing those words, he realized what he was doing, then stopped, and backed off. "No, I'm sorry. I just. . ."

When he stopped being so aggressive, things turned around. We both settled down and took a long breath. He lit a cigarette, and I told him I would now have that glass of wine. We sat down at the table; there was a long, uneasy silence between us.

I knew he was embarrassed for his ungentlemanly-like behavior. His blue-blood upbringing, along with his mother's demands for proper manners, were drilled into him all his life. I felt sorry for him, for he knew he had stepped out of line!

I remembered his words, "I am now ready to make a commitment." Those words lingered with me. Those were the words I had wanted him to say for years, and now he finally had the courage to say them. I should have been elated, and I was! We just did not get started off very well that night. Because I loved Alex so deeply, I didn't want the night to end with him feeling bad about sharing his heart with me.

I sat my empty glass down and moved closer to him. Getting right into his face, I started kissing his forehead, eyes, nose, cheeks, mustache, and then on to his lips. My tongue was circling his mustache and lips, then into his mouth, in and out of his mouth with French kisses. I took his left hand and placed it on my right breast as I dropped my bra strap, exposing my small breast. He massaged it gently, circling my nipple with his fingertips, we continued to kiss deeply. It sent waves of warm, salacious tingles down to my garden. I was getting rapidly delirious to make love to my one and only lover!

He looked into my eyes and softly said, "Are you sure you want to?"

"Oh, yes!" I was begging.

Alex picked me up and gently laid me on a nearby bench in his galley. I pulled my skirt up to my waist and took off my bikini panties, sexposing my full bush. He took a moment to view my half-nude body before going down on me and kissing little Eva with loving care. His tongue was circling my clit, very softy and rhythmically. He blew hot breathy air all around my clit; then suddenly he licked it hard, causing me to convulse with acute gratification. He moved in and out of my garden, with his hot, hard tongue. Oh! It was giving me goosebumps. It was divine and doing strange and delicious things to my insides. I raised him up and kissed his face, then spread my legs, awaiting his entry. I wanted him inside of me-----I was so aroused; I needed Big Boy inside of me!

I was lying on my back with my legs spread. He was holding my left leg on his right shoulder; my right leg was resting on the mattress of the bench. He was straddling me; in a scissor-like position. Both his feet were touching the floor as he was in a semi-standing position.

His shorts came off, and I noticed he was not wearing underwear; he was already prepared. Big Boy was hard and throbbing; little Eva was wanting him to enter my Garden of Pleasure. Then, Oooo! I felt heady when he rushed Big Boy into me, causing me to momentarily tense. He paused, waiting for me to settle, then we continued

This was the perfect position for Big Boy to touch my G-Spot. I spread my legs further, and he worked and pumped his ass, forcing Big Boy to the sexact spot where he wanted it. He knew precisely where and how to place Big Boy, to make me smolder for more.

This scissor-like position did not allow mouth kissing, but we did not need it. We were in a hurry, so this quickie was in order. It was probably one of the fastest quickies on record in the history of humanity! I was so damn scared of getting caught when I got home; it heightened my sexcitement. I wanted this man all for my very own. I wasn't going to ever let him go.

Just a little of Big Boy goes a long way! As soon as he entered me and started his sexy movements, I went wild! Man! This position was heavenly. How did he know about this position? He must have invented it! What a lover! I rocked back and forth with him as hard as I could. At one point, he stopped and stood there while still inside of me and watched as I did all the hunching as fast or as slow as I wanted. He held my leg over his shoulder with my ass in the air. It was an aphrodisiac for Alex to watch me riding him, getting all of him that I wanted.

His eyes were blazing down at me, and I knew he was about to climax! His neck relaxed back, and his mouth opened with a loud groan of complete contentment as his hot semen spurted into me like a hot flowing fountain from a volcano! On and on, Alex pumped harder, and his sperm released again and again; until. . . then I started my release with him. Our eyes were still locked on one another's in a dreamy, loving sort of way. We both knew what we were doing for one another was sexceptional and out of this world! Oh! What a release! My lower belly was cramping with waves of delight.

When we finished, he relaxed and laid on top of me. He started giving me thank you kisses. I was looking into his eyes when he told me how beautiful I was. I knew the pillow talk was getting better. Once again, I remembered those wise words from my past:

"Pay close attention to the way a man treats you <u>after</u> he has had sex with you, and you will know how he feels about you."

The clock was ticking. . .

I got dressed as quickly as possible. Alex slipped on his shorts and lit a cigarette.

I proceeded to leave his boat and get my ass home before all hell broke loose, should Cody still be awake! As I was exiting the companionway of his boat, he immediately started throwing off the lines. Then he started the engine! I knew then and there he was about to leave the dock with me still on the boat! *What the hell*!

Quickly, I jumped off his boat and onto the dock. He came over to me, "don't you want to go for a midnight sail with me?" He caressed my hand, and lovingly looked into my eyes.

Oh God! Yes, I wanted to go sailing with this wonderful man whom I loved so profoundly! I wanted to sail with him under the star-lit sky all night! I wanted to sit cuddled his arm and hear the quiet water rushing past the bow of his boat and hear the rustle of the sails as we tacked. I wanted to sail away with him forever!

At that moment, all I could say to him was, "I would love to go sailing with you; but someone is waiting for me at home."

With a sad heart, I left him standing there on his yacht, watching me, as I walked down the dock and into the still, silent darkness of midnight.

Chapter 17 The Columbine

The columbine represents a deserted love.

That night after I left Alex on his boat, I hurried home as quickly as possible. All the way home, I was conjuring up in my mind excuses as to why I was so late getting there. I came up with the perfect excuse: *we had a flat tire when we left rehearsal and had to call for a service to come and repair it.* I was lucky. When I arrived home, all the lights were out, and everyone was asleep. No one knew when I arrived. So, all was well, and I was relieved that I didn't have to lie. Undressing quietly in the dark, I slipped into bed next to a man with cold hands and a cold heart.

I laid there in my bed all night reliving those scary, yet wonderfully exciting moments with Alex on his beautiful yacht. It seemed, at last, Mr. Wonderful and I was getting somewhere. Where? I did not know, but we were going there anyway. He was finally beginning to open up to me. Then I had another thought. Did he mean those sweet tender things he said, *"I have been avoiding you for a long time. . . I've had these feelings, and I don't know how to deal with them, I am ready to make a commitment."*

My mind started to play tricks on me. I concluded it must have been the alcohol talking. I decided the next day I would write a note to him and send it to his business. It read, "I hope you meant what you said last night---or was that just a moment of weakness?" The envelope was marked *personal and confidential.* I hoped that no one else would open it. There was no reply. It was over a year before I heard from him again.

I later heard around town that he was no longer working at his hardware store. He had sold his shares of stock to the other partners and had taken another job as district manager of a large building supply company located in New Orleans. It seemed that he had disappeared off the face of the earth.

A year later, in October 1987, I had almost given up all hope of ever seeing Mr. Wonderful again. Then it happened. I walked into the local bank to make my daily business deposit. As I walked in, I noticed through the glass window, that he was chatting with the bank president. I immediately looked away from him. I continued to step up to the bank teller and go about my business. I wanted to get the hell out of there as quickly as possible, without him seeing me. It didn't work; he saw me and walked over to speak.

Alex looked so damn handsome that day in his navy pinstripe suit; he smelled good too! I was embarrassed to be seen talking with him. I told him so. "I know every girl in this bank, and they all know me, and they all know that I am married," I said.

"I know them too," he said. "Well, let's step outside." We walked outside the bank and onto the town square where he held up his left hand and said, "look, you don't have to be afraid of me, I'm married too."

My heart nearly failed! I stood there in disbelief, holding my breath, blinking my eyelashes and trying to hold back a cry.

Looking him straight in the eye, and before I could stop my tongue, I said, "I thought you were going to wait for me." He quickly responded, "you were never going to get a divorce." I felt my eyes squint as I was staring at him. Then a cry swelled within my throat, choking me. I said, "you don't know what I would have done for you."

My upper lip started to quiver. I felt my throat tighten more; I had to turn my eyes away from him. There was a long silence. I was overwhelmed with sorrow and helplessness.

He said, "do you remember the last thing you said to me that night on my boat as you were leaving?"

Dispiritedly, I answered him, "yes, I told you I had to go because I had someone at home waiting up for me."

"**_Up_** for you?" he repeated my words back to me. "You did not say *those words*, you merely said, you had someone *waiting for you.*"

"Let me remind you," he said. "That night on my boat, I finally summoned the courage to pour my heart out to you as I had never done to anyone. Then, as you were leaving, the last thing you said to me was, '<u>I have to go, I have someone at home waiting for me.</u>' How do you think that made me feel? What was I to think? I had just offered you my heart; then you said those words. I could only surmise that he cared for you, and you cared for him."

I wanted to cry, but I held it back as best I could, then I said, "that's not how I meant it, I only meant that he was awake, and I could get into trouble by arriving home late."

Alex's words were racing through my mind and heart as I remembered that night on his big beautiful boat, "I am ready to make a commitment." I was wondering, *how did we have such miscommunication? How did we let this one slip away?* Now, the most wonderful man that I had ever known belonged to another woman, the new Mrs. Wonderful!

Knowing it was now definitely too late for us; I felt I needed to avoid any more humiliation. Looking up at him only slightly and trying to smile, although I felt like crying, I said, "I have to go." I waited a few silent seconds, no response. His head was hung low too.

My eyes were blinking through tear-filled eyes as I turned my head away, looking down so he could not see I was starting to cry. There was nothing left for me to do so I turned and walked down the street toward my car. I never looked back at Mr. Wonderful. My heart was totally broken; <u>I wanted to die!</u>

You know. . . you cannot wish death into existence; sometimes you must live through and with the pain. That was one of those times, and it lasted for what seemed an eternity. Like the Columbine flower--I was a deserted love--his deserted love. Yes, I was his deserted love, but my love for Alex would never die! It would still be there for him when he returned.

On December 23, 1987, he was again in town. While driving my company van, I had just picked up Nathan's Christmas present, which was a custom-made dirt bicycle. I was on my way home to hide it when I passed Alex on a neighborhood side street. He pulled over, and I knew that was a sign for me to do the same. Reluctantly, I pulled over too. He walked over to my van, put out his cigarette, and began to talk as if nothing had ever happened. He gazed into the back of my van, and asked what was covered up? I told him it was my son's

Christmas present, a custom-made dirt bike. He asked, "how old is Nathan?" I told him, "Nathan is 14 years old." He said, "my son is the same age." I wasn't sure until that moment that he had a son. We tried to carry on a conversation, but I couldn't talk much or look at him because I was hurting. I was hurting because he had gotten married. He had gotten married, and I loved the hell out of him! I had never told him that I loved him. I thought he knew. I thought he could see it in my eyes. I guess I was wrong.

Then I made a big mistake; I asked what he was going to give his new wife for Christmas. He said, "a diamond Rolex." I sighed, held my breath, and my heart sank! I smiled, nodded at him, and looked off. I had never received such a lovely gift in my life! I wish I had never asked! It only added to my torment.

I don't know why he stopped me that day. Was he still interested in me or what? I felt my whole world had gone down the drain forever, now that he had gotten married, it seemed like I was condemned to live with a dull, controlling man for the rest of my life.

Two days later was Christmas day, and once again I thought of him. I wondered what he was doing with her. I thought of how happy she must have been as she opened the new Rolex that he had given her. I imagined they made hot, passionate love that Christmas evening by the fireplace, as they sipped champagne.

Have yourselves a Merry Little Christmas, Mr. and Mrs. Wonderful!

Chapter 18 The Gerbera Daisy

The daisy is the birth flower for April.
The gerbera flower's message Is:
Let happiness be your compass!

My rose had his own secret flower. He called her Daisy. Unknown to me, he had been seeing her in private since his first marriage and all through his second marriage. She was a psychologist; Dr. Gerbera was her real name. Being the likable and informal guy that Mr.

Wonderful was, he always made up nicknames for all his friends, and everyone liked it. Even the fine shrink lady loved and accepted his pet name for her.

I always wondered why they called psychologist and psychiatrist "shrinks," so, I looked it up. It simply means that it's a way a therapist can listen to your problems and talk to you about them. Hopefully, she can help you "shrink" your problems or make them smaller. It made sense to me. Daisy eventually helped to make sense of Mr. Wonderful's dilemma and showed him how to shrink his problems down to only two easy decisions. He just had to decide on one of the two. Her words made it simple for him. I am eternally grateful to her for her smart and thoughtful insight.

Mr. Wonderful first started seeing Daisy when he was married to Mrs. Not-so-wonderful, his first wife. Alex just <u>had</u> to marry this girl while he was still in college. When he married her, he had to forfeit his athletic scholarship at Georgia Tech and transfer to Mobile to finish his degree at the USA. His mother begged him not to marry her, but he was in heat, and they married anyway. Mama Wonderful did not go to the wedding. The day after the wedding, Alex woke up staring at the ceiling and said to himself, *Alex, you've done it now! You have gone and made a big mistake!* It was too late. The grass was not greener on the other side of the fence like he thought it would be.

Mama Wonderful had nothing to do with the new Mrs. Not-so-wonderful. She would not speak to her. She would not even look at her. One day, Mrs. Not-so-wonderful decided she would go over and talk to Mama Wonderful about the situation. When she got there, she found Mama Wonderful in her car, ready to pull out of her driveway. Mrs. Not-so-wonderful rushed up to Mama's car, stopped her, and tried to talk. Mama was a feisty little lady, weighing a total of 85 pounds soaking wet. Mama Wonderful was extremely smart and not easily fooled. She was not the type person that anyone should agitate. Well, Mrs. Not-so-Wonderful was also Mrs. Not-so-smart because she forced herself onto Mama. Mama was infuriated and wanted nothing to do with this young hellcat, who had ruined her son's chances for future success by seducing him into marrying her at an early age.

So, Mrs. Not-so-wonderful (aka Mrs. Not-so-smart) tried to converse with Mama. I guess she thought if she could get Mama to talk to her, she could convince Mama to like her. Mama was not going to be forced into doing anything that she did not want to do! If you can imagine the scene, a little gray-headed lady is sitting in her big Oldsmobile, whose steering wheel she could barely see over. She was in her driveway, ready to pull off--when up pops the unwanted daughter-in-law. Mama was trying her best to get away from this pushy young thing, but Mrs. Not-so-smart was persistent and kept on yapping at her. Mama Wonderful did what she had to do. With great dignity, she did not say a word; she just glared at the girl and pulled away, leaving her standing there.

As Mama was driving away, she looked in her rearview mirror and saw the little hellcat screaming to high heaven, jumping up and down, waving her arms crazily! It appeared she was pitching a temper tantrum. It made Mama mad as hell to see her acting so ridiculous on her driveway, so Mama continued to drive away and left her standing there, acting like a fool! It greatly embarrassed Mama for this girl to be acting so crazy in her yard for all the neighbors to witness! Mama Wonderful found out later that evening that she had run over her daughter-in-law's foot! Mama's only comment was, "well, that's what she gets!"

Now to add to all this fun, along came the first grandson. Grandmama Wonderful did not go to the hospital to see Grandbaby Wonderful, but Granddaddy Wonderful did. Alex and his father had always had a close relationship. Granddaddy Wonderful came over to visit the new grandson almost every weekend but Grandmama Wonderful did not.

The marital bliss started to deteriorate shortly after the honeymoon and did more so after the baby arrived. Alex had to stick it out. His pride couldn't let it be known to Mama Wonderful that she was right about her predictions of marital failure. (Mamas are always right, you know---well, they are never wrong!)

Mrs. Not-so-wonderful worked in a doctor's office. Strangely, she started to get sick with all sorts of illnesses. She had to go to this doctor, for one thing, then another doctor for another problem. Then another new one, on and on. She was a hypochondriac. She loved the attention of doctors. Some doctors said she did not have any physical problem; they were all imagined and made up. So---enter the shrinks! After years of doctor visits, the couple was getting deeper into financial difficulty because of her medical bills, all because she seemed to like the attention. More than once it was suspected she had affairs with the doctors. Yes, she wanted their attention all right! It didn't take much longer before Alex concluded she was a real "nutcase." A self-induced nutcase. She could be sane when she wanted to be, then sick as a dog when she wanted otherwise. Go figure! Sex had long been gone from their marriage. Well, for a man like Mr. Wonderful, that is a heavy load! But he would try to cope with the situation.

Enter, Daisy. After several therapy sessions with Mr. Wonderful and Mrs. Not-so-wonderful separately, it was finally decided a divorce was inevitable. The not so happy couple finally got their divorce. But what about the son? The child stayed with his mother. Guilt was plaguing Alex about leaving his son with the nutcase mother. He wondered if she would influence his son. Of course, she would! A child learns what he lives. Remember, "the nut doesn't fall far from the tree." Alex's son was another load of worries for Alex. Thank goodness for the wise insight of Daisy.

After the not-so-happy-couple got divorced, Mama Wonderful was once again on good terms with her wonderful son. Mr. Wonderful was trying to balance his professional career in his businesses, trying to keep a relationship with his son, his parents, and his private life. It was, indeed, a balancing act. He assumed the personality of "The Iceman." It was as if he would not let anyone get close to him; he had his guard up all the time. No one could penetrate his shield. Ice flowed through his veins. He did not want to get hurt again, so, he would let no one know his thoughts nor his personal feelings.

Enter, the *lovely little violet* in 1984, who would slowly but surely melt that ice.

Then Mr. Wonderful made another impulsive mistake. It was in May 1987, when out of the blue, he married Mrs. "Let-me-tell-you-how-wonderful-I-am!"

One day Alex had an appointment with Daisy. He told her he had married Mrs. "Let-me-tell-you-how-wonderful-I-am." Daisy was shocked. She already knew about the lovely little violet and Alex's interest in her because he had discussed her with Daisy in previous sessions. She couldn't believe Alex had made such a hasty decision to marry again to someone else. Daisy knew he had remarried for some reason, but what could that reason be? Boredom or loneliness? She knew he did not love this woman. It would take ten more years of therapy that Alex and Daisy would go through together before she could shrink his problems. Remember the message of the Daisy:

"Let happiness be your compass."

Chapter 19 The Azalea

The azalea represents good qualities of personalities, but it also symbolizes specific emotions or events. Many people feel this flower means:

- Remembering your home with fondness or wishing to return to it
- Taking care of yourself and your family
- A passion that is still developing and fragile
- Femininity and feminine beauty
- Abundance, especially of beauty or intelligence

It was two years later, and it seemed like an eternity with no contact with the love of my life. *Hanging on in limbo* was the only way to describe my numb feelings.

The year 1989 was probably one of the saddest years of my life. It was a roller coaster of emotions that had to be dealt with daily. I felt like my lover had died but had no funeral.

It all started in the fall of 1988 when the Glee Girls won the Southeastern district competition in Atlanta. Now, that was a good thing! We were on top of the world! Out of fifty choruses, we were number one! From that success came fame and glory. We were invited to participate in U.S.O. shows for the troops in Europe, Germany, and Sweden in 1989. Man! You talk about excited! I felt like I had made it to stardom for sure! Cody hated it! I saved my *slave money* to pay for my airfare and all other expenses that would inevitably occur.

While in those countries, the Glee Girls were invited to stay in various homes of other Glee Girls choruses. Staying in multiple homes would help defray some of our costs. We were honored to receive an invitation to entertain our military men abroad! It was indeed a chance of a lifetime for an ordinary girl such as I!

The Glee Girls had a fabulous show package that year. We performed and sang many songs with choreography from the 1950's Do-Wop, to the 1960's Rock-n-Roll and ending with 1970's Disco. Our costume changes ranged from poodle shirts, saddle-oxford shoes, and ponytails, to barefoot, hip-hugger bell bottom pants with scarfs around our heads. The best costume change of all was for the grand finale, 1970's Disco red hot sequin palazzo pants with matching halter tops. The heavier girls in the back of the chorus did not wear halter tops; they covered up more with cute bolero jackets. We couldn't have enough glitz, glitter, and sequins on those costumes! We wanted to **WOW'em** while we were on stage. I loved every minute of it.

We had to work very diligently to get our routines down perfectly. By this time, I had worked and earned my way to the front row of the chorus, which was an honor! The front row was the twelve dancers who sang and danced out toward the audience so that the people could get a close-up view of them. A requirement for becoming a front row girl was that you had to own almost a perfect body shape.

Not only had I made it to the front row, but I was now a "bookend." A bookend was one of the two top positions in the chorus. We stood on the left and the right ends of the front row. We were the official spokespersons for the chorus. Between segments, the bookends would walk out toward the audience and talk with one another to set up the next few songs. My best friend, Barbie, and I were the two bookends, and we were good at it, we fed off one another! I loved it! Cody hated it! I didn't care!

Our finale for the U.S.O. show package was a real showstopper. . .we meant for it to be! The song we sang was called "Night Fever." It was written in 1977 by the Bee Gees. It goes like this:

Night Fever
Bee Gees

Listen to the ground
There is movement all around
There is something goin' down
And I can feel it
On the waves of the air
There is dancin' out there
If it's somethin' we can share
We can steal it
And that sweet city woman
She moves through the light
Controlling my mind and my soul
When you reach out for me
Yeah, and the feelin' is right
Then I get night fever, night fever
We know how to do it
Gimme that night fever, night fever
We know how to show it
Here I am
Prayin' for this moment to last
Livin' on the music so fine
Borne on the wind
Makin' it mine
Night fever, night fever
We know how to do it
Gimme that night fever, night fever
We know how to show it

The best part of that song was the chorus:
"Night fever, night fever, We know how to <u>do it.</u>
Gimme that Night fever, night fever, We know
how to <u>show it</u>."

Our choreography was performed using the steps from the famous dance of the seventies called the 'Horse,' as we pranced out toward the audience. Then an occasional pelvis thrust, only once or twice, just to add a little flair for the guys. When dancing back toward the chorus, we turned slightly, and a little bootie shakey-shakey was thrown in for added spice. Those two suggestive moves were not in our standard show performance package; they were just added in for the troop's entertainment. I was sure there might have been some masturbation going on in the showers that night after the show.

Anyway, that was our show package. We continued to work hard to get it perfect. I continued to plan for the big trip and save my *slave money* all year.

My twentieth high school class reunion was held in the late spring of that year. I would be unable to attend because I would be out of the country on this most important trip of my life. I sent my classmates my regrets and stated why I would not be able to attend. For the class directory, I was asked to write a synopsis about myself; where I was living, and what I was doing, etc. I wrote it and sent it in. It seemed impressive that I would be entertaining the troops for the United Service Organization in Europe, so I was told.

It was only a few weeks before the departure of the big trip, and I needed to have my passport made. All hell broke loose! Cody put his foot down and told me I could not leave the country! I could not believe what I was hearing! After all that time of my planning, and rehearsing, he never said a word of disapproval. <u>I not only wanted to die. . . but I wanted to take him with me!</u> I cried and cried until I could cry no more! You have no idea what humiliation that put me through with the other girls! They depended on me and my position in the group as a speaker. All along, I thought I was going with the chorus! I was included in the group number for the reservations made abroad. Cody's silence fooled me, he never told me differently. The humiliation that I was feeling among the girls was nothing compared to the letdown that I was feeling of not being able to go on this fabulous trip of a lifetime! I hated him for denying me this honor and privilege. How selfish of him!

One of my other friend's husband unpredictably did the same thing to her. There were five girls left behind that summer, while the other sixty-five lucky girls had a great time without us. Several of my friends brought me back a souvenir. I guess it was an *I'm sorry you could not go gift.* It didn't make the hurt feel any better; I was still grieving. I never forgave Cody for doing that to me. He was a cruel and selfish man.

With my saved-up *slave money,* I bought myself a gorgeous grandfather clock. Every <u>time</u> I look at it to check the <u>time</u>; I remember that <u>time</u>, and that wonderful trip--to Europe entertaining the troops--in the U.S.O. shows--that I <u>never made!</u>

Oh, one other thing. Remember my other friend whose husband would not let her go? They soon got divorced. Then he came over one early morning and shot her, then killed himself. They left behind two beautiful daughters. Some controlling men are just like that!

All hopes of ever seeing Mr. wonderful again had vanished when he got married. I was heartbroken, but I never stopped thinking about him. Having known him made me realize even more what a lousy marriage I was living in and barely existing! I knew I wasn't going to continue to stay there much longer. At that point, Nathan was 16. It wouldn't be much longer; he would be out of school and off to college.

Nathan could now drive and had he own car. Occasionally, I would let him use my new conversion van. Loaded with band instruments and his other band friends, they would go to various band activities. He was a good son, and he could be trusted. I did not have to worry.

It was a Friday night; Nathan was 15 minutes late coming home from one of his events. Cody had been drinking heavily and was waiting up, lying in wait for him. Nathan had been smoking cigarettes. When Cody smelled that he had been smoking, he blew up and started his ranting and screaming! Most of the time, when Cody started his verbal abuse, Nathan would go to his room and close the door. It was his way of escape and a coping mechanism. Nathan never had a defense, so why bother to respond to Cody? It only made matters worse if Nathan got into a battle of words with his father. He had tried that before. He had stopped trying to reason with his father when he would pitch a fit of drunken anger. That night was different.

Nathan listened to Cody's senseless ranting and screaming for a very long time. He never said a word. His father's threats of restrictions and punishments were harsh, getting in Nathan's face, pushing and shoving him around the living room. When Nathan had taken enough of his father's verbal and physical abuse, he got up and slowly walked into my bedroom, opened the top drawer of my dresser, pulled out the .38 revolver and stuck it to his head! I almost passed out! I screamed, "please! Nathan! Put it down! Please! I love you! Please don't do it!" was all I could cry out! I could barely mumble; I knew not to move toward him. I was so weak, I felt like a wet noodle and about to pass out from fear.

Cody started to say something. I turned toward him, gritted my teeth and with fire in my eyes, authoritatively I said, "get the hell out of here and shut up! Don't you say another word!" Cody never said another word; he never moved another inch. He just pitifully watched as I handled the horrible situation. It's incredible how a bully will back down when confronted!

I continued to plead with my son. "Please, son, don't do it! If you pull that trigger, I will die with you! You are everything that I am living for! Do you want me to die too? If you kill yourself you will be killing me, do you want that? Please don't do this! I love you more than life itself!"

My begging went on for quite some time, with Nathan not saying a word, nor moving. I was sobbing out of my damn head with grief! I still could not make a move toward him as I knew he might do something more irrational, to reinforce his point. I did not know what to do, other than to plead with him and tell him that he was truly loved.

He slowly began to speak, as he too was crying, he said, "I am tired of living like this; it's not the way a home should be. There's no love, no civil conversation. We have got to get help."

"I promise you. I will do whatever it takes to make things better. Just please, Son, give me the gun. Please! I love you with all my soul! Please!" I was crying so hard I could hardly speak, I was so damn weak, I fell to my knees, looking up at him. "You are my heart; you are the best part of me. I carried you under my heart for almost nine months. Please, give me the gun, and let's end this."

I don't know how long this pleading went on back and forth between Nathan and me, but he wasn't easily convinced to put down that gun. He demanded that I make an appointment for family counseling immediately, which I did. I got on the telephone as we were standing there. The counselor asked if we could come that night? Nathan agreed. After I got off the phone, he handed me the gun, which I immediately unloaded. Then I hugged him and kissed him for a very long time while we cried in each other's arms. Cody joined in the family hug. We all cried together. We then drove to the crisis center, where Nathan spent the night for safety reasons.

It was not I who drove Nathan to act so irrationally that night. It was Cody's fault for his continual nagging and verbal abuse to both of us. There was never a happy moment in our home!

If I *did not like* Cody before that night for his selfishness. . .and if I was *indifferent* toward him for the many other various things that he had done to me in the past. . . and if I felt *harshly* toward him for not allowing me to go on the European trip. . . then you have no frigging idea the amount of *hatred* I felt toward him for having pushed my son to the verge of suicide that night!

My life with that man was totally over! I would find a way out of that marriage one way or another, and it would not be much longer---so help me, God!

P.S.

We lived through that night. Nathan seemed to bounce back to his normal-happy-go-lucky-self after a few sessions with a good male-role-model counselor. I guess young people are just like that. I was greatly relieved.

I never mentioned that night again. I never kept the gun loaded either. I also made damn sure that Nathan knew how much he was loved, no matter what was going on around him in our house. If he came home late, even if he had been smoking, I didn't say a word. After all, smoking cigarettes isn't the worst thing a young man can do. Some things are just not worth fighting over. We must choose our battles very carefully. I decided to keep my son!

Chapter 20 The Lily

The lily of the valley represents the birth flower for
May.

The lily flower's message is: Take a regal stance
and embrace your power. Remember that renewal is
just around the corner and that the end of one thing
heralds the beginning of another.

137

It was still the year 1989. I was working very hard in my pool business, trying to win a trip to Hawaii. We had just become new dealers for a mechanical pool sweep/cleaner. This new-fan-dangle-device was selling like crazy in our town. My company was the only swimming pool business in the county. I made it a point to contact every business and resident that owned a swimming pool in my selling area. Then I made an appointment to demonstrate this great new device. Because it was a tremendous time-saving item, I sold nine out of ten that I demonstrated. By the end of the season, I had made enough sales to win the trip! I was ecstatic! I had never been to Hawaii. It would be a ten-day trip, all expenses paid for two people. The trip would take place in March of 1990. Of course, Cody did not deny me this trip, because he would be taking it with me.

All during that summer, while I was working my ass off trying to sell this new product, continuing to raise my very active teenage son, and caring for the Old Bat, I continued to think about Mr. Wonderful. I was still in love with him. I could not get him off my mind and out of my heart. Although I had not seen him since December 23, 1986; who could forget a man like that? My heart longed to be with him. I wanted <u>so</u> to see him, to simply talk with him or look into those brown bedroom eyes. But I couldn't because he was now happily married to Mrs. Wonderful. So, I had to move on with my life and make the best of it, for what meager existence it was. Nathan was still in high school. Therefore, I felt the need to stay where I was, for now.

One morning out of the blue, I received a phone call. The voice was a man on the other end of the line. It was not Mr. Wonderful. I did not recognize the voice, but he knew me. *What the fuss?!* After a short while, he revealed to me who he was. It was an old flame from high school. He had gone to our 20th class reunion and saw I was not there. He read my synopsis and looked me up. He said he was in the middle of getting a divorce and was wondering how I was doing. We talked for a short time. Then he asked if I might have lunch with him, for old time's sake. I thought about it. I concluded that it would not harm me to have lunch with an old friend. Although I certainly did not tell Cody.

.

11:30 sharp we met at a little restaurant on the beach. As I got out of my van and walked up to the restaurant, I spotted him. There he was; I recognized him right off. Same tall build, same face. Only, he was a white-haired old man! What the hell? What a turn off!

Well, I was disappointed with his looks, but I was courteous and polite to him anyway. We were glad to see each other. We gave each other a slight little hug, hello, then we went into the restaurant and were seated. It was a very casual restaurant, but very crowded. I concluded the food there must be good. I ordered the daily special. You can't go wrong with that, right? It was his time to place his order; he said, "I won't be eating, I'm fasting. Just water, please." *What the fuss?* I could not believe what I had just heard! Why in the hell did he ask me to lunch if he wasn't going to eat? He could have just as easily asked me to have coffee. Then I had a weird thought, *I wonder if this son-of-a-bitch is going to expect me to pay for my lunch since he is not eating?* I was prepared to do so, just in case.

So far, nothing was working out too well in his favor! I only nibbled on my food, because I was uncomfortable eating in front of a hungry man! He watched me take every bite. I wondered if I should have offered him a taste, or maybe I should have given him the rest of my plate? But I didn't; I just stopped eating. Besides, he's fasting, remember?

He told me he had been married twice before, and this was his third marriage from which he was about to get a divorce. I thought, *not too stable, huh?* He loved to talk about himself, so I let him go right ahead and do so. I was getting sicker by the minute at his boasting and bragging. As we were getting ready to leave, he handed me his business card, and said, "Here's my number if you ever want to get together again, call me. Just tell my secretary you are Dr. Israel's nurse, and you are returning my phone call. She will put you through to my private line." I took his business card and replied, "Thank you," I smiled back politely. I was thinking, *Yeah! If I ever want to have lunch again, and you watch me eat?*

The waitress asked if I would like some home-made apple pie for dessert, "No, thank you." I replied. Then she handed him the check. He took it. I almost snickered under my breath!

As we walked out of the restaurant and toward our vehicles, he asked me a couple more personal questions. We were standing in the parking lot beside my van when he asked me, "How is your marriage?" I said, "Not too good." "Have you ever had an affair?" he boldly blurted out. I knew where he was leading, and I wasn't going there. I was not interested in starting it up with him again. So, in a few short words, I told him about Mr. Wonderful.

"I have been very unhappily married for a long time. I am not proud to say that yes, I have been unfaithful to my husband. I met a wonderful man and fell deeply in love with him, but all he wanted was a good lay."

With those few words, I smiled at him and said, "Thank you for lunch. It was nice seeing you again. I hope things work out for you and your present wife."

I could now finally put out that old flame and never think of him again. In my heart, I knew there was still someone out there for me who would love me as much as I loved Mr. Wonderful. As sure as the sun comes up tomorrow, it is another day, and there is always hope for a new beginning. I still had hopes of seeing Mr. Wonderful again someday.

Chapter 21 The Dahlia

The dahlia symbolizes:
Staying graceful under pressure, especially in challenging situations.
- Drawing upon inner strength to succeed
- Traveling and making a significant life change in a positive way
- Standing out from the crowd and following your unique path
- Staying kind despite being tested by certain life events

142

- Finding a balance between adventure and relaxation
- Commitment to another person or an absolute ideal

Finally, March 1990 arrived. Cody and I went on the very much appreciated vacation trip to Hawaii that I had earned from selling swimming pool sweepers. Cody's aunt, who lived in Texas, came to take care of the Old Bat while we were away. She also helped run our business. Nathan was a junior in high school and self-sustaining.

While in Hawaii, I was constantly reminded of the romantic beauty of those islands. It was truly heavenly! Everything there was centered on having fun and light-heartedness. Love was in the air everywhere we went. Couples were vacationing on their honeymoons there. It seemed that all the island entertainment was about love songs and love dances. Flowers were worn in the hair of the native women, which symbolized love. It was, indeed, a beautiful experience. I was saddened, realizing I was doing all the right things with the wrong man. I could not enjoy the love and romance of Hawaii with a man I did not love. I didn't even like him. There I was, pretending to the world that I was happy with a jerk. All the while, I had Mr. Wonderful in my heart.

We were away on the trip for ten days. We returned to New Fort late on a Sunday night. Because of the time change, I was exhausted and worn out, but I still went to work the next day. Cody stayed home to visit with his aunt before taking her to the airport to catch her flight back to Texas.

That day I wore a long, linen, mid-calf, cream-colored skirt, a pink button-down blouse, and a pretty tapestry and silk vest to match. Cream colored heels and cream-colored pantyhose finished off the attire. I had jet lag! I was sitting on a barstool behind the front counter of my store, attempting to pin on a brooch. I was tired and was fumbling with it when the front door opened and in walked Mr. Wonderful! OMG! I nearly creamed my panties! Mr. Wonderful looked gorgeous! As the song goes, "looking better than a body has a right to." He had on a navy pinstriped business suit with a deep red tie and highly polished black shoes. His black salt and pepper hair made him look distinguished. Damn! Alex was a first-class man!

He walked over to me; I tried to act as calm and graceful as I could under the circumstances. I did not know what to say. I just smiled and asked softly, "how have you been?" He said, "fine, and how about you?" "Well, not too good right now. I can't seem to get this damned old brooch on!" He leaned in and started to help pin on my brooch. He smelled good. I looked up at him as he was hovering over me. We were once again in close contact with one another. The warm electricity started flowing between us just as it had done so many times in the past. I was saddened. I almost wanted to cry at the site and scent of him. I loved him so deeply, I wanted him so badly! Why did he keep coming back into my life, teasing me, and torturing me?

As I was gazing up at him while he was pinning on my brooch, he looked down at me and softly said, "I've missed you." I looked away because it hurt so badly to see him again. Yes, I had missed him too. I missed him greatly! All I could timidly say was, "I have missed you too," as I was slightly shaking my head in a 'yes' direction. I didn't know what to say or what to do at that moment. The ball was in his court. If we were to go anywhere with this "whatever-it-was," he had to make the next move. I had long since given up hope of ever seeing him again, now that he had gotten married. I never mentioned anything about his new marriage. Nor did I ask any questions about why he was there to see me. Knowing that he was a newlywed, I could only assume that things must not be perfect at his new home or he would not be there with me once again.

He was still standing very close to me as he finished pinning on my brooch. When he had finished, with his right hand, he took my chin and lifted it, forcing me to look up at him. My eyes were teared as I looked into his brown bedroom eyes once again, the eyes that I dearly adored. Then he slightly cupped my cheeks, making my lips pucker; I felt them open and separate. He leaned into me for a kiss, I did not resist. I accepted his soft lips and mustache as he tenderly started to make love to my mouth. Both of our mouths were getting more and more passionate with tongue French kissing, back and forth. Yes, we both had missed one another greatly. I could tell this man was not getting what he needed at his new home. He needed the same thing from me that I needed and wanted from him! He slowly slipped his right hand up my leg, as we continued to make love with our mouths. He almost made it up to the bad girl in my panties, who was desperately luring him closer. The good girl inside of me knew we had to stop; although she was not resisting anymore. I didn't know why this man was continuing to torture me, but the bad girl in my panties loved it, even if it was only for the few risqué minutes that we had.

The good girl inside of me made me stop kissing him. Then with all my heart, I sincerely asked, "what do you want Alex?"

He asked, "what do <u>you</u> want?"

I unashamedly proclaimed, "I want a hot romantic love affair. . . with no strings attached." (I knew I had to add that last part to keep from scaring him off. Remember---the "little deer running" thing?) I further added, "we must agree there will be <u>no others</u>, except our spouses. I do not want to come home with anything unexpected. Do you know what I mean?"

He knew I was referring to V.D. With that uncomfortable last comment, he quickly agreed to the commitment. From that moment on, we had a miniature marriage. No one else would ever be in our sex lives, just us. Except for our spouses, and those two did not count. Mr. Wonderful was the only man for me from then on.

Yes, I had to have sex with Cody, out of duty and to keep him from getting suspicious, but I hated it! Sometimes I cried after I had sex with him as I went to my restroom and douched.

Mr. Wonderful was the <u>real </u>man to whom I was devoted.

After Alex and I agreed to our hot romantic love-affair, he gave me his beeper number. He told me to call him anytime that I could get away to meet him, and he would make arrangements on his end. At that time, he was living and working in Mobile. As district manager of the company that he worked for, he sometimes worked out of town in New Orleans two days a week. We had to plan strategically around those days. I cheerfully took his beeper number. He told me he would always call me back unless there was a situation where he could not return the call at the moment. Otherwise, I should wait for his return call. I felt confident about him and this new arrangement. He had opened up to me somewhat, or so it seemed at that moment.

After that short-little-miniature-marriage-love-affair-commitment-ceremony was taken care off, he said he had to go; hc had only stopped by on his way to Pensacola. He said he couldn't pass this way without stopping in to see me. I was more than happy he did. He said he had stopped by several times prior, but I was not in the store. I must have been on one of those many appointments selling the new swimming pool cleaning machines that helped me win the trip to Hawaii. We continued with a little short kissy-smoochy session for a little longer, to remind us of what was waiting ahead for us. Then he left, out the front door he walked, the same way he came in... *"Looking better than a body has a right to!"* I felt as though I had been dead, and now, I was alive again.

It had only been a few days when I had the opportunity to give him a beep. We met halfway between our two cities at a Welcome Center. He parked his car, and we went for a ride in my van through the countryside to talk and get caught up on what had been going on in our lives for the past two years. I did not ask why he married so hastily; he very casually explained it to me.

He said, "can we go back and continue our conversation that we were having the day when we were standing outside the bank? It concerned me that we did not finish our conversation that day. We were talking about our last night on my boat, and our last conversation while on the boat; do you remember that conversation?" I was apprehensive, but I said, "yes."

He continued, "when you said *you had someone waiting for you at home*, I thought about that statement for the rest of the night. I, too, wanted to have someone waiting for me when I came home every night. At that time, I thought you were never going to get a divorce. You had previously told me you would never do anything to mess up your marriage as long as Nathan was a minor.

I was tired of being alone. I thought you took what I said too flippantly that night, and my feelings for you meant nothing. Well, I guess that's one reason I made some hasty decisions."

I was astonished at his words. What could I say to that? I couldn't imagine where we had gone wrong. We were like two ships passing in the night, so close, yet never seeing where the other was coming or going. I thought he was so far away and out of my reach, and he was thinking the same about me.

I finally asked, "how did you meet your new wife?" He said he had known her most of his life. She was a debutante and beauty queen in public high school; he went to a private military school, however, they never dated. In December 1986 they crossed paths again, and she invited him to a Christmas party that her company was having. They hit it off and started dating. In May 1987 they were married. He never said anything negative about her, but I could tell he was not in love with her. Otherwise, he would not be back in contact with me. From everything he said about her, I knew she fit the bill for the perfect Mrs. Wonderful-in-the-public's-eye. Looking good and proper manners were very important to him and his family. Excellent education and sophistication were drilled into him all his life. Mama Wonderful had set her standards high, and he was to follow those standards at all cost! In a family of high achievers, there was nothing wrong with that. The only problem was, I did not think that I quite came up to his standards for the perfectly well-educated, sophisticated, and well-mannered lady that would make him look good in his high-powered business and public life. I never knew how I stood or ranked with him.

While driving around, we found a little dirt road that led to nowhere, or so it seemed. We pulled over and parked where we could have privacy. That short dirt road was where the heavy conversation ended. I was tired of hearing about his new wife; I was a sick jealous wreck. I never let on to Alex that I was jealous. I needed to turn his attention to me. After all, he <u>was</u> with me and not her. If he had wanted to be with her, he would be with her. He wanted to be with me for some reason, and there we were! Just like old times. I knew I needed to give him what he wanted and needed, and that was more of me! His new wife may have been giving him what he wanted in public, but she was not giving him what he needed in private. So, the question is this: which is more important?

Remember: A man wants his lady to be two ladies in one.

> **"A man wants a lady in his living room and a whore in his bedroom."**

I <u>can</u> and <u>will</u> be both for this man one day!

I was not so much a whore that day in the back of my van, just the warm and receptive lover that he needed me to be in return to him. This man needed a lady to give him hot passionate kisses in return for his, to let him know he was desirable. <u>Desirable</u>---he was! Paying close attention to the physical ways he was leading me, I responded positively on his every move. Knowing this was what he desired from me. He loved to tease me with his eyes before closing them and leaning in to meet me for our soft kiss, wet, let's-get-started-kisses. I could tell his eyes were talking to me even when words were not spoken. His pupils would dilate with lust, and his penis would get erect at the same time.

150

I kissed and returned my tongue to him; he sucked on it. My breasts were getting engorged, I wanted him to suck my nipples, so I started unbuttoning my blouse as a hint. Then I unbuttoned his white, crisp starched shirt so I could see his big hairy chest that I adored! My vagina began to flex and contract with desire. I moved slowly down his chest and started rubbing my nose and face through the thick hair, stopping momentarily to lick his nipples and belly button. He seemed to like it, as he let out a sigh of pleasure. With my right hand, I couldn't help myself, I had to feel his bulging penis through his pants, it was full, and I wanted it! I knew it would soon be deep inside of me! Feeling his penis made my Garden of Paradise, vagina, flex even more with desire for him. I moved slowly up to his face, and we began to kiss more passionately. He began unzipping his pants, and we both started taking off my panties. We seemed to be in a hurry as his lips sucked on my throbbing nipples until we could not stand it any longer. We had waited long enough! We had to have each other! We both wanted and needed the physical loving that we had not been getting at home or anywhere else since the last time Alex and I were together so long ago. Only he and I knew how to give it to one another the way we both needed it.

We were in the back of my air-conditioned van where the back seat unfolded out into a queen size bed. I nudged him gently as a message for him to lie on his back. He took off his trousers and boxers. I went down on him softly and tenderly, brushing and swooshing my hair along his chest and belly until I reached Big Boy. Taking

Big Boy in one hand, I started kissing him on the head very softly, then taking him into my mouth a little at a time.

When I had half of Big Boy in my mouth, I started using my talents. Alex pulled my hair back and gently tucked it behind my ears, so he could have a clear view of my face. He wanted to watch as I was giving him a full-mouth-to-dick, kissy-kissy, sucky-sucky, hard-blowjob.

Sucking lightly at first, then using my tongue to swirl around the tip of the head. When I reached the top, I flicked it and teased him with my teeth. Gently, very gently with my teeth, dragging my teeth down Big Boy tantalizing him. Energetically going up and down Big Boy several times was all it took. On the way back up sucking harder and tickling him with my tongue, then stopping at the top to suck harder than ever while licking the back side of Big Boy with my tongue until he groaned and almost climaxed. He begged me to stop.

"Baby, stop. You're gonna make me come. I don't want to come like this. I want to feel every part of your body and enjoy every part of you. I want to be inside of you."

I stopped, lowered my eyes, and slowly flashed my eyelashes once, as I looked up at him. With a sinful smile, I said, "did you miss me?"

"Oh, hell! Did I ever miss you! You will never know how much I have wanted to see you and be with you these past months!"

Alex pulled me to his face and started kissing me. I mounted him on top, spreading my knees around his hips. Then I laid on top of him and continued to kiss him. We hunched back and forth, but he was not inside of me yet. I was riding him back and forth, rubbing my clit up and down on his Big Boy--that was hard as hell!

He said, "I love the close-up view of your breasts swaying above me as we make love. I can kiss your tits until my heart's content." I was getting wet, and I was ready for his Big Boy to give me what I needed. I reached down and took Big Boy firmly and squeezed, he groaned, then I led him inside me. Oh! How wonderful it felt! I started rocking up and down; he was meeting me halfway. We both knew how to tango-sex-dance together. What great rhythm we had! It was feeling so warm and cozy; it was overwhelming! Then he had the urge to thrust deeper into me he had to get a little more, just a little deeper, and deeper, and harder and I bounced back on him into a frenzy that almost hurt.

He grabbed a handful of my ass and pulled me toward him as he was thrusting deeper. He stopped momentarily, and breathlessly, he said, "you are the most tantalizing woman I have ever had the pleasure of riding me like this! Don't ever stop!"

With those words, I could not hold myself back from needing to climax. I knew I was keeping him on edge for a long time without him being able to do much about it. Oh, God! I did not want it to end. He was looking me straight in the eye. He seemed to love and watch me enjoying the very act of bucking him. He was so damn fine! I couldn't help but feel intimidated by this gorgeous man, and we were screwing the daylight out of one another. I kept riding him and squeezing Big Boy with my vagina muscles as he was thrusting deeper for more until I could stand it no longer! The climax was there! I didn't want to peak so soon.

I wanted to screw him all day and all night too. But there it was, he touched that particular little G-Spot that sent me over the hill, and I was climaxing higher than ever before! I let out a muffled scream! "Oooooh! Oooooh!" It was a great release! Toward the end of my climax, he released too, like a mighty lion! Harder and harder, he pumped and thrust me like never before! I collapsed on top of him. I was embarrassed because I was sweaty. It had been a long time since this man had enjoyed sex and I knew it. Me too, for that matter! We continued to kiss softly as his semen was leaking of out me and onto the upholstery. At that moment, I didn't care nor worry about it. I would clean it up later.

"Thank you. Thank you," he said.

"You don't have to thank me; I was on the receiving end; I should be thanking you!" I responded breathlessly.

"You just don't know how much I have missed you," he said, with a half-smile on his sassi-fied face. He lit his cigarette, nodded his head, and winked at me.

"Baby, I knew all along how much I was missing you," I quickly responded.

"Well, we won't let that ever happen again," he said. Those words were like music to my ears.

We departed our little dirt road, honeymoon rendezvous with promises to get together again as soon as possible. We had a lot of catching up to do. He would be waiting for my next beep. I was now the official "Mistress Wonderful," and I loved it.

Chapter 22 The Hyacinths

The hyacinth flower means:
- Sincerity (blue)
- Victorian meaning is play or sport or engages in the sport
- Jealousy (yellow)

It was the end of the summer of 1990 when I drove home from work one afternoon. Cody and I lived about fifteen minutes outside New Fort. Our house set about 300 feet off the road. As I drove down the long driveway toward my house, there seemed to be a mirage of something in my front yard that appeared to be a sailboat on a trailer. Was I dreaming, or what? The illusion got bigger as I was continuing to drive farther into my yard. What the hell! It <u>was</u> a sailboat! There were no other cars in my driveway; now I was beginning to wonder from where did this boat come? It was a 26-foot MacGregor sailboat, with the centerboard retracted and the mast laying on the deck.

Curiously, I circled the boat in amazement when Cody came out of the house smiling. He said a friend from Birmingham had come down to Gulf Shores on vacation with his wife to sail for the week. The boat was practically new. His wife hated it and would have nothing to do with sailing. She wanted him to sell it. To keep from having problems with his wife, he wanted to sell the boat for the balance due on their loan: $17,000. It sounded like a great deal to Cody, so he took this guy up on his offer, and bought the boat without consulting me. He just went to the bank and withdrew the money, gave it to the man, and he left the boat in my front yard. That might have been a good thing, except there was one problem. Neither Cody nor I knew a damn thing about sailing!

Not liking the fact that Cody made a financial decision without talking to me first; I thought to myself, *that's okay, I can get a lot of mileage from him spending $17,000 without first consulting me. After all, I contributed to our income as much as Cody. Just wait until I want to do something the next time!* I did not say a word. What Cody did not know and understand was that he was opening a world of more communication with Mr. Wonderful and me. I would now be entering the sailing world arena.

As the song goes. . . "Movin' on up!"

We needed a place to dock the sailboat. It needed to stay in the water if we were to use it frequently. Cody suggested we join the New Fort yacht club. *What a great idea!* I thought. Now Cody had no idea how he had opened the lines of communication between Mr. and Mistress Wonderful! We could now see one another almost every weekend. Of course, we would act as if we did not know each other around the yacht club. But we would keep eyes on one another.

Up until that point, Alex did not know me very well personally: my intellect, my talents, or my abilities. He only knew we had two things in common, good looks and outstanding sex. I needed to prove myself worthy of his love if I was ever to become the real Mrs. Rosenberg, aka Mrs. Wonderful.

I set out to let it be known to him who I truly was. The Commodore of the yacht club liked me as soon as he met me. It wasn't long before he asked me to be the editor of the monthly newsletter for the club. I was the first lady to have that title for the club, and I liked that. Being the editor of the newsletter meant that I had to speak at the monthly meetings to give my report. Usually, ladies did not speak at the conferences. Alex always attended the meetings. It wasn't long before the Commodore asked me to sing in the yacht club band. I would be disingenuous if I told you I did not like feeling this new importance, singing and showing off and flirting just a little bit in this new environment. I wanted to let Alex know other men also thought I was pretty. It worked. He was always watching me. I never thought the tables would turn on me! When I saw him talking a little too much to other girls, I got jealous as hell! It was a no-win situation!

Taking private sailing lessons were most beneficial to me, and I was getting good at this sailing thing, although seasickness was a real problem! My doctor prescribed a solution, which was a band-aid placed behind my ear. It took care of my seasickness. We started racing our little sailboat, and I liked it. I was always a competitive type person, I wanted to win, and I was a sorry loser. Well, we were not too good at this racing thing in that type of boat. I don't know if it was the boat or the sailors that caused us not to win. I'm leaning toward the inexperienced sailors being the reason for the loss. It wasn't long before Cody lost interest in racing and decided to sell the boat. He wanted to buy a bigger boat, so we could go cruising and sleep aboard. That suited me fine. Again, he had no idea how much more he had opened the door of communication for Alex and me.

We started shopping for a bigger sailboat.

Chapter 23 The Endive

The endive represents frugality.

In December 1990, I had the opportunity to take a trip to New York City, along with seven of my other girlfriends who were also Glee Girls. It was a fabulous trip for four days and three nights. The trip was jammed packed with fun events, with almost no time for sleeping. We attended five Broadway musicals and operas, including the Rockettes Christmas show. We had brunch at Trump Towers, lunch at Tavern on the Green, and visited Rockefeller Center. One evening, we traveled by horse-drawn cart to Times Square for dinner at a fine penthouse restaurant. On Saturday night we saw Saturday Night Live after waiting in line for several hours earlier that morning for tickets. It was worth the wait; there were seven famous hosts on the show.

The weather was frigid and snowy. It was the way I had imagined New York City would be at Christmas time. One day we had a little time to get in some Christmas shopping. We were all in Saks Fifth Avenue shopping, and I had grown weary of the usual mundane merchandise, so I told the girls I wanted to go down the street to one of the other little unique shops. I said I would not be gone long. I secretly wanted to get a Christmas gift for Mr. Wonderful. While walking down the street, I noticed a fine men's clothier, so I decided to drop in. As I approached the door and turned the knob, I noticed the sign: "Appointment only." It was too late. Uh-Oh! I knew I was about to step into something over my head! I had already opened the door and taken a step in.

The doorman was dressed in a gray wool suit with gold shiny brass buttons down the front of his coat and a little pillbox hat. "Yes, may I help you?" As if he was asking me, *do you have an appointment?* "Oh, I just noticed your sign that read 'appointment only'" I responded embarrassingly.

A voice from behind me said, "yes, but that's all right; we can still help you." It was an extremely well-dressed salesman in a black silk suit. *My! New York men are so handsome!* I thought. "I am shopping for a belt," I said. I could hear myself in my head use two syllables as I said the word, "ba-ult." "This way, please." He led me to another room and offered me a plush, wingback chair. A bottle of what looked to be fine wine was on the adjoining table. I took notice that I was not offered the wine. I was astonished by my surroundings. The building had high ceilings with old ornate carved crown molding and high gloss wood floors that pinged as I walked across them. I was definitely a fish out of the water. "Madam, what type of belt shall I offer you?" I should have known better than to go any farther! I should have said, stretch, or vinyl, but I didn't! I just continued to step right on into it deeper. With all the sophistication I could muster, I said, "alligator, size 36." He nodded politely, turned, and walked away. In just a few minutes, he returned with the most exquisite alligator belt I had ever laid my eyes on! It was displayed in a leather box, wrapped in white velvet. It was the perfect gift for a man like Mr. Wonderful! It was at that moment; I was reminded of that old cliché:

**"If you have to ask how much it cost, you
probably cannot afford it."**

But that didn't stop me. I was already into it too far to back down now! So, I decided to go right ahead and step into it as deeply as I possibly could! I looked at him, and with my sweetest southern smile, I said, "okay, so here's the question: how much is it?" Without batting an eye, he said, $2000.

As dignified and gracefully as I could, I handed back the beautiful, exquisite, expensive alligator belt, wrapped in white velvet, and still untouched in its leather box. I then stood up and said, "thank you." As I was walking toward the front of the store, I knew this northern man was only toying with me the whole time. He had already sized me up as a person who could ill afford to shop in his upscale store. Therefore, I continued to play along with his silly little game. I looked up high at the beautifully carved moldings and then slowly looked around his fancy store, as if to be scrutinizing. Then I gazed back at him with a sweet little southern smile and asked, "What type of people shop in your fine store?" In his condescending voice, he responded, "people like the Donald Trumps." I felt my mouth smirk in a downward motion, and my left eye winked as I nodded my head in a 'yes' agreeing type of way at his last response. I continued to slowly walk out of his store, but not before turning back to him and saying, "I don't think they have stores like this in Alabama." Then he blasted me, "yes ma'am; <u>I'm sure they do not!</u>"

POW! I know now why we call 'em 'damn Yankees'!

I thought, *Well, Hell! I could have well afforded to purchase his damned old belt, had I wanted to. But I would have been a fool to pay that exorbitant price!*

When I arrived back home in New Fort, I made it my personal responsibility to research and find one of those fine men's clothiers. What do you know? We had one right there in my hometown. I had never noticed! There were only a few differences. As I walked into that beautiful, hundred-year-old, well preserved business, there was no concierge to open the door for me, nor to ask if I had an appointment. Good! I didn't want nor need an appointment anyway.

A beautiful blonde southern lady immediately walked up to me, and in her sweet, charming voice offered assistance. There was no condescending attitude, she knew I could well afford to shop in her fine establishment, and she wanted my money.

Honey was dripping from her sweet, red lips as she showed me around her lovely clothier. I told her I was in the market for a man's alligator ba-ult, size 36. She asked me, "Wh-ult cul-lar?" I told her, "Brown, I gues-us." She knew exactly what I needed and reached un-da one of the displays and pulled it out. There it was, the same ba-ult; the only difference was, it was in a nice cardboard box, wrapped in white satin. I did not need to ask the price; I was glad. I could see the small tag hanging on the edge of the box that read: $375. I smiled with my bright blue eyes as I said to her, "I'll take that lovely thing!" She said, "yes ma'am, how would you like to pay, ca-ish or credit card?" I said, "ca-ish." She rang me up with a smile. I was smiling too.

After the sale was completed, she thanked me in her sweet southern style and asked me to, "please come back." I promised I wou-uld. As I was walking out, I noticed the floors pinged in her store, just as they did in the store in New York. So, what was the difference? Was that leather box worth the difference in price? I think not!

You know, what northern men don't realize is this: they think we southern women are not so smart. Well, we have more sense than they give us credit for having. I had more sense than to let go of my hard-earned money that day and overpay for his ba-ult!

Remember the old southern cliché:

"You catch more flies with honey than you do with vinegar."

Chapter 24 The Cactus

The cactus represents maternal affection and love.

I found myself entering the year 1991 in the same way I had entered the previous year. But this year, I had great anticipation because Nathan was graduating from high school and ready for college. It was during the spring band concert that I nearly lost it. The senior band members played their last concert after all those years. During the last song, they were to exit the band while the rest of the band continued to play the song, "If You Leave Me Now" by, Chicago. The lyrics go like this:

"If You Leave Me Now"
By: Chicago

If you leave me now, you'll take away the biggest part
of me
Ooohh no
Baby please don't go
And if you leave me now, you'll take away the very
heart of me
Ooohh no
Baby please don't go
Ooohh girl
I just want you to stay

I was sitting on the front row; I watched as Nathan placed his saxophone on his instrument platform rest for the last time. He picked up a long-stem red rose and exited the stage. That was my cue to meet him at the front of the stage. He handed me the red rose, and then he kissed my hand. Nathan was the second man ever to kiss my hand. I honestly lost it as we walked down the aisle and out of the Coliseum! All those years of hard work in that school band had finally paid off. He had now received a full virtuoso scholarship to the University of Alabama. My only baby son would soon be out of my home and on his own, to prepare for his future. It seemed too fast, and I was not prepared. I cried. I then remembered this was the moment I had long waited for, the moment I could now have my freedom. Freedom to be with Mr. Wonderful. The only problem was, Mr. Wonderful did not have the freedom to be with me. It was a vicious cycle.

Nathan graduated in May of that year. College was only a few short months away. He would be moving to Tuscaloosa and entering the University of Alabama on a full scholarship. He was also taking a full-baggage-girlfriend. She did not have a scholarship, nor the money to attend college. She had only enough money for one quarter. I was surprised she had the grades to enter. I assumed she was accepted on the prerequisite that she takes remedial courses.

We had a girl-to-girl talk about contraceptives before they left for college in August. I knew they were sexually active. I could feel it as I knew electricity was in the air when they were together. A mother knows these things, so I told her if she needed to go to the doctor and get a prescription for birth control pills, I would help her. I told her I did not want anything to get in the way of my son's college education; he had five long years ahead of him. She assured me she had everything under control. She was beautiful, but not too bright. I wondered what she meant by 'under control.'

In January 1992, the Old Bat gave up the ghost. After ten years of torturous bellringing, and hop-to-it-demands from her, I was finally relieved of my duties. All the Adams family came to my house for the sad occasion. Nathan came home from college to attend his *sweet, beloved* grandmother's funeral as he was a pallbearer.

Nathan was in his private room, staying to himself, suffering alone. One of the aunts noticed, came to me, and said, "Nathan is taking his grandmother's death hard, isn't he?" I asked, "why?" She responded, "because he is staying in his room, away from the rest of the family so that he can handle his grief alone." I knew that was far from the truth! The Old Bat never gave a crap about him, nor did he care for her! She only cared about herself and what she could get others to do for her. Nathan stayed away from her most of the time to avoid conflict.

I entered Nathan's bedroom without knocking. "Nathan, what's wrong; why are you not out with the rest of the family?" He was sitting at his desk, rolling a pencil and tapping it on the desktop, like a drumstick. He said, "Mama, we need to talk." I said, "WHAT?" As I gritted my teeth and screeched out those words under my breath. I knew and feared what he was about to say.

"Peggy is pregnant."

"Nathan, I told you!"

"I know." He said.

"How far along is she?"

"Four months." He said quietly and humbly.

"Didn't you use. . .

"Yes."

"Then, how?"

"One broke."

"It only takes one!" I screamed in a muffled whisper to him, so no one in the house could hear. I almost burst a blood vessel in my neck, I was so mad!

I started to cry, and so did he as we held each other tightly in one another's arms. We were sadder about this situation than we were the funeral. We never told the other relatives. They never knew why we were so upset, they just assumed it was because of the death. Well, in a way it was. . . it was almost my death!

Somehow, we made it through the funeral that weekend with dignity, with no one knowing the awful news.

In February 1992, the young couple were married, much to my regret. I cried and cried during the small ceremony and did not make any apologies about it!

In July, at the ripe old age of 41, my son turned me into a grandmother. John Frederick Adams was a beautiful baby boy. He called me 'MiMi.' After two years of marital bliss and hell, the young bride and groom ended in divorce; she returned home to her parents with the baby. Nathan continued with his college education. Although my son paid full support for his son, he rarely had the opportunity to visit with him because the mother refused to live up to the court order.

We do not see or visit this child today; his mother has made us out to be the villains. Nathan has tried to have a relationship with his son, but there is little that can be done if the connection is one-sided. His son has no interest in his father, nor his grandparents. He will only call if he needs money or wants something, like a car or a new computer. He lives just 10 miles away from us with his other grandparents. This child has no idea what a blessing he is missing out on in life, and his inheritance to say the least! He is my only grandchild, and I would have been a fabulous grandmother, had he only given me a chance.

Young mothers have no idea what damage they are doing when they purposefully turn their children against their fathers.

Chapter 25 The Fig

The fig represents an argument.

In the spring of 1992, Cody and I found the perfect new sailboat, a 32' O'Day, racer/cruiser. She was pristine and beautiful! Her hull was gray like a dove, and her deck was white. On the inside her upholstery had navy ticking. Teak and holly flooring and walls were throughout, beautifying the interior. We named her *DreamBoat*.

We had a yacht christening at the yacht club and invited everyone except Alex and his wife. We were not supposed to know them, remember? I was friends with the town mayor and his wife, who were invited to be on board for the blessing and christening as I smashed the bottle of champagne off the bow of my beautiful new sailing vessel. It was a lovely evening with a three-piece jazz band playing gently under a small gazebo near the food tables. The yacht club catered the food exquisitely. Champagne and wine flowed freely from a silver fountain. Other alcoholic beverages were also available. All our guests were invited aboard to tour our new yacht. She was beautiful inside and out. I made sure every piece of brass was highly polished from the lanterns, clocks, barometers, bells as well as the smallest ashtrays and beer openers. The galley dining table was set with new yachting dinnerware, flatware, and stemware along with matching napkins on display. Fresh flowers graced the center of the table. I was so proud to show her off that day.

As we were celebrating the big event, Alex and his wife walked up. She was inquisitive as to what was going on. No one had ever had a yacht christening at the yacht club before that day. I looked at her and sized her up right away because I knew who she was. She had no idea who I was. I was friendly and invited them to be part of the evening. She wanted to decline, then I said, "oh, didn't you see the open invitation on the bulletin board in the lobby? Everyone is invited." She suddenly felt better about staying around and talking with the other influential people. She was underdressed for the occasion; I was delighted that she was. They stayed for a while, and she drank more than her share of champagne. Alex had one beer. She came aboard, toured my boat, and told me everything about everything that I would ever need to know about sailboats and sailing. She knew everything, and I do mean <u>everything!</u> If I did not know something, I should ask her. I could tell she would be glad to let me know how knowledgeable she was. With her vast amount of knowledge, I felt free to call her at any time, even at midnight!

A week later, Alex and I had another date. He told me his wife wanted to invite us on a 10-day cruise with them and another couple. They would be sailing east along the coast and stopping in various ports along the way to dine and spend the night. "The water along East Florida is crystal clear, green and blue. In twenty feet of water, you can see the sandy bottom," he said. "I would love to see you swimming out there in a white bathing suit." At that time, he handed me a package from Victoria's Secret. I opened it, and in it was a pretty, white, one-piece, swimsuit. On the front of it was a metallic gold seashell. It was simply gorgeous! What good taste he had in ladies clothing! I excitedly thanked him with a hug and a kiss.

The trip sounded like fun, and I wanted to go with him. Although I was apprehensive about spending such a long time with him in his wife's presence; this was truly dangerous. Either she or Cody might notice the interaction between Alex and me at any time. It did not matter to me; this was the trip of a lifetime. I wanted to be near this man continuously for ten days.

A day later, she called and invited us on the cruise. I talked it over with Cody, and we agreed to go with them. We met with them and the other couple, who was going with us, at the yacht club to make our plans. One of our plans was that we would take turns hosting dinner and cocktails on each of our three boats at various points along the way, while we were at anchor. On the other nights, we would be eating in fine restaurants. Alex would be the lead boat, as he was an excellent navigator. My boat would be second in the line as it was faster than the third boat. I was excited about the trip. I shopped for three days for new clothing and more swimsuits. I wanted to look good every day and every night for Alex.

On a beautiful sunny morning in May of 1992, we departed from the New Fort yacht club on our 10-day cruise. We left very early, as it would be a long sail before our first stop. All three boats stayed within viewing distance of one another. Along the way, we were always chatting with one another on the radio. At the end of a very long day's sail, we made it to our first destination, which was a heavenly place called Redfish Point. All three boats anchored for the evening. The sun was setting over the sea oats covered sand dunes. A blue heron was casually fishing along the beach for his dinner as the sea breeze gently cooled the evening.

I hurriedly began to set up for my dinner party, as I was the first hostess. A luau was my plan. The food and drinks coordinated with my decorations. Since I had recently returned from Hawaii, I knew some excellent recipes. Blue Hawaiians were the choice cocktail of the evening. Grilled filet mignon wrapped with bacon served over rice and slathered with a secret Hawaiian soy sauce was the main entrée. Edamame was served on the side. Fresh fruit on skewers was mostly for beautification.

I wore a matching floral halter and sarong to add to the festivity. I knew I looked sexy in it since my thin little tanned midriff was exposed. I pulled my hair back in a French braid. Colorful, large wooden flower earrings topped off my attire. When Alex stepped aboard my boat, I could see his eyes begin to dilate as he looked at me. I could also tell he was uncomfortable being around Cody and me, along with him and his wife. All four of us together made a poisonous mixture, more like a Molotov cocktail! He stayed in the cockpit and conversed with Cody and Sam, the other guy who was on the cruise. Cody was finishing grilling the steaks, while Alex was finishing his cigarette and cocktail. Alex could carry on a conversation with anyone, even my jerk of a husband. I was embarrassed for him to get to know Cody.

Meanwhile, I was below deck with Leda, the other girl who was on the cruise, along with Alex's wife. Alex's wife was very complimentary of everything at first. I was surprised! Then she couldn't stand it any longer; she just had to start talking about herself! She began with, "oh, I brought a beautiful sarong along on the cruise too. If I had known you were going to wear one, I would have worn mine also. My sarong is so gorgeous! Alex bought it for me while we were in the Virgin Islands on our honeymoon." I could feel my face turning red, and my eyes turning green with envy! I knew this was going to be a very long trip, just hearing her irritating voice was like fingernails screeching down a blackboard!

Despite her boasting, we had a great time that night. For all the trouble in preparation, I wished my guest had stayed longer, or maybe I just wanted to spend more time with Mr. Wonderful. We were all tired from the long sail in the hot sun, so it was understandable that they made an early departure.

The next night we had dinner and cocktails aboard Alex's beautiful boat. His yacht was the largest of the three and the most beautiful. The inside upholstery was white leather, with solid teak and Holly walls and floors. I was reminded of that night when Alex and I made love aboard it before he married her. The dinner was elegant, by candlelight. Alex made the grilled chicken tasty with sweet-honey barbeque sauce. Alex was a gourmet cook. He had reggae music playing through the stereo. His wife had nothing to do except elegantly set the table, and sit back, relax, smoke and brag about the boat. I was jealous of her. I was learning a few lessons about how and what Alex expected of his lady. I was also learning a lot about her. She talked nonstop about herself. I did not have to worry about carrying on a conversation with her. It was all about her and her's. "*I-I-I-me-me-me-and-mine-mine-mine.*" I realized then, that her real name was, Mrs. "Let-me-tell-you-how-wonderful-I-am!"

The third night, we stopped by a little harbor that had a tiki bar and grill. We could hear the steel-drum band playing on the beach as we entered. We had to anchor a long way out because it was too shallow close to shore. We used our dinghies to go ashore, where we would have dinner. We sat under a tiki hut and enjoyed listening to the band. The greasy burgers and fries tasted great after a long day's sail. Several Margarettas washed down the burger and fries very well. We continued to tank up on more Margarettas, just because they tasted so good. The girls were having more fun than the guys. We girls were laughing and getting drunker by the minute. It was around that time that I was thinking, *I might be friends with her if things were different.*

The night was approaching, and the guys decided it was time to take the dinghies back to the boats before the wind kicked up and made it difficult to do so. The girls wanted to stay and continue with the fun. I especially wanted to stay and better get to know Mrs. "Let me tell you-how-wonderful-I-am." The guys warned us they would not come and rescue us if we could not make it back to the boats, should the wind kick up. We assured them, we could take care of ourselves, and they should go back without us if they did not want to stay with us. So, they left us there on the beach to continue our fun and drinking.

Mrs. "Let-me-tell-you-how-wonderful-I-am" was having the most fun of all. It was at that time I realized she had a drinking problem. The more she drank, the bigger she got. The more she drank, the more beautiful she got. So, I just let her drink herself into beautiful. She could actually drink herself into gorgeous! As the night went on, the wind started to build, so we decided we should head back to our boats, but not before going to the restroom. When we went to the restroom, Mrs. 'Let-me- tell-you-how-wonderful-I-am' left her wallet on the side of the stall outside of the restroom with a great deal of cash hanging out of it. I saw it and rescued it for her. When I gave it to her, she began to scream hysterically, "where's my $750 gold Monte Blanc pen that Alex gave to me?" Hell! I didn't know! I never saw the damn thing! I just found her wallet before someone else had the opportunity to steal it. It seemed she was not thankful that I had returned her wallet. She was more concerned about making a scene to all those around her about her expensive lost pen and making a point to let everyone know the value of it. She embarrassed me and made a fool of herself with her drunken crying.

We made it back to our boats that night in my dinghy; albeit, the wind was working against us. I took Mrs. "Let-me-tell-you-how-wonderful-I-am" to her boat first, then Leda to her boat. When I got to my boat, Cody was waiting up for me, and he was mad. I did not care. The next morning her pen was found in the bottom of her own dinghy. It must have fallen out of her wallet before she made it to shore. What a drunk!

The next several days were much like the first. Every night we dined; all I could hear was Mrs. "Let-me-tell-you-how-wonderful-I-am" talking about herself. It was "I-I-I-me-me-me-and-mine-mine-mine" for nine straight days. I was sick and tired of her mouth! I was also sick and tired of seeing her and Alex together. I was sick and tired of seeing her having fun with the man I loved so profoundly! One of those nights, I watched them dance together on the pier beside our boats. They were good dancers together. They moved in and out of one another's arms with excellent coordination, and their feet were in perfect timing. They looked like two tango dancers that had practiced together for years. I was green with envy. I wanted to be in his arms, dancing, and having him hold me like he was holding her. I wondered if their dancing was a prelude to their lovemaking. It was almost more than I could bear to see. I silently cried myself to sleep that night.

On one of the evenings, we stopped by a sister yacht club and spent the night. They had a just-for-fun sailboat race. Then afterward, we grilled steaks on their outside grills: the yacht club furnished baked potatoes and green salad. While the guys were grilling our steaks, Mrs. 'Let-me-tell-you-how-wonderful-I-am' and the girls were sitting around the dock talking. Mrs. "Let-me-tell-you-how-wonderful-I-am" had been drinking wine all day and was full of herself. She was bigger than life! She began to belittle Alex to Leda and me. She said, "he would be nowhere if it weren't for my family and me." I wondered about those accusations. Was she just mad at him about something? Leda nor I made any comment as she went on and on. At one point she even called him 'Mr. McGoo'. What an insult! We just listened with amazement. We could not believe what we were hearing.

Why would a woman want to run down her husband? Notably, a man like Alex. Did she think by tearing him down; it would make her look bigger or better? Well, it worked the opposite as far as I was concerned. It only made her look small. I would belittle my husband in public. . . not even a jerk like Cody! It always makes people take sides with the underdog!

On the ninth day of our trip, we cruised on the outside, in the Gulf of Mexico. I had never sailed in the Gulf of Mexico, in the deep blue water. I did not know what to expect, so I wore my life jacket the whole time and kept my engine running. I knew if I kept my engine running while the sails were up, I would have better control of my sailing vessel in case something unexpected should happen.

After a long day of sailing in the Gulf, we made it back into a safe harbor for the evening. This harbor was on a lagoon adjacent to a very nice condo complex. One of Alex's friends owned the complex and said we could use three rooms for the night to freshen up before heading back to New Fort the next day. That afternoon, I was lying out by the pool and I watched Alex and his wife as they played together flirting in the Jacuzzi. He was splashing her in the face, she splashed him back, smiling and laughing. I knew this was foreplay. It ate my heart out! I could not stand to see it anymore.

I left the pool and walked to my condo room. I made a concerted effort at getting dolled-up for dinner. I wanted Alex to see me looking great. That night I wore a white sundress and white sandals. My freshly shampooed hair was down on my shoulders, and my dark tan was radiant. Extra make-up and lots of mascara with red lipstick were a must! Only a splash of perfume was needed for the evening.

That night we were dining at a local steakhouse. We were all sitting at the same long table, and Mrs. "Let-me-tell-you-how-wonderful-I-am" was sitting across from me. I had just placed my order. In front of everyone, she asked, "Eva, how did you like sailing in the Gulf?" I responded, "I loved it, *DreamBoat* responded very well out there." Then she blasted me! "Well, you're going to have to turn off that engine if you're ever going to <u>truly learn</u> how to sail!" That was the final straw!

After nine days, I had enough of her boasting, bragging, and know-it-all-mouth! I blurted back at her a little too loud, "no, I don't! My boat comes with an engine, and I can use it whenever I choose!" With that being said, I realized I had made a scene in front of everyone. I left the table and walked outside and sat in a chair under a tree. I was about to cry, but I would not allow myself to do so. After a long while, she came out and said, "Eva, I don't know what I said to upset you so." I answered her, "you are overbearing. I have a lot of friends, and none of them talk to me the way you do. I do not allow it." She did not know what to say, so she turned and went back into the restaurant. I never went back to the restaurant. Cody was mad. He was angry because I had ordered and not eaten. I didn't give a damn, as I was mad too!

The next day was Sunday and day ten of the cruise. It was the day we were to return to New Fort. Instead of waiting for the other two boats, Cody and I got up at daybreak and were preparing to disembark. Alex heard our engine and got up to see what was going on. Cody told him we needed to get back early. He told him I had a flight to catch early Monday morning, going to Las Vegas to attend a weeklong convention. I needed to prepare for my trip.

Alex could tell I was still upset after the debacle from the night before. I would not look at him nor speak to him. I had been crying, he could see through my sunglasses that my eyes were swollen. I continued to prepare for departure and ignored Alex. He remained standing close by on the dock while staring at me.

At last, he tossed my lines onto the boat to Cody, as he watched me standing at the helm of my big beautiful yacht. I slightly looked back at Alex only once with an empty sadness in my heart. I then steered my boat away from the dock and out of the harbor. . . with my engine running!

Chapter 26 The Hydrangea

The hydrangea's message is being a rare beauty can lead to frigidness unless you express your true emotions. Don't inflate your ego with bragging, stay humble to become prosperous.

With a grieving heart, I packed my bags and left for the Las Vegas convention on the following Monday morning, June 1, 1992. I was heartbroken that the man I dearly loved was married to a woman who had spent the past ten days praising herself and berating her husband in front of others. Alex had no idea she was speaking unkindly of him when he was not around, and he did not deserve her ridicule. It seemed that she thought if she put him down, she was building herself up. She would say things like, "I make more money than Alex. He could never do my job because he cannot work with people as well as I do." She was brought up in a much higher-class neighborhood as a child than he. On and on she would go, bragging about herself. By the end of the trip, I was sick of her mouth, and so was my friend Leda.

Then, there was also this thing about how much she knew. No one knew more about anything than she! If you don't believe me, ask her! She knew everything about everything and everyone. Just let her tell you. No one could get a word in edgewise when around her. She did most of the talking while getting drunker and drunker, and drinking herself into beautiful and more *'beautifuler.'* and even more *'beautifulerer'*. . . which was most of the time. I guess that is why I blew up at the dining table that last night. I'm not sorry for what I said back to her smartass remark, even though it made me look bad in front of Alex.

I was sitting on the airplane, very sad and distraught. I worried Alex was in love with his wife and was probably just using me as a sex kitten. I could not figure him out for the life of me!

Upon arriving in Las Vegas, I checked into my room, then checked out the reception Welcome Center in the convention hall. I did not stay long because I was mentally and physically exhausted. I rose early the next Tuesday morning and dressed for my first class. I wore a short, above-the-knee cabbage rose suit with a' three-quarter length sleeve jacket that was cropped at the waist with a wide elastic band. A matching cabbage rose lace camisole peaked out from under my jacket, which buttoned only twice from the bottom up. Cream heels and pantyhose completed my attire.

As I walked into my first class, a very handsome, tall guy offered a chair next to him on the front row. He pulled the chair for me to take a seat. Hmm! That was nice. We began to talk before class. He was from upstate, New York. I already knew some of the best-looking men I had ever seen were from New York. Remember, I visited there once with my friends. I also knew that New York men could be very crude and rude, but not this man. I guess northern men can be extremely nice when they want something from a southern girl, such as myself.

I found out he was a very successful businessman and was one of the featured speakers. He sold commercial indoor swimming pools to hotels all over the Northeast. He later taught a class at the convention on how to sell commercially.

Every day for the next couple of days, I kept running into this good-looking man, and he would make it a point to stop and make conversation. I think he may have been stalking me, but I don't know for sure, but he sure knew where I was most of the time. It was a large convention, and I don't know how he could always find me in that big crowd. On Thursday of that week, he asked if I might go to a dinner show with him after my last class. I considered it and concluded there could be no harm in it, especially since Mr. Wonderful was so happily married, and there was no chance of a future with him. It was almost like a revenge date. Besides, who could turn down a free dinner and show with a good-looking man who was well mannered? Right? I sure did not feel guilty concerning Cody.

We were seated down front at a private table, complete with fine linens, china, and candles. The dinner was the same as served to everyone at the show; it was delicious mystery meat with two sides, coffee/tea, and dessert. The show was very entertaining if you like Wayne Newton. When the show was over, it was getting late and time for me to head back to my room. On the way, we stopped at the outside courtyard to talk. We stayed there for quite some time. He kissed me. It was nice. I could tell he wanted to take me to bed. Let's face it, girls! We know these things. I told him I was not interested in going any farther with him. I already worried that our kissing had gone too far with us exchanging bodily fluids! Remember this HIV thing?

I told him all about Mr. Wonderful and our ten-day cruise fiasco. I also told him I was deeply in love with Alex. You talk about a selling job! This man told me every reason on earth why I should forget about Mr. Wonderful, and how he was using me. He said to me if Mr. Wonderful cared about me, he would have never allowed his wife to treat me in such a way, on and on with the selling job he went. I then realized why he was a successful swimming pool tycoon. Anybody who can sell swimming pools in upstate New York has to be a good salesman! He sure tried to sell himself to me that night. It didn't work; I would not give him my room number. I left him in the courtyard and walked back to the north tower, which was all he knew about where I was staying.

Friday was the last day of the convention. I had one more class on my agenda, then the final banquet Friday night. After that, I was to catch a red-eye flight home at 11:45 PM. I decided I had enough of Las Vegas so, I did not go to my last class on Friday. Instead, I checked out of the hotel early and took the hotel limousine to the airport in hopes of catching an earlier flight

.

Remember the old saying;

"What happens in Vegas, stays in Vegas."

Well, I'm here to tell you, nothing happened in Vegas worth the talking. Now, in New Fort---Now, that's worth the talking! So, let's get on with the story.

It all worked out, and I caught that earlier flight and was back in my comfortable home at New Fort by midnight that Friday night. I was still heartsick over Mr. Wonderful. Love does that to you, you know.

I was exhausted over the weekend, so I relaxed and enjoyed some time with Nathan, my "Sonshine." He was out of college for the summer, and at home awaiting the birth of their baby. Being with Nathan brought me out of my funk. He always had a way of cheering me up when things were dark and dim in my life.

On Monday, the following week, I was armed and ready to go back to work and apply the new selling skills that I had obtained in Las Vegas. I was now attempting to win a Caribbean cruise to the Bahamas by selling a new pool chemical. I was excited about this new product. I knew I would be successful, but it would take a great deal of effort to change my customers over to this new product. I enthusiastically told Cody all about this new product and how to sell it so we could go on the cruise. He agreed we should try for the trip.

When I arrived at work that Monday morning, there was a small blue envelope on the front desk addressed to me. I opened it. The stationery was beautiful; the back of the envelope was embossed with her return address. Her monogrammed initials were embossed on the front of the card. I knew the letter was from Mrs. "Let-me-tell-you-how-wonderful-I-am." It was her feeble attempt at an apology. I read it, then put it in my purse as a reminder that I needed to order stationery like that except in a classic cream color for myself. The apology was ignored.

Around noon, what do you guess happened? Yep! *"Looking better than a body has a right to"* walked straight into my store! He was smiling as if nothing had ever happened. Cody spoke to him as if they were good-old-buddy-old-pals. I ignored him. He pulled out a big envelope of pictures from the cruise and handed them to Cody. I immediately said, "I have to go to the Marina to see Tony." Without giving Cody a chance to ask me why I was going, I walked out the back door to my car. As I was leaving, I heard Mr. Wonderful say, "I have to go too. . . I just dropped by to bring you these pictures. I'm on my way to Pensacola." I knew he was going to follow me.

I drove directly to the city pier and parked, as he pulled up beside me, he motioned for me to come to his car, so I did. There was tension in the air; I was still mad as hell, and he knew it. It was hard for him to begin the conversation, but he did. It wasn't a good start. He said, "did you get that note from Susan (Mrs. Let-me-tell-you-how-wonderful-I-am)?" I said, "yes." Then he made a big mistake! He said, "that was first class!" As he winked his left eye and made the 'okay' sign with his fingers.

That was like throwing cold water onto my face! It added insult to injury! My immediate response was, "FIRST CLASS? You call first class getting sot drunk in public and berating your husband behind his back? Is bragging about yourself and low-rating other people first class? If you call that first class, I want no part of it. If you are so happy with that fat, ugly faced, monkey-mouthed, FIRST CLASS-BITCH---then I suggest you keep her and leave me alone!"

I got out of his car, slammed the door behind me, and never looked back.

Now, <u>that</u> girls. . . is how you make a FIRST CLASS exit!

Chapter 27 The Petunia

The petunia flower symbolizes anger and resentment, especially when they are presented by someone with whom you have recently had a heated disagreement. They can also express your desire to spend time with someone because you find their company soothing and peaceful. According to some sources, petunias are also a symbol of not losing hope.

You know, it doesn't matter how mad you are at someone, if you genuinely love them, you will always forgive them.

"Love covers all sins." (Prov. 10:12)

Love does conquer all and covers all misfortunate things that we would rather forget. It didn't matter to me that Mr. Wonderful had hurt my feelings; I understood that he just did not know how to express himself to this sensitive woman. I needed to teach him how to treat me. I knew he was trainable, and there was still hope for our future together if I would not give up on him. I just had to hang in there and not lose hope. It was hard at times.

It was a shame I had waited so long for the time to come when I could have my freedom to be with Mr. Wonderful. Now that Nathan was officially reared and out of the home, it was now my opportunity to leave. But I had nowhere to go. Mr. Wonderful was with his wife; so why should I make a move and mess up the applecart where I was? I had an economically comfortable lifestyle, although I was miserable with Cody. The time still was not right to make a move to be with Mr. Wonderful. As long as I was living with Cody, I could again see Mr. Wonderful on the weekends around the yacht club.

It was July 1992, and I had known Mr. Wonderful for eight years. At times I thought we were getting close, then at other times, I did not know anything for sure about him. He was such a mystery; he always hid his feelings. I read an article once in Cosmopolitan magazine that said,

"The longer an affair goes on, the more damage it does to the marriage."

I held on to that hope. Hope that it would continue to do damage to his marriage. My marriage, if you could call it that, was already beyond repair. I wanted Alex, and I wanted him badly. I was willing to wait for him as long as it took. I dearly loved him and desperately wanted to hear him say that he loved me too.

But. . .

<u>A person cannot give that which he does not have</u>.

He could not say he loved me, because he did not have it to give at that time, at least I did not think he did. It would be like me asking him to give me the keys to my car. I could ask all day long for him to give me my keys and he still could not give me my keys, if he did not have them. It is the same with love; I could ask him to love me all day long. If he did not love me, he could not say those words, not at that time; I had to be patient.

That morning in July, for the first time since our big argument, Alex called and asked what I was doing that day. I knew what that meant. He was available, so could we meet? I had a very good older friend who was a Glee Girl and owned a river estate near my home. I confided in her about my affair. She gave me the key to her river cottage and said we could use it whenever we wanted; just let her know when that might be, in case they may be out there. This plan worked great. We now had a secret rendezvous. She also told me I might want to take fresh sheets, just in case. She was a very savvy lady. I could tell in her younger days she surely must have had a great deal of fun, in all areas of life.

The beautiful river estate was set on a peninsula. The land alone was worth $1 million. Although the three houses on the lot were very old, they were still in reasonably good shape, but not well-maintained. You could tell at one time in the past, this location was a favorite place for significant social events, probably in the 1940s and 50s.

I always arrived first and unlocked the massive front iron gates, that bore the family crescent. On each side, the gates were guarded by two large concrete lions, each with one foot raised into the air and his mouth open as if to be roaring, "Stay out, No Trespassing!" When Alex arrived, he would re-lock the gates. The same key that opened the gates also opened the front door to the big house, which was more like a small mansion.

The long winding, cobble-stone driveway was lined with azaleas and dogwood trees on the right side, while palmettos graced the left along the riverside. Giant cypress trees hovered and drooped over the spacious property, as well as oaks with Spanish moss hanging and drooping along with the many overgrown vines of wisteria. A pebbled nature walking trail which led down to the water was still usable if you were not afraid of snakes. The stately, swirly six-columned Porte-cochere led us into the old courtyard, then on farther to the big house.

As we approached closer to the house; we found a big frog pond which was overgrown with seaweed and vines. In the center of the pond was a non-working fountain. The fountain statue was that of two naked dancing babies with their hands in the air. A big bullfrog could constantly be heard croaking, "Ba-rump. Ba-rump," as if to say, "welcome lovebirds, enjoy your visit." I never saw that bullfrog, but I'm sure he saw us.

Once we reached the front of the grand old mansion, the arched, wooden, double doors had fancy double columns on each side of them. At the top of the double columns, there laid a resting lion on each side, to guard the magnificent old entrance.

Since I was always the first to arrive, I immediately went into the big house and opened the jalousie windows and turned on the paddle fans to circulate the air. I carefully spread my fresh silk sheets on the living room couch and lit a scented candle, then placed it on the old coffee table by the massive fireplace, which was much taller than I. Alex was always close behind me, never late.

This location was quiet and peaceful. We could hear the birds singing outside the windows. One day we heard a critter scratching at the back door; it alarmed us, so we went out to investigate the noise. It was a baby armadillo. In my silk lingerie; I reached down and lightly touched the back of that baby armadillo, but it ran away. That was a moment I shall never forget.

We met at that old location over a hundred times over the years. It was at that secluded, romantic place that

Alex Rosenberg fell in love with me. He never said those words verbally, but I could see it in his eyes.

After several weeks of not speaking, and still, with very hurt feelings, Alex and I met at our secret, secluded love nest. After the usual walk in and enthusiastically kissing; we went right to making love. It would not take long to come that day because it had been a long time since we had been together. Alex took me by the hand and led me to the old couch, we sat down. I straddled his lap, we continued to kiss deeply and exchange our tongues, softly at first, then more aggressively.

I could tell he had missed me. I had missed him too, as always! I started missing him from the moment we parted until we would meet again. So, there we were, once again, in one another's arms, making love, and making dreams come true.

He started unbuttoning my silk blouse. I could always depend on my lace, push-up, underwire bra, to make my tiny breasts look like mountains in his face. I pushed them closer, enveloping his nose and filling his nostrils with my sex-scent. I lifted my left breast out of the cup and into his mouth so he could suck on my nipple. He took it with his right hand and cupped it into his mouth and licked it tenderly with his tongue, then massaged it with his mustache until it was almost raw. Man! I loved that soft hairy mustache rubbing against my nipples. If this was the sin of lechery, then I'll ask for forgiveness later! But for now, his pleasuring me was sending waves of anticipation down to little Eva, who was ready and yearning for my Big Boy to work his magic. He continued licking, kissing, sucking me softly on both my breasts, causing me to writhe. I was ready to receive what I came for. . . a good sexercise like only Alex could give me!

I am not sure who was having more fun, him or me; but I sure as hell was enjoying every minute of his teasing and tickling my tender nipples. By now, my blouse was ultimately off as well as my bra. He was unzipping my skirt, and I was pulling off my lace bikini panties. My completely nude body was totally exposed; his to do with as he pleased. I was his willing sex toy.

Alex was caressing me gently along my neck and shoulders; it felt so sexsational that I had forgotten to undress him. I started unbuttoning his shirt, and there was his big hairy chest. The chest that I dearly loved and adored! I don't know what it was about his chest that turned me on, but it did! I guess it's because I knew that a hairy chest and body was a sign of high testosterone levels in a man. And high testosterone he certainly had---validating that theory! I guess he could make love all night if we had the time. One day, I would find the time to let him do me all night. But for now, we had to make the most of the short amount of time we had, and it was always sextastic!

When his shirt was completely off, I unbuckled his belt and then unbuttoned his pants. I could feel through his pants that his erection was full. I loved to hold his penis with my hands and caress it gently, then more firmly. As I rubbed it more aggressively, it seemed to please him more; he moaned under his breath, he liked hard pressure on his penis. I stroked it on the backside, then over the top several times; he quivered as he rested his head on the back of the couch.

"I like it when you do that. You know how to make me beg for you. . .don't you," he whispered.

I wanted him to beg for me; just as I wanted and begged to have his penis inside of me. But not before I showed Big Boy how much I missed him. I slid off the couch to my knees, and onto the floor, with his penis still in my hands. He was looking down at me as I was gazing up to him. I lowered my eyes sinfully, then licked hard up the backside of Big Boy. I again flashed my eyelashes slowly up at him, Alex moaned and leaned his head back, relaxing for the ride. His erection was hard and tight as I continued to lick and suck up and down, over the top and back again and again. Scrapping it with my teeth.

"Baby, you're gonna make me come. Get up here, I want to be inside of you!"

Slowly, I helped him slide Big Boy into little Eva. Shallow at first, so I could feel the head of his throbbing penis as it was stretching my engorged vagina. The first strokes of his penis were always the most sexsational. Then more deeply, I would accept him into my Garden of Paradise with every loving glide.

"Aargh!" He moaned as we continued to make love to one another, with my naked body straddling his lap.

On my enthralling upstrokes, I would squeeze his penis with my vagina muscles, then relax on the teasing down strokes. Tighten, then back up again. All along I was arching my back and luring my nipples into his mouth. We were sucking and naughtily playing with one another in shameless euphoria. With me on top, I could place his Big Boy penis wherever I wanted it to go, right on my G-Spot. And I knew how to do it with precision. Deeper and harder, we pumped back and forth with one another; we were in lover's ecstasy. He massaged my clit with his fingers until I could not contain myself any longer!

With no one around to hear, we both climaxed together with voices like those of wild animals mating. I guess we were. . . wild animals mating!

Chapter 28 The Snowdrop

The snowdrop is also one of the birth flowers for January.

The snowdrop flower's message is typically positive, signifying hope, rebirth, and a bright future. It symbolizes purity; it comes only in white.

In February 1993, Cody and I were in Salt Lake City, Utah, snow skiing with some wealthy friends. Both couples owned several charming condominiums in that state, also other states. One friend bought and sold ships to the United States government. The other couple was a doctor and his wife. Both wives liked to spend their husband's money.

We were invited on a two-week winter vacation with them. Every day we would rise early and head to the slopes. The other two couples had been skiing for many years; they skied on the black slopes. Cody and I needed to take lessons at first. I caught on quickly. Thus, I advanced off the green slopes and on to the blue slopes in no time. That left Cody to hobble around, slip and slide around by himself on the bunny slopes most of the day with the kiddies and the old ladies. It was pitiful; he looked like a newborn calf skidding around and busting his ass in the snow! It embarrassed me to see him! It did not matter to me if other people knew who I was; I did not want to be seen with him and didn't care that I left him alone. He never stopped using that stupid "pizza-wedge- form" to stop himself. I liked to ski fast, and I wasn't going to waste my time with a ball and chain. Besides, I did not want to be around him anyway. I was growing weary of him controlling me every minute of my day. His selfishness and over-bearing attitude were more than I was willing to accept any more.

One day he wanted to ski the blue slopes with me. What could I say? He was able to go anywhere he wished to go to at that large resort. So, he followed me up to the blue ski lift. When it came time to exit the chair, he fell flat on his face and had to be dragged out of the way as not to hinder the next skier who was about to exit the lift. His falling flat on his face was so embarrassing! I quickly skied down the mountain trail, and he slowly followed. I felt duty bound to check on him. There he was, pizza-wedging and wobbling slowly behind me. He was stopping along the way to catch his breath, and I'm sure he was trying to get up his nerve to head down the mountain. The trail began to get a little steeper, and it was narrowing at one point. I slowed down, stopped, and waited for him. He had almost caught up with me when I heard a *crash-ca-boom! Bang!* Then I heard a screech and him yelling, "Ahhh! Ohhh!" As he was tumbling down the mountainside. I had no idea where I had lost him. I took off my skis and, in my boots, I walked back up the trail to see if I could locate him. I could not see nor hear him moving anywhere. I called out to him; there was no answer. God! Could I be so lucky? I continued to walk up the mountain to search for him, still no sound. My hopes were getting higher on my luck. Hell no! I wasn't so lucky, after all! Finally, I found him sprawled, flat on his face in the snow, hanging on to a small tree off the cliff of the mountain. He was motionless; I called out to him. Maybe he was dead? Hell no! He looked up at me with a pitiful look on his face with dead brown leaves hanging from his mouth. He had lost his skis. They were down the mountain somewhere.

I could see he was about to cry. What I could not tell was whether he was seriously hurt. He was a bloody mess with bruises on his face and hands. I should have left him there, but I couldn't. I would be disingenuous if I told you I did not think about further shoving him down the mountainside. But I couldn't live with myself had I done that. Besides, he probably would have survived that too! I reached for him as far as I could and offered him my ski to hold on to as I pulled him back up the mountainside and back onto the trail. From tree to tree, he climbed and hobbled back up. He had not suffered any broken bones. He did, however, suffer a broken pride! I was happy; it broke him from wanting to ski the blues with me.

That night while we were dining, Cody was complaining about having lost his expensive skis and how much it was going to cost him to replace them. When the guys had heard enough of his whining, one of them said, "Well, Cody, I saw the Lodge had skis on sale for 20% off." Then the other guy pitched in, "Yea, and the kiddy skis are 50% off. Why don't you check those out?" Then the first guy added, "That's a great idea, and I'll bet they'll add training wheels on'em for free if you ask them." I was embarrassed that they all had a good laugh at my uncouth husband's expense!

Every morning, I would go directly to the ski lift that lifted me to the blue slopes. Then I would ski down one level to a resort lodge and get three dollars changed into quarters. I would head to the nearest phone booth and call Alex. I could only talk for about two minutes, so I spoke to his message/recording system. I reported in with him each day and told him what events we had planned. I always ended with how much I missed him and wished he were there with me. I also ended with, "I love you."

When I came home to New Fort, Alex told me how much he looked forward to those phone messages each day. He listened to them over and over. Unknown to me, while I was away, he was at home each night making me a love-song-tape. A collection of 20 love songs that said everything he wanted to say to me, but he could not verbalize at that time. It was the most romantic thing anyone had ever done for me.

While in Utah, our friends told us about a significant financial business venture in which they were going to invest. The Winter Olympics were scheduled to take place in Salt Lake City, Utah in 2002. There would be over 2,400 athletes, their families, and other families visiting there for months at a time. That did not include the many tourists who would be attending the winter games. Thousands of condominiums were under construction at that time in preparation for the big event. Both other couples were going to invest in condominiums while the prices were low; maybe we would like to do the same? Cody thought it was a good idea, so we bought a new condominium, which was near completion and located in Deer Valley. The other two financial wizards assured us that when the Olympics came to town, the condominium would more than pay for itself ten times over, by renting it out to tourist. I could only hope they were right!

As long as we were married, Cody and I went back to that condominium in Deer Valley, Utah every winter to snow ski. We usually invited other friends or his family. I hated every minute of it! Remember: "doing all the right (fun) things, with the wrong man."

We employed a property management company to keep it rented for the rest of the year. I was surprised it rented in the summer months. Biking and hiking are almost as popular a sport as snow skiing in Utah. It truly is a beautiful state. I always worried if we would be able to make the payments on that damn condominium. With the help of that management company, we were able to do so. When I divorced Cody, I let him have the condo on his side of the asset settlement. I had no interest in ever using it again nor continuing to make those payments. I have no idea whether he sold it or kept it and made a mint off it when the 2002 Olympics came to Salt Lake City, Utah. I genuinely hope he kept it and made gazillion dollars! After all, money was the only thing that ever made him truly happy; I sure as hell never could!

Chapter 29 The Bindweed

The bindweed represents philander, quidnunc, and perseverance.

The years 1993 and 1994 were rocky years for Alex as well as me. Those two years were a roller coaster for me, and I made it hell for Alex as well. To say that I am a jealous person would be stating it mildly. I had good reason to be, or so I thought. Hell! Alex was the best-looking man in the town, and every woman was making eyes at him. I was perceptive enough to see it! Mrs. "Let-me-tell-you-how-wonderful-I-am" was so conceited, she only had eyes on herself. She refused to believe other women were trying to make out with her husband. She had such a high opinion of herself; she thought no other woman *could* take her husband. She was wrong. Women were trying all the time, right under her nose; I could see it!

The yacht club was under new management. We now had two managers, a husband and wife team. Two for the price of one, or so we were told. Their names were Claude and Maude "Mo-fo-yo-money." He did the cooking and ran the kitchen; she tended bar and ran after the men. I could see it plain as day that she had set her eyes on Alex. She couldn't keep her hands off him when he was around. She was always winking and blinking her long eyelashes at him as she served his drinks. Then she would always be leaning over to show off her D-cup cleavage, which was very well tanned and firm, as she asked him if he would like another drink? She was friendly with everyone, but that didn't matter to me! I was only concerned that she was too flirty with Alex!

Mrs. "Let-me-tell-you-how-wonderful-I-am" thought the new manager was so sweet because she now had a new audience that would listen to her brag about herself, and what all she had just bought, and what all she knew, and what all do you want to know. Because Mrs. "Let-me-tell-you-how-wonderful-I-am" knew it all! Of course, the new manager would listen to her, then poke her full of more alcohol. The drunker Mrs. "Let-me-tell-you-how-wonderful-I-am" would get, the less she would pay attention to how much "Maude-Mo-fo-yo-money" was rubbing her tits on Alex. I guess Alex thought I was as dumb as his wife, but I wasn't. I took notice!

One day after a sailboat race, I saw "Maude-Mo-fo-yo-money" prissing her tanned-tight-high-ass down the pier of the yacht club in very short shorts. She was on the way to Alex's boat with a tray full of Bushwhackers that she had prepared for Alex and his crew *on the house*. Of course, this made her look good to Alex's crewmembers. I knew what she was doing! She stayed and visited on his boat for a long time. That was highly unprofessional for an employee to fraternize with club members in this manner. I was a sick jealous wreck! Plus, she looked too damn cute in those short shorts!

At other times, during the monthly general meetings, she would stand a little too close to Alex in the back of the room and whisper in his ear while the meetings were being conducted. She never did this with ugly men.

I decided to take matters into my own hands. I asked a close friend to pen a letter to "Maude-Mo-fo-yo-money." Using my friend's handwriting to formally warn her to, "Stop being so cozy with my husband, if you value your job." The note was unsigned. "Maude-Mo-fo-yo-money" received the letter, and it slowed her down for a while, but it didn't stop her.

Not only did I have a problem with the manager, but I also had a problem with another lady sailor who thought Alex was attractive. After sailboat races, they were always laughing and flirting at the bar. I got word one day that Alex said to her, "I sure would like to see you in a swimsuit." Well, you can imagine how much I liked that comment! I walked over to Alex while he was having fun talking with her, and I joined in the jovial conversation. When I got him to myself, I quietly said to him, "you're burning the candle at both ends, aren't you?" He had been drinking quite a bit and had a Bushwhacker in his hand. He laughed and made a joke of what I said. Then he responded, "yeah, just walking that thin line, right down the middle." When he said that, before I could stop myself, I hauled off and slapped that Bushwhacker out of his hand, slamming it against the wall, and splattering it back onto him! I guess you know by now, I turned and walked out of the yacht club, without another word!

I went outside and sat under a tree where sailors sometimes gathered, relaxed, and talked after sailboat races. I was alone when Ms. "Good-body-sailor-like-to-see-you-in-a-swimsuit" came out and asked, "what was that all about?" I responded, "Alex is always trying to make out with every woman in this club! Well, he's not going to get what he wants from me!" I said that to her in hopes it would send a message that she was not the only woman Alex was flirting with; I was also in his group.

Ms. "Good-body-sailor-like-to-see-you-in-a-swimsuit" continued looking good around the club for the rest of that year. Still, my most significant threat, or so I thought, was "Maude-Want-mo-of-yo-man"! After talking to other club members, I found out there were other members who were unhappy with this two-for-the-price-of-one team. I was glad to hear there was a movement underway to get rid of them. I cheerfully joined in the campaign. Being the outspoken person that I was, I probably said more than I should have. . . especially about her.

It was October, and time for the new Commodore to be elected. I knew him; he also did not like the couple, which delighted me. I knew he would fire them as soon as he took office. The two managers knew this fact also. Because I was a friend with the new Commodore, it appeared that I had influenced him to fire them. I don't think I had anything to do with it, nothing of any consequence anyway. There were more influential people than I who were outspoken about their inept management skills.

Toward the end of November, Alex and I were on a date at our beautiful river rendezvous. We were getting ready to depart when the conversation about the firing of the managers came up; he thought I had something to do with it. He said, "this may come around and slap you in the ass before it is over." I did not know nor understand what he was talking about. I also did not know why he was upset, but I certainly did not like his comment! I left mad that day!

About a week later, Alex called and asked, "what are you doing today?" I knew what that meant. I was still mad, but I softly said, "I guess you want to go somewhere and fuck?" He smoothly said, "yeah." I answered curtly, "then go fuck yourself!"

Yes, you guessed it. I slammed down the phone without another word.

Cody and I were away snow skiing at the end of December and the beginning of January. When we got back home, there was a letter in my mailbox. It was from the board of governors of the yacht club. They were requesting Cody and me to appear before them at their next meeting. Because Cody was the official member, the formal complaint was filed against him, because of me. We received the letter too late; the meeting had already taken place while we were in Utah. I called the new Commodore and asked what the situation was. He and I met at the yacht club, and he explained to me that someone had written a letter of complaint to the board of governors because I had been so disgruntled about the previous managers and consequently resulted in them getting fired. The new Commodore assured me he had handled the whole situation on my behalf with the board of governors. After all, it was his idea that the managers should be fired. (We both knew we were in cahoots,) So he covered for me. He refused to tell me who the member was that wrote the letter of disapproval. I later got it out of him; it was Alex! Alex wanted Cody and I brought before the board of governors of the yacht club and reprimanded! I knew Alex was upset because he liked the little hussy manager's attention. Well, now she was gone, and I was still there! Maybe I did help to get rid of her just. . . a tinge. Sometimes, revenge is sweet.

Men like to have their egos stroked with the attention of beautiful women, even though they may not do anything about that attention shown; they still want to flirt around with sexy ladies. I would not allow Alex to enjoy it in my presence nor to my knowledge!

"If you let your man walk on you, he will most likely run (around) on you."

The comment that Alex made, "this may come around and slap you in the ass before it is over," stuck in my mind. Well if you ask me, it came around and slapped *him* in the ass, because I did not speak to him for eight months after that!

Chapter 30 Wow! The Amaryllis!

The amaryllis flower's message is:
if you've got it, flaunt it!

In January 1994, I was still mad as hell at my rose, Alex Rosenberg. I would not answer the telephone in the mornings when I knew he would call for us to get together. He called and called every day for weeks; he finally got the message and stopped calling. I was teaching him a lesson on <u>how not to treat me!</u>

New Fort celebrated its centennial year in 1994. A friend from the yacht club gave my name to the city development officer and told her I would be a good asset for the Centennial committee. She called and asked if I would meet with her. We hit it off right from the start. I was always looking for things to do to get away from Cody; this was an excellent outlet for me to meet people and have fun.

There were six significant events planned for that year, one of which, "First-Night" had already taken place at midnight on January 1. That remained five events to follow, all of which were celebrations of the city. The next event was around Easter, and it was celebrated for the children with a parade with various Disney characters on floats. I was chosen to be Sleeping Beauty, sitting on a big bed. *How appropriate,* I thought, that I would be flaunting myself around the city on a bed!

The next big event was held in May, and was called, "Celebrate the Bay." Celebrate the Bay was the event of which I was the chairperson. It was an all-day affair with all events held at the city pier. The event had sailboat races going out of the yacht club and around the bay, with the awards ceremony finishing at the pier that night. Three large powerboats were enlisted to take people out into the bay for a sightseeing ride along the coast as some people had never seen the land from the water. A colorful tethered hot air balloon was there to take people up and down on short trips. The local amateur Shakespeare actors performed "A Mid Summer's Night Dream" later that afternoon under the large shady oak trees. The Glee

Girls were hired to perform in another part of the park at noon. Horse-drawn carriages and a small train transported guests from one end of the park to the other while various sports and entertainment were carried on all day long. A roller derby and dance contest were the highlight of the afternoon, held just before the old-timey bathing suit/beauty contest. A $2000 college scholarship was awarded to the high school senior girl who won the beauty contest.

That night, as all events were coming to a close, the big event took place. There were two giant stages erected in front of the city pier/bayfront, and decorated beautifully like an old fish camp, with large colorful fish, crabs, and shrimp all along the walls. Nets, crab traps, anchors, buoys and all sorts of old boats framed the sides of the double stage. This bayfront location was where the trophy presentation for the sailboat race took place. Also, where the $2000 scholarship money was awarded. There were over 50 door prizes given away before the band cranked up.

Everyone was encouraged to wear white, as that was the color most people wore back in the early days, to keep cool. I wore a white sundress with white heels. My tan looked darker in that white dress that dipped low in the back; (my long blonde hair covered up most of my back.) I wanted to look great that night because I knew Alex would be there for the sailboat race trophy presentation. There were thousands of people gathered around the big stage that night as the mayor came forward to officially welcome everyone.

He called me onto the stage as the chairperson of the event. He introduced me and thanked me for having done a great job. The crowd embarrassed me with roaring applause. I then helped with the trophy presentation and awards, as well as the door prizes. While standing there on the stage with the mayor, I spotted Alex in the crowd of thousands. He never took his eyes off me; I could feel it! He told me months later he was eaten up with jealousy. He was jealous because, at that time, I was no longer his.

When the mayor and I had finished, the mayor introduced the band, and they immediately kicked off, and the crowd continued to enjoy the night. As I was exiting the stage, Alex was trying to work his way through the crowd to get to me; I could see him trying. I kept moving along with my mission of finalizing the night's business. I would not give him the pleasure of speaking to me.

In July, the next big event was "Celebrate the Country." The owner of the shopping center where my business was located, was chairman of this event. He was also the primary benefactor to finance it. He and I were good friends; he was quite wealthy and had a slew of girlfriends, but none of them knew about the others. I knew about all of them because he would always bring them by my place of business and introduce the newest one to me. I would always compliment his ladies and tell them how beautiful they were. I would also mention how lucky he was to have such a gorgeous lady. He liked those comments. I kept his little secrets and never told the other girls that he was a philanderer. He was just out for a good time, and they were out for his money. He always won. The girls won too; they usually left the relationship with a very nice engagement ring. He knew all along he was never serious about marriage.

For this big event, the city park and waterfront were once again used for the location on July 4th. A country music star was brought in to perform that night, but not before the committee flew to Nashville to check her out. This new and upcoming country music star was my young friend from the past, who was formerly a Glee Girl. She indeed was working her way up the ladder to success in Nashville. My landlord, chairman of this event, wanted to hear her perform before paying her those big bucks. So, he flew my friend, the city development officer, and me, along with himself and one of his girlfriends to Nashville in his private airplane for the evening. When we arrived in Nashville, there was a black limousine waiting at the airport to take us to downtown Nashville where she was performing live. I was proud to say that I was personal friends with this young lady. He liked her singing ability and the way she could get the crowd involved; he hired her on the spot. During the flight back home to New Fort that night, we further discussed our plans for the big party over drinks while on his nice airplane.

We were excited. Our team of workers worked steadily to set up an old country town setting for this event. Three 40-foot tents were erected to protect the crowds from the hot summer sun, so they could eat and drink in comfort.

A \$15,000 stage was rented and assembled at the bayfront. Giant speakers were all around the stage. When this beautiful, little performer, with her mighty voice, made her way upon the stage, the crowd went wild! They knew who she was, and they loved her! New Fort was indeed fortunate to have a country music star of her caliber to perform in our little town. Everything was going great until her band blew out one of the giant speakers and shut down the show! But that was okay, we just went right into the fireworks display, and everyone was happy. It was a very successful party.

I continued to ignore Mr. Wonderful, going into our eighth month of not speaking. When I would catch him staring at me at the yacht club, I would turn my head and walk away. It was hard for me to do!

Every Friday evening, I went sailing and racing with the guys at the yacht club. I was the only girl among six guys. We each raced on a small one-person boat called a sunfish. When it was light air, I had a chance to win, because I was a lightweight person. But on the heavier air days, one of the guys always won, because they were stronger and had more weight to balance their vessel.

I loved racing against those guys. I loved it, even more, when Alex and Mrs. "Let-me-tell-you-how-wonderful-I-am" showed up on Friday nights to spend the night on their boat, and Alex would see me out there with the guys having fun. He always made it a point to see where I was and find out what I was doing whenever he came to the club. That night he saw me with the guys having fun.

It was a late August evening, and we had finished our sunfish races; I was sitting on the beach having a few drinks with a friend. Cody came over and said he was ready to go home. I told him to go on, and I would be there shortly. I continued to talk to my friend. It was getting late when I saw Alex walking with one of his crew members to his car. My car was parked beside his car. I had just enough drinks to "let it all hang out!" I told my friend I had better be going; she decided to do the same. We both headed to the parking lot, got into our cars, and proceeded to drive away.

One minor exception, or should I say deception? When I reached the top of the hill, I turned around quickly and drove back down to the yacht club just in time to catch up with Alex as he was beginning to enter the breezeway at the back of the clubhouse.

I got out of my car, drunk as a skunk, in my wet bikini, with salty damp, matted hair. I caught up with Alex behind the club. There in the privacy of the still, hot, tropical, summer night, I quietly called out to him, "Alex, Alex." He was sauntering along, he turned around. Then in a low voice, I whispered, "let me show you what you've been missing!"

With that being said, I backed them up against the wall of the janitorial mop closet and unzipped his shorts. Uninhibitedly, I reached into his shorts and firmly grabbed his Big Boy with both hands! It was already as hard as a rock! I went down on my knees and unashamedly licked and sucked on Big Boy with all my might! I sucked harder and harder, on and on. Then I rolled Big Boy around in my mouth and thrust it back and forth. I licked down the backside vein while wiggling and tickling it with my tongue.

Alex leaned further against the wall of the closet as he convulsed and held on to my head firmly. More and more, I licked back up and down his penis like it was a sweet, tasty lollipop; then I tickled him on the head with my tongue. Alex groaned softly with excitement. I took Big Boy even deeper into my mouth and throat, pulling it in and out a few times and scraping it dangerously, yet gently against my teeth.

I was losing all sense of myself when I sucked it harder, deeper, and faster again over and over until he climaxed uncontrollably in my mouth. I swallowed quickly as not to embarrass him, (or me.) I stood up and kissed him on his lips with my lips, still with the taste of his semen on my breath.

"Now! That's what you have been missing!" were my final words as I was strutting away.

"You'd better answer your damn phone, or I'm coming to your house!" I heard him say as I was out of sight.

I put my drunk-semen-breath-and-wet-salty-bikini-clad-ass, in my car and drove away.

Yeah! If ya got it. . . Flaunt it! I thought.

I smiled all the way home!

Chapter 31 The Filbert

The filbert represents reconciliation.

"It is harder to fight against pleasure than against anger." *Aristotle*

I would be lying to you if I told you I was not sitting next to the telephone the following Monday morning at nine o'clock, waiting for his call. Promptly at nine, his call came through. I did not answer on the first ring; I waited for it to ring two or three times to give him a little more anxiety. He did not know whether I would answer or not; coyly, I answered the phone. I was happy that Alex and I had finally made up after eight long months of not speaking, but I wasn't going to let him have the satisfaction of knowing that I was happy. The fact is, I was ecstatic that we got back together. I had missed him as much as he had missed me. You see, I was teaching him a lesson. The lesson was as hard for me as it was for him because I had missed the hell out of him! But the lesson paid off! What lesson do you ask? Girls, I would tell you this once, and I trust you will listen well!

<u>You teach people how to treat (respect) you.</u>

If your man does not already have proper respect for you, you must teach him how you expect to be treated like a lady. Sometimes that means withholding yourself from him, (which is something good) until he realizes he wants you badly enough to behave and earn your company back. You had better teach him to respect you at the first sign of his disrespect, or his bad behavior will continue, then eventually the bad behavior will turn into a habit of disrespect. When that happens, you will have a decision to make, to stay with him, or move on to someone who will respect you for the lady who you are.

If you love him, it is better to teach him to love and respect you at the very beginning of the relationship. If he refuses to treat you in the way you want to be treated, Girl. . . you'd better move on before it is too late!

Lesson two and another piece of advice, as I have stated previously:

If you let your man walk on you. . . he will most likely run (around) on you.

You see, Mr. Wonderful really was terrific. His only problem was, he liked the attention of beautiful women. His mindset did not sit well with this little southern lady! *Of course*, other women thought he was handsome because he was! Even though he was married, he was mine, and we both knew it! Therefore, what is mine is not yours! So, you get the picture here. If a man's heart belongs to you, he will not purposely hurt you. He will treat you like the queen that you are; he will treat you the way you want to be treated. You will not have to demand this but once to get your message across. It only takes once, other than that, you turn into a whiner. Once you have established your strong place of love and respect in his heart, you need not worry about him running around on you with other women. Until then, remember my words from above. Write them down and put them on your refrigerator as a reminder.

Okay, lesson three, and this one is free:

<u>Don't be a whiner.</u>

When you have stated your demands once, stick to them and never back down or back off. If you back down, you are playing the <u>victim,</u> and he will walk on you. Keep in mind, I'm speaking of that certain man who is trainable. Some men do not care, so leave that man alone and move on before it is too late, or you will live a life of misery! But, if your man is the type who is caring, but needs a little tweaking, then this works every time.

Keep in mind, you are in the "catbird seat"! Use it--- and use it to its fullest, because you are sitting pretty!

"The catbird seat" is a phrase used to describe an inevitable position, often in terms of having the upper hand or greater advantage in any dealing among parties.

https://www.wikipedia.org/wiki/catbirdseat

That's enough of my lecturing for now. Let's move on with the story of Mr. Wonderful's phone call. He called and acted as if nothing had ever happened; no apology was offered. I did not expect one, nor did I ask for one. Sometimes you must let go of things to move on in a relationship. I wanted reconciliation with this man whom I loved dearly. I was willing to overlook his inability to talk about a bad subject. There was no need to beat a dead horse. It was over, and we both were ready for new beginnings together.

He now had accepted another employment position with a business friend in Mobile who wanted him to buy into his business, reorganize it and help him run it. It seems that everyone wanted Alex's genius brain to work with them.

It was convenient that he was working locally; we could see each other more often. There was one problem: I had to drive to Mobile and meet him at a hotel. It didn't take long before the clerk at the front desk caught on to our little shenanigan. I finally told her one day, as I was handing her a $100 bill, "I am not a bad girl. I'm just in love." She said, "Honey, you don't have to tell me anything! I know within two minutes, there's going to be a black Mercedes to come around that corner, then in two hours, both of you will leave. Next week, the same thing will happen. You don't have to worry about me." I knew I had made a friend.

We met at the same hotel for months and had heavenly blissful lovemaking for two hours at a time.

Chapter 32 The Rhododendron

The Victorians labeled this bloom "beware," — which is appropriate since <u>they're quite poisonous</u>.

<u>Beware!</u> How often do we hear that word and not take heed?

<u>Beware</u> definition: Be cautious and alert to dangers. Be on your guard, watch out, look out, mind out, be wary, be careful, be cautious, be on the lookout, be on the alert, keep your eyes open, and keep a sharp lookout.

Think how many times a day someone is watching or looking at you and you are unaware of them doing so. If we could feel it when someone looked at us, we would know it, but we can't do that. Therefore, we go around all day feeling safe until something unfortunate happens. We, as ladies, should be more aware of our surroundings to be safer in this world. I had a real scare one day. It happened this way:

I was on the way to meet with Alex at our favorite hotel. I told Cody I had to make a pool chemical delivery to another pool dealer in Mobile. By that time, Cody was getting suspicious about my weekly activities. He may have been stupid, but he was no fool! He questioned me thoroughly from time-to-time, then at other times, he said nothing. It was the times that he said nothing that concerned me.

That day I was dressed in a short, off-white straight skirt with an embroidered, pull-over sweater. White stockings with white heels, along with all the Victory's Secret matching, white lace bustier, garter belt, and bikini set were worn underneath. The short skirt may have been too sexy, although it was only about 2 inches above my knee.

After making the pool chemical delivery to the dealer, who was located in a large shopping center. I promptly left and drove straight to the hotel, where I checked in with my friend at the front desk. I paid her the usual $100 cash, which Alex always reimbursed me for. Then I went straight to my room and beeped Alex the room number. Within a few minutes, he was at the door.

We were always so excited to see each other. We always stood at the door and kissed and kissed and kissed for a long while before getting down to business. That day we had barely made it into the bed, and we were still fully clothed when the telephone rang! What the hell? That had never happened before! My heart nearly stopped! My eyes widened! Alex and I looked at one another in shock. I picked up the receiver, without saying a word, I grunted, "Ah-huh" as if I were clearing my throat. On the other end, in a low soft, mysterious voice, the office clerk said, "Don't you open that door!" I hung up the phone and relayed the message to Alex.

About that time there was a *Rap-Rap-Rap* on the room door. Alex looked through the peephole. It was a man dressed in a business suit! I peeked. It was no one that either of us recognized! Then, *Rap-Rap-Rap* again, only more demanding than before! No, we were not about to open that door to an unknown man! Once again, he persisted, *Rap-Rap-Rap-Rap-Rap* he pounded harder and harder! That son-of-a-bitch wanted me to answer that door! I wasn't about to! He finally left.

After he left my door, I phoned the front desk and told the clerk he had gone and to get his tag number when she saw him exit. She did and called me back. She said shortly after Alex had time to get to my room, the stranger came into the office to talk with her. He said he was a private detective and was looking for me. He knew my tag number, name, and description. He said she should give him my room number, or she would be in trouble for not cooperating. His mysterious ways scared the hell out of the clerk as well as Alex and me! Had Cody hired a private detective to catch me? Or possibly, could Mrs. "Let-me-tell-you-how-wonderful-I-am" have done it? Then I thought, *Absolutely not! She's so full of herself, she'd never believe Alex would mess-around on her!* So, she didn't do it; that left Cody.

Alex and I both left the hotel. Alex tried to hunt down the son-of-a-bitch, but he could not find his car. We both called our spouses on the telephone for a casual conversation. Nothing was out of the ordinary. So, it seemed everything was okay there, but Cody could always cover things up so well with a lie!

That night I had planned a surprise 40th birthday party for Leda at the yacht club. Alex and Mrs. "Let-me-tell-you-how-wonderful-I-am" were invited. Alex and I agreed that we would go along with our plans to be there and act as if nothing at all had happened. Everything was cool. No one acted out of the ordinary. The party was fun, and everyone had a good time; everyone was relaxed . . . everyone except Alex and me! We were still worried like hell about who that son-of-a-bitch was that was trying to get into our room.

Monday morning, Alex had one of his connections trace his tag number. He was not a private detective! He was a salesman from a local grass farm, and he had evidently spotted me at the shopping center. He got my tag number, traced it, and got my name. He then followed me to the hotel and fabricated that lie to the clerk to get my room number. I don't know what he thought I was doing at the hotel, but he wanted in on the action! He had no idea there was a big man on the other side of that door with me! I don't know who would have been in more danger *should* that door been opened. . . me or him when he met Alex!

Chapter 33 The Zinnia

The symbol of the zinnia flower is endurance. The zinnia's message is: setbacks are only temporary, the heat of the moment will pass, and you will be able to move graciously through any obstacle to reach your goal.

Well, here we go again! Just when I thought everything was 'peachy – dory,' and Alex and I might have a future together; along comes another setback! Alex was such a private person. Sometimes it seemed that he would be close to me and tell me personal things about himself and what was going on in his life. At other times, I would be broadsided! I had no idea what was about to happen on that summer day in 1995.

I was at the yacht club one weekend when I noticed that Mr. Wonderful's boat was not there, nor was he. I was disappointed because we usually spent the weekends on our yachts and messed around at the club with the club activities and sailed around the bay together separately in our boats. I wondered where they were because their sailboat had not been in the harbor for several days. It was late on that Sunday afternoon; I was on the bow of my boat cleaning the deck, getting ready to pack up and go home. I looked up and entering the harbor was a brand-new, more prominent than ever before sailboat with Mrs. "Let-me-tell-you-how-wonderful-I-am" at the helm! This sailboat was gorgeous! Alex already owned the largest boat in the harbor; now, he owned the largest boat that had <u>ever been</u> in the yacht club harbor! Mrs. "Let-me-tell-you-how-wonderful-I-am" was grinning from ear to ear as she docked this brand-new beautiful yacht in its slip! I was not only green with envy. . . I was not pea-green with envy. . . I was emerald green with jealousy! All I could say, as I yelled out to them from across the harbor was, "nice boat!" She, with her Cheshire cat grin, responded, "thanks." I wanted to toss her flat-ugly-ass into the water! I continued to pack up my boat, then we got the hell out of there! I wasn't going to give her the opportunity of showing that great boat to me and rubbing it in my face! I don't think I could have stood to hear her brag one minute about how great that new bigger boat was, and how much better it was than anyone else's at the yacht club. I am sure she would have had the audacity to have done so!

The next Monday morning, Alex's phone call came through as usual. I was still hurting with jealousy, but I tried not to show it. Knowing now that they had this new boat, there was no way he and I would ever have a chance of being together. It was *as if* he and Mrs. "Let-me-tell-you-how-wonderful-I-am" had just announced that she was pregnant with child. The new boat cinched the deal of their marriage forever! *What a great insurance policy*, I thought. Before they were married, Alex owned his yacht, and it was in his name only. Now, this new sailboat was in both of their names because they were married.

Well hell! I'm sure he had no idea what was going through my mind all along, my future dreams of one day becoming Mrs. Wonderful. Remember, it was 1995, and up until this point, he still had never said those words, "I love you." So, yes! I was hurt to see he had bought his wife a new yacht! Who wouldn't be hurt and jealous? I had invested 11 years of my life and love with this man whom I dearly loved. Now, it seemed he was well grounded with Mrs. "Let-me-tell-you-how-wonderful-I-am." I was beginning to think she was just that. . . something wonderful! Why else would he continue to stay with her? I concluded I must be the fool here! I was being used as a pretty little sex slave and toy, and dumb ass for putting up with this cad!

When he asked, "what are you doing today?" I knew that was his way of asking if we could meet. I merely told him I had other plans, and we would not be able to meet that week. I just could not bring myself to meet with him and have sex with a man who just bought his wife such a wonderful gift! I was not rude. I was, however, a little curt, and I cut the conversation short before I showed my ass and started talking about that big new boat.

You would have done the same thing . . . Right?

Chapter 34 The Gardenia

The gardenia flower's message is one of purity and love. Whether it is an expressed love, a secret love or love for friends and family, it is pure. It is elegant. It is love!

I got over my jealousy and met with Alex; he explained he was the one who wanted the bigger boat. He did not buy the boat for his wife. Since 1992, he and his crew had been racing his boat to Isla Mujeres,

233

Mexico out of Pensacola, Florida every other year. They wanted and needed a larger boat for safety reasons, also for racing faster. I believed him, but I was still jealous to see her behind the helm from time-to-time!

I finally allowed them to show off their beautiful new boat to me. I swallowed my pride and suffered through the tour. All along, I secretly was continuing to make my plans for a life together with Mr. Wonderful. Now, I could include this beautiful new boat in my dreams! But not yet! I had to keep dreaming a few more years. He wasn't quite ready for me.

I will never forget the date: it was August 26, 1995, on a Saturday afternoon. We were at the yacht club working on the boat. Cody was sitting, plotting a course at the navigation station. I heard a tap on the deck of the boat. I stuck my head out of the companionway to see who it was. It was Alex. (Keep in mind, he was only eight feet away from Cody and within hearing distance.)

Alex was very nervous as he said, "Can I tell you something?" I responded, "yes." He continued, "I love you!" I nearly fainted! But I had to act as if nothing out of the ordinary had happened. I just said, "yes, it's over there." Then I turned and went back down below. Cody wanted to know who it was and what they wanted. I made up a lie and said Alex wanted to borrow our water hose. Cody believed me. My heart was about to come out of my chest! That was the happiest moment I had ever lived in eleven years! What a time to say those unique words! Right there within hearing distance of my husband! Alex later told me he had been feeling it for a very long time and could not hold it in any longer and had to let it out then and there.

For the rest of the evening, Alex hung by my side like glue! We had dinner together as two couples, then sat together at the bar, then sat together under the tree outside the club. Mrs. "Let-me-tell-you-how-wonderful-I-am" was busily drinking herself into beautiful at the bar and bragging about the new boat. She did not notice Alex, nor what he was doing with me. Occasionally, she would get up and bump into the walls as she made her way to the restroom. Cody was being his usual dull self, drinking himself into oblivion.

While Alex, Cody and I were sitting under the tree that night, we could hear music coming from the cliff that sounded like a wedding party. Mrs. "Let-me-tell-you-how-wonderful-I-am" closed the bar, and there was no one else to listen to her, so she wobbled down the pier to the new boat for the night. I was hoping she would fall into the water on her way, but she didn't.

As we continued to enjoy the evening under the tree, listening to the distant music, Cody had the drunken brilliance that we should go skinny-dipping in the bay. That idea embarrassed me to no end! It proved his stupidity, low-class, and red-neck ways. Of course, Alex and I declined his offer to do such a poor judgmental activity. No one had ever done such a despicable thing at the yacht club and I sure as hell was not going to be the first! That did not stop my crazy-ass husband from striping down and showing off his tiny penis in front of my boyfriend, God, and everybody! I wanted to crawl under the nearest rock, but there were no rocks on that sandy beach.

Alex and I walked along the beach, hand-in-hand as we laughingly watched my silly husband swim naked in the bay. I told Cody to swim out to the first buoy, then back. That would have only been one mile out and one mile back. I don't know why he couldn't make it! That was just my luck! He came back, safe, and sound. Naked, cold and displaying his shriveled little penis once again to my boyfriend! Had that thing been any smaller, I could have called him my sister. Anyway, it was a disgusting display of his uncivilized, despicable behavior. It reminded me why I wanted a divorce.

August 26, 1995---A romantic night I will always remember! The night Alex Rosenberg said those three little words, "I love you" (within hearing distance of my husband.) Later, Alex and I were watching my husband display his tiny penis to the universe and stars, as Alex and I were walking along the beach. I squeezed his hand as I repeated those three little words back to him, "I love you too."

It would have been much more romantic if the husband-penis-thing had not occurred!

Don't you think?

Chapter 35 The Peony

The peony represents the birth flower for November.

Remember how your actions reflect on yourself and others, and always strive to act honorably and respectfully. Don't be afraid to apologize if you make a mistake and share your love with others to improve their lives as well.

Girls, I am now going to tell you a story that I am not proud of. I do not suggest that you try this, for it never works. I will tell you the lesson before I tell you the story.

Lesson:
<u>No matter how badly another person may behave, your acting out because of it will always overshadow their bad behavior; then you become the villain.</u>

- First, never wear a pink sequined cocktail dress to a party. It will get you into trouble!
- Now, if you are a Barbie doll in a hot pink sequined cocktail dress going to a party, I can guarantee you will get into trouble!
- And, if you happen to be an overly confident, drunk, Barbie doll, wearing a pink sequined cocktail dress, and going to a party. . . Girl! You will regret it for the rest of your life!

The night started when Cody told me not to wear that damn pink sequined, cocktail dress. He said I was overdressed for the occasion. I did not care. I had one man in mind that I wanted to see me wearing it, and I was dressing for his eyes only. I wanted to knock his eyes out.

The occasion was the Commodore's Ball of 1995. The night started like all the rest had gone in the past several years with boring speeches and presentations. After the formalities had concluded everyone was free to mingle and have a pleasurable time for the rest of the night. Complimentary hors d'oeuvres and drinks were never-ending. Never ending that is unless someone should become inebriated, then they were cut off from the bar. But that did not happen very often.

Everyone was dancing the night away, as was Cody. He certainly did not know how to dance, but he enjoyed shuffling and shifting around the dance floor with anyone who would let him drag them around, rhythm or not! Mrs. "Let-me-tell-you-how-wonderful-I-am" was perched on her roost at the bar, just waiting for the next unsuspecting victim to walk up and ask for a drink. Then she would pounce on them and start up a conversation about herself or maybe about their new boat, (my new future boat.) She had no idea what Alex was doing, nor did she care.

What Alex was doing was chasing me around. He caught up with me and whispered in my ear, "You look absolutely gorgeous tonight!" I coyly said, "Thank you," then promptly walked away. Men don't know how to take it when a woman plays hard to get.

I walked over to the bar and started talking to Mrs. "Let-me-tell-you-how-wonderful-I-am." We had a small talk for a while, mostly about her, then I noticed that we both had on the same Gucci, black satin stilettos. I asked her what size she wore. She said she wore size eight. I wore size seven and a half, except my left foot was slightly larger than my right foot. I asked if I might try on her size eight. She handed me her left size eight, and it felt great on my larger size left foot. When she did not notice, I handed her back my size seven and a half-left Gucci. For the rest of the night, I was in foot-heaven, and she was in foot-hell! I wasted no more time with her. So, I then started to mingle wearing my new well-fitted left shoe.

When Alex saw that I was alone, he casually walked over to me, breathed softly and blew in my ear, then whispered, "Would you like to meet me in the men's shower house for a little while?" My heart rate spiked instantly; his voice sounded so seductive. How could I turn him down? That seemed like a safe place; no one would need a shower at that time of night. As much as I craved his body, my good-girl-subconscious was rebelling, *you might get caught!* I thought about it about two seconds, then I walked out the back door to meet him.

We met in the shower house, in the dark. He locked the door behind us. Alex was dressed exquisitely in a black tuxedo. Man! Did he ever look great in that tux with his salt and pepper hair! You already know how I was dressed . . . to kill!

When we entered the shower room, our pheromones were released, sending out scents that made both of us almost combust with arousal! We could barely contain ourselves as we started kissing hot and heavily. We could not get undressed, because of the circumstances; but we wanted to make good use of our time. I was hot as hell to ride his Big Boy. He was kissing me with his 'jock-type' kisses because we were in such a hurry, but I didn't care, he tasted so damn good!

He was sitting in a chair, with his legs apart. I was straddling him. I lifted my left foot and rested my left high heel on the nearby sink. Then he rewarded me when he slipped his hands into my panties, with his sexpert fingers, he started to finger-fuck me. His middle finger was inserted while his thumb was circling and caressing my already erect clit. His fingers were about to make me come, but I wanted more; I wanted his Big Boy inside of me as soon as possible. He was kissing me and rubbing my clit while he was still fingering me. His other hand moved up and down my leg, past my black lace-top stockings, until. . . then. . . there it was, I couldn't help it, I climaxed! It was smoldering as I was hunching on his hand and hugging his head. My belly was cramping with delight

His fingers were softly continuing to massage my oversensitive clit as I was settling. My bikini panties were still pulled to the side as I reached down and unzipped his trousers and out sprang his big beautiful Big Boy that belonged to only me! We were continuing to kiss. I wasted no time when I slipped Big Boy into me ever so slowly and deeply one glide at a time. Oooh! The gliding and sliding inside of me felt good! My little pink dress was pulled up to my waist. His left hand was on my ass, and his right hand was massaging my clit as we continue to make love with our mouths, exchanging tongues back and forth. Our tongues were doing what our penis and vagina were doing; enjoying one another's bodies to the fullest.

Up and down, I was gliding on his penis, in and out it was going with the greatest of ease. Little Eva was wet; my fluids were flowing freely. My breasts were screaming to be touched, to be sucked, but we couldn't undress that far.

Our lovemaking didn't last long, because we were already sexcited and afraid of getting caught. That only added to the sexcitement of the lovemaking. Alex had little moving to do, as I had full control, sliding up and down on him. . . hard! He closed his eyes tightly and gritted his teeth, to muffle the sound of his climax. But when a man has a really good release, he can't do it quietly. He must groan and moan with his whole body, as his semen flows out of himself and into his lover. Just knowing we were being very mischievous, so close to everyone, also hearing Alex enjoy our sex, sent me over the hill again! I climaxed again! Both of our climaxes were the best because we knew we were naughty! And we were naughty so close to everyone around!

Climax, but don't scream! Climax, but don't make any noise that would draw attention to us! We both tried to muffle our wondrous, thunderous ending with a long, wet kiss into each other's mouths.

"Aaah!" I lifted myself off Alex., cupping myself to catch his semen from falling onto him. Then I wiped him off with a damp paper towel, so it would not leave any residue of semen on his black tuxedo trousers. (I should have licked it off.) I quickly cleaned myself; one final long kiss goodbye, then we left the shower house as if nothing ever happened. He walked off one way, I stepped off the other. A few minutes after he had smoked a cigarette, he entered the side door of the club with a sassy-fied smile on his face. He winked at me from across the room; I sinfully smiled back in contentment.

I went directly to the bar and had another Top Shelf Margarita, which was a mistake because it made me drunk. Alex and I were very cautious not to send out any 'red-flags' by acting too friendly in public. Therefore, we never danced together at any of the yacht club dances. But Alex made a big mistake that night, he danced with an old girlfriend from the past. I knew he had dated this girl, but Mrs. "Let-me-tell-you-how-wonderful-I-am" did not know this fact. Another mistake that Alex made that night was, he continued to drink and get drunk. We <u>all</u> did!

Now, I have told you what Alex was doing, but I have not told you everything that I was doing. It was as if I was prancing around, showing off my cocktail feathers in that pink cocktail dress! I think that damn dress must have been demon possessed! You see, I didn't like it that Alex was flirting with Ms. "Girdy-Old-girlfriend-from-the-past," so I decided to flirt with every old bald fat guy I could find. I didn't think anything of it, because I certainly was NOT interested in them. It was okay for me to try and make him jealous, but it was NOT okay for him to make me jealous. He could always top me!

I went back to the bar and had myself another Top Shelf Margarita and pretended to chat with other members. What I was doing was keeping a very close eye on Alex and Ms. 'Girdy-Old-girlfriend-from-the-past'. Another Top Shelf Margarita was my next-to-the-greatest-mistake! I looked across the ballroom, and there sat Alex on the couch with Ms. 'Old-girlfriend-from-the-past' chatting cozily. Then he leaned over and kissed her on the side of her cheek. I went berserk! I could not stop myself!

In my hot-pink-demon-possessed-sequined-cocktail-dress (freshly stained with his semen); I pranced my drunk, Barbie Doll smart-ass over to her. I hauled off and gave her one-full-faced-teeth-shattering-slap up beside her head! (I should have slapped Alex instead of her.) Then I turned and strutted my cocktail-feather-drunk-ass back to the bar as if nothing had ever happened. Alex promptly got up and fled the scene, leaving Girdy sitting there, holding her head and crying.

When I returned to the bar, the past Commodore, with whom I had been conversing said, "Why the hell did you do that?" I suddenly became stone cold sober! Before I could stop my tongue, I said, "Because she was kissing Alex." He said, "SOOO?" Then I thought, *Yea! So is right! Now, what the hell am I going to do? Oh shit, what the hell have I gone and gotten myself into?*

I was sober, but I continued to act drunk, and as if I did not know what I had done. Cody came over, got me, and said we had to go home right then! I remembered that I still had on Mrs. "Let-me-tell-you-how-wonderful-I-am's" left Gucci. I went to her and had the decency to exchange those expensive shoes with our correct ones before I left the club. At that moment, she had no idea what had gone on.

Cody and I left the club as other members were consoling Ms. "Girdy-old-girlfriend." Actually, she was so drunk; she didn't exactly know what had happened. I think she thought the sky was falling or something. After that night some of the guys called me Rocky.

On the way home, Cody asked me, "Why the hell did you do such a thing?" I continued to act drunk and said I did not know why, and I certainly did not remember doing it. I knew full well what I had done and why! But I wasn't going to start talkin'-and-catchin'-my-own-self-tellin'-lies!

Cody continued to add to my misery by telling me that before the next day was over, I would probably be visited by the Sheriff with a warrant for my arrest for assaulting her.

That night I laid wide awake in my bed; I could not sleep. Around four o'clock a.m., I called my best friend and said, "Can I come over? I need to talk." She said, "Yes." It was freezing! In my flip-flops and jogging suit, I left my house, with Cody still sleeping. When I arrived at her house, we went for a ride, and I told her what had happened. She already knew that Alex and I were having an affair. She listened intently, then she offered one piece of advice, "Eva, you have got to come up with a good story about why you did it. Then stick to it!"

"Truth is truth, as long as it works, it is the truth.
When it fails to work, it is no longer the truth."
David Hume

I took her advice. Slowly driving back to my house, I could not think of a single thing that I could say as to why I did that stupid action. What kind of lie could I tell that would sound like the truth and make it work? Not a damn thing could cover up for my stupid actions. I was doomed for jail, or maybe worse. . . Hell? Or even worse than all that---having to live the rest of my life with Cody!

When I arrived back home, it was still early morning. No one was awake yet. I slipped into bed without Cody, even knowing I had been gone. I was still wide awake when he got up, but I played opossum; not one move did I make. He tried to make as much noise as he could to make me get out of bed, but it didn't work. I was not going to allow him to put me through his fifty questions ordeal. I was scared to death and still waiting for the sheriff to come and serve me with assault papers. My head was about to split open with a pounding headache. When I heard Cody go outside, I got out of bed and took something for my pain. Then I used the bathroom, brushed my teeth, and went back to bed to think. I desperately needed to sleep, but I could not. I stayed in bed for the rest of that day.

Finally, the truthful lie came to me why I had done that dastardly, terrible thing to that poor little unsuspecting girl! Well hell! She deserved it! *After what she had said to me in the bathroom! I had a right to slap her!* I might as well go on and fess up to Cody why I did it and take my medicine!

About six o'clock that evening, I got out of bed and came into the living room where Cody was watching television. Before he could say anything, I started, "Cody, I want to explain to you why I slapped Girdy last night." He turned off the television, turned around in his chair and glared at me, then sarcastically said, "Let's hear it!"

I started out humbly by saying, "I know you told me not to wear that pink dress and I wore it anyway without your approval. I shouldn't have." (I had to eat crow on that one!) He lit in on me, "Well maybe next time you will listen to me, you never . . . on and on, etc."

I lowered my head and nodded in humble approval as I had to listen to his verbal punishment (only because I felt I had to.)

When he stopped his ranting and raving, I continued with my <u>absolutely</u>, <u>positively truthful lie</u> that I had just made up. "Well, what happened was; I was in the bathroom last night, and I heard someone in the stall next to me say, 'Looks like a whore in pink.' When I heard that, I knew whoever it was, was talking about me. I did not know who it was that said it. So, I looked under the stall and saw her shoes. I was so mad, I slammed my fist against the stall door, and she ran out of the restroom before I could get out of my stall and see who she was. When I came out of the restroom, I was furious! So I went to the bar and ordered another drink. I started watching for those shoes that I saw under the bathroom stall. I had almost finished my Margaretta when I spotted "Girdy-old-girlfriend" sitting on the couch. (I didn't mention that she was smooching with Alex.) When I saw those shoes, I knew it was Girdy that had said, 'Looks like a whore in pink.' Before I could stop myself, I walked over and slapped her. I am sorry, I couldn't help it; I was so mad at her for calling me that!"

That was my story, and I was sticking to it! It was the truth, and I was going to make it work! I don't know if Cody believed it or not.

Poor "Girdy-old-girlfriend" She never knew what hit her! She was so drunk; she never felt a thing, nor did she remember anything the next day. I was relieved. Some of the other club members did remember, however! I had to strategically tell my story to key people to save my reputation, and it worked. It is helpful if you have *a town gossip*. "Gabby-D-Gossip" was one of the best at getting the news out. If you want your true rumor to spread especially fast, you must always finish telling your story (rumor) with, "Now please don't tell anyone that I told you."

After I had told "Gabby-D-Gossip" my true rumor that I had made up, one of my friends called me a few days later. She said, "Gabby-D-Gossip," told me she heard "Girdy-old-girlfriend" call you a whore in the restroom."

I replied to her, "That's correct! But I can't be going around talking about it. So, if you hear anyone else repeating it, tell them what Gabby told you about what she heard Girdy say in the bathroom."

Remember: Truth is truth as long as it works.

I never received that visit from the sheriff. I also did not receive a letter of reprimand from the board of governors of the yacht club. I thought surely, I would have gotten a reprimand. I was later told that everyone was drunk that night and memories are very short. I had a great deal in which to be grateful!

Remember the lesson:

<u>No matter how badly another person may behave, your acting out, because of it, will overshadow their bad behavior, then you become the villain</u>.

After all that, I was still in a quandary concerning Alex. It seemed that our relationship was like a melodrama, unhurried, and relaxed at times. Then at other times, it would crescendo into something like that of a tune from the top forties hit parade. Somedays I felt caught in one phrase of the play, especially a mournful phrase, where the music seems unbearably sad, then onward it moves, at a deliberate speed and with great effort. Nothing in our relationship was predictable or the same. The very act of *waiting* itself works and nourishes in us qualities of patience, persistence, trust, gentleness, and compassion. It would take more trust and time. Sometimes we do not get what we want as soon as we want it. A little more time was needed for me to continue to tame my rose. He wasn't quite ready for me yet.

Let the music play on, play on.

P.S. I donated that little pink dress to the Goodwill, semen stains and all.

Chapter 36 The Narcissus

The narcissus represents the birth flower for
December.

The narcissus message is this: nothing bad can last
forever because spring is always just around the corner.
You can recover anything if you focus on the positive,
and good things are already on their way to you.

Alex and I did not see nor speak to each another for several weeks. He was as embarrassed as I was. But I was also mad at him. He did not know how to approach me after that night. I found myself in hibernation for the rest of December 1995 because I had shown my ass that night at the club. I had not heard any bad rumors about that night, nor had I suffered any severe repercussions because of it. So, I decided I might as well head on out and show my face again. I thought maybe I should try to make amends for my misbehavior the month before, by attempting to do something good for the club. That way, the members would think positive of me, instead of the last negative actions that I had previously displayed.

In the spring of 1996, the yacht club was to host a national championship sailboat race. Since I had a lot of experience at planning events and parties, I told the Vice Commodore I would help him with this big event. He welcomed my expertise and put me in charge of the Friday night skippers party. It would be the most significant event the yacht club had ever hosted, and the management wanted it to be memorable. I knew if I worked on this committee, it would put me back into good standing with everyone.

I worked my ass off to make sure the party was fun and perfect for all the sailors. The theme was "Caribbean night." I set up a small Caribbean village on the club parking lot. This village was complete with a stage which set on a flatbed trailer and decorated to look like an old

Polynesian hut with bamboo growing around it. Jumbo painted shrimp, fish, crabs, and seashells were displayed along the fence and walls of the stage. All sorts of old nautical items were stuck into nets along the fence and walls. A steel drum band entertained on that beautiful stage Friday night. Also, in the village, there were smaller Tiki huts where girls were braiding hair for everyone who wanted their hair braided into cornrows, like island girls.

Some of the guys had their hair also braided into cornrows. When the guys exited the hut, they looked like "Buckwheat," (the little boy character in the old time TV show "The Little Rascals.") But they didn't care; they were too drunk to notice. A large 12 x 12 Tiki hut was used as a quick service bar. All the sailors could walk up and quickly get their libations, then get on with their dancing or whatever they were doing previously. The food was fabulous, including a roast pig in the ground. A hula girl was there teaching the guys to hula; then later she led everyone in a limbo contest. Over 1000 tissue paper flowers were hanging all over the village, along with many artificial parrots. A real parrot was brought in by a club member for everyone to talk with and adore. The only thing the parrot could say was, "Ahhh shit!"

Everyone was encouraged to wear Caribbean clothing. The party lasted into the wee hours of the morning, which was not such a good idea for the serious racers/sailors who were competing the next day.

I was one of those sailors. By that time in my life, I was now racing an all-girl sailboat racing team on my very own J-24 sailboat. We were very serious about winning and were training for the Women's Championship Cup which was to be held that summer in Florida. We had some outstanding male coaches. The next day, we were to race in the big race, and one of the coaches was going with us, to critique and fine tune our skills, but not work.

Earlier that evening, before the party ended and while the sun was setting, I noticed Alex was walking hand-in-hand with Mrs. "Let-me-tell-you-how-wonderful-I-am" toward the beach where there was a dinghy pulled up on the sand. He was pointing to their new beautiful sailboat, (my future sailboat.) They were admiring it. The tide was out, and the water was too low, that meant they would not be able to get the boat out of the harbor the next morning to race. As a precautionary measure, Alex moored the boat out in the bay for the night; they spent the night on it. A few minutes later, a beautiful, voluptuous, blonde joined them, and Alex put his arm around her too! Well hell! Here we go again!

A little later that night, Alex came up to me and whispered in my ear, "couldn't you just make love on a night like this?" I was mad as hell when I looked him straight in the eye and said, "Hell, no!" Then I walked off and continued to finish the business of my party and close it down.

The next morning, I was exhausted from all the setting up and working during the skipper's party, but I didn't let my crew down, I raced my sailboat anyway. We had four girls and one coach. We were a tough gang!

The racecourse was 17 miles, one way down the bay. It took three hours to sail the course. Alex's boat was a go-fast boat in heavy air, but slower in light air. My lightweight boat performed well in a light breeze, but we usually took a beating in heavy wind.

The race started with strong wind, so off we headed down the bay. Alex was a reasonable distance ahead of me, which he very well should have been in that big boat. But that afternoon, the air died to almost nothing, and I caught up with him because my boat could move with little air. I spotted his boat on the South end of the course and sailed toward him. My coach wondered why I was not steering toward the finish line. Paying no attention to the coach, I kept driving my boat towards Alex's boat. Approaching Alex's boat from behind, he looked over his right shoulder and saw me with a surprised look on his face. Then the surprised look came upon my face! That beautiful, voluptuous, blonde was in a teeny weenie white bikini on the bow of his boat, sunbathing! I nearly died! I steered my boat as fast as I could to get away from that cad! Talk about mad? Girl, you have no idea how insane I was! Feeling like I was about to bust a blood vessel in my brain, I steered my boat as fast as I could. We ended up beating Alex to the finish line! Our crew took first place in our class. I don't know if it was because of my anger or the light air that helped us win that day. I want to think it was because of my excellent crew.

When we arrived at the island, where the trophy presentation was to take place, I was drained. Not only was I tired from the night before, but also the strenuous sailing down the bay all day. Cody was already at the island on our other boat, *DreamBoat.* He brought her down so my crew would have a comfortable place to sleep for the night, before racing back the next day.

There was another party on the island that night, along with the trophy presentation and dinner. I was not in charge of those festivities, so I stayed on *DreamBoat* and rested for the evening. I was mad at Alex, and I did not want anything to do with him, nor did I want to be seen by him.

Once I peeked through the bow window of my boat and saw him dancing on the beach with another girl to the song, "Brown-Eyed Girl." Again, another reason to be madder! Alex came to *DreamBoat* later and asked when we were going to dinner? I told Cody and the crew to go without me; I was too tired to eat.

I was exhausted, but more than that, my heart was hurting because of Alex.

When will this ever and? Will I ever be able to trust this man that I call Mr. Wonderful? What is it about beautiful women that men just can't get enough of? Is it the attention the women give them that feeds their ego?

That was 1996; I still had a little more time to tame my rose. I wondered if I could hang in there.

Chapter 37 The Calla Lily

The calla lily flower's message is to focus on the beauty around you and remember that it will return even if it disappears for a season. Hold onto your innocence and grace as you move through the world and conquer your challenges.

The following Monday my party volunteers and I disassembled the Caribbean Village at the yacht club. Tired or not, it had to be done. Well, at least now I had redeemed my reputation from the fiasco of the prior December. Occasionally, one of the guys still called me "Rocky."

It was over a week before I would answer my phone knowing Alex would be calling. I couldn't bring myself to do it! But I finally did answer the phone. We met in our usual love nest hotel the following day. Only, this time, I would not let him off so easy. I asked who the blonde was that was on his boat. He sure did have a way of explaining away things! She was a local newspaper reporter who was covering the story, and she wanted to sail on the largest boat. He let her ride along as long as she would stay out of the way. Sure! She stayed out of the way, but certainly not out of sight! In my humble opinion, she was just a trollop, trolling for a pole! But that was just my humble opinion, what do I know?

Listening to his story carefully, I accepted it as fact, then we moved on. After all, if our relationship was going to grow and move on, we must overcome our challenges, right?

It was a few weeks later, Alex and his crew raced to Mexico out of Pensacola Florida. The race was over 350 miles in the Gulf of Mexico. They were gone for a couple of weeks, if you count the days racing the boat down, partying while there, and sailing the boat back home. I missed him while he was gone. The wives and girlfriends flew down, joined the crew, and partied for three days. I was overjoyed when he returned home safely. They won a trophy. Alex said he did not have a good time while they were there; he missed me. I believed him. Alex had a way of making me feel extraordinary!

In August of that year, there was another race at another yacht club in our association. Cody and I sailed *DreamBoat* down and towed my J-24 race boat behind her. Alex and Mrs. "Let-me-tell-you-how-wonderful-I-am" were participating in the race also. Both couples met at this other yacht club. Alex got there first and reserved a spot for me next to him in the harbor.

Cody and I got there around 4 p.m. on a Friday. I quickly showered and got all dolled up so I would look sexy for Alex. He invited us to step over to his boat for cocktails before taking the dinghy over to the yacht club for dinner and the skipper's meeting. We accepted his invitation. They had their air conditioner on, and it felt great because it had been hot in the blazing sun while sailing down. The cold Bushwhackers tasted delicious! Everything was going well when Mrs. "Let-me-tell-you-how-wonderful-I-am" decided she would let-me-show-you-what-a-great-time-we-had-in-Mexico.

She promptly shoved a video into the television VCR. She now had a captive audience. I was watching the video of Alex not having a good time in Mexico, leading the Mardi Gras parade as the head strutter down the town streets to the town square. There he and a few of his crew members forced themselves not to have a good time while they performed the "gator" dance for all to watch. Then they continued not to have a good time while they were dancing with the local senoritas. It was truly awful, watching Alex suffering, <u>not</u> having a good time at those fun parties while he was in Mexico. I could feel his pain!

While watching the video intently, the bikini contest (a.k.a. the booty contest) appeared, this made my interest peek! They were 15 or 20 contestants competing for the title of, "Miss Purdy-Bootie" or What-ever-the-title-was. Representing Alex's boat was. . . Who do you think? That gorgeous, voluptuous, blonde newspaper girl!

"Oh, she just flew down to cover the race event," or so I was told. There she was, in a yellow bikini this time! Mrs. "Let-me-tell-you-how-wonderful-I-am" did not think much of it. "She's pigeon-toed," was her remark as a critique and as if to be speaking poorly of her. I assume she did not notice those double-D cups. Anyway, that's not the worst of the story!

The bikini/booty contest winner was a beautiful, well-rounded, well-tanned, girl from Fort Worth, Texas, wearing an American flag bikini. There were a lot of high mountain ranges peeking out of her flag at the northern part of her territory! So, there she was, posing, grinning, winking and blinking with her trophy (which was nothing more than a bottle of Mount Gay rum). As she was having her picture taken, there was Alex, standing right beside her, adoring her mountain range and pledging allegiance to the flag of Fort Worth, Texas! Seeing it, fired me up! Mrs. "Let-me-tell-you-how-wonderful-I-am" had no idea what Alex was doing and what she was seeing as she was videotaping. I noticed immediately what Alex was doing. It was like he was chasing a dog in heat!

Upon seeing the evidence of what fun, he <u>did not have</u> while in Mexico, I immediately became too tired to do anything else that evening. Excusing myself, I said I needed to get rested up before the race the next day. I went back to *DreamBoat* and cried, vowing not to show my face again for the rest of that night. Cody stayed on Alex's boat and continued to enjoy the free drinks.

It was getting late, so Cody took Mrs. "Let-me-tell-you-how-wonderful-I-am" in the dinghy across the bay to the host yacht club for dinner and the skipper's meeting. Alex stayed on his boat. Shortly after that, a couple of Alex's neighborhood friends from Mobile showed up at his boat. A few minutes later, Alex knocked on the hull of my boat. I did not answer. He knew I was in there, so he continued to knock. "Baby, come out." He said. I stuck my head out of the companionway; he could tell I had been crying. "I want you to meet someone," he said.

"No," was my quick reply. "Baby, my best friend has driven from Mobile, and I want him to meet you." Alex always had a way of convincing me to do whatever he wanted me to do, so I agreed and said, "Give me a few minutes."

Quickly I got dressed into a white denim mini-skirt and a white halter top that had a rhinestone anchor embedded on the front, both of which showed off my dark tan. Slapping on more make-up, I got myself collected and stepped over to Alex's boat, barefoot. Alex introduced me as one of the most excellent lady sailors on the bay; he was blowing smoke, but I smiled and said nothing, shaking my head in denial. His friend was with his wife, who was very lovely and unbelievable friendly to me.

We visited for a short time, then I made a snide remark, to jab at Alex. "Has Alex shown you his video of the Mexico trip? He has it right here if you would like to see it." The couple burst out in laughter. The wife remarked, "Oh, yes! We've seen that video---more than once! Every time we go to their house or boat, she has it ready to shove into the VCR." They were tired of seeing it.

After a brief visit, it was time for me to return to my boat. I let Alex's friends make my acquaintance, and now that was over. No more "Ms. Nice-Girlfriend-Wonderful!" On my way out of the companionway, both the guys stepped outside with me. Alex was trying to speak to me, but I ignored him. Stepping off his boat, I heard his friend say, "She has a beautiful body!"

Hmmm! Why would he feel free to say such a thing about me to Alex? I wondered. Alex told me later that he had already confided with both of his friends about his feelings for me and that we were having an affair!

Shortly, his friends departed, leaving Alex and me alone on our two boats, and up to our own devices! Cody and Mrs. "Let-me-tell-you-how-wonderful-I-am" were roosting at the free bar across the harbor at the skipper's meeting and having dinner. They would stay until the wee hours of the night and come back drunk, if they made it back at all, without falling out of the dinghy into the water and drowning!

Alex knocked on my boat, I curtly said, "What do you want?" "Want to go for a walk?" he asked. We walked hand-in-hand along the vacant pier for a long time; he knew I was hurting because of what I saw on that video. I made a sharp comment about him, "pledging allegiance to the flag of Ft. Worth, Texas." He knew what I was referring to; his only response was, "Well, she was just the pick of the litter." We both laughed at his reply, inferring that she was a dog in the first place!

It was another obstacle, another challenge, and we jumped over it just fine. We still loved one another, and it wouldn't' be much longer.

Chapter 38 The Tulip

The meaning of the tulip flower is:
- Perfect, enduring love
- Undying passionate love

It was a steamy summer day in 1996 when Alex called and asked if I would meet him for lunch in Mobile. What a surprise! We never met alone in public, just the two of us, for lunch or anything else for that matter.

Once we meet in public at an outlying hotel on the beltway in Mobile one evening. Alex wanted us to enjoy a cocktail in the lounge, but I refused to be seen in public with him; so, we took the cocktails to our room. Whenever we might be seen in public together, we were always seen as two married couples; usually at the yacht club, but never he and I alone. This invitation to lunch made me nervous, but I agreed to meet him.

We met at a trendy restaurant which was owned by one of his sailboat race crew members, which also made this a horrible idea. A lot of people that we both knew would be eating there. Arriving on time, Alex was already there sitting at the bar chatting with the owner. Walking in, Alex acted as if I happen to be coming in for lunch, and he motioned for me to have a drink with him at the bar. Going along with his act in front of our mutual friend, I sat down beside him. After a few minutes, Alex casually said, "may I buy lunch for a pretty lady?" Right in front of our friend, the owner. Acting resistant but finally agreeing, we were seated. Nervous as hell, I ordered the best cheeseburger in town, Alex did the same. After all, the cheeseburgers were what made that restaurant famous. They were so good! I was very nervous about being seen in public with Alex. Therefore, not but two bites were taken from that burger. Guilt was written all over my face, knowing for sure the owner was aware of what we were up to.

Because of my nervousness, I kept shredding my napkins instead of eating. It embarrassed me when I noticed what I was doing with my napkins. Now I had nothing to wipe my mouth with. It was about that time when Alex made it clear why he had invited me to lunch. He wanted to talk about our future together.

You could have blown me away with a feather when he asked, "how much money does it take for you to live on?" Bewildered by his question, I answered him with another question, "why do you ask?" "Well, if we are ever going to be together, I want to make sure I can support you in the manner in which you are accustomed." I nearly dropped my sweet tea!

He continued by telling me how much money he made, which was absolutely none of my business! He made a hell of a lot more money than I had ever lived on! Trying not to act surprised or overwhelmed, I replied, "I am not a high maintenance type of girl." I continued to nervously play with my paper napkin, making unnecessary circular motions with it, then folding it into small squares, then unfolding it again. "Well, you appear to be," was his quick reply.

Do I? I questioned myself. *Hmm*! I put the worn-out napkin in my lap and held down my fidgety hands. Then I remembered:

While the old cliché is true, **"It is—what it is."**
However,
**What *"is—is" does not count.* What does counts is
how it appears to be.**
(You gotta think about that one.)

You know girls, it's all in the presentation (and perception.) No one must know from whence you came, or how much money you do or do not have. Don't talk about it and you will go farther than you ever thought you would, or ever expected! People are always comparing you to themselves . . . looks, intelligence, and financial worth. It's like a chicken pecking order, and everyone is trying to figure out who is on top. Don't talk about it and carry yourself well. Just be the *best you* that you can be. Don't try to be anyone else, only you. Who knows? Maybe you will end up on top?

P.S. I found out a long time ago that people with *real money* never talk about it. People who do not have much money are the ones who go around bragging about having it.

This break-through with Alex was something I never expected would happen. He was making plans for our future, and I had no idea. By humbling himself and confiding in me about his salary, he was informing me of his future plans with me. Keeping up the encouragement, I told him I was not expensive to maintain; I used drug store make-up and could color, cut, and style my hair. If a specific dress was needed, and it couldn't be found in a store, or if I could not afford it, then I would sew it myself. You see, Alex saw me as the spoiled brat of New Fort, who got whatever she wanted because I put up a good front. He knew nothing about my background; he only knew that everyone liked and respected me, that I was smart and pretty. He was won over by my style. I was the type of lady that would make him proud to be seen with in public. That was important to him as well as his family.

Unlike Mrs. "Let-me-tell-you-how-wonderful-I-am," I would never belittle my man. She was always in competition with Alex. That is not the way a marriage should be. A marriage is a team of two people working together, not vying to see who the best is. Working together as a team brings out the best in both people.

After shredding half a dozen napkins and not eaten but two, maybe three bites of that cheeseburger, it was time to go. My sweaty palms were worn out, as well as my flushed cheeks. When the waitress asked if I wanted a go-box, I almost said, "yes," because I was starving, but that would have been evidence of where I had been.

We said our short little good-byes there in that public restaurant for all the world to see, as casual friends.

To me, this occasion was his official proposal of marriage, only without the engagement ring. Our future together was certainly looking brighter!

Chapter 39 The Gloxinia

The gloxinia means love at first sight.

Do you believe in love at first sight? Yeah! Neither do I. Well, in a way I do believe in love at first sight because I was infatuated with Mr. Wonderful at the very first sight of him and never stopped thinking of him since that very first day. But that's not the case for everyone.

My son tried to convince me that he and his new girlfriend were in love at first sight and wanted to get married as soon as possible. Okay, maybe they were in heat at first sight. He said she was, "hot-to-trot"! She thought she was "hot-snot!" I-thought-not! Anyway, they just had to get married! What could I say in the matter? Nothing! Nathan was a full-grown man, so in September they were married.

Nathan continued to work part time and go to college part-time. It was a no-win situation. He now had a full-time bride and a full-time marriage. There was no time left in the day, according to my calculations. Upon visiting them, I observed their poor living conditions, and it broke my heart. He was barely making enough money to make ends meet while living in the married student apartments. He had initially started college in the fall of 1991. Now was the fall of 1996. By this time, he should have already graduated, but with all his setbacks, he continued to drop courses and work more hours to pay the bills. His student loans were piling up, but college credits were not. Finally, the question came up, "Nathan, are you going for a doctorate or what?" Nathan was no fool; he knew what the inference was about. Therefore, he offered no response.

After talking to Nathan and "Bride-number-two-hot-to-trot-n-hot-snot," they were convinced to move back to New Fort and help manage the family business. They could continue their education in New Fort while Nathan would be able to make more money in the family business than he would ever be able to make working part-time anywhere else. After some quick 15-minute consideration, they both said, "yes."

After the fall quarter had ended, they both moved back to New Fort. They lived with Cody and me only a few days before finding a small rental house which they leased for six months from January until June 1997.

Everything was going great for the newlyweds. Then one day they saw an advertisement for new homes in our area, the builder was offering low down payments and low closing cost. Nathan had no money saved up, so Cody and I gave him the *gift money* to cover those costs. It was only a few weeks, and the newlyweds moved into their new home. With them moving, that left their rental house vacant. Now we had a problem; the landlord would not release them from the lease. They had to continue to pay the rent until June, plus the new house payments. They did not care; they moved into their new home and started enjoying it in February. I would have done the same.

While being happy to have my son back at home, because he was a delight to be around, "Bride-number-two-hot-to-trot-n-hot-snot" was another subject!

You know the old saying:

A daughter is a daughter for the rest of her life.

A son is a son until he takes him a wife!

It has been said that <u>*a boy grows up and marries a girl just like his mama*</u>.

Well, there was room for *only one of me* in this family. "Bride-number-two-hot-to-trot-n-hot-snot" was nothing like me. I wondered if she and Nathan would make it after that "hot-to-trot-thing" cooled off.

270

Chapter 40 The Magnolia

The magnolia symbolizes dignity and nobility.

In ancient China, magnolias were thought to be the perfect symbol of womanly beauty and gentleness.

Mr. Wonderful and I continued our plans for the future together as husband and wife, although we did not know when that time would be. We just talked about it in general, where we wanted to live, etc. The most crucial plan was that he would get his divorce first, then let the dust settle; afterward, I would follow suit. Nothing was set in stone. The time wasn't right just yet.

In January of 1997, Alex called with disturbing news, and he was quite upset. His beloved Springer Spaniel, Abbey, had gotten sick during the night. He took her to the vet for emergency surgery, and she died in his arms. He started to cry as he told me the sad story. Feeling so sorry for him, I was crying along with him. But there was nothing I could do to take away his pain. It is not enough to say, "I am so sorry." Words are a poor medium at a time like that.

I had no idea how closely attached a person could become with an animal. My parents would not allow us to have pets because they could barely feed the kids, much less feed a pet.

Nathan had a dog or two while growing up, but they stayed outside. My thinking was a dog should be kept outside due to sanitary reasons. In retrospect, it was a foolish thing to think! Therefore, I never was attached to a gentle, loving creature such as a dog and never knew how much love I was missing out on.

It was later when I realized this lovely Springer Spaniel was the same beautiful show dog that I had met on that first night when Alex and I were together. He loved her dearly. That sad incident was one of the first times I saw the tender, caring side of Alex. I wanted to reach through that telephone and grab him and hold him with all my might to comfort him in his loss and sadness, but I couldn't.

Chapter 41 The Aster

The aster represents the birth flower for September.

The aster is a symbol of patience and elegance

The Winter Series Sailboat Races were scheduled toward the end of January 1997. It came by no surprise that Alex asked me to crew on his boat. The races were held on three consecutive Saturdays, with the skipper's meetings held on the Friday nights prior to each race. It was the last weekend of the races. On that Friday night, I went to the yacht club and spent the night on

DreamBoat, so I would be there early the next morning for the final race. Cody stayed home that weekend.

After the skipper's meeting and dinner, I retired to my boat alone. Later that night, I heard a knock on the hull of my boat; it was Alex and a guy whom I had met on the 10-day cruise but had not seen since. He lived in Pensacola and was there crewing with Alex for the final race. Welcoming them aboard, I offered them a beer, and we chatted for a while. Alex had also told this friend about me. It was hard to believe how many friends Alex had confided in concerning me. That would be number three, to my knowledge.

You see girls, men talk too! When something is on your mind, you must talk about it. It was as if he had a trophy and was showing it off to this guy. After a short while, the two of them departed and went back to Alex's boat for the evening.

Knowing Alex would be paying me another visit later that night, I showered, powdered slightly and put on light makeup. Adorning myself in a sexy blue baby doll negligée for the night, I waited for Alex. Before falling asleep, he came walking aboard my boat. Quietly he slipped into my stateroom. "Is there room in there for one more?" He asked as he was taking off his pants and shirt, then climbed into bed beside me. "Only you," I responded, welcoming him with warm and tender arms.

"What about your wife?" I asked. He said when they returned to the boat, she was drunk and about to pass out, so he put her to bed.

His friend was sleeping on Alex's boat for the weekend. He promised to keep a check on her, to make sure she did not fall overboard while looking for Alex. We were safe once again with his friend acting as our watchdog.

In the south, it is cold during January, but it was hot under the blankets of my boat, especially with our two hot-blooded bodies rubbing against one another. In the warm comfort of my boat, we loved and kissed the night away until almost dawn.

Our tongues could not get enough of one other's mouths. In and out of each other's mouth, we were exchanging saliva and continuing to lick lips. I loved his mustache, tickling my lips and face. His hands were so smooth as they caressed my breasts and circled my nipples. He lowered his head under the blanket; I knew what was coming next! His mouth sucked on my nipples, that were standing erect. They were sensitive, and I was about to explode with desire. Reaching down and slipping him out of his boxer underwear, I took hold of Big Boy and started massaging it to give him pleasure while he was pleasuring me. He was already erect and full; this made me more excited to feel and hold him knowing he wanted me. Spreading my legs, he laid between them, kissing his way down my belly slowly and stopping only at my bellybutton to tease me, then back up to my breasts to suck more. My pelvis was rubbing against Big Boy so I could massage my clitoris, which was throbbing for his touch. I was in erotic torment, waiting and wanting him. He kept holding off.

Stopping momentarily, I gave him a surprise. I reached into the top drawer of my stateroom and took out my vibrator. "Have you ever seen one of these?" I asked. "I sure have, let me show you what to do with it," was his instant response. It surprised me that he was not intimidated by the introduction of an adult sex toy into our romantic play, but he was familiar and certainly knew how to use it. It takes a <u>real man</u> not to be intimidated by an adult sex toy. He took it out of my hand and turned it on.

He began by vibrating and massaging the back of my neck, then my shoulders very slowly on low vibrations. There was absolutely no rush to go anywhere with that tool. What precision he had; he knew right where to place it that would make me sing with melodious harmony with his movements. Moving from my shoulders, he gently rolled me over onto my stomach, where he vibrated down to my breasts, where he circled them slowly and softly with B.O.B. (my battery-operated-boyfriend.) My body was quivering with ecstasy when he moved farther down to my lower abdomen.

Desperately wanting to kiss his lips, all I could do was lie there and enjoy his massaging me. He loved to watch me going crazy with desire for him as he was tormenting me erotically. He gently rolled me over, up onto my knees, my ass was exposed high in the air. He opened my pretty little fun spot with one finger to prepare me for his penetration. It felt wonderful and I started rocking back and forth on to him, letting him know I was ready. He slipped Big Boy into me ever so slowly, with each stroke going deeper and deeper. My head and neck arched backward as we began our rhythm of pumping together. He turned the vibrator to a high-pulsing mode and with sexpertise, he reached around and placed it on the crown of my already engorged clitoris. It was so sensitive, I could not stand much more, but we continued rocking and pumping and taking each another to euphoria. The vibrator on my clitoris and the stroking my G-Spot at the same time was more than this small-town girl could stand! The constant vibrating, the continuous pumping, the rocking back and forth was heavenly! Oh my! I wanted it to never end.

My vagina was free flowing with vaginal fluids, and I was sweating all over, I knew I couldn't last much longer. Our rhythm of pumping was: one-two-three-four. One-two-three-four. On four, he would thrust deeper into me, hitting my G-Spot HARD! It nearly drove me out of bed and out of my mind! We were like two sex maniacs because we couldn't get enough of one another. Then, there it was, the climax of the century! I screamed but tried to muffle it, to no avail. He kept pumping and pumping until he climaxed hard and long, groaning with pleasure as he released inside me. Aaah! Hot semen shooting into me over and over! Alex could come forever it seemed He gradually turned off B.O.B., and we collapsed on the bed in total exhaustion. We were both panting as he slowly pulled out of me; his semen flowing out of me and onto the bed.

Now <u>that</u>, girls, is how to have an orgasm!

Holding me tenderly in his arms, we kissed for a while longer after our lovemaking was finished, then we both knew he had to head back to his boat before it was too late. We were saddened as he dressed to leave that night, knowing it would be a long time until we could be together again.

Leaving my boat, he turned briefly and looked back at me, then said, "Oh, by-the-way. . . that vibrator thing. . . don't try that at home alone!" We laughed because we both knew what he was referring to.

With a sinful smile, I replied, "I'll try not to."

Chapter 42 The Hibiscus

Youth, fame, and beauty are very much like hibiscus flowers, which have short lives. Although the flowers may die, they do grow back if the bush is cared for properly.

Mardi Gras was in February 1997. Alex was in a mystic organization and had been for many years. Tickets to the ball were supposed to be given away, but some members sold their tickets. Alex had given Cody and me tickets for several years, that year would be no different. We stayed at the same hotel every year as Alex and Mrs. "Let-me-tell-you-how-wonderful-I-am," which was across the street from the auditorium where the ball was held. The parade started down the street not far from the hotel. A group of us walked to the float where Alex had his throws loaded and was ready to roll and throw his trinkets. Alex was juiced up, pumped up, excited about parading down the streets and throwing his trash to the spectators, who loved catching that stuff! That year the mystic society's theme was "Kings and Kingdoms." Alex's costume was that of a farmer. (Don't ask me why.) I assume it represented the king of the field or something? Anyway, he looked cute wearing his coverall's and straw hat.

Alex knew where I would be standing on the parade route, and he would be looking for me. When the time came and his float passed by my location, I called out to him. He spotted me and flooded me with a case of red silk roses. What a surprise! To be inundated with 144 red roses from my rose! I only got to keep a few of them; the crowd picked up the majority. But I knew they were all meant for me.

The mystic societies enforced a strict dress code for all ball attendees: *costume de rigueur* was stated at the bottom of the invitation, which meant white tie and tails for men and full-length dresses for the ladies. Cody hated to dress up; he called it a 'penguin suit.' He was such a redneck! I loved to dress elegantly. On that night, I wore a full-length, black velvet strapless, well-fitted gown with a long-rounded train in the back. Formal length gloves and black high heels finished off my attire. A lady always looks sexy in a simple black dress.

Alex also gave tickets to my best friend and her husband. This best friend was a Glee Girl and the other Bookend with me. She knew all about Alex. That night, our husbands did not want to go to callouts; they stayed in the hotel room and continued to drink before walking over to the ball. My friend and I loved to watch callouts from the balcony. We watched as Alex and Mrs. "Let-me-tell-you-how-wonderful-I-am" strutted out from the stage and showed off. She was showing off her new annual gown, which was always stunning. They disappeared into the crowd before the first dance took place. The next thing I knew, Alex was ushering a friend around in a wheelchair right below me. I called out to him, and he spotted me. It was unbelievable when he left his friend in the wheelchair and started climbing up the railings to get to me! Worrying that he would fall and get hurt, I said, "no! Don't!" But he kept on climbing higher and higher to get to me. When he was within touching distance, he handed me an expensive set of Mardi Gras beads, which were collector's items from his organization. Shouting, he said, "I love you!" As he climbed back down to safety. While I was relieved that he was safe, it was unbelievable he said those words with hundreds of people around. He was in costume, wearing a mask, and only I knew who he was.

Later that evening at the ball, the three couples were in Alex's hospitality room. Suddenly, he grabbed me by the hand and dragged me out of the room before anyone knew we were gone! Into the crowded corridors, we disappeared and slipped into a side ballroom where a band was playing. There we danced arm in arm, with our bodies so close you could not pour water between us. We kissed passionately the whole time we were dancing, nonstop. His farmers straw hat was used to cover our faces so no one would know who we were. We danced in the middle of the crowded dance floor, so no one entering the room would spot us right off. No one else in that ballroom was paying any attention to us. We were just another couple enjoying the night at the ball. We danced and kissed slowly and got sweaty as hell for about 30 minutes when the band took a break. At that time, he said, "here, I want you to have this." It was another gift, another collector's item, a lady's brooch from his organization. We then departed, I went one way, and he walked off another.

Walking back in the same direction from which I came, which was toward Alex's hospitality room, I ran into Cody. He was mad and raging when he asked, "where the hell have you been? I have been looking for you! I'm ready to go home!"

I said, "I have been in hospitality room number ten visiting with some of my other Glee Girl friends. No, we are not going home; come on, let's go dance." Dragging him off to the main ballroom got him into a better mood;

he continued to drink until he was drunk. Now he had a good time.

Before going back to the hotel that night, we once again ran into Alex and Mrs. "Let-me-tell-you-how-wonderful-I-am." While complimenting her on her newest ballgown, she was doing the same for mine when she noticed the brooch that I was wearing, the one that Alex had just given me. She knew that brooch was only to be worn by the wives of members. She asked me, "where did you get that brooch?" I said, "I just found it on the floor, isn't it pretty?" She said, "yes." Immediately turning to Alex, she asked, "where is my brooch for this year?" Alex coyly answered, "they were sold out by the time I got to the meeting this morning." It made me feel good to know that I was now "Lady-number-one-Wonderful."

Oh man! I <u>do</u> love this man that I call Mr. Wonderful!

Chapter 43 The Stock Flower

The stock flower's message is: enjoy the life you have before it is gone. Love and beauty are both eternal if you believe in them.

My family home had been for sale for over two years. Assuming it was overpriced and that was why it had not sold after so long, the value finally caught up with the market. It was a charming four-bedroom, 2 ½ baths ranch house with a swimming pool, built on four acres. Finally, a single man came along and made a cash offer that we could not refuse. The cash offer meant we would be closing within ten days; he also wanted immediate possession upon closing. We agreed. Cody wanted to move closer into town and build a larger house on a smaller lot. Keeping silent about the matter, I had no plans of building another home with him. I could not see me building another house with a man whom I did not love. When the home sold, it was a big breakthrough, and then I had a big decision to make. After all, life is too short, and that was my chance to change my future before it was too late. We only live once, and I was not getting any younger.

As stated previously, I have purposefully kept my silence concerning the negative things about Cody. This story is not about him. In spite of all that, to validate my reasons for wanting a divorce, some things must be brought out. Some nasty secrets have been hidden concerning him and protected because it is incredibly embarrassing to share. *Coup De Grace!* Well, here goes!

Cody was obsessed with watching porn movies. He liked to watch them, then have sex with me, not out of love, but out of lust. . . lust for the women in those videos. I was used as his vehicle to bring about his ends. It escalated into him demanding that I watch them with him, then have sex with him during the watch. I hated it and resented him for requiring this of me, it was getting worse. It was a weekly ordeal, but I felt compelled to go along with his demands. I reluctantly complied with his requirements in order not to do anything that would send up any red flags. Not having sex with him would have indeed set up a red flag!

I was very tired of this disgusting activity that he was demanding and forcing me to participate in with him! I felt that having sex with Cody was being unfaithful to Alex. Many times, after having sex with Cody, I would rush to the bathroom and douche and cry. I hated it!

It was on a Friday night when all hell broke loose; it was my final straw! I had had enough of his bullying me and demanding that I participate in that deplorable act with him! When he put the porn video into the VCR, as if that was his foreplay, I took charge of my life and said, "I am not interested in that!" He got mad and started to pitch a fit of anger like a baby who had just had a sucker pulled from his mouth! After 28 years of enduring his controlling and bullying me, I now had the courage to stand up to him.

Without another word, I packed a small bag, left the house, and went to the yacht club to spend the weekend on *DreamBoat*. There was a race that weekend at the yacht club, so it was not out of the ordinary for me to spend the weekend on our boat. Cody did not like it that I left, and he was furious, but so was I! When I left the house on the way to the club, surprisingly he did not follow me, I was greatly relieved!

Friday night was spent on *DreamBoat*. The next day, I raced my J-24 with my all-girl crew. Saturday night, I once again spent the night on *DreamBoat* without going home. Then Sunday afternoon during the trophy presentation, he dragged his sorry ass to the club. He proceeded to follow up and continue our Friday night argument. He surprised me when he said, "the only way I will sell this house is if we sell the house, split the money, and split the sheets!" It greatly surprised him when I yelled, "fine! Get your shit and get out!" I advised him I was not kidding. "Don't come home tonight either! You can stay in Nathan's rental house until you can find another place. I'm going home, and I do not want to see you there!" He did not show up there; he did as I ordered.

While driving home, I called a friend and asked if I might use his storage warehouse to store my furniture after we moved out of my home because Cody and I were getting a divorce. He could not believe what he was hearing, although he seemed a little pleased at the news. I was ecstatic!

This sort of messed up mine and Alex's plans; I could not help it, the cards just fell into place, and it was the right time. Our original plans were for Alex to divorce first, then I would follow suit. Now Alex felt compelled to make a hasty move, which he did not need to do and should not have done. Without talking to me and within a few days, he moved out of his home and moved onto his boat. Big mistake! Can you hear the rumor mill? After all those years of not getting caught while messing around, Alex goes and does something stupid like that! Our two separate actions caused people to assume we are having an affair, and the gossip got started with no proof! We were the talk of the town, with no substantiated evidence, only speculation.

With absolutely no proof of adultery, Cody and I continued with our plans for a quickie divorce on the grounds of incompatibility. Within 12 days of his smart-ass remark on the boat, we signed divorce papers separately, using one mutual attorney.

Our house was sold and closed within 10 days. We separately signed the closing papers in another attorney's office. After receiving my half of the equity money, I rushed to the bank and invested all of it in a high-yield IRA for 6-months. All our assets were divided right down the middle as I proclaimed them to be. Taking a piece of notebook paper, on one side of the page was "HIS" and on the other side of the paper was "HERS." It was an easy arrangement; he agreed to exactly what I put on paper because I gave him most of what I didn't want anyway. He agreed to the things I wanted. The IRAs and annuities were already in separate names, so that was no problem.

There was one mistake that I made. I gave my half of the family pool business to Nathan. That put me completely out of the family business. I knew I could no longer work there with Cody. Besides, I felt that I could go anywhere and gain employment. I would soon learn differently.

When I went to the attorney's office to sign the divorce papers, he asked me, "is there any way this marriage can be saved?" I unequivocally said, "NO!" He then said, "sign here." That was that! My 28 years of mortal hell was finally over.

I wondered how my adult son, Nathan, would take all of this. He was saddened that his parents were getting a divorce after all those years. He understood my feelings because he had lived through hell, along with me. He also empathized with me and my reasons why. What he did not like and failed to cope with, was the news his mother had been having a 14-year affair. I guess young men can't fathom their mothers having and enjoying sex. I wonder how they think they got here in the first place.

Word got back to me that Cody said I 'had P.M.S. one day too many' and that was the reason for the divorce. Another person was trying to make me feel guilty when she told me Cody said he would never marry again because he *could never find another woman as perfect as his first wife.*

I laughed as I told her, "You do know I was his second wife, don't you?"

Chapter 44 The Frangipani

The frangipani flower's message is: being delicate and beautiful doesn't mean you are weak or incapable of rising to meet a challenge.

I bet some of you girls are going to think this storybook fairytale is about to have a sweet little ending. You know, where the Prince comes and sweeps her off her feet. Then they ride off into the sunset on a white horse, like the Disney Princess, that-happily-ever-after-thing. Well, I have never had that Disney Princess mentality, and never will have. It was at that time in my life that I had to embrace the Warrior Princess attitude.

There were more turbulent waters that had to be crossed. So, girls hold on to your tiaras a little longer.

The day the closing papers were signed on my home, the new buyer wanted immediate possession. Everything was packed, and we were moved out on time. All my furniture was placed in storage, except a few light pieces which I could easily move around myself should I need to. My good friend allowed me to move into that beautiful river rendezvous love nest until I could find a more suitable residence.

My son and "Bride-number-two-hot-to-trot-n-hot-snot" were happily living in their new home by that time. I asked them if they would help me move my personal items, wicker furniture, and a single bed to that beautiful river cottage. They sadly agreed. Only a few of my art pieces were taken to ensure their safety, also to beautify wherever I would be living. I made my son promise not to tell anyone where I was living. Knowing that Cody was a violent and angry man, he might seek me out and kill me, now that he had heard about the rumors of Alex and me having an affair. Nathan promised he would keep my secret location to himself; he had the river cottage telephone number should he need to contact me.

Upon moving into the river cottage, I immediately began cleaning and sanitizing it; it took all day. That night, Alex came to visit. We sat by candlelight, holding hands on that old couch, and talked for hours about our problems which he had just stirred up by prematurely leaving his wife. We talked about how we were going to solve them; there was no easy solution. We were both too worried to think about making love that night.

I promised him this, "Alex Rosenberg, you will be the *last* man in this world that I will ever have in my bed for the rest of my life." We hugged, and he kissed me. Then we said our goodbyes, and he went back to his boat where he was staying.

Not knowing what to do for the next few days, I wondered if I should start looking for a job. My best friend advised me to do nothing. She said I needed to stop and rest and think; there was no rush to do anything. I took her advice, well, as long as I could. There was nothing to do at that river, except listen to that bullfrog. This time he wasn't saying, "welcome lovebirds, enjoy your visit." This time he was croaking, "Well, Sista! Hope you know what-the-hell-you-done-gone-and-done-did!" He didn't have the nerve to show his face and say those words to me in person. I would have probably made some mighty fine fried frog legs out of him, had I caught that son of a bitch, err. . . son-of-a-toad? Oh hell! That, "son-of-a-what-ever-you-call-a-female-bullfrog"!

I was getting tired of being alone at that beautiful old secluded location. The nights were especially scary. Sometimes, I could hear critters crawling across the floor. Not knowing what type of critters they were, I certainly did not get out of my bed to find out. Thinking it might be some sort of a big old cockroach, dragging its belly across the floor, or something. Then, worrying that it could be some kind of a snake, dragging its belly across the floor, or something. Or maybe a big fat rat, dragging its belly across the floor, or something. It was a no-win situation for me! I was not getting out of my little single bed to find out what type of critter was dragging its belly across the floor in the middle of the night! I was just glad I wasn't sharing my bed with them. . . as far as I knew!??

Alex called me daily when he arrived at work, telling me of any news that he might have heard. While continuing to live on his boat, it was obvious he was getting worried. I had been living at the river for about two weeks at the time.

There was a sailboat regatta at the yacht club that weekend. I hated that I would not be able to race with Alex and his crew because it would not look good. It was best that I continue and stay in hibernation until the smoke settled. Mrs. "Let-me-tell-you-how-wonderful-I-am" was not part of the crew because she was now, Mrs. "Not-so-wonderful" and separated from Alex.

While waiting all day that Sunday for Alex to finish the race and visit with me at the river, I sunbathed on the pier as long as I could, then took a nap. It was getting late into the afternoon when I woke up from my nap. Still, no Alex. I wondered and worried about why he was taking so long to come to me. Finally, around 7 o'clock, he drove up. It was obvious there was something on his mind, but he wasn't talking. We had a drink together, but not much conversation as he fell asleep on my bed. This too concerned me.

That was the night Haley's Comet passed over our region at 9 o'clock. I stepped out the front door of that old magical place and watched the black, star-covered sky with awe; it was a once in a lifetime experience that I will never forget. With my cocktail in hand, watching Haley's Comet cross over the still, dark, night sky, I breathed deeply and smelled the faint scent of the azaleas and dogwoods in the April air. Suddenly a deep depression was upon me; I felt I was losing the love of my life. Words cannot explain the feeling that was deep inside my heart. A prick from the thorn of a rose was nothing compared to the hurt I was experiencing. It was excruciating, and I had to live through that pain.

After watching Haley's Comet alone for about an hour, I sadly walked back into that beautiful old mansion where Alex and I fell in love and had made love over a hundred times. He was still sleeping. I woke him and told him it was time to leave. I knew he was going to leave anyway; I might as well be the one to ask him to do so. He got up and sleepily stumbled to his car, leaving without saying a word. I knew what he was going to do; I cried all night without sleeping.

The next Monday morning, he did not call as usual when he got to work, which validated my fears. He had called his wife and asked if he might come home and reestablish a relationship with her; she agreed, welcoming him with open arms.

It took a few days for all the trauma to sink into my already muddled brain. I needed to talk with Alex desperately, but I couldn't call and argue with him while he was at his workplace, so I had an argument with him anyway. I had a lengthy argument with him for leaving me and going back to his wife. Point-by-point, I laid it out to him, where he was wrong, and I won on every single point. . . And he wasn't even there, nor was he on the telephone.

I had to get up, brush myself off, and pull myself together! I was mad as hell at that point! I packed up everything he had ever given me: every piece of jewelry, every piece of lingerie, every piece of crystal, every piece of artwork, every bottle of perfume, and every love card. Then I put it all into one big plastic bag. In the middle of the night, I went to the yacht club and placed the package on the bow of his boat. The next morning, I called Alex, and in a straightforward statement, I said, "I left a package on your boat." He was trying to inquire what it was when I hung up; he knew he had better get to it before Mrs. "Let-me-tell-you-how-wonderful-I-am" found it!

The satisfaction of having done that dastardly deed lasted only a day; then I was back into my deep depression. There I was now divorced, alone, with no job, and the love of my life had gone back to his wife! It was Good Friday, and I felt my whole world was caving in on me. Looking like hell, and with swollen eyes from having cried so much, I stopped in to speak to my son, where he was working in the family swimming pool business. Then I went straight to the liquor store and bought a bottle of vodka and peach snaps; I was going to drink myself out of self-pity, contemplate my future, and contrive a plan. Drinking never gets you out of depression nor self-pity; it only makes it worse. I was about to fall asleep when my best friend came to check on me because my son had called her and told her that he was worried about me. We talked for a while, and she too became concerned about me. She made me leave the river for the weekend and spend Easter at her home and with her family. It was the right decision, and it got me out of my funk. It certainly helped clear my head of self-pity. After talking with her, I was able to make my plans for moving forward with my life, without this man called Mr. Wonderful, the one whom I still loved dearly.

The Warrior Princess in me realized that you cannot depend on another person for your happiness in life; you must start your own fire every day. Once again, as it had happened to me several times in my life previously, I found myself alone in the world with a fresh new start.

The following Monday morning, I called Alex at his place of employment; he answered the phone promptly. I told him, "I have a message for you, I am going to hang up and then call you right back. Don't answer; I will leave my message on your answering machine. I want you to be able to listen to it repeatedly, so you will get the full effect of what I'm saying to you." I then hung up.

When I called him back, the message was this, "I don't blame you for going back, I know it was a tough decision for you to make. I *am not* and *will not* go back to Cody. I got my divorce for <u>me!</u> I am moving ahead with my life with or without you. I love you with all my heart, and I will wait for you---for a while. But if you are not the man for me, there <u>is</u> a man out there who is the right man for me. . . and when he finds me. . . he will know he has hit the jackpot!"

Chapter 45 The Geranium

The geranium flower appears to have some conflicting meanings, which means you must rely on both the circumstances and their color to refine their meaning. Some of the most common meanings are folly or stupidity, gentility, ingenuity, melancholy, preference, and true friendship.

297

The next few weeks were a roller coaster of emotions for me, full of ups and downs. Being extremely happy to have my freedom to go and do whatever I pleased, with no one asking where I was going and when was I going to return. That was fabulous! Then realizing, there was no place to go and nothing to do. It was time that I started looking for employment, and it was not as easy as I once thought it would be. I had not been employed outside of my own business since 1979. The lady at the employment agency was quite cold when she said I was not marketable because I had been encapsulated in my own business for 18 years. Having been my boss for so many years and not having been in the open workforce for so long was not a good thing. Continuing to search on my own, I went on a few interviews when I suddenly realized that the longer the potential employer interviews you, the better are your chances of obtaining the job. If your interview is over very quickly, most likely you are not considered for that position.

Another agency sent me on an interview with the University of South Alabama as an administrative assistant. The salary range was from $12 an hour, up to $25 an hour. Assuming I was worth the $25 an hour position, that was what I expected, so I went on the interview. That was about the amount of money I could live on as a single girl. I certainly had all the skills to fill the position, and my chances looked good for obtaining the position. My interview lasted over 30 minutes; then another person came in to talk with me about the job. After a short while, I was told they would like to hire me. I was smiling along with the manager until he said, "we are going to start you out at $12 an hour and..." I stopped him in the middle of his statement. "I was told the position started at $12 an hour, ranging up to $25 an hour. I was expecting a higher amount." He started stammering around when I stood up. Knowing he was not going to back down on his hourly wage, we were getting nowhere. So, I said, "you know, I'm probably not worth $12 an hour, but I have more expenses than that. I do appreciate your time, but I think I need to seek employment elsewhere." I smiled, shook his hand, and continue to search for employment elsewhere.

After sending out resume after resume, it became obvious I was not best suited for a secretarial position, I should be in sales. After all, I had been very successful in winning trips to Hawaii and the Bahamas by selling my products in the swimming pool business. Sending my next resume to one of my friends in the car business, I received a call immediately from him asking me to come in and talk. He hired me that day. I was now officially a car salesperson! After a week in training, it was time for me to hit the sales floor. I soon learned that selling cars is a dog eat dog business. But this dealership was fairer than others; they required that each salesperson take their turn on the sales floor. Walk-in customers belonged to the salesperson on duty at that time. Still not knowing much about selling cars, or trucks, an old established salesman took me under his wing and pulled me along, teaching me the tricks of the trade. He told me the right words to say when and when to shut up.

He told me I would be best at selling trucks since they were the hottest selling vehicle that year. He thought I would be able to sell a lot of trucks to the young men who came in because first of all, they would like to talk with me. He took me to the truck lot and taught me this: you gotta remember to find out what is most important to the customer, is its safety, or beauty, sport, or is its economy? Then talk to the customer about the item that he is most interested in. While we were on the lot, he started showing me the biggest Chevy truck and how to demonstrate it. He started talking to me as if I were the potential customer, "now this here Chevy Silverado K 1500 pickup is one of the finest in its kind." As we approached the truck, he leaned in, touched it, and rubbed it gently with his hand along the side of the truck to feel the paint job, without saying a word. The customer would do the same; it was contagious, or so he told me. I felt the paint job too, he was right, it <u>was</u> contagious.

He walked around to the back of the truck as he continued to talk. "Our base model here has rear-wheel drive transmission, but this here extended cab has a four-wheel transmission, which'll getja better gas mileage. It gets 13 miles per gallon in the city and 17 on the highway. The fuel tank holds a whoppin' 34 gallons." He dropped the tailgate as he said, "see this here bed, has a payload of sixteen-hundit, fidty-six pounds!" I said, "un-huh."

His next move was his closer. We walked to the front of the truck as he popped the hood. "V-8 engine, 255 horsepower at 466 rpms." Then he slammed the hood without another word.

I asked, "is that all? What about the inside, the radio, the air conditioner, automatic windows, and cruise control?" He answered me, "men who want a real truck don't care much 'bout that stuff. They knowed what wuz under that hood before I even popped it. That's all you need to show'em." "What about a test ride?" I asked. "Well, if you have to, go right ahead, little lady, but it's a waste of time to a serious truck buyer. They knowed what they wanted by the time they got here." Wuz wot, he said.

"Well, alrighty, then!" I said as we started walking back into the dealership. Then he added, "oh, another thing I'd likc to scc you do is this; you know that billboard out there on the highway with my ad on it?" "Yes, I remember." He said he had one more month left on the lease; then he would need to put up a new advertisement on it. He suggested that if I would go in halves with him on the cost, I could put my picture on the billboard, advertising that I was a new salesperson selling trucks at the dealership. That would get me a lot of business, especially from those young cowboys. It sounded like a great idea to me.

Paying close attention to everything that old salesman told me that day and rehearsing every word of my sales pitch so I would be proficient when the time came to use it, I even practiced that "slam-the-hood-thing." I had to practice that several times because the first time I crushed my finger while "slamming-the-hood-thing" and catching my scarf in the lock. Finally, I got it right.

While trying to think of a way that I could customize the old guy's sales pitch to fit my style, I thought maybe I could incorporate my past modeling experience. Maybe leaning against the truck and posing, tilting my head slightly and smiling as I stroked the paint job. How would that be? (Well, no.) Then I was thinking about maybe kicking the tires once or twice as I was walking around the truck. I ruled that one out too. Both ideas seemed too much of an over-kill-gimmick. I wouldn't want to make anyone feel high pressured into buying a truck; you know what I mean? Besides, I didn't want to scuff up my stilettos.

Finally, my lucky day came around for me to be on the sales floor. Up walked an old man who could barely get around with his cane, even with his wife helping him. "Welcome to New Fort Chevrolet," I said with a beaming smile on my face. "My name is Eva. How are you?" After a short conversation about their health, both not feeling too good, I finally concluded they were interested in a new truck. It truly was my lucky day!

We were walking toward the truck lot, (I was walking, he was hobbling, and she was helping him hobble.) Like I said, as we were walking toward the truck lot, I started my sales pitch, which I had mentally rehearsed and memorized without stuttering a single word. "This is a base model rear-wheel drive Chevy. . ." (She interrupted me,) "do you have one in red?" I continued, "yes, yes we do, this way." We hobbled across the lot to the red extended cab four-wheel drive transmission.

"Now this is our red, extended cab, four-wheel drive transmission. . ." (he interrupted me again,) "we don't care for naron extended one." I quickly looked the large lot over and finally spotted a red, base model sitting on the back of the lot. "Okay, we have just what you're looking for, a red base model sitting on the back of the lot. This way, please." I was leading them toward the rear of the lot when he said, "Lady, you're wearing me out, all this walking around this here lot." Knowing I was about to lose them, I said, "why don't we go back inside where it is cool and more comfortable, and we can talk a bit?" We were all three hobbling back to the dealership by that time.

We sat down in my small cubicle, and I offered them a soda and said, "I'll be right back." Rushing over to my "good-ole-buddy-ole-pal," salesman friend, I told him my dilemma. None of his sales pitches were working out for me with this couple. He chuckled and said, "let me see what I can do." He walked to my desk in his old country style, he sat down and started talking to the worn-out old couple. "Howdy, I'm Wes. My friend here tells me ya'll are interest'd in our red Chevy truck."

"That's right." The old man said.
"Now, you know you wanna buy that truck, now don't ja?"

"Well, yeah."the old man responded.

"Well, you know you wanna buy it, and you know I wanja to have it."

"Well, let's get right down to the lick-log."

Without going back to the lot, he sold them that same red truck that I was trying to show them, sitting on the back of the lot! He told me to get the keys and drive it around to the front of the dealership so the lady could get a look at the interior color.

I was a little upset that he outsold me that day. I sorta felt cheated, like he was holding out on me. He never told me about that lick-log-closer-thing! But that was okay; I still got my half of the commission.

My half that is, after tax, tag, title, delivery charges, dealer prep, and "all-those-other-surprise-charges-that-no-one-ever-expects-to-pay" (until they see all those charges added on at the end of the contract.) Of course, the salesman's commission is never listed at the bottom of the agreement. In this case, it was $56 for me and $56 for the other fine old salesman.

If you ask me that $56 was not enough money for all my niceness!

Chapter 46 The Clematis

The clematis is a symbol of ingenuity.

On my next day off from strenuously selling trucks, I made an appointment at Glamour Shots to have my portrait made to go on top of that billboard representing the dealership. Upon arriving, the professionals at Glamour Shots styled my hair and did my makeup. From the studio wardrobe, I picked out a cowgirl shirt and hat to wear for the photo, thinking that would be the appropriate attire for a truck advertisement. The picture turned out reasonably good, but it needed touching up before the final product could be sent to the billboard company. Secretly I wanted Alex to see my face on that billboard every time he passed it coming and going to the yacht club. To hell with the advertisement!

Finishing at Glamour Shots, I decided to pay a visit to my friend/clerk at the downtown hotel where Alex and I had been meeting for the past couple of years. I wanted to explain to her why she had not seen me for a long time. Walking in, she smiled and hugged me. "Where have you been?" I replied to her, "you will not believe what I'm going to tell you!" She quickly responded, "you got married to him!" I started crying as I told her the sad story of what happened. I had gotten a divorce; he left his wife, and then he went back to her. Now I was alone. We talked for a long time, and I gave her all the details.

She sadly looked at me, then with her savvy squinting eyes that seem to see straight through me, she said, "go see him." I replied, "no, I can't." Once again, she suggested, "go to where he works and take him a cup of coffee." I assured her that I would do no such thing. Then with her knowing-all-things-advice, she very slowly and deliberately said, "he wants to smell your perfume." Breaking down, I knew she was right, for I wanted to smell his scent too.

That day I wore a below the knee navy suit with pearl buttons down the front and navy high heels. My hair and makeup were already perfectly groomed by the professionals at Glamour Shots, so that day was a great day for him to see me. I just needed to contrive a sly reason for showing up at his place of employment. Then it dawned on me why I needed to talk to him.

As I walked into the main office at his place of business, in my most professional, polite tone of voice, I said, "I would like to see Mr. Rosenberg, please." The receptionists said, "yes, ma'am." She then telephoned upstairs to Alex; he must have asked her who it was that wanted to see him because she turned to me and asked, "May I ask who is calling?" I responded, "no." She looked shocked at my answer but relayed it to Alex. He must have then asked for my description because she stated, "a tall blonde in a business suit." The helpful receptionist then turned to me and said, "he will be right down." I said, "thank you." I turned around and faced the door, so he could not see my face when he entered the room.

Within a minute, his footsteps were descending the stairway. When certain he was down, I slowly turned around and smiled at him. He smiled and breathed a sigh of relief in a sad, broken-hearted sort of way. We were both feeling the same. I said, "I believe you still have my sailing shoes in the trunk of your car?" He said, "yes, yes, I do; let's go to my car and get them for you."

Walking to his car, he opened the trunk, and there were my sailing shoes safe and sound, right where I had left them after our last race together. We stood there and talked for a short while. He seemed glad to see me but said he could not speak long, because his partner had also heard the rumors about us. He asked if he could call me at the river, and I said, "yes." Giving him my business card from the dealership, I told him he could call me there too. A good businessperson should always be alert for opportunities to pass out her business cards. You know, just in case he should ever need a good car or truck. . . or in his case, a good lay.

The wise little lady from the hotel was right; he <u>did</u> need to smell my perfume!

Chapter 47 The Lotus

The lotus flower represents a sense of purity which arises from the flower's growing habit of rooting in mud and pushing up through the water to bloom.

Among its other many meanings are peace, mysticism, direct spiritual contact, the emptiness from desire, victory over attachment, love and compassion for all things, self-awareness, and rising out of suffering.

Toward the end of June 1997, a friend who was a property manager of a large apartment complex was waiting on a vacancy for me. She called and said an apartment would be available for me on July 1. Quickly, I prepared to move away from that beautiful river rendezvous love nest.

Sadly, I started packing all my worldly possessions (what were not already in storage). I started taking inventory to make sure I did not leave anything out there because I knew that would be my last visit to that lovely old place.   My list was short:

Three racks of hang-up clothing–*check.*

My "Imelda Marcos" collection of boxed shoes–*check.* It has been said, "you can tell a woman's age by how many pairs of shoes she owns." I counted my age; I was close to a hundred years old! Some of my shoes were antiques from high school, but I kept them anyway, just in case. You know, in case I needed that color for something.

Then there was my makeup kit–*check.*

Toiletries–*check.*

Single bed–*check.*

Linens–*check.*

Wicker furniture–*check.*

Artwork–*check.*

Then last, but not least, my vibrator (which was hidden, nicely tucked under the stuff in the first aid kit)–*check.* I thought that was an appropriate place to hide it because, on the front of the box, it read:

"In Case of Emergency."

310

I rented a U-Haul truck for $19.95 per day, local and around town only, plus mileage. Why pay *Two-Men and a Truck* when this one Southern woman could do the same job? I certainly needed to save my money. That $56 commission from selling that truck the previous week did not go very far.

This time, I did not ask Nathan and "Bride-number-two-hot-to-trot-n-hot-snot" to help move me. Knowing I could do the job myself; I did not want anyone around while saying my final farewell to that lovely river love nest.

After everything was loaded onto the truck, with a melancholily heart, and tear-filled eyes, I started walking around that beautiful old place, remembering all those romantic times spent out there with Alex. That lovely old place was where Alex fell in love with me. We spent many days making love, talking, and laughing with one another. Memories of the time I made Alex take a nature walk down the trail with me were on my frontal lobe. He was afraid of snakes and sort of acted silly. I recalled the day of that extraordinary experience when I touched the back of the baby armadillo, wearing only my silk teddy underwear. Of course, there was that humble old bullfrog constantly croaking to us, just as he was doing----exactly at that very moment!

I started searching for him, thinking surely if I looked closely enough, I could spot him. After searching for quite a long time, I was thinking,

*what if I did find him? Would he let me touch him too,
like the baby armadillo? Maybe he would let me kiss
him!*

*Would he then turn into a handsome young Prince?
Perhaps he was the Prince I had been searching for all
along!*

<u>*What would happen then*</u>*?*
My mind began to daydream as I was thinking
*if I kissed him and he turned into that handsome
young Prince that I had been waiting for all along---
Would he sweep this Princess off her feet. . .?
then would we hop off together and live
"hoppily-ever-after" . . .on his lily pad?*
<u>Uh—Dud!</u>

After coming back to my senses, I got into my rented
U-Haul truck and drove away to my own, new
apartment/pad.

Chapter 48 The Lisianthus

The lisianthus represents calmness.

Have you heard the old expression, *the calm before the storm*? Have you ever experienced the fear and anticipation of suffering through a hurricane, waiting for the eye to pass over? That eye is the portion of the storm, the center, where it is dead still and very calm.

Having lived in the South all my life, I have lived through many hurricanes; all of them were different. It

313

was by the grace of God that I moved away from that beautiful river cottage when I did because Hurricane Danny hit 19 days after I moved away from there. The flood waters rose quickly overnight to 32 feet, completely gutting and washing away that beautiful river love nest rendezvous. Included in that loss, I'm sure was my favorite bullfrog. Had I been asleep in that cottage, there would have been no way to escape from those rushing flood waters. Someone was looking out for me. It wasn't Alex, and it sure as hell wasn't Cody!

It was unbelievable when my son called me the next morning and told me the bridge near that cottage was covered with water. The bridge was 32 feet above the river. The river had never risen that high. But a hurricane had never hung around for four days before either.

Hurricane Danny hit the Gulf Coast on July 19, 1997. It hung around for four days and four nights with constant, heavy rain and high winds. The hurricane packed heavy flooding for four days and four nights, I never saw the eye of the storm, nor the calm in the center. Had I been closer to the Lord at that time, I'm sure he would have instructed me to build an ark. I never heard him speak. But, then again, I am hard of hearing. I only saw it rain and rain and rain for four days and four nights! Not light rain. . . I mean heavy, flooding, lightning crashing, scary raining, for four days and four nights! Do you get the picture here? It was a long and boring, go nowhere, do nothing, stay at home with no power, for four days and four nights!

It was on that day, July 19, 1997, when I became extremely sick. Being too ill and too weak to get out of bed for a glass of orange juice to take a pill for my pounding headache was tough! My fever was 101. All I could do was sleep through my pain and the rain.

Occasionally I would wake up and maybe stumble to the nearby bathroom. One afternoon, I opened the blinds in my bedroom to see outside. The destruction at the apartment complex was not too bad, but there were a great many fallen limbs all around the grounds.

During the third day of continuous rain, lightning, and flooding, some of the tenants in the apartment complex were getting cabin fever from having to stay indoors for such a long period. From my sick bed, I was watching out my window at them in the street. There were 20 or more in the group, having a hurricane street party in the pouring rain. There they were, with their ice chests full of beer and wine or whatever, with their portable boomboxes playing loud party music. They were standing around, some were dancing and celebrating the storm. Some were sharing their stories of the horrors they had experienced the past two days. All were laughing and joking about their situation as the wind was howling and blowing ferociously, causing limbs to fall all around them.

Suddenly, the wind whipped around, and the power lines got entangled with one another, making a loud electrical sparking and hissing sound as the lines were swinging wildly above the crowd. Then one line broke free and fell to the ground and continued to spark and hiss. The crowd went wild! They started running and screaming in 10 different directions with her arms in the air!

One woman fell to the ground and started flouncing and wallowing around, jerking her head and legs, generally acting a fool! For a moment I thought she had been struck by lightning; then I thought maybe she was having a seizure. She just laid there for about two minutes and rolled around on the wet, soaked ground, moaning as if in severe pain. When she saw no one was coming to her rescue, she got up and started acting normal again.

After a few moments, the crowd reassembled in the street, and the party continued. I wondered if one of them might get close enough to touch the fallen, sparking powerline. You know, just to see what would happen when they touched it. I was ready to call 911.

That was the most entertainment I had during those four days and four nights of enduring Hurricane Danny. I must say it was funny, but I was too sick to laugh.

Chapter 49 The Dandelion

The common dandelion has different meanings:
- Healing from emotional pain and physical injury alike
- Intelligence, especially in an emotional and spiritual sense
- Surviving through all challenges and difficulties
- Long lasting happiness and youthful joy
- Getting your wish fulfilled

Since the dandelion can thrive in difficult conditions, it is no wonder that people say the flower symbolizes the ability to rise above life's challenges.

317

The dandelion flower's message is: do not give up, even if those around you keep trying to get rid of you. When things seem bleak and dark, stick it out and remember the cheerfulness of a sunny summer day.

It was a little concerning when I received a call from Alex, wanting me to meet him at our downtown hotel. He said for me not to worry because he only wanted to talk. *It's about time!* I thought. As Ricky Ricardo would say, "Lucy, you got some splainin' to do!"

Getting all dolled up that day, I wore a navy pinstripe dress which was above-the-knee and double-breasted in the front. Neutral stockings and navy high heels were worn to look businesslike. Underneath were a navy silk slip, lace bra, and bikini. But that was not supposed to be seen, remember? We were merely going to talk.

Arriving at the hotel, the clerk was glad to see me with the good news of "whatever-it-was-for-why-we-were-meeting." Alex was only minutes behind me arriving at the room. We passionately kissed at the door. Then we both sat down at a little round table by the window to have our heart-to-heart conversation. It was that day that I realized how much we were so much alike. Our problem was our lack of communication. If you can imagine the Scarlett O'Hara and Rhett Butler couple; they truly loved each other, but had a hell of a way showing it. . . or should I say not showing it?

I let Alex do all the talking that day, after all, he had called the meeting. We were both sad and happy to be together once again. The first thing he said was, "stand up; I just want to look at you." I stood up. He looked at me for a few moments, then he reached out and grabbed me by my waist and hugged me tightly; I thought he was going to cry, but I would not let him. I leaned down and kissed him tenderly. Then I sat back down in my chair beside him, and we continued with our conversation.

He reached into his side jacket pocket and took out an envelope which contained a three page, single-spaced, typed letter that he had written, and handed it to me. I gave it back to him and said, "read it to me." I thought if he had something to say to me, he should say it to my face and verbalize it out loud where I could hear it! I had no idea what he was about to say.

I will not tell you all the details of his heartfelt letter; that would not be fair to him. But I will give you a synopsis of what he said. There were several points he covered that were bothering him concerning us as a couple. What was peculiar to me was the fact that I had the same exact feelings and thoughts about him. I had no idea he was feeling and thinking the same about me!

Number one: <u>Jealousy</u> - We were both jealous types and had exhibited this behavior on past occasions. We both did things to make the other jealous. Come to find out. . . neither of us liked it! All we did was hurt our relationship. Remember the many months at a time that we were apart?

We were at cross-purpose!

Alex felt that I dressed too seductively in public; he didn't like that. I thought I was dressing that way for him! He said he wished that somehow, I projected an image of being extremely beautiful but untouchable. He feared that other men were mentally undressing me when they saw me. What he did not know was, I <u>WAS</u> untouchable! I was his and his alone! No one could turn my eyes away from him!

Number two: <u>Trust</u> – Relationships are built on honesty and trust. We both had the express ability to sneak around undetected for significant periods. We both were the best at it and had done so for the past fourteen years. Could we totally trust each other in the future should another person come along and cause one of us to misbehave? He assured me he would not. What he did not know was, there was no other man for me. . . ever! He was the one and only love of my life! I knew I would never be unfaithful to him.

Number three: <u>Sex</u> – He thought I was the sexiest thing he had ever imagined in his whole life, and he worried about keeping up with me. What he didn't know was sex to me was only great with him, whenever we could find the time to be together. I didn't want or need it every day, as he thought I would. After all, chocolate cake is good, but you don't want or need it every day either. . . often is enough of a good thing.

Number four: <u>Creature Comforts and Money</u> – He knew that I had already taken a financial loss when I got my divorce. Now he knew for sure he was about to also take a financial bath. That meant we would be starting over from the start, with nothing. He worried about starting over with a new mortgage, new retirement, etc.

What he did not know was, I came from poverty as a child. So, I learned how to survive! I could lose it all today and gain it all back tomorrow. That was my mentality all my life. I knew, for I had proven it in the past.

Number five: <u>Public Opinion</u> – Alex came from a respected old family name in "Old Mobile." He had a lot to live up to; he guarded his family's name and reputation. He did not want to embarrass his mother and father. Although I was never as affluent as he, I would never want to embarrass him either; we were together on this point.

There was one other topic of great importance that was not discussed that day. He later told me about the other lady involved in the equation of their divorce. I could compete with Mrs. "Let-me-tell-you-how-wonderful-I-am," for she was not so great in the beginning. It has been said, "Another woman cannot take a woman's husband away from her. . . unless she lets her." In this case, she was giving him away to me, especially when she would make statements to her friends like, "Alex isn't worthy of dusting my shoes."

It was a sad awakening when I found out the reason why Alex went back to his wife. It was on the advice of his attorney.

A friend of Mrs. "Let-me-tell-you-how-wonderful-I-am" phoned Alex one day. She said that Mrs. "Let-me-tell-you-how-wonderful-I-am" (told her) that she was going to 'clean-Alex's-clock'! Alex knew that meant financial disaster. Alex's attorney advised him that if he went back to her for just one night, that meant she had forgiven him of his infidelity, and she then would be unable to divorce him on the grounds of adultery. Therefore, she would be unable to 'clean-his-clock.' So, Alex went back, and they started over.

Now, let's talk about this other lady that meant so much to Alex, and why she was brought up in their divorce discussions. There were three ladies involved, only two of which Alex loved and wanted to keep. I knew I was his lady number one. Alex had to plan a strategy of how he was going to get his divorce from his wife and keep lady number three. . . *Lady in Blue*, his beautiful sailing yacht!

Chapter 50 The Orchid

The orchid represents both male and female sex organs.

The ancient Greeks thought orchids were a symbol of virility. They were so convinced of the connection between orchids and fertility that they believe orchids with large tuberous roots symbolized a male child, while orchids with small tubers symbolized a female child.

We have all heard the phrase: "Men are from Mars, and women are from Venus." What does it mean? It means we are strong opposites in many ways, and it is as if we live on two separate planets. You might be surprised to find out just how much we are closely alike when it comes to sex!

Some of you girls think sex starts at erection and ends at ejaculation. As I have previously said, that is such a penis thing! That leaves little Eva out of the fun! Did you know that not only can a woman have an orgasm, but she can also ejaculate? It is two separate functions, just as a male.

According to a study from:

https://www.everydayhealth.com/columns/lauren-streicher-midlife-menopause-and-be

Female Ejaculation/ spurting

For a guy, orgasm is synonymous with ejaculation. The notion that women sometimes spurt fluid at the height of orgasm has been debated for centuries. We know things get pretty wet during sex. The question is, is the fluid urine or lubrication from the vaginal walls? Or is there a spurt of fluid from one of the lubricating peri-urethral glands?

Reports show that somewhere between 10-54% of women (depending on the study) report fluid expulsion during arousal or <u>orgasm</u>. Fluid could simply be from increased vaginal lubrication, but when most women describe "ejaculation," they are referring to a gush or spurt that occurs with orgasm as opposed to increased vaginal wetness from sexual activity. This emission is generally a result of one of three phenomenons:

- *A small gush of whitish fluid from tiny glands on the side of the urethra called Skene's peri-urethral glands, but also sometimes referred to as the "female prostate."*
- *Urine expelled from the bladder. Coital Incontinence (CI) is divided into two groups: women that have problems with <u>incontinence</u> in general, including during sexual activity, and women who lose urine only during orgasm. Women who squirt urine only during orgasm usually don't identify it as urine because it is far more diluted and doesn't smell or look like urine even though it comes out of the bladder.*
- *A combination of both*

This is harder to study than it sounds since most studies rely on questionnaires and a woman's perception of where the fluid is coming from rather than visual confirmation. Masters and Johnson recorded only rare instances of female ejaculation in their observation of over 3000 couples.

Experts all agree that many women experience "female ejaculation'. There are enough scientists that believe female ejaculation from lubricating glands to be a true phenomenon. Clearly, women expel a variety of fluids during sexual activity and orgasm. So, if you do notice a spurt or gush of fluid at the height of ecstasy, it is nothing to worry about. Enjoy it!

2. Another similarity that male and female have in common is **Testosterone.**
https://www.everydayhealth.com/sexual-health/sexual-dysfunction/testosterone-and
https://www.healthline.com/health/lowtestosterone/testosterone-levels-by-age
https://www.drtami.com.2014/04/04/the-untold-testosterone-story-for-women

Testosterone is a powerful hormone in both men and women. It can control sex drive, regulate sperm production, promote muscle mass, and increase energy. It can even influence human behavior, such as aggression and competitiveness.

As you grow older, the level of testosterone in your body gradually decreases. This can lead to a variety of changes, such as reduced sex drive. While lower testosterone levels may be concerning, it's a natural part of aging.

Testosterone maintains sex drive. It is known as a male sex hormone, but women have levels of the hormone in their system as well, just as men have low levels of estrogen in theirs. The hormone is part of what drives desire, fantasy, and thoughts about sex, and even helps provide the energy for sex in women. It lifts women's sex life. Testosterone improves sex drive and sexual response in many women and can increase sexual thoughts, fantasies, activity, and satisfaction.

The normal level of testosterone in the bloodstream varies widely, depending on thyroid function, protein status, and other factors. For men ages 19 and up, normal testosterone levels range from 240 to 950 nanograms per deciliter (ng/dL). For women ages 19 and up, normal testosterone levels range from 8 to 60 ng/dL.

For your information:
** One nanogram is a billionth of a gram.
** One deciliter is 3.381402 oz.

Testosterone levels reach their peak around age 18 or 19 before declining throughout the remainder of adulthood.

So, you see, men are not from Mars, and women are not from Venus after all! We are both from Earth, co-existing with one another on a wonderful planet and attempting to know one another better. <u>Most of the time, our biggest problem is communication with each other</u>.

Remember, the *love of your life* comes only once in your life! He will blow up your skirt and force you to stand up, which will prove what true love is. A true love adores you, yet he challenges you to become the <u>best you</u> possible.

It isn't always smooth sailing. . .
It isn't always a bed of roses. . .
<u>It's sometimes roses with thorns</u>.

Chapter 51 Love-In-The-Mist (Nigella)

The nigella represents perplexity and delicacy.

The sickness I had during the hurricane did not go away. It hung on for days; then it turned into weeks, it seemed I was getting worse instead of better. After going to the doctor and taking high powered antibiotics to no avail, my temperature was continuing to run 101 and 102

328

every day. The doctor seemed perplexed, with no answer as to what was wrong with me. Yes, I was very sick, but I had to keep going, sick or not.

I learned while working at the car dealership that it takes years to build a good clientele of repeat customers to make good money. I couldn't wait for years to eat. Nor could I get that-lick-log-thing down!

I had turned in my resignation at the dealership because I still believed that with my many talents, I could get a good job. I was wrong! Most of the interviewers told me I was over-qualified.

So, there I was, sick, with no job and little hope of getting employed. As if I didn't have enough problems! I had a short-term lease on my apartment and would lose it soon. What is a single girl to do?

I went to the bank.

I planned to build my own home. An advertisement in the Sunday newspaper featured new homes for affordable prices. Being a single lady, a smaller home was all that was needed. I contacted the builder, and we made plans to start building a 1500 square foot house on my newly acquired lot which had been cleared and ready to start construction.

Going to the bank for approval, I told the loan officer about the C.D. which would be maturing in a few months as she could use it for collateral. That was fine, but there was one problem. My $56 commission working at the car dealership was not enough earnings to be approved for my mortgage, no matter what amount was needed! It ended up that I needed to go back to work in my family business to prove my past track record of earning potential.

At that time, Cody had moved from New Fort to a nearby town and opened another pool business. He left Nathan to manage the New Fort operation.

I asked Cody to give my portion of the company back to me. He said, "no, but I will sell it back to you." (*Son-of-an-Old-Bat*!) If I was going to be eligible for the bank loan, it was necessary for me to get my old job back, to prove my earning potential from my past record. So, I accepted his outlandish offer! Cody took Nathan, his own son, and me to the cleaners! I had to buy back my own company for $250,000, which I had just kind-heartedly given to him-----ka-ching! It just gave me another reason for having divorced him---the greedy bastard!

Working back at my own business with Nathan, who was absolutely a pleasure to work with, was better than before. There was one problem; I continued to be sick every day! I was barely able to drag myself out of bed and drive to work as my head was pounding, and the fever was raging. But I had to keep going because I needed to make those sales if I was going to earn a paycheck. So, every day, I would get out of bed, go to work, and come home. Sometimes I would cook dinner, other times, I would grab a burger. It was hard to eat; I had no appetite and was losing weight, now dropping down to 95 pounds. That was not a good thing when a person is 5'8". Every day after coming home totally exhausted, I would take a shower and go straight to bed. That was my life for weeks on end.

The next day, the same thing. Get out of bed, get dressed wearing no make-up, and drag my skinny ass to work. My hair went neglected, although it was always shampooed and clean, it was not styled. Why bother? Alex was back with Mrs. "Let-me-tell-you-how-wonderful-I-am." Alex and I were talking regularly, and he was supposed to be making his plans for divorce, but that seemed to be dragging out too long.

One day a long-time customer came into the store and said, "Eva, what's wrong with you?" I told her about the divorce, which she had already heard about. Then explaining to her about my illness that I could not shake, her response was, "Eva, fix yourself up! You look terrible!" Well! That was encouraging! If I felt like fixing myself up, it would have already been done. Hell, I could barely get around, much less care about 'fixing myself up'!

Continuing to go back to the doctor, time after time and demanding of him to try this or try that, I was getting desperate to get well. At one point, I requested that he test me for HIV! After reading that the HIV virus could stay in your system for seven years and knowing Alex had had many women, it was a reason for concern! I knew where I had been. . . with him! The reports said you are not just having sex with that one person, you are having sex with every person that they have had sex with, and everyone that those people had had sex with. I felt I had reason to worry. I just knew in my heart that

Alex had had sex with every woman in three counties (except the ugly ones.) The doctor reluctantly gave me the test, and it came back negative for HIV, I was relieved! My illness continued to rage on!

The doctor thought because of my divorce and the stress involved, he should put me on an antidepressant, so I quickly started taking them. Within two weeks, I was happily sick with a headache, fatigued, and a temperature of 101 every day.

A lady pool sales representative paid a visit to the business one day. As we were talking, she noticed I was sick, weak, and very frail. She asked me to explain my symptoms. I explained to her all the details starting on July 19th during the hurricane. Since then, I felt like my head might explode, I was totally exhausted, the fever was non-stop, and all I wanted to do was sleep, but I couldn't do that either. I could barely keep going, much less think about living. I told her I had been to the doctor time after time, and he could not figure out what was wrong with me; he was totally perplexed.

She said, "Eva, doctors don't know what is wrong with you, all they can do is run tests to find out what is _not_ wrong with you." She then went on to tell me her own real-life story concerning her son, who had the exact same symptoms. The doctors had a difficult time diagnosing his illness. After many office visits, the doctor finally tested him for the 'Epstein Barr virus.' Her son tested positive. It was then that the doctor was able to treat his illness. She said, "Have your doctor test you for the 'Epstein Barr virus.'"

After taking that insightful woman's advice, I visited my doctor and requested that he test me for the Epstein Barr virus. His immediate response was, "Eva, you're trying to diagnosis your own problem!" That statement fired me up! Glaring across the examining table at him, I curtly remarked, "Dr. Get-well-soon" if you will please just test me for this virus, I promise you, I will not bother you again!" He reluctantly took a sample of my blood and ran the test.

In a few days, "Dr. Get-well-soon" called back with the results. You would have thought it was his bright idea to run the test. He had found the solution to my illness! "Eva, the test results are back, you have antibodies in your bloodstream for the Epstein Barr virus. I now know how to treat you."

"Dr. Get-well-soon" further stated I had chronic fatigue syndrome. *Whoopee!* That was great news to know that I had a dreaded illness! Now, how do we get rid of it? It would take more months of suffering through headaches, tiredness, and fever before I would have a full recovery.

One remedy to treat my illness was to juice a lot of green and orange vegetables and force them down, three times a day, along with high-potent natural vitamins. Like it or not, it had to be done if good health was to return to my thin, delicate, frail body. I did it.

Chapter 52 The Dog Rose

The dog rose represents pleasure.

After finally solving the mystery of my illness and while continuing to recover from Chronic Fatigue Syndrome; I went about my business of going to work each day and putting me first by taking good care of my health. Drinking that juice three times a day was no easy task, but by holding my nose, I was able to gulp it down.

The best thing that got me through that ordeal was a friend called and told me she had a litter of English Springer Spaniel puppies that were born premature, and they needed bottle feeding and special care. The mother's milk was not producing, and she asked if I would help her. She assured me that by my caring for a new puppy, it would ultimately lift my spirits and result in my own health improving. She would give me my choice of the four puppies if I helped her. At first, I resisted her offer because no pets were allowed in my apartment complex. I then remembered Alex's beautiful show dog, Abbey, a Springer Spaniel, whom he loved and had lost.

Taking her up on her offer, I snuck two black and white female puppies, which were only three weeks old at that time, into my apartment. These two tiny babies did not yet have their eyes open; I fed them faithfully every hour or two with a tiny bottle. They slept under blankets, close together to keep warm, in a cardboard box. At night, they seemed to get cold and would cry out, so putting them in bed with me and placing them under my armpit solved the problem. Then they would settle down and go comfortably back to sleep. My friend was right, the joy of taking care of those two tiny puppies brought joy and pleasure back into my life.

I was purposefully staying away from Alex because I did not want him to know how sick I was, nor how badly I looked with the weight loss. But, one weekend he called and said he needed to come over to check on *Lady in Blue,* and could he stop by to visit for a while.

I had not mentioned the new puppies to him because I wanted to surprise him with his new daughter; this was the perfect occasion to make the introduction. I laid both black and white tiny puppies in a large basket on a white, soft towel. A thin pink ribbon was tied around their little black and white necks, with their eyes still unopened. I placed a warm blanket over the top of the basket to keep them warm until Alex arrived, then I hid them in my closet.

Quickly I showered and dressed all in red---red bra, red bikini, a red short see-through top and a red silk scarf around my waist.

When Alex arrived, I immediately closed the door behind him so no one would see him visiting me. We kissed, then I said, "I have a surprise for you," as I took the red silk scarf off my waist and tied it around his eyes, blindfolding him. Making him promise not to peek, he agreed, then with a devilish smile of anticipation on his face, he said, "I know this is going to be fun!" Leading him to the bedroom, (he knew the way,) I sat him on the bed, once again, warning him not to peek! He was getting erect; he was wondering what I was up to.

Creeping to my closet, I took the basket of puppies and set them on my bed, then I took off his blindfold. We were <u>both </u>surprised as hell to see his surprise! He was surprised to see the two beautiful black and white English Springer Spaniel puppies. . . and I was surprised to see them lying in a pile of poop! All I could say was, "That was not the presentation I expected to make!" We both laughed with pleasure that afternoon as we played with the two tiny baby puppies. One puppy seemed to catch our hearts, and we knew that day which puppy was ours; it was as if she had chosen us.

Sex was not thought of after meeting Alex's new daughter. My red outfit nor my weight-loss was noticed after meeting "Misty Morning's Windy" that afternoon.

Because the puppies were born during Hurricane Danny, we named her "Windy." It thrilled my heart when we learned that, her sister, the other female puppy was adopted and named "Abbey."

I never knew how much pleasure a dog could bring into my life. Alex had no idea that he encouraged me to have a dog. I wanted that tiny little puppy for him, knowing how much he grieved after the loss of his dear show dog, Abbey, a few months prior.

I loved little Windy right from the day I laid eyes on her, she would prove to be my 'ace-in-the-hole' very soon.

Chapter 53 The Lemon Blossom

The lemon blossom suggests discretion.

It was around the middle of September 1997. I decided it was now time to put myself first and take the best care of me---*for me.* No one else was looking out for me. . . only me. Whatever Alex decided to do with his life, he would do in his own good time. I simply had to live with it. I could not and would not let Alex rule my

338

life and my emotions. My health was first and foremost of importance. Second was to finish my new home, which was under construction.

It was late one Saturday night, and I was exhausted. I had worked all day in my business, then went to my new home, still under construction, and cleaned up. After a quick shower and a hamburger from a fast-food joint, I was in bed by eight o'clock.

Around nine, I was in a full fledge snore when the phone rang. I knew who it was because no one ever called me, much less called me that late. So, I answered as sexy as I possibly could. On the other end, Alex was drunk as a skunk when he said, "Hey! What are you doing?" I coyly said, "Who wants to know?" "What'd ya mean 'Who wants to know'?"

To add more fire to the conversation, I said, "Oh! Is this Alex?"

"Yes, who were you expecting?" Seeing he was getting jealous, I let him know I was glad he had called, and we started talking.

He had been on a sailboat race from Gulfport, MS. to Pensacola, FL. Mrs. "Let-me-tell-you-how-wonderful-I-am" had been drinking all day and had drunk herself into "Queen for The Day." She had successfully shared with all the crew members every dirty little secret of the problems between her and Alex. She told them how Alex was no longer sleeping with her. He was sleeping upstairs, and he was not returning her affections. All her attempts at sexual intercourse with him were being turned down, and she did not know why.

While they were racing to Pensacola, Mrs. "Let-me-tell-you-how-wonderful-I-am" started off with "poor-pitiful-me" stories. Then the conversation turned into her bashing Alex behind his back to his six best friends/crew members. Not only were the unfortunate circumstances of their sexual life divulged, but she also took the opportunity to brag to the crew about how much money they had, and what she was planning to keep. . . should they decide to split the assets. Of course, the crew said nothing to her face; they simply relayed her messages of despair to Alex.

This greatly infuriated Alex. He did and said nothing about her unladylike display of drunkenness. His only remark was, "It's obvious she is unhappy."

Upon arrival at the Pensacola Yacht Club, after the finish of the race, the crew members abandoned ship like a mischief of rats. Alex and Mrs. "Let-me-tell-you-how-wonderful-I-am" was alone with nothing to say. She continued to drink and get bigger, braggadocio, and more beautiful. Alex only watched and resentfully listened to her empty chatter. When she fell off her stool, dropping her cigarette, and burning a hole in the oriental rug, Alex had stomached all he could take. He took her cigarette lighter (so she could no longer smoke and possibly set the boat on fire), then he fled the ship himself.

It was about that time when Alex called me. After talking briefly, he went into the yacht club for a short while, then he called me again. I had not entirely fallen asleep, it was easy to tell he was missing me and wanted to talk. He was using a pay phone so we couldn't talk long.

Around eleven o'clock, the phone rang again, it was Alex. I said, "Do you want me to come to you?"

"Yes," he replied in an emotional kind of voice.

"I will be there as soon as possible."

Immediately I got out of bed, took a quick shower, and got all dressed up for him. It took about an hour to drive to the yacht club from my apartment.

Upon arriving at the Pensacola Yacht Club, I waited outside the gates in my car. I did not want to be seen on the grounds because rumors were going around that Alex might be having an affair with me. Discretion was of utmost importance at that time in our lives.

After waiting for almost an hour outside the gates and not seeing Alex anywhere, I decided to drive in. There he was waiting for me by the front door of the yacht club. The club was closed, and no one was around. . .. we were safe. He got into my car, and we drove away.

After a little discussion about why it took me so long to get there, and why Alex wasn't at the gate waiting for me, we both agreed we should have communicated a location to meet.

He was exhausted, sweaty, drunk, and glad to see me. It didn't matter that he was tired, sweaty, and drunk, I was delighted to see him! We drove around the corner to a vacant lot and parked to visit. He told me what had happened all day during the race. He was embarrassed that Mrs. "Let-me-tell-you-how-wonderful-I-am" had acted out in front of his crew. Her actions only made him more determined to end the marriage. She had lost respect for him, and now it was mutual.

We loved one another for a short while. Kissing and petting were as far as we could go because Alex was so tired and drunk. When he fell asleep in my arms during the wee hours of the morning, we both knew it was the time that we should part. We kissed goodbye, and he went back to the lioness den. Sleepily, I drove home.

On Monday morning when Alex called me, he told me about the return sail back to New Fort that following Sunday. Not only had he taken Mrs. "Let-me-tell-you-how-wonderful-I-am's" cigarette lighter and tossed it into the bay so she could not smoke all day; he also hid the aspirin. She had a terrible hangover all day with nothing to relieve the pain for the eight-hour sail back home!

We both thought it was funny! Yeah! She deserved it!

Then I thought, *I hope Alex never does anything like that to me!* That was a side of him I had never seen! "The Get-Revenge-Alex." I knew not to try and compete with that side of him.

Again, I thought, *If you love someone, you will never seek revenge.* Love conquers all . . .and I did truly love Mr. Wonderful!

Chapter 54 The Gerbera Daisy

The gerbera flower's message is:

Let happiness be your compass!

Alex was befuddled with the dilemma of what to do about his future. It was a big decision. He could stay where he was comfortable, with a great retirement and where he was financially secure. This meant he would be forced to live with a woman who did not love him; but he could get along with her as if he were living with his sister. But he would not have a sex life. At least, he would be able to keep his beloved yacht, *Lady in Blue,* and enjoy her all the time on cruises and races with friends.

Well, this way, Mama Wonderful would not be upset about Alex getting another divorce, albeit, she did not like Mrs. "Let-me-tell-you-how-wonderful-I-am" either. Mama Wonderful did not like her boastfulness, nor her drunken behavior. It seemed that Mama Wonderful would rather turn her head to Mrs. "Let-me-tell-you-how-wonderful-I-am's" uncouth behavior than for there to be another divorce in the family.

Another option Alex had was to make a significant change and start over with me. This meant the possibility of losing his beloved *Lady in Blue* in the great divide. It would mean starting over from the beginning with a new woman, a new home mortgage, along with all the financial worries. Alex was not so much worried about the money, because he knew he could earn that all back. He also was not too concerned about his mother, because he felt sure she would be understanding over time. She would be glad for him after seeing he was happy with the new change. But losing his yacht was still weighing heavily on his mind.

Alex decided it was time to go see Daisy (Dr. Gerbera). After many therapy sessions with her, it was getting down to the line. Alex had to decide whether he was going or whether he was staying. Mr. Wonderful had to make a decision that would affect him for the rest of his life, and it was not easy. (Remember that Law of Cause and Effect thing?)

Daisy, (Dr. Gerbera), very intuitively looked him in the eye and said, "I <u>cannot</u> tell you for sure if you go to New Fort to be with this lady, (whom you say you love,) that you will be happy. What I <u>can</u> tell you for sure is this; if you stay where you are, you will continue to be unhappy."

That statement was all it took.

Remember the meaning of the Gerbera Daisy is this:

"Let happiness be your compass!"

Chapter 55 The Sunflower

The message of the sunflower is: stand tall and follow your dreams. Focus on what's positive in your life and don't let anyone get you down.

I was feeling somewhat better from time-to-time, even though my illness was lingering. I continued to go to work, although I was still running a slight fever and constant headache. After work, I would go back to my apartment, change clothes, then check on the construction progress of my new home. At that point in time, Alex had not made any final divorce arrangements, so I planned to get on with my life with or without him. Remember that 'little-deer-running-thing'?

One day at work, an old classmate popped in that I had not seen him since graduation. It was good to see him; he was one of my favorite friends back then. We laughed and visited for a while, then he got around to the reason for his visit. He said, "Mackie told me to tell you he wants to go out with you." Mackie was a popular football player in high school, and I had a crush on him back then, to no avail. Word gets around when women get divorced. All men regard divorcees as fair game, I guess.

It surprised me to hear he wanted to go out with me. Of course, I was not about to take him up on his offer. I was absolutely and totally devoted to Alex, and my heart belonged to him alone. No one could turn my head away from the love of my life!

My only response to my friend was, "tell Mackie that in high school when I had a crush on him, he wouldn't give me the time of day. Well, I know what time it is now. . . *it's too late for him.*"

What I was *not* saying was more truth than he wanted to hear. The fact was this: In the first place, I was in love with Alex, and I would never go out with him. In the second place, I just do not care for bald men that drive beer trucks! But I was too sweet to say that.

Meanwhile, Mr. Wonderful planned to make Mrs. "Let-me-tell-you-how-wonderful-I-am" so miserable that <u>she </u>would be the one who would ask for the divorce. It was slowly working. Finally, I told Alex, "don't call me again until you have a divorce!" hoping that would speed up the process.

Several weeks passed, and he did as I had ordered, he did not call. I continued to focus on my future, with or without him. I was moving on with my plans for my life and trying to stay positive. A few men asked me on dates, but I turned them down because I was still in love with Alex. I wasn't going to do anything that would jeopardize our relationship.

My focus was on getting my house finished. Also, on the weekends caring for my new puppy, Windy, and her sister. One hot, muggy Saturday afternoon, I took the two pups, in their cardboard box, and went to the new house. I also took along an ice chest of various libations for myself. All the workers were off work for the weekend, so I had the house to myself to do with as I pleased, which was mostly sweeping and cleaning up after the workers. After planting a few shrubs, where it was safely out of the way of construction, I came inside and started sweeping the floors.

The puppies were running around the inside of the house, chasing one another, yapping and having a good time. The windows were up, and two box fans were blowing to keeping the house as cool as could be expected because it was a hot September. Some would say it was 99 degrees in the shade. At that time, I had no shade trees.

Working at that house gave me a sense of pride because it was my first house that I had built solely on my own, and it was all mine! There really wasn't much work to do there, but I enjoyed going there and dreaming about the day I would be moving in with Windy.

I was hot, dirty, and sweaty from working in the yard, so I sat down on the concrete floor and drank a soft drink. The puppies ran over, started to crawl and jump all over me, and lick me on the face. I laid back on the cool concrete floor, getting even dustier, but enjoying laughing and playing with those little rascals. Wearing only a tank-top and short-shorts, my body was covered in dirt and dust that clung to me with sweat, but I didn't care…I didn't care that is; until I heard footsteps walking through my garage! It startled me! *Who-the-hell?*

I looked up, and it was Alex! How did he know where to find me? How did he know where my new house was located, for I had not told him? Besides that, I told him not to call me until he was divorced! Now, did I care that I was hot, dirty, and sweaty? Yes! Trying to divert his attention away from me, I said, "look at what I have!" while lifting one of the puppies. His smile was of love coming from his eyes as well as his lips, as he loved on the puppies with me. Loving on the puppies did not last long.

We both laid our puppies down. Alex took me in his arms, and we kissed sadly-tenderly for we had missed one another so. I responded to his kisses as I had always done in years past, exchanging tongues and making love with only our tongues, lips, and mouths. I was tiptoeing to reach his lips; my sweaty arms were locked around his neck. Both his arms were grasped tightly around my waist as we continued to kiss for several minutes. The puppies were yapping in the background, and my heart was choking me to death because it was in my throat and about to leap out of my body with joy and happiness . . . happiness to be again in the arms of Mr. Wonderful!

We talked for a short time, and he updated me about the progress of his divorce. Mrs. "Let-me-tell-you-how-wonderful-I-am" had finally filed divorce papers. It would not be much longer, and he would be free. The division of the assets was the last thing that needed to be fine-tuned. We were both elated that he was able to keep *Lady in Blue*, his beautiful sailing vessel.

Alex demanded that she drop his last name and use another. I wondered if she might go back to her original family name or if she might change it to Ms. "Wuz-wonderful-once-now-justa-wannabe" . . .or something like that.

Chapter 56 The Larkspur

The larkspur represents the birth flower for July.

The larkspur has many meanings, including love, affection, strong attachment, lightness, pure heart, sweet disposition, and desire for laughter.

My lovely little house was finally finished in October of that year. My son and Mrs. "Bride-number-two-hot-to-trot-n-hot-snot" helped me move into it, along with two others who were my son's friends. It only took one day of moving, then the fun of unpacking began. My furniture had been in storage for several months and was in dire need of cleaning and polishing, which I joyfully did.

Now was the time that my new puppy could move in with me. Windy was twelve weeks old and almost housebroken, which saved me a lot of grief.

For the first time, my life was finally getting to a peaceful state of being. I had a real sense of pride in owning my very own home . . . and it was ALL MINE! Like the old cliché goes, *"I was happy as a lark."* I found myself smiling more, and my self-confidence was beginning to return.

About two weeks after moving into my new house, I was on the way home after work one day. I was about to drive out of the shopping center, where my store was located, and I had stopped at a red light. While waiting for the light to change, it occurred to me at that very moment that I did not have a headache. "I don't have a headache!" I almost laughed out loud and screamed it while sitting alone in my car. After four long months of constant headaches and temperatures of one hundred-one degree, my illness of chronic fatigue syndrome appeared to be coming to an end.

No more feeling weak and tired all the time. No more wanting to sleep all day and all night. I knew I would now be able to focus on life again. My ambitions would come back. I knew my appetite would return, and consequently, I would gain back my weight. I was back on the road to the vibrant health that I once had, and so desperately wanted it back again.

A person just doesn't know what she is missing until she loses her health. It is something we all take for granted. We shouldn't! We think ill health or car accidents only happen to the other person. It does . . . until it happens to you!

Never take your health for granted! Be very thankful for the good things you have been given each day, for tomorrow you may not have them.

Chapter 57 The Begonia

The begonia flower's message is don't be lulled into a false sense of security and stay vigilant for danger. Always repay the favors given to you with appropriate gifts, or you'll end up with no help at all.

It was November 1997, and Mr. Wonderful had finalized his divorce papers. He was able to keep his beloved *Lady in Blue*. Can you spell r-e-l-i-e-f? Just having the papers signed did not mean it was over. There was a 30-day waiting period so the other party could come back and change anything in the divorce agreement if they found something, they thought was not right. We had to be very careful not to be seen together in public because Ms. "Usta-think-I-wuz-wonderful-once-now-justa-wanna-be-again" might vindictively refile against Alex and take back the boat. We were not safe yet.

Alex was living with his mother during the week, then he told her he was sleeping aboard *Lady in Blue* on the weekends. Actually, he was sleeping with *this other lady* on the weekends along with Windy, our new Springer Spaniel puppy.

I gave Windy to Alex to help him heal from losing Abbey, his beloved show dog that had died in January. Although Windy was my dog, Alex was quickly stealing her heart and winning first place with her. I had never owned a dog of my own. Therefore, I did not know how to raise a puppy. I was raising her according to the rulebook that Leda had given me. At night she slept in a doggy crate, but not before yapping a while. Then she would settle down and doze off to sleep.

One Friday night, Alex was spending the weekend with us. I had put Windy down for the night in her crate. She was yapping and crying to get out. I told Alex not to worry, she'll stop in a minute. He said, "she sure will." He got out of bed, went and got her out of her crate, and put her in bed with us! He was right! She sure did settle down! She slept comfortably under his arm for the rest of the night. From that night forward, she slept in our bed. When he was there, she preferred to sleep under his arm. But when he wasn't there, she tolerated sleeping with me. She never slept in that crate again.

Alex spoiled her. Can you imagine how he would have spoiled a human baby girl? That puppy had Alex wrapped around her little paw! When she wanted to go outside or go for a walk, she would go get her leash and bring it to Alex. He usually hand-fed her on weekends. I now had another lady to compete with. One was his wife, (she gave him to me!) Two--was *Lady in Blue*, his beautiful sailing vessel. Now, three—this cute, spoiled, female puppy demanding his time. I had to play the last place in Alex's heart again! Or so I thought. Actually, I was first place, I just had to share him with the other two. I didn't mind it though, I loved Windy and *Lady in Blue* as much as he did!

Girls, it never helps to be jealous of things you cannot compete with, i.e., a boat, a dog, a stepchild, etc.

Another word of advice and this one is free.
**You cannot compete with a stepchild, so don't try! Never be jealous of one. I know that is a hard pill to swallow, because I have been there, and have suffered the torment of vying to be number one. You cannot compete against blood. You must work around the circumstances and find your own special place of love in your man's life. You cannot take the place of anyone or anything, you must share.

Now, you have every right to be jealous of another woman! Go full speed and defend your territory! If you don't, she'll take him away from you every time!

Chapter 58 The Ranunculus

The ranunculus flower means radiant charm, you are charming, and you are attractive.

Mr. Wonderful and I spent Thanksgiving 1997 aboard *Lady in Blue*. I prepared an abbreviated Thanksgiving dinner, and we sailed away for a holiday cruise to the Chandeleur Islands which were located about fifty miles east of New Orleans and thirty-five miles south of Gulfport, Mississippi in the Gulf of Mexico. These uninhabited, barrier islands serve as a great fishing location for many people. But for Alex and me, they just served as an excellent anchorage for our first romantic cruise together.

I tried to make this first holiday with Alex as unique as I could. So, I used my best white linen tablecloth and napkins, china dinnerware, silver flatware, and crystal stemware. These items should not be aboard a sailing vessel most of the time because of their fragility, but I did not care, this was a special occasion that I did not want to forget, and I wanted it to be memorable for Alex.

We dined by candlelight and feasted on roast turkey breast, Cajun cornbread dressing with gravy, stirred-fried green beans with onions and bacon, sweet potato souffle', home-made rolls and pecan pie.

After dinner, Alex scurried around and helped me clean the galley. Having never had help in the kitchen before, that was a real treat. I was impressed.

Alex was excellent at making Brandy Alexanders (a.k.a. panty droppers.) After dinner, we sat on the couch under the oil lantern, sipping Brandy Alexanders while listening to a Grover Washington C.D. being played through the boat intercom system. It was warm and romantic, being snuggled up with the man of my dreams.

Alex was the only man who could touch my mind and heart with his gentle, caring ways; he made me feel like the most beautiful woman in the world! Only he could make love to me and send me into la-la-land, and there was no hurry that night. We were all alone, together in our own little private world. We could make love as long as we wanted, or as many times as we wished, with no interruptions. And we did just that . . . on our first official Thanksgiving together.

We moved from the galley couch and proceed to take a bath together. Slowly, Alex undressed me, then himself. We stepped into a whirling warm pool of delightful smelling bubbles. Tenderly, Alex began soaping me all over with slow, massaging strokes all over my neck and shoulders, then on to the lower parts of my body. I was lying on my stomach in a tub of warm foaming suds, as Alex rubbed my neck up and down, then more profoundly around my shoulders. It felt good to release the tension in my muscles. I was putty in the hands of the master artist. He worked his way down my back and rubbed my waist and hips, my buttocks were next to be part of the rapture. He kissed his way down my back as he was caressing me.

He softly and lightly mounted me on my back, then he brought his hands around to my front side and started massaging my clitoris as he was kissing the back of my neck. I arched my hips and neck to give him room to work his magic. We were warm and slippery in those suds. I felt myself hunching back on his fingers as he was caressing my clitoris. Umm, it was delightful. Then he inserted his middle finger into my Garden of Pleasure, while he continued to massage my clitoris with his palm. OMG! He was finger-fucking me; it was so good; I couldn't stand it! I was about to climax. . . stop, stop!

I raised up onto my knees, so I could accept his full load when he was ready to give Big Boy to little Eva. I yearned to kiss him on his lips. I wanted to taste him and feel his rugged mustache on my mouth. I wanted his tongue inside my mouth when I climaxed. But I also wanted to fuck him this way, so he could do me deeper and massage my clit harder. The warm slippery suds made his fingers slide over my clit faster and harder. It made me even more sexcited. Little Eva was craving her Big Boy that was erect, hard and stabbing her in the rear. He was just teasing, waiting for an entrance. Little Eva was wanting and desiring him in her Garden of Pleasure. . . all of him! I spread my legs further and pushed back onto Alex, welcoming my best friend, and his Big Boy into my tight little Garden of Pleasure. Alex filled all of me solidly with his thick, heavy penis. We began making love in perfect hunching and rocking rhythm. I reached under and between my legs, grasping his scrotum, then I massaged it as we continued to be one. He grabbed my shoulders and moaned with overwhelming emotion as I massaged his sudsy, slippery scrotum, while Big Boy was buried deep inside of my Garden of Pleasure.

Each deep downward stroke that he was giving me was returned with an equally balanced hunch upward to meet him. Our Mambo-love-dance was in perfect timing. The head of Big Boy was caressing my G-Spot on every loving stroke. Sometimes he would stop because he was about to come. Then he would start back up again, just like brand-new. It seemed he could make love all night!

He knew how to make lovemaking feel magnificent, heavenly, and last as long as I wanted or needed it to last. At one moment, he pulled out of me and kissed his way starting at my neck, down my back, then all the way down to my ass. It was warm and sooth, like a baby's butt. Then he reinserted Big Boy, and we began hunching harder and faster than before. His fingers were caressing my clitoris again, I was going wild with ecstasy, I knew I was about to climax any moment, and I wasn't going to stop this time.

There it was. . . just release and release and release! It was a good, hard climax; my body was flexing with that feel-good, tickle-so-fine feeling. I could hear myself groaning with heavenly pleasure as I was tightening my vagina, squeezing him and pumping him for a little more. My lower abdomen was flexing and rolling as the climax was carrying me away.

While I was squeezing Big Boy when Alex started his release. He closed his eyes and let out a low roar. I could feel Big Boy get bigger and harder, as he was shooting hot semen deeper into my swollen vagina. What a lover!

He collapsed on top of me; we were both hot and sweaty. The warm, sudsy water felt relaxing and soothing to our worn-out bodies. He slid off and laid beside me. After we caught our breaths, he smoked a cigarette. We laid naked in the sudsy tub, staring at the moon and stars as a gentle sea breeze was blowing through the hatch window. We could hear the halyards tingling against the mast as the boat rocked on the waves.

We retired from the tub and went to our king-size bed. Then it was time for round two. . . then three! Soon it was daylight, and we slept most of the day.

What a Happy Thanksgiving it was in 1997!

There was no Black Friday shopping for us!

Chapter 59 The Star of Bethlehem

The star of Bethlehem flower is associated with the birth of Christ and symbolizes the traits of Jesus: innocence, purity, honesty, hope, and forgiveness.

It is often used in religious ceremonies as a symbol of the Christ Child, but it can be used for other occasions, too.

It was December 1997 and I had not been back to the yacht club since my divorce earlier that year. Although my friends invited me, I thought it best to be discrete to preserve my reputation, what little I had left.

Alex now felt comfortable about the finalization of his divorce; she could not come back and change the agreement. So now was our time that we could be seen together in public as a couple. Where do you think we were seen together first? The Commodore's Ball! I had not been to another Commodore's Ball since the night I slapped "Girdy-old-girlfriend-from-the-past." Needless to say, I dressed very conservatively. No little hot pink sequined (demon-possessed) cocktail dress for me that year! A simple little black cocktail dress with pearls made an elegant statement. Alex was handsome as ever in his black tuxedo.

When we arrived, we were amazed that no one was surprised to see us together. Everyone knew us, and we were both loved and respected as individuals, now we were loved and recognized as a couple. I actually think everyone liked us better as the new couple we were, instead of the two couples we were previously. (Our two previous spouses were jerks, and not many people liked either of them anyway.)

We loved to dance close to each other, whether the music was fast or slow. It was as if we were making love standing up, moving in and out of one another's arms in perfect timing. Alex was a good dancer; I was not so great, but I could follow his lead. I loved gazing into his brown bedroom eyes as he mopped up the ballroom floor with me. After one of the dances, a male friend came up to us and said, "I can tell you've danced together before."

Alex and I just smiled at one another, because the only other time we had ever danced together was the night we secretly danced at the Mardi Gras Ball the year prior.

We were now together for our first Christmas; it would be a quiet and simple one. Just the two of us plus Windy. Now that we had one another, there was nothing that we wanted or needed as far as gifts were concerned. We still wanted to exchange gifts anyway. We decided to set a limit on how much we would spend on one another's Christmas gift. Alex would not say, and I would not say what that amount should be; we were at a standoff. We decided that we would both write down a number on a price of paper, then exchange with one another. We would then take the two numbers, add them together, and divide by two. That would give us the amount we would spend on each's gift and no more.

We both wrote down a number on a piece of paper. I wrote down $500 because I did not have much money. Also, I did not want Alex to spend much money on me. We were ready to exchange. I opened Alex's paper, and it read, *"A Number."* I nearly fainted! "Alex, you cheated!" I exclaimed. "Well, you said to write down *a number*, so I did." He was always so bright!

That Christmas wasn't about us and gifts. We heard about a young boy and girl who were in need. Their father was in prison, and their mother had just died from cancer. They were living with their grandmother, who was also in financial need. These children had been going without the essentials for a long time.

When Alex and I heard about them, we decided to give them their Christmas. Alex shopped for the boy, and I shopped for the girl. The grandmother was also included in the shopping and giving.

The story was that the mother was dying from face cancer, and there was no cure. Metastatic cancer had moved from her face and into her brain. The father heard about a doctor in another country who claimed he could help her. So, he robbed a bank to take her to that country for treatment. He robbed the bank and escaped on a bicycle. He was apprehended but not before hiding the money. He plead not guilty but was convicted anyway and went to prison. The money was never found, and he's not talking!

At Christmas time, we have so much to be thankful for. Just look around you. We have so much, yet we want more. There are so many people in need, yet we don't see nor do anything to help them. How many times do we look the other way when we see a homeless person? If we don't look at them, we won't see them. Therefore, they are not there, and we won't know about their needs, then we won't feel guilty for not helping them.

Christmas celebrates the birth of Christ, the one who came to help us all.

We should celebrate Christmas every day.

Chapter 60 The Bird of Paradise

The bird of paradise represents festivity, celebration.

"Laissez Les Bons Temps Rouler"

is a Cajun French phrase that is literally translated
from the English expression:

"Let the good times roll."

Mardi Gras is the annual carnival celebration in
Mobile, Alabama. It is the oldest annual carnival in the
United States. Actually, most people think Mardi Gras

366

was founded in New Orleans, but it wasn't; Mobile preceded New Orleans by fifteen years, starting in 1703.

Mobile has a tradition of elaborate mystic societies, with formal masked balls and elegant costumes. The public parades are where masked members of the secret societies ride on floats or horseback, toss gifts, (known as throws) to the general public. Throws include necklaces made of plastic beads, doubloon coins, decorated plastic cups, candy, footballs, frisbees, whistles and in my case—silk roses.

At the masked balls, the non-masked invited adult guest men are required to wear a white tie (full dress or *costume de rigueur*) while the women wear full-length evening gowns. The members of each particular secret society hosting their ball must remain in mask and costume to conceal their identity.

One of the most popular parades in Mobile is the M.O.T.---The Mystics of Time who parade out on the Saturday before Mardi Gras Day and release smoke-breathing dragons onto the streets of the city. The M.O.T. is one of the city's oldest mystic societies, being founded in 1948.

It was now the year 1998, and the M.O.T.'s were celebrating their 50th anniversary. Alex had been looking forward to this year for a long time; so was I, for it was our first official Mardi Gras Ball together as a couple.

I searched several days for the perfect evening gown and finally found it. It was silk fuchsia, tightly fitted, fully beaded and silver dangling epaulets. It was cut a little low in the front for my small breasts, but thank goodness there were pads sewn in. The back dipped down to my waist, and the whole gown fit like a glove. I hoped to look stunning in it, to make Alex proud; I knew he would want to show off his new trophy girl to his friends.

The time was rapidly approaching for the big event, and Alex had made his preparations. His throws were purchased, his costume was fitted, and he had given out his guest tickets. We were excited to be making our first formal debut to the world as a couple.

The week before the ball, I started getting a flu-bug. Not the severe flu, just the type where the doctor could prescribe an antibiotic to treat it. I was determined to get well in time for the ball. I was not going to miss that party if my life depended on it. They would have to bury me in that beautiful fuchsia dress!

I took that prescription precisely as prescribed. . . but it wasn't helping that much. Well, maybe it helped a little, or was that just in my head?

Saturday morning came around, and I was packed up and ready to move into the elegant hotel for the weekend celebration. The not-feeling-so-good wasn't just in my head. It was now in my stomach! The antibiotics did nothing for my flu-like-symptoms, but they sure did a number on my tummy! There was a storm building in my abdomen that would not go away. Well hell! I could tell it was not going to be a romantic weekend!

That Saturday morning, Alex went to his society's breakfast celebration and came back with my commemorative brooch, similar to the one he had secretly given me the year prior. My stomach was roaring and rumbling, but I said nothing to Alex. I merely asked if he would take me to a drugstore. Being the well-mannered gentleman that he was, he did not ask any questions.

We got into his car, and he drove me there. I bought a large bottle of Pepto Bismol and swigged down about a third of the container. Then we stopped for lunch, which was a mistake. I was only a little hungry, but that big, greasy, home-made, grilled, cheeseburger was good! I ate every bite of it and the French fries as well.

Uh-oh! Before we could make it back to the hotel, I needed to stop and you-know-what! Where-in-the-hell was I going to stop and go? I was about to have a blow-out. . . and I'm not talking about a tire!

I couldn't ask Alex to stop at a service station or a convenience store to let me use their facilities. You never know how sanitary they are, you know? Besides, he was such a high-class guy, I didn't want him to visualize me sitting on one of those public things. (Stupid, right?)

Anyway, we made it back to the hotel, he pulled up to the front entrance, and I rushed upstairs ahead of him. He was lagging, talking to the valet service. Finally! Peace and quiet as I relieved myself; well, peace anyway.

I freshened up a bit, and after a while, Alex came to the room. We had a cocktail on the balcony with some other revelers. That was another mistake! A girl should never mix alcohol with diarrhea. It was slightly afternoon when Alex said he needed to rest before the long night ahead of him. He suggested we take a nap, I wondered if he might want to make love. I was glad sex was not on his mind, because another big storm was brewing in my belly!

We laid down together, and he was about to doze off. I could feel my stomach rumbling up a big fat opportunity to flatulate. Oh no! I just couldn't do such an un-lady-like-thing anywhere near Alex! That would end our romance for sure! Maybe even end our love affair?

When Nathan was growing up, I told him that *girls don't do those smelly things*. One day he came home from his four-year-old kindergarten class. He was quite indignant and adamant when he said, "Uh-huh Mama! Girls <u>do</u> poot! 'Cause Kristy did it today in the sandbox!" I felt so embarrassed for that little girl. I could just imagine the sand flying, scooting, and puffing out from around her short little legs as she sat there. . . sandblasting my little boy! I don't think Nathan ever played with Kristy again in that sandbox. Poor little girl!

I could just imagine that Alex would never play with me again (in my box) if I did such a thing around him.

Anyway, I was in a mell-of-a-hess! So, what was I going to do? It was as if there was a dragon inside my belly clawing and gnawing and raging to get out! The bathroom was only three feet from the head of our bed and certainly within hearing range. I would never want Alex to hear me make such scary noise, it might scare him to death or scare him off. You know, sounds like some ghost might make in a horror movie, screaming "Booooo," or something like that. I could only imagine the sounds that might come from that bathroom. It just wasn't worth the risk! I just had to suffer in silence.

Finally, my only choice was to wake up Alex and ask him to leave the room and give me some privacy for about fifteen minutes. I did just that. He was bewildered at my request, but he knew I was stomach sick. Being the gentleman that he was, he agreed and left the room without question. Great!

My privacy did not last long. Within three to four minutes there was a knock on the door, and it opened with, "Helloooo!" It was Alex's friends from Mobile whom I had met on his boat the year prior. That ended my moment of private relief!

It was no secret that I was stomach-sick that weekend, but Alex acted as if nothing was wrong and overlooked my rumbling stomach. What a sweet, well-mannered man I was in love with! His look-the-other-way at my embarrassing situation made me love and appreciate him even more! **Teaching lesson:**

Never kill the romance in your relationship by letting your man know or see your defects. That means, never point out to him that you think you are ugly, or fat, or have crooked toes, etc. He will always remember those defects that you point out to him, and he may remind you of them one day.

As in the story at hand, never let your man see you doing your private, personal business, or any embarrassing thing, like sitting on the potty. No one over the age of three ever looked cute sitting on the potty.

Making love + romance + potty = ? Nope! They just do not go together.

Next, do not let him know anything negative concerning you, he will remember you in that way if you do. Let him think you are the perfect, sweet lady that he wants and deserves. Then he will appreciate you for being just that.

About three o'clock, Mr. Wonderful headed to the auditorium with his costume in hand, ready to begin his big night of fun and folly. Finally, I had six hours to get myself collected and prepared for the parade and ball. That night I stood at my usual location to watch the parade. There, Alex flooded me with a case of 144 silk roses. It was the symbol of his true love for me. The crowd caught most of the roses, but I knew they were all meant for me.

After the parade, I rushed back to the hotel and dressed in my beautiful evening gown. By that time, my stomach was cleared of everything, and I was feeling much better. I met Alex in his hospitality room before the doors officially opened to the general invitees. He pinned me with his annual commemorative brooch as he kissed me. We then made our way to the long line for callouts. I was so proud to be on his arm as we pranced and danced our way out into the auditorium for the first time as a real item.

Mardi Gras 1998 in Mobile, Alabama, was one of the best ever for Alex and me. It was our first Mardi Gras Ball together and the 50th for his mystic society.

I will never forget it, diarrhea and all!

Chapter 61 The Cedar Leaf

The cedar leaf asks you to 'think of me.'

Alex and I were living and loving large back in those days. May 1998 came around quickly, and it was time for Alex and his crew to race *Lady in blue* from Pensacola, Florida to Isla Mujeres, Mexico. This regatta took place every other year and included approximately fifty sailboats, with about three hundred brave sailors. The three hundred-fifty miles across the Gulf of Mexico usually took three to five days, sailing – racing hard day and night. Sometimes the weather and seas might be calm, some days it could be very treacherous! I hated it when Alex went on these dangerous races, but he loved the excitement, thrill, and challenge of doing it. It was a man thing I concluded; I just could not see why he wanted to put himself in harm's way when he could avoid it.

After the race, a three-day party on Isla Mujeres ensued; the crew member's wives or girlfriends flew down for the festivities.

Alex and his crew had worked diligently for weeks preparing the vessel for the long voyage. Safety was the first and foremost item on the agenda. Then making sure the bottom hull was clean and slick to sail fast. After all, it <u>was</u> a race! Their meals were catered and stored in dry ice; Alex prepared them for the crew each evening. His crew dined each evening on elegant meals such as crown roast, Cornish game hen and other gourmet feasts.

When the day came for the big departure, I placed a bouquet of red rosebuds on his boat with a note. In the middle of the real rosebuds, there was one silk rosebud (one that he threw to me from his Mardi Gras float.) On the outside of the envelope, it stated, "Do not open until midnight."

On the inside, my love letter read:

To My Dear Alex Darling,

These buds represent my goodnight kisses to you while you are away.

This silk bloom represents my undying love that will be waiting for you the moment you arrive in Isla Mujeres.

May God bless you and your brave crew. May he keep you safe and return you to Windy and me as soon as possible.

Have a great time! I will think of you every waking moment, and I shall dream of you each night!

Words cannot express my love for you, I only hope you know that you are the only reason my heart beats!

Sail fast, my Love!

Eva

Alex's big, beautiful, sailing vessel started the race, along with the other fifty gorgeous boats; my good friend, Tina, and I watched from a distance, out of the way on a guided tour boat. Tina's husband, Jon, was one of Alex's best friends and was also on his crew making the voyage. Our hearts were about to come out of our throats as we watched with excitement, while the giant spinnakers were hoisted into place and the sailors were jockeying their vessels into position for better wind. Alex's crew worked in perfect timing with one another; all six sailors were excellent at making *Lady in Blue* obey their every command. Within a few minutes, the sails were set, and the boats were off and sailing fast for Mexico. Tina and I both cried as we headed back to land; we already missed our men and the loves of our lives. It would be three to five long days before we would see them again.

Each night Alex would call me on the single sideband radio and tell me where they were in the Gulf of Mexico. I, in turn, would call each of the wives and relay the message. I also had the pleasure of calling Mama Wonderful to keep her informed.

The first night that I called her, I was very nervous because I wondered if she might know about mine and Alex's love affair. After all, Alex had only been divorced seven months at that time. I dialed her number, and she promptly answered; she was expecting my call. I started out with, "Mrs. Rosenberg, my name is Eva Adams, I am a friend of Alex's." She responded in a cheerful tone, "Yes, my son has spoken very highly of you. He told me you would be calling me this week to let me know how he is doing in the race." That was all it took; we were instantly friends; I was glad. Come to find out, she never liked Mrs. "Let-me-tell-you-how-wonderful-I-am" in the first place. I guess she did not wish to listen to all her bragging any more than the rest of us did! I was mindful not to talk about myself while around her, ever!

During the days while waiting to fly down to meet Alex, I made a pendant flag for his boat to surprise him. The flag was a beautiful mermaid with a blue, swirly, sequined tail. She had big blue eyes, enormous bosoms with seashells that covered her nipples and red, lustful lips. Her hair was blonde braided dreadlocks that flowed loosely when blowing in the wind. I thought she was the perfect representation of a *Lady in Blue*.

After three days, Tina and I caught a flight to Mexico to meet our men. We were so excited! We landed in Cancun, Mexico. From there we took a taxi to the waterfront. From the harbor, we went by ferry to the small island across the bay where our men would be landing soon. While in the taxi, I asked the driver where I might be able to buy a Cuban cigar. I did not understand his Spanish, but he understood my southern English dialect very well. He knew just the place to purchase the cigar, and he stopped in front of a little store where he went in and came back out with my prized gift for Alex. I thanked him and tipped him very well for his courtesy.

In no time we were on a quick ferry boat ride to the small island of Isla Mujeres, Mexico.

We arrived at the island, Tina and I went straight to the hotel and checked in. Then we went to the regatta/race headquarters to check on the location of our boat and sailors. Some sailors had already finished the race, but our crew had not, they were still about a day out. The festivities had already started with music, food, drinks, and laughter. Everyone was having a great time. Everyone except Tina and me that is. We were still waiting for our men to arrive. We had dinner and a couple of drinks while listening to the stories of the other sailor's adventure sailing down. The weather was great for them, and we were glad they had a good time. We now only hoped our men would make it safely to the island the next day.

After our long flight, we were ready to turn in early and get some rest. The next day was to be our big day of once again seeing our men, our very much missed loved ones.

Bright and early the next morning Tina and I were up at the crack of dawn and at the regatta/race headquarters checking on the location of our boat and crew. They were still a few hours out. So, Tina and I had breakfast, did a little shopping, got our hair braided, and headed to the beach to get some sun. From the beach, we could see when our boat was approaching. The harbor was marked by a beautiful red and white lighthouse. This was our focal point to keep a check on.

We hired a small fifteen-foot water taxi to be on hand when our boat entered the bay. They would take us out to meet our big boat and follow along beside them, down the bay to the customs dock. That was our plan. We waited and watched for our boat. Hour upon hour, the time was dragging on. The water taxi driver was beginning to wonder if we actually had a boat to meet and follow. We assured him that we did and to please be patient. Tina and I enjoyed too many margaritas that afternoon and got too much sun. We were getting bored waiting for our boat.

Finally, some entertainment arrived. A couple of young sunbathers came along and set up camp not too far from us. They spread out their beach blanket, popped up their sun umbrella and turned on their radio. The beach attendant quickly came and took their order for drinks. Two beers were brought back to them promptly as he was beginning to rub her down with oil, slowly and sensually. This was a topless beach. Therefore, the girl was free to take off her teeny-weeny yellow bikini top, exposing her full double–whatever-they-were-cup-breasts! He slowly rubbed oil all over them. Then he licked it off, first the left, then the right. She rolled over onto her knees, and with one hand, she pulled her G-string bikini out from between her much tanned, firm buttock cheeks, and popped it in his face. He lovingly, yet firmly slapped her on her ass, they laughed sinfully and kissed. It looked bootylicious! Then they stood up and walked out to the water to cool off; he followed behind her, watching her every step. Tina and I were watching his every step. He was a young and very well-built man. His tan accentuated his six-pack abs which were just above his black speedo. I usually don't like speedos on men, but this speedo looked very sexy. We could tell that he was well equipped by the size of the package he was carrying around in that little black speedo! Well, we could only imagine that he was well equipped . . . that is. One never knows for sure about those things. (Not until it is too late.) We could only hope it wasn't a potato he was carrying around or something like that.

Well, the sexy young couple made it into the water. They played and splashed around for a while; more kissing began. Fondling followed; she obviously was sitting on his lap as the two began to have full-blown sex right there in front of us and everyone else who might have been watching. They did not care! They were enjoying the sex to its fullest, and we could tell they were! The look on both their faces was proof of what was going on below the water line. Pure ecstasy! She was riding him up and down in the water with all her might. All he could do was to hold on to her because she was pumping him like a bucking bronco! That sexual experience went on for about fifteen minutes. Tina and I were embarrassed. We were embarrassed because we both were enjoying watching them make love right there in front of us. I never knew I could get into voyeurism and we weren't turning away from watching them. It made us horny as hell for our men!

After the sexual excitement was over and the couple had gone, I was looking through the binoculars. There was one little speck of a white sail on the horizon near the lighthouse; I knew it was our boat! We rushed to get our beach bags together and find the water taxi driver. He was nowhere to be found! Finally, we found him. He had given up hope on us and our boat. We rushed into his small little powerboat, and off we puttered into the middle of the bay to meet our majestic sailing vessel and our brave men who were aboard.

Tina and I found a bamboo pole and hoisted our pendant flag. As our small water taxi boat was approaching our big sailing vessel, the six guys on the big boat were ecstatic when they saw us rushing up toward them with our pendant flag blowing in the wind. Tina and I were screaming and blowing kisses wildly to our mighty brave sailors! We could not board the big boat until it had cleared customs; they were still in quarantine. So, we continued to follow alongside them for the duration of the ride down the bay. Our hearts were racing with anticipation; we were so eager to get into the arms of the men that we loved and adored so dearly.

That was a moment in time that I shall never forget. My heart still races when I think back on that exact moment when Alex and I locked eyes in the middle of the Isla Mujeres Bay. He was so surprised to see me out there. Alex had made the same trip two times prior, but Mrs. "Let-me-tell-you-how-wonderful-I-am" had never met them anywhere. Alex had to dock his boat and go find her when he arrived. She was usually drunk at one of the local bars.

When the boat docked at customs, the customs officer immediately boarded *Lady in Blue* and asked for the proper documentation papers and passports of all crew members. When he was satisfied that the crew was all legal, he released *Lady in Blue*, the quarantine flag came down, and Tina and I stepped aboard. Alex and I kissed and locked lips for what seemed several minutes. We had truly missed each other. He said that he had thought of me every moment; and especially all night when he was sailing his watch duty.

It took no time for the crew to secure the boat to the dock and suspend the new mermaid pendant flag to the forestay. She looked pretty flying in the wind, telling the world that *Lady in Blue* had arrived in Mexico! After four days at sea, the guys were glad to get off the boat. We were then off to rent a golf cart for the duration of our visit on the tiny paradise island.

The guys had a good race down to Mexico, until near the end when they were becalmed, that being the reason for their later arrival time. I didn't care, they were there, and they were safe. That was all that mattered to me at that moment.

When Alex and I made it to our hotel room, the first thing he did was to take a monumental shower. I did the same to get the salty beach sand off me and shampoo my hair. In bed, we kissed and made love tenderly and lovingly. It was over quite quickly. Alex was ready for me! Then we rested in bed for a little while as he told me of his adventure on the sea. He honestly had a great time; I could tell he loved those adventurous days with the guys. I knew I would never deprive him of those manly pleasures.

Soon, it was time to meet the crew for dinner at the race headquarters. Once again, the food, the drinks, and the music were excellent. But this time it was all the better because I had the man of my dreams with me and I was locked in his arms.

After dinner, Alex and I sat together in a double swing, under the Mexico moon and stars, as he enjoyed his Cuban cigar. We sipped our cocktails, and he continued to tell me of his adventures on the sea until we fell asleep in one another's arms.

What a 'fairy-tale-happily-ever-after-life' I was beginning to live!

Chapter 62 The Saffron

The saffron flower symbolizes voluptuousness--be cautious about excess pleasures.

As I, the author, was beginning to write this next chapter, I was stopped by this flower's symbolism. . .

Voluptuousness--be cautious about excess pleasures.

I realized that in my previous chapter, for the sake of adding stimulating sexual reading pleasure for you, the reader; I told you a down and out lie! I made up the story about that sexy couple on the beach in Mexico. Well, I didn't make it <u>all</u> up . . . I just embellished it a little. I felt guilty about telling you that lie! The truth is, I didn't want to gross you out with the real story! Well, I must now tell you, my readers, the truth about what really happened that day on the beach while Tina and I were waiting for our boat. It really happened this way:

Finally, some entertainment arrived. A couple of rotund sunbathers came and plopped down not too far from us. They were nasty slobs and low-lives! They spread out their tattered quilt with its cotton-filler hanging out of it at various spots. Then they shoved two sticks into the sand to hold up an old beach towel that was to serve as a make-shift umbrella, to shade them from the hot afternoon sun. Then they turned on a portable radio/CD player that was playing something that sounded like Polka music. A Styrofoam cooler lid was lifted, and two cold beers were popped open; they started slurping down the brews. They were set to enjoy themselves for the afternoon when the beach attendant arrived and advised them that personal coolers were not allowed on the private beach, because the beach was owned by the hotel; they were supposed to purchase their libations from her. The beach attendant did not mention the fact that they should also rent the beach umbrella from her, instead of using that soiled beach towel and sticks! The couple did not like the rule, but the man ordered two draft beers anyway. After gulping down the draft beers, they refilled their plastic cups with regular beer from their personal cooler, when the beach attendant wasn't looking.

After they had swigged down those next two or three beers each, it was time for them to rub oil on one another. It was a topless beach, so she was at liberty to expose herself to the world as she saw fit. She was sprawled out on her back when she pulled down the top of her size double X, maybe triple X, large floral print, bubble top bathing suit. She pulled it all the way down to her waist. As she pulled her bubble-top-swimsuit down, her flabby breasts spread out and rolled off her chest and onto the quilt, forming a puddle of fleshy mush-o-breasts. I dare not guess what size they were! Even though it was a topless beach, it just wasn't fitting that she should sexpose those flabby, bodacious, boobies to anyone. It was a down-right disgusting sight; we tried not to look, but we just could not turn away! Besides, her left nipple was just lying there in its own puddle of mushy breast, staring back at me!

No one cared to look at them. Only Tina and I were watching discretely through our sunglasses. I don't think they could tell we were observing them. We were laughing as quietly as we could. The sight was repulsive, even amusing, but we couldn't draw our eyes away.

She rolled over onto her stomach so he could rub oil on her back. He coated her back, and then it was time for him to make it around to the front and anoint those babies with oil. She sat up and slapped his hands, then took the oil bottle away from him. She then proceeded to rub her own breasts with the oil; he just watched with lust as she rubbed over and under both of her own breasts . . . all the way down to her belly button. Her breasts took up all of her chest and stomach area. Tina and I felt like we were cheated out of the blessing of big breasts, and she had gotten our share; what a waste!

Anyway, after a while of heated oil rubbing, beer chug-a-lugging, and lively Polka music, it came time for them to get into the water. She rolled over onto her stomach, like a beached manatee, and with a deep-throated groan, she made it up onto her knees. Finally, he decided to help her, but he could only half-ass drag her up to her feet. Her bubble top bathing suit was still dangling there around her waist, as were her saggy, wrinkly old breasts. It was a pitiful sight to behold! Tina and I watched in amazement as they waddled together, knocked-kneed, out into the water--deeper and deeper. From the rear-view, they looked like a couple of sea turtles walking upright on their hind legs going toward the sea.

Rotunda-and-Roland splashed around with one another playfully for a short while, then things turned serious. Tina and I couldn't tell if they were having sex or using the restroom. They may have just been taking their occasional bath, who knows? Anyway, it didn't matter what they were doing below the water line; it was a private matter, and we did not need, nor did we want to know which it was! I guess big folks like sex too, but these folks were so big and nasty! The rows of blubber appeared so thick! We wondered how they could find a penis in all those folds, much less get it in anything should that little thing be found. I wondered if a little thing so small could bring pleasure to a big thing so large. Tina and I concluded that he must have been only pleasuring himself; she was just his vehicle. One would never know, nor care to know! But we all know that it happens all the time . . . some girls are used as vehicles to bring about the ends for other's pleasure. Sad but true.

There is another known fact: It doesn't matter what size a penis is, it always brings pleasure to the male who owns it.

Oh well! When they had finished whatever-it-was-that-was-going-on-below-the-waterline, they started to wade and waddle back toward the beach. Tina and I certainly did NOT want to be caught staring at the entertainment. Tina exclaimed, "Oh! Here they come, quick; act like you are napping!" We both fell back on our beach blankets and closed our eyes, as to not be caught in the act of voyeurism! Not that we enjoyed watching this flabby old slob couple having sex or whatever-it-was-that-they-were-doing-out-there-in-the-water. It's just that we couldn't stop looking at what we were seeing! It <u>was</u> great entertainment; even the Polka music was a sort of different and strange entertainment that we did not expect in Mexico!

Am I a snob? Maybe so --- and I do feel a little guilty that I had watched that nauseous display. I also realize that everyone, no matter their age, size, social status, income, or body cleanliness, they all need pleasure. It just seemed that they should have had their pleasure in private as most normal people do!

Now you know the real truth of what really happened that day on the beach in Mexico! So, you see, it was the same story, different people. Same circumstances, but a different outcome. Go back and re-read the previous chapter and decide which couple you like the best---Who had you rather watch or read about?

Now on to the rest of the story. The next day. . .

While we were in Mexico, I was a little worried that Alex might revert to his old habits such as enjoying the bikini contest or enjoying dancing with the young Mexican senoritas at thc town square party and drinking too much. But I said nothing about any of those things. I just kept my peace and watched him for the duration of our visit. He surprised me.

Alex had no interest in attending the bikini contest. I was the one who wanted to attend it. I wanted to see what it was all about. I was glad that I did; I imagined it to be more than it was. When we attended it, I realized it was just a big fun and foolish event for laughter that they did each year for entertainment. There really wasn't much of a contest. I guess you could say it was mostly elimination of the "worstest," to the "worser," to the worse looking girls who entered themselves in the contest. Now you get the picture? Only the best-looking pig survived to win the bottle of rum, which was the trophy! And all along, I was jealous of Alex for having fun at that pigini contest! Who would've thunk?

Some of the girl's bodies looked pretty good, but their faces left a lot to be desired. One girl with a beautiful body put a brown paper bag over her head! I thought she should have won. Then some of the girls had pretty faces but did not have a voluptuous body that was needed to win the prized bottle of rum. One cute older lady, who was just a little chubby, wore an over-sized tee shirt. On the front and back of that tee shirt was painted a perfect body in a tiny bikini. That cute little gal modeled her tee shirt as if it were her own body that she was showing off. The crowd cheered her on as if it was. It was indeed elimination of the pigs, in my humble opinion . . . but what did I know? I was just a jealous girlfriend, standing with my man, who was looking at all those other women's bodies! Mmmm!

After the pigini contest had satisfied my curiosity, Alex and I were walking back to the hotel. We stopped along the way and went into a little shop where he purchased two white silk scarves. I concluded one must be for me and one for his mother, but I wasn't sure; he said nothing about his purchase.

That afternoon was the time for fun and festivities for the Isla Mujeres children and adults of the small town. The parade ended at the town square, where the people put on a party for the sailors with food, drinks, music, and dancing for all to enjoy. The American sailors brought decorations to beautify their golf carts, which were used as our floats. Also brought down was candy and throws for the children. The sailors wore masks and colorful make-shift costumes.

All the children in the town were dressed in white clothing. They were clean and very well behaved. They were very polite, and all were smiling and friendly. I was driving our golf cart in the parade. I had a whistle in my mouth and was blowing it wildly when one little boy about the age of nine approached my golf cart. (The children are supposed to stay on the side of the street, out of the parade traffic.) This little boy very politely, with a big, shy, smile on his face, gently took the whistle out of my mouth. He wanted that whistle for himself. I smiled back at him and let him have it.

So, if I was driving our golf cart, where do you suppose Alex was? He was the self-appointed-self-anointed-Head-Strutter of the parade! He wore one of his previously used Mardi Gras costumes and mask as if he was the king of the event. He cut a large palm frond and used it as his scepter. He carried a portable CD player playing Mardi Gras celebratory music as he strutted down the streets, getting the people into a festive mood. Alex was excellent at getting everyone to smile and have a good time.

Behind Alex was the lead golf cart driven by the two beautiful daughters of the president of the little island. In the back of their golf cart riding were two chubby senoras. All four ladies were decked out in colorful Mexican regalia. When the parade concluded, and we all had arrived at our destination, (which was the town square) the two chubby señoras quickly grabbed Alex and mopped up the town square dancing with him. It was all he could do to keep up with them! I watched in amusement. He had indeed met his match with those two women! I don't know who had more fun; Alex showing those two señoras a good time . . . or those two señoras having a great time, laughing and dancing with the best-looking man on the island!

After the party was over, we were walking back, trying to find our golf cart. I was surprised to find that the children had robbed all the carts of decorations and had taken them back to their own homes. Alex said that it was a tradition. That little town was impoverished, and the children appreciated the beautiful decorations. We were glad they had stripped and cleaned the golf carts for us.

When Alex and I made it back to our hotel room, you would have thought that we would have been exhausted after a long day of fun and celebration and ready to turn in for the night. Tired, no! Rejuvenated, yes!

Alex and I took a long, sudsy, sensual shower together. First, he soaped me down slowly all over my body, starting at my neck, moving slowly down to my breasts as we kissed softly. My arms were wrapped around his neck and back as I was massaging him gently. Our mouths were making love in the down-pouring of the refreshing shower water. The conclusion of the shower led us into the bedroom, where he showed me the reason for his buying those two white silk scarves.

I laid naked on the bed, with the Mexico moonlight shining through the window. I watched as Alex brought out those two silk scarves from under his pillow, without saying one word. My heart started to race, as I knew the master of lovemaking was going to introduce me to something new that I had never experienced.

He had a rather pensive look on his face as he asked, "Is there *anything* you do not want to do?" All I said was, "No, I trust you."

He still hesitated. Then, slowly, he placed the first silk scarf around my eyes, snuggly, but not too tight. I was in total darkness and at his mercy and complete control. Slowly, he then rolled me over onto my stomach, stretching my arms behind me, he bound my wrists. I felt a jolt of apprehension as my heart was beating rapidly. "Are you alright?" He asked instantly. I nodded, unable to speak. I felt unbelievably vulnerable. Every sense was heightened, except sight. I could smell the sweet hibiscus blooming just outside our open window, mixed with the slight tinge of his expensive cologne. I could feel the soft sheets below me, sliding across my skin. My nipples dragged as I rolled slightly on them.

I could feel the warmth of his palms dancing just millimeters away from my skin, not actually touching me. The hair on the nape of my neck prickled as I felt his breath against my shoulder and neck. It made me quiver with excitement and anticipation of what was to come next.

Alex rolled me onto my back, the awkwardness of my bind made my chest jut forward. I could feel his breath and mustache between my breasts, teasing them, taunting me, making me want him. At that exact moment, he took my nipple into his mouth. The juxtaposition of feelings (uncertainty and pleasurable) was like an electric shock! I gasped as he began to suck, drawing my nipple deeper into his mouth. The pulsing pull of pressure was sending waves of delight all over my skin. He switched breasts, increasing his ministrations. I rubbed my thighs together, suddenly they were wet from my growing arousal.

He moved his hands smoothly down my body . . . lower, until he spread my thighs. His fingers teased their way between my damp folds as he was stroking and stretching my legs apart. He moved his head lower, pressing hot, wet kisses into my solar plexus, my stomach, then toward the area where his fingers were moving so industriously. His mouth found my clit, his tongue manipulated it skillfully. Waves of sensation were pulsing up from within my lower stomach, and inner thighs. My heart was beating like a hammer! I moaned softly as I lifted my hips and hunched up to him, enticing him to give me more, as I was ready for his Big Boy to be inside of me!

I had no idea how long he was going to keep this up— it seemed interminable. I was burning in a flame of desire for him and he knew it. I had never felt this hot before;

when would I find my release? When would he finally give me what he was teasing me with? Every time my breathing sped up and got to the edge of orgasm, he would pull back. He would then adjust my position and give me time to cool down. Once again, starting over with kissing my breasts, hips, and legs.

Finally, he unbound my hands when he turned me over, onto my knees with my hips and ass in the air. I shivered, knowing he was going to finally enter me with his Big Boy, my beloved Big Boy! He began by slightly penetrating my vagina with his finger, giving me a foretaste of the real penetration, which was to follow. The actual penetration which I wanted and needed desperately! "Alex, please. . ." was all I could say when I felt the smooth, sensual glide of his Big Boy inch by inch inside of me. I felt my head lolling as my hips were thrusting back and hunching to get every inch that I could get of his Big Boy deeper and deeper inside of me. I was shivering as we were escalating into a chaotic frenzy of desire and pleasure for one another.

"Alex!" I screamed quietly through clinched teeth as he started to thrust harder, with deeper penetration. He groaned; his pace frenzied as I was bucking against him. He cupped my breasts; I could feel his chest against my back as his hips were jerking against mine. The feel of his warm kneading of my breasts, the unique feel of his hard, thick, heavy Big Boy inside of me, it was finally too much. The orgasm exploded through me like a grenade, and I shrieked in pure animal pleasure. His loud groan of pleasure made him shudder as he spilled himself into me over and over again.

We fell to our sides, kissing, sweaty, and breathing hard. Alex removed my blindfold, I felt dazed, and my whole body was twitching.

He kissed my hair, face, and shoulders. Our hot, passionate, sex had turned into a blissful, loving after-glow. "Did I hurt you?" he asked. "No. I've never felt anything like it." I said. "You can do it again whenever you like."

He pulled me ever so tightly into his arms. I curled up with him, knowing I would always be safe with this man that I called "Mr. Wonderful."

"I don't deserve you. I love you. I will never betray you," were his last words as he drifted off to sleep.

"I really love you!" I responded as I kissed his beautiful face. The moon was still shining through our window, as I too was dozing off. I sighed a sigh of pure contentment, although oddly sad because it was our last night in our little paradise called Mexico.

Chapter 63 Adam's Needle

Adam's needle represents best friends.

The next morning, we were up bright and early to make the most of the day, because our stay was quickly coming to an end. Alex took me sight-seeing all around the beautiful, tropical island paradise in our golf cart. Then we did a little shopping for our friends and relatives back home.

Later that afternoon was the highlight of our trip. The sailors were invited to a cocktail party and reception at the president's home. I knew it would be an extraordinary event, so I bought a unique dress for the occasion. Not having experienced such an event, I was really unsure as to how I should dress. Alex assured me that whatever I wore would be just fine. I, on the other hand, was not so sure. A simple white, strapless sundress and white beaded sandals made an elegant statement for the afternoon event. I learned a long time ago that it is not <u>what</u> you wear, it's <u>how</u> you wear it.

When we arrived at the president's home, I was astonished! The house was made totally of rock. A long rock walkway led us out into the water for about two hundred yards or more. We could see many species of colorful tropical fish swimming freely on each side of the rock walkway as we journeyed along. Finally, we reached his beautiful home, built in the middle of the crystal blue sea of Mexico. The president and his lovely wife welcomed each of us at the entrance of their open-air home. The gulf breeze flowed through their open house, cooling it in the hottest of days. Mexican art, paintings, sculptures, and large seashells graced the home throughout. Gourmet food and drinks were never-ending, served by humble servants wearing starched white attire.

After the sailors had a time of mingling together and adoring the president's beautiful, unique home, the president gave his words of welcome and made his presentations and awards to the sailors. I was proud of Alex as he walked forward to receive his trophy. Everyone applauded as I snapped his photo with the president. My heart was full of pride, as my best friend and the love of my life reached out and received his engraved silver tray trophy. I wondered, *what did I ever do to deserve this man? How on earth did I ever get here?* God! I love this man that I call Mr. Wonderful!

The next morning was our last day in Mexico. Tina, Jon, Alex, and I joined our secondary crew at our beautiful *Lady in Blue* as they were preparing to disembark for home. Alex went with the crew to the customs office to ensure that all crew members were given back their passports.

On a previous trip down, the passports were misplaced, and oddly, the officials in the customs office could no longer speak English. When Alex demanded to see the president of the small town, the passports were immediately found, and the crew members were released to sail for home. There was no problem with the passports this year, thankfully!

Lady in Blue was loaded with food, fuel, and supplies to last for the duration of the trip back to Alabama. We sadly watched and waved good-bye as our crew, and our beautiful sailing vessel left the Isla Mujeres harbor sailing back to America. All we could do was pray for our friends to have a safe voyage on the sea.

Later that afternoon, Alex's best male friend, Jon and my best girlfriend, Tina (who was conveniently married to each other,) Alex and I, all boarded our airplane to return home. It was a bitter-sweet experience. I was sad that the time-of-my-life had come to an end. Never-the-less, I was taking with me fond memories that I would cherish for the rest of my life!

Chapter 64 The Daffodils

Gift these cheery blooms to someone celebrating a new job, a new home, or a new addition to their family — daffodils stand for "new beginnings."

We landed in America just before midnight and made it back to my house in the early morning hours on that Sunday. We were glad to get home; Alex and I rested most of the day. Around three o'clock, it was time to pick up our fur-baby, Windy, from the trainer where she had been for the past ten days.

We dearly missed our little girl! When we arrived at the trainer's home, he was outside working with her. She was observing him and obeying his every command. When she looked up and saw us, she started whining for us, but she would not leave the trainer's side. I was proud of her accomplishments and obedience to him; but now it was time for me to take over! She was my puppy, and I was ready to love on her and have that sweet little puppy love and lick my face! At that time, I didn't give a damn what the trainer said! I went down to my knees, held out my arms, and said, "Windy. Come!" She broke loose from the trainer's leash and ran to us full speed! Right into mine and Alex's arms, she landed!

We laughed and cried in joyful reunion for quite a long time. She was excited and whining with happiness to be back with her family that she knew for sure loved her and cared for her more than anything in this world!

That night, you can bet she was right between Alex and me in bed . . . cuddled up tightly under Alex's strong arms. I was cuddled up with her on the other side. She was our baby girl, and we truly loved her!

**Windy lived to be fourteen and a half years old. God bless and rest our dear, sweet, *Misty Morning's Windy Rosenberg.*

The following Monday morning was back to the grindstone. Our time of playing and loving in paradise had come to an end. The reality of the real world was now settling in on me. It was now toward the end of May 1998. Alex and I had known one another since the spring of 1984. That was fourteen years, and our relationship had come a long way. He now was able to freely say, "I love you." I had been divorced for over a year, and he had been divorced for half a year. Still, there were no concrete plans for us to get married. It was true I thought Mr. Wonderful would never say those three little words, "I love you." Finally, he did, and I nearly fainted when he said it that afternoon with my husband only eight feet away. Now I was wondering if he would ever make the next move and ask me to marry him. It seemed like an eternity of playing this game with him. Then I remembered:

"Lifetime is a child at play moving pieces in a game. Kingship belongs to the child."
Heraclitus

I wondered who was moving the pieces in this game of life that I was playing. Was it Mr. Wonderful, or could it be me?

About mid-day, I received a phone call from Alex. In a simple sentence, he asked, "Do you think it would be alright if I stayed with you for a while?" My heart nearly exploded with joy as I said, "Of course!"

We were at a new beginning in this game of life that we were playing with one another. I then knew who was moving the game pieces and to whom the kingship belonged. It was Alex. Alex was the king who was moving the game pieces in our game of life. He was the manly leader that I had always wanted. Therefore, I did not begrudge him this power. He was the type of man who would do things in his own time; no one could force him into doing anything that he did not want to do. I was the one who had to gently persuade him to do those things and make him think it was his idea. . . without him knowing it. If I should force my views on him, he might reject them. I knew; however, I could always lovingly appeal to him and get what I wanted. If he thought something was the best for all concerned, he would think of the variables and discern the best move. He was like that.

That was Alex! Those were some of the reasons that I so loved him! He was seven years older than I, more intelligent and certainly more experienced in the ways of the world in which I had little experience. I knew I could depend on him to love and protect me. I could rely on him to make crucial decisions in our game of life. I knew I had definitely chosen the right man this time around. I just had to convince him that I was the right woman for him to spend the rest of his life with.

Although I did not have the opportunity to attend expensive private schools and I wasn't experienced in the finer things of life, as was Alex; what he didn't know was--what a savvy little gal he was dealing with. Yes, I had chosen, 'Mr. Right'. What he didn't realize--he was playing the game of life with 'Ms. Always-Right'!

"Much learning does not teach understanding."
Heraclitus

Eventually, we would learn who truly was moving the game pieces . . . king or queen?

Chapter 65 The Camellia

The camellia flower speaks to the heart and expresses positive feelings. Its most common meanings are desire or passion, refinement, perfection & excellence.

The lovely Camellia flower is the state flower of Alabama. It is an easy to grow evergreen flowering shrub of smoothly polished leaves with breathtaking beauty.

These attractive sweet flowers bloom from November to March, peaking in January and February.

This beautiful flower is *one of the reasons* why I love living in the south. The south has warm weather almost year-round and mild winters to afford lovely flowers to continue to grace the south with their beauty.

Warm weather is not the only reason I love living in the south. Life moves at a more peaceful pace here. The people speak kindly with refinement and gentility most of the time. I say most of the time; please don't get our good manners confused with stupidity. Just because we overlook other people's rudeness does not mean that we must stoop to their level of gross repugnance and reply with the same. Most of the time, we do not; that does not mean we did not take notice. We were just better self-controlled with our tongues. Sometimes.

I love living in south Alabama, which is about as southern as you can get. It opens to the Gulf of Mexico, which is heaven on earth for sailors like Alex and me.

The summer of 1998 was filled with sailing days and nights on *Lady in Blue.* Alex was excellent at sailing *Lady in Blue;* I went along as his first mate. We made a good team. From raising the sails, tacking, jibing and setting the anchor in the evening. We worked in unison with one another on the boat as well as we did while making love. There is a lot to be said about cruising topless on a sunny day with the wind in your face; sitting beside the man you love while sipping a refreshing glass of wine.

Windy had become quite an excellent little sailing companion. She thought the blue rubber dinghy was her very own small boat. When we stopped for the evening, we would set the anchor, drop the dinghy into the water, and take Windy ashore. The minute she saw Alex touch that dinghy, she would start yapping with excitement. She knew it was time for her boat ride to shore to run, chase birds and play. Alex was her boy and she had him wrapped around her little paw.

As Windy, Alex and I walked along a deserted sandy beach near sunset, I knew that was an experience I would never forget. It could never be replicated. It could only be held dear to my heart as another one of those best times of my life. Sadly, I could never go back to those exact precious days for:

"You can never step into the same river twice."
Heraclitus

After a late afternoon stroll along the beach, watching Windy chase the seagulls and sandpipers; we puttered back to *Lady in Blue*, where she was securely anchored for the night. A quick freshwater shower and we were set for the continuance of a lovely sunset and dinner aboard our beautiful sailing vessel.

Dinner was always something easy on the grill while dining outside in the cockpit. On that particular night, it was filet mignon with grilled zucchini, squash, onion, and carrots cooked together on the side (in foil). Green salad and French bread completed the meal. While Alex was grilling, we sat in the cockpit and listened to his favorite island music while watching the sunset and sipping our cocktails. Alex usually had Appleton Estate Rum with a splash of lime on the rocks. I always enjoyed a cool refreshing flute of champagne. What a relaxing evening. Windy was snoozing in the cool evening breeze as we enjoyed our dinner while sitting near the oil lamps.

Alex was always so helpful about cleaning up afterward. I never spent time in the galley or kitchen alone. I could not ask for a more loving and caring southern gentleman!

After the cleanup was completed, the night was still young. I went into my stateroom and freshened up, for I knew what was to follow. When I came out, he did the same.

The moon and stars were shining brightly on that clear, late September night. The boat was open as the fresh, salty sea breeze flowed through the hatches. Aaron Neville was singing "Don't take away my Heaven" through the boat stereo when Alex took me by the hand, and we began to slow dance together. . . very slowly and closely. He began singing along with Aaron Neville in my ear. Oh my! He could stay right on pitch! That was so damn sexy! Then he pulled me back and looked me straight in the eyes as he was singing the words:

Don't Take Away My Heaven
By Aaron Neville
Oh, baby, I found heaven when I found you
And this heaven is somethin' I don't want to lose
I only know that if you ever said goodbye, I couldn't

stand the pain
These eyes would cry, cry, cry like the rain
And the sun would have nowhere to shine
And the stars would all fall from the sky
Baby, please
Don't take away my heaven, oh, no
'Cause this world would stop turnin', I know
And I'd lose my whole world if you go
Baby, don't
Don't take away my heaven, oh, no……

When Alex stopped singing, we started kissing while continuing to slow dance to the music. That was the most salacious kissy-dance I had ever embraced! I couldn't help but reach and touch him through his shorts on his Big Boy. It was hard as a rock! I was delirious with desire to have him inside of me. We kept on slow dancing to the music as I caressed him more firmly. Eventually unzipping his shorts and taking him firmly into my hand, flesh-to-flesh. He sighed with pleasure as I stroked and squeezed him on the crown of his Big Boy. Our kissing was deeper and deeper, tongue-n-tongue. His mustache was teasing my little bird lips, giving me goosebumps down my spine. I slipped off my loose-fitting sun blouse, exposing my fully tanned breasts. My nipples were standing erect, luring him to come closer and taste the sweetness I was offering him. He lowered his head and started to suck on the left nipple. I groaned with pleasure, wanting more and more. He took more of me into his mouth and sucked harder and deeper sending waves of passionate desire down my belly, past my bellybutton and on to my clit. My clit was getting full and erect like a small little penis, just wanting and yearning to be tickled and touched. I was hunching back on him; my juices were flowing freely. I was wet and ready for my Big Boy. He took me by the hand and slowly led me to the stateroom and laid me on the bed.

Slipping out of my miniskirt, exposing my white lace bikini panties, I laid there, my back began to arch, projecting my breasts toward him. Watching him undress, my pelvis started to slightly hunch toward him, letting him know that I was craving his passionate, hard love-making that only he knew how to give me. Spreading my legs and bending my right leg upward, with my left hand, I slid my bikini panties to the side and with my right hand, I began to slowly caress my labia, unashamedly exposing it fully for his viewing pleasure.

He slowly continued to undress and stood beside the bed, watching me, wanting him. His bedroom eyes began to dilate. He had a slight smile as he watched me stroking myself, advertising myself to him. He too looked so damn good! His full hairy chest and mustache with his dark tan were driving me delirious with longing for him. He leaned into me and kissed me on the lips then he took over the stimulating and teasing me with his warm fingers on my clitoris. I spread my legs farther for a deeper massage, while I was rocking and hunching back to him. He laid beside me; his warm body felt good, I rolled over and got on top, placing my nipple in his mouth. He sucked harder and harder while still caressing my clit with his right hand. I was about to orgasm, but he wouldn't let me. He kept pulling back.

I kissed my way down his hairy chest, past his belly button, slowly licking, while brushing my long blonde hair back and forth on his belly as I moved down him. I kissed and licked my way all the way down until I got to my Big Boy. I took him in my hands, grasping him tightly and stroked it up and down. He groaned with pleasure as I took him into my mouth, flicking him with my tongue, sucking harder and harder around the crown and licking the back-side vein hard with my tongue up and back down, then back again and again. He seemed to get bigger and harder and redder the more I sucked and licked and flicked. I was sinfully driving him crazy, as he was me earlier. My tantalizing him was arousing me more and more.

When I could stand no more, I crawled up on him and took his Big Boy into me as deeply as I could, as quickly I could. I was wet, he slid into me with ease, hitting my G-Spot on the first glide. *Ahhh!* I sighed with ecstasy; hesitating for only a few seconds to squeeze him and savor the moment. I began to ride him up and down. Placing his Big Boy on my G-Spot every time I stroked him downward. I leaned down on my elbows with my butt upward and continued to pump and hump him. He was hunching upward to meet me. He didn't have to hunch too far, because his Big Boy was so damn, heavenly large! I was able to take in as much of him as I wanted and needed. He loved watching my face as I was enjoying myself getting all of him that I wanted and desired. He took my breast into his mouth and sucked it harder and harder.

Our pumping and hunching were heavenly intense! He was driving me crazy when he reached up and massaged my engorged clitoris! I climaxed like a wild-ass hyena! I screamed and tried to suppress it, but I couldn't. I didn't care, there was no one around to hear us. His release was explosive, hot, and long-lasting, as he filled me with his semen. It felt good; Big Boy got bigger and more powerful as he released inside of me. Alex groaned with pleasure over and over as we continued to hunch one another slowly to the loving end while staring into each other's eyes. My vulva was wet and dripping with my juices as well as his semen.

We rolled over from exhaustion. We were both breathing heavily, trying to catch our breath. The lovemaking with that man was so damn exciting! I am never going to stop having sex with this wonderful man!

Girls, I gotta give you a bit of advice. If you have a man like this that can make love to you and make you orgasm like that . . . <u>Don't dare go around bragging about him to your friends! They will try to steal him away from you every time!</u>

Chapter 66 The Holly

The holly represents the coming of joys.

My! How times flies! It seemed like no time and the holidays were upon us. Alex and I enjoyed a small Thanksgiving gathering with my son and his wife, also Alex's son and his girlfriend. Of course, Thanksgiving dinner was the usual menu with turkey and all the trimmings. I was slowly learning what a terrific gourmet cook that Alex was. He especially enjoyed cooking Creole and Cajun dishes. His Cajun cornbread dressing was absolutely out-of-this-world! We made a great team in the kitchen. We worked in unison chopping and dicing, then cleaning up as we went along. Yes,

Thanksgiving dinner was quite a joyous and pleasant experience with Alex in charge of the kitchen.

The Thanksgiving dinner was divine! At times we had to suffer through empty conversation with our young men the table. Nathan had never had a problem making friends and conversation with anyone. But it seemed that Alex's son, Chad, had little interest in making friends with his future stepbrother! It was bewildering to Nathan and me alike, why this young man wanted to act condescending toward Nathan. It was their first opportunity to meet one another. A person has only one time to make a good first impression. In this case, Chad blew his chance by acting like he wanted nothing to do with Nathan. We couldn't figure it out! Maybe it was because he was jealous that Nathan might take his place, which of course, he could never do. Nathan had a cordial and friendly relationship with Alex. Chad still had a sour and bitter attitude toward his father because his mother had taught him to do so. Bad manners never get anyone anywhere.

"You can get more bees with honey than with vinegar."

(Simply put, you can make more friends by being sweet and charming than you do by being rude.)

Chad still had a great deal to learn about getting along with others and making friends. As I stated in a previous chapter, the nut doesn't fall too far from the tree. He was very much like his mother.

Dinner was over in no time, and the sons were eager to go their separate ways. I was glad. It wasn't the most comfortable setting I had ever been in. Maybe time would bring the two together?

After Thanksgiving, it was time to plan for Christmas. The next day I began to decorate my home; I always enjoyed a real Christmas tree. Alex, Windy, and I went to the nearby tree farm, to pick out our first tree together. Windy was running and playing through the many rows of sweet-smelling fir trees. It was hard to keep track of her. We only had to find a child, and there she would be, enjoying a loving, friendly petting.

We found the perfect tree, a nine-foot, well-rounded fir. Alex had it delivered to my house that afternoon.

When it arrived, we had already re-arranged the living room furniture to make a spot for the tree beside the fireplace. The fire was popping and sparkling from the glow of the fresh smelling oak logs. The many boxes of decorations were brought down from the attic, and we were all set to start our annual project of decorating our traditional Christmas tree. Alex made hot rum toddies for our enjoyment as we worked together that evening. Alex wasn't interested in decorating that tree; I found out!

One hot rum toddy turned into several frozen Margaritas for me. I was really feeling the Christmas spirit, or maybe it was the spirit from those Margaritas? I was busy placing ornaments on the tree, when Alex took one out of my hand, laid it back into the box, and started to slow dance with me. He was looking me in the eyes when he said, "This is the best Christmas ever!"

I felt my Garden of Pleasure starting to throb with desire, lust, and want for his Big Boy. Alex kissed me long and hard with his tongue and mustache lovingly caressing my lips. His hand was stroking my neck as we continued to slow dance. I could feel through his trousers that Big Boy wanted to come out to play. Little Eva was anxiously inviting him into her Garden of Pleasure.

He slowly rubbed his hand up my leg to the top of my silk-lace-top stockings and unbuckled my red garter belt. My breasts started to ache for his touch, my nipples were hard and erect. I unbuttoned and slid out of my blouse so he could see what I wanted him to see, my red bustier. I slid the strap down, exposing my right breast as I arched my neck back with anticipation of his suckle. He read my sign and went down on me. Oh! It sent waves of electricity through me and down my solar plex as he sucked harder and harder, then on to the other breast. Wow! He could suck those babies so fine!

I took off his shirt, exposing his beautiful hairy chest that I loved so much! I rubbed my tits on his chest as I gazed into his eyes. He liked it; he smiled as he bit and sucked my left nipple again. We were both ready to enjoy one another. He led me over to the dining room table and lifted me up onto it. I laid back and he took off my skirt, exposing my red bikinis, red garter belt, red bustier and stockings. "Lady, you have got the most gorgeous body in the world." He said. "I want to make love to you every day for the rest of my life! I will love you forever!" Those words ignited my fire even more! I couldn't wait to get him inside of me!

I was lying on my back with my ass right on the edge of the table; he was standing. It was just the right height. He drew my knees up as he slowly entered me. I hooked my legs around his hips. Since he was standing, he could move almost any way he wanted. We were moving in concert with one another as he was stroking my clitoris with his thumb. Oh! It was heavenly. I wanted it to never end! Then he did something unexpected! He reached over and lifted me off the table! We continued to hunch and pump. It was the most exciting and surprising thing to ever happen to me. It was something that I had fantasized about, but never thought it would ever happen to me. But Alex was a big strong man, and I was small, so he could easily lift me and hunch at the same time. It was an experience that was out of this world! All I could do was hold on for the ride.

Our lovemaking was coming to a close when he laid me on the table again. Suddenly a feeding frenzy resumed. He was roughly rubbing my clit, and I was reaching for more and more, I couldn't get enough roughness as I began to orgasm! But---Wow! What was it that just spurted from my urethra? OMG! I think it was the first time I had an ejaculation! It was the best damn thing that I had ever experienced in my life! It came as a surprise! It was something that *just happened*---you cannot *make it happen*---it's a phenomenon!

Alex was right! It <u>was</u> the best Christmas ever!

Chapter 67 The Valerian

The valerian means---readiness.

It was February 1999 and Alex's 54th birthday. I had planned a birthday party for him that evening after work. Only a few close friends were invited, twelve to be exact.

The close friends were his crew members and their wives.

I made his favorite deep-chocolate-fudge-cake for his special day. Leaving the tempting cake sitting on the bar area of my kitchen, the delicious, sweet, aroma filled my small house. It wasn't a pretty cake, sitting lop-sided, but it smelled yummy; Windy thought so too. When I wasn't looking, she jumped up on a barstool and onto the bar. She had eaten almost half the cake before I knew what had happened. What wasn't eaten was scattered all over the bar and floor. Dogs are not supposed to eat chocolate. After forcing a couple of tablespoons of peroxide down her throat, she vomited up the cake, and she was fine. We were lucky it did no harm to her.

After that debacle, I rushed to the nearby bakery and purchased another generic birthday cake for the party. That cake was much prettier, but it was not as tasty as my deep-chocolate-fudge-cake. I know, because I had plenty to taste as I was cleaning up after Windy's private party. When Alex arrived home, he thought it was cute-as-pie that his little girl got the first and only slice of his birthday cake. I did not think it was so cute! Windy could do no wrong as far as Alex was concerned!

Heavy hors d' oeuvres were served at the party along with a variety of cocktails, mostly beer for the men. It was the first time I had the pleasure of inviting all of Alex's boat crew to my home for a small soiree. Everyone was having a light-hearted evening, joking and reminiscing about the fun times they had on boat races in the past and looking forward to future ones.

Everyone at the party was friends and had known each other for years. That meant everyone knew a lot about each other's private lives. Everyone knew about mine and Alex's secret love affair, which had gone on for years. It was no longer a secret. It was as if the whole world knew about us, and no one cared; it was our private business.

Our good friends Tina and Jon were among the invitees, as well as Sam and Leda. Out-of-the-blue, Tina did a "show-stopper." When the conversation came to a lull, she looked at Alex and asked, "When are you going to set a date for marriage?

My eyes widened, and I held my breath; the room fell silent. All eyes were on Alex. I almost peedinmypants and wasn't about to speak for him. He was in the hot seat, and Tina put him there. I was still holding my breath in anticipation of his answer when he said, "We're gonna elope!" That took the edge off the conversation, and we all laughed . . . sorta.

Tina further insisted, "No, you are not!" After all these years, you're not going to deprive us of an opportunity to have a party!"

"Yeah, we want a party!" Sam said. "And a big one at that, with lots of wine and beer!" said Leda.

Tina left the room in search of a calendar. She returned with my large desk calendar, and in front of everyone at the party, she handed Alex a magic marker and said, "set a date."

Remarkably, he took the marker from her hand, ready to mark a date. He looked over and motioned for me to join him. He asked, "What day would you like to become my bride?" "Today!" I answered!

"See, I told you we're going to elope!" Alex laughingly said to the crowd.

"No, you're not, we want a party to celebrate this special occasion! We have kept this secret for too many years! So set a date!" cried Tina.

Tina continued to encourage, "Here, I will make it simple, any time after April 15th. That way, tax season will be over, and we can all relax, settle down, and celebrate!"

Alex turned the calendar pages to April. The next Saturday after the 15th was the 17th. So there! That was simple! Alex signed mine, and his name on April 17th, 1999. Hooray! I wanted to kiss Tina! Instead, I put my arms around Alex and kissed him deeply as the party applauded.

Alex and I were both ready to get married, but I wasn't about to rush him into it by nagging. After all, it was not the first rodeo for either of us! It just took a little encouragement from a friend to get the ball rolling. It was the best thing for both of us. But, believe me, if Alex had not been ready for marriage, he would have never signed that calendar!

Lesson:

Girls never nag at your man. It will only turn him off, and he will usually do the opposite of what-ever-it-is-that-you-want-him-to-do. In my case, I wanted him to ask for marriage, but I could not badger him about it.

Another example: *You want your man to stop smoking.* If you nag at him constantly about it, it will be a source of irritation, and he will never stop doing it. But, if you say nothing, he will stop in his own good time. Believe me, he already knows of your displeasure.

In bed that night, we reminisced about the party and continued to make our plans for our wedding day. There were only eight weeks before the most important day of my life. All I could think about was the party, the dress, the ring, etc. Alex had bigger plans on his mind.

Alex said, "Now that you are going to be my bride, don't you think it would be a good idea if I bought us a bigger home?" *Oh Wow! Well. . . Yeah!* That was about the last thing on my mind at that moment.

We agreed to immediately put my house for sale and start building our dream home together. Because I had sold real estate while living in Birmingham, I knew the process and how to make the deal entirely from start to finish.

The next day I put a 'For Sale by Owner' sign in my front yard. Word got around fast! One of our single male friends from the yacht club had been working and living in Greece for the past two years and was now back in New Fort looking for a home. He asked if he might look at my house. Of course, I said yes. It was just what he wanted and needed, so we signed a contract that week. He went to his bank, and it was all set; we were to close the sale in March. He wanted immediate possession upon closing. I agreed. But where were we going to live until we got our new home built?

No problem. Alex talked to the board of governors at the yacht club and explained that we were to be married soon, and we were going to build a new home. He asked if we might be allowed to live aboard *Lady in Blue* until our home was completed. It was approved.

Not only did I have a wedding/party to plan, I now had to pack up my home and prepare to move. That was okay, I could do it! Life was moving at such a fast pace; I couldn't help but be elated! There was nothing to complain about; it was precisely what I had been waiting for! Could this really be happening to me?

I must be dreaming! Somebody pinch me and wake me up!

Chapter 68 The Spider Flower (Cleome)

The spider flower (cleome) means: elope with me.

You might think you have your man/rose tamed---but that doesn't mean you have him wrapped around your little finger! He is still a man, and he can always think on his own and make decisions for himself. Sometimes that means he can and will change his mind completely.

Life is never a bed of roses; remember, those rose blossoms have stems with many thorns that can prick at any moment!

Wow! Who could have thought a birthday party would have turned into an engagement party? It all happened so fast! Now there were only seven weeks left in preparation before our wedding day, the day that I had dreamed of for years!

But who could have predicted what was going to take place before the wedding?

Now that my house was in the process of being sold, the next item on the agenda was to buy an engagement ring. Not just any ole engagement ring mind you! I declared that it had to be extraordinarily beautiful and outstanding. A ring like that could not be found in the average jewelry store. Alex decided it had to be exceptionally handcrafted by a jeweler. A visit to our friendly home-town jeweler was the ticket. A two-carat diamond was the official engagement stone in the center, and one diamond for each year I had waited for him. The total was fifteen diamonds; fourteen smaller diamonds surrounded the one center engagement diamond.

I designed the mounting and called it *"As Love Grows."* Have you heard of an add-a-bead necklace, where you add a bead for different occasions until the necklace is full of beads? That was the same idea for this ring, only with a different twist.

The mounting looked like a closed flower. The flower opened as a diamond was added (on different occasions). Alex bought the fifteen diamonds, and everything was set for the jeweler to work his masterpiece.

Within a week the ring mounting was crafted, and the diamonds were set; the ring was finished and ready for delivery. The jeweler called, and I anxiously drove down and picked it up. When I tried it on, I was surprised to see that it took up half of my ring finger! Uh-Oh! *What the hell?* Not what I expected, but I loved it! I quickly put the knock-your-eyes-out-ring back into the beautiful velvet box and thanked the jeweler for a job excellently done.

When Alex came home from work that night, I told him about the arrival of our new treasure. He was anxious to see his investment. I handed the beautiful velvet ring box to Alex so he could place that gorgeous knock-your-eyes-out-ring on my finger.

He opened the box, his only comment was, "That's quite pretentious, wouldn't you say?" My heart sank.

"Uh-huh----and, I'm keeping it!" I put the knock-your-eyes-out-ring on my own finger and proudly wore it!

When Ms. "Let-me-tell-you-how-wonderful-I-am-or-who-usta-be" heard about my knock-your-eyes-out-ring, she commented, "it sounds as if it's *gouty*."

I told the person (who told me what she said) "Tell her------"it is gouty, and I'll bet her gouty ass wished it was hers!"

Next on my list was to find the perfect dress. White was out of the question; I was not going to pretend to be the blushing bride, but I did want to look elegant on this beautiful day when I was going to become "Mrs. Wonderful." I searched diligently for days. My first stop was in a-fancy-upscale-bridal-boutique. It didn't take long to figure out that I was not going to find my perfect dress among the hundreds of white-fluffy-ruffles-puffy-Disney-like-dresses displayed throughout the fine shop.

While in that exquisite boutique, I was made aware of how fortunate I was that Nathan was a son and not a daughter. I couldn't help but overhear the loud, argumentative conversation between Bridezilla and Mamazilla while choosing their perfect dress. It was not a pretty scene. Yes, the bride was beautiful, and she knew it. The family obviously had money to spoil their little princess and must have done so all her life. Sometimes it is a good thing to spoil your children, but when the tables turn—and that child demands more monetary luxuries from you, it is a different scenario. Bridezilla was pitching a fit with Mamazilla over which dress she wanted. Mamazilla wanted the princess-look, and Bridezilla wanted the sexy look. It was a no-win situation.

What was barely audible from Mamazilla's final words as they stormed out of the boutique were, "I don't believe in abortion, so I brought you into this world. You are not yet twenty-one and full-grown; I can still abort you anytime I want to. . . so you'd better watch your tongue, Missy!"

All I could think of was how thankful I was that Nathan was a boy instead of a girl. Had he been a girl, he most likely would have acted and talked just like me. And I probably would have aborted him too sometime around the age of thirteen years old!

Not finding my perfect dress in that bridal boutique, I visited another little shop called *Puttin' On the Ritz*. Evening gowns of all colors and styles were carried there. Not wanting anything too flashy, it took a while to find something bridal, not too sexy and yet classic. Since this was Alex's third wedding and my second, I didn't want to be flashy. I knew Alex would not like that.

There it was, what appeared to be the perfect dress. Very simple, formal length and form-fitting, sleeveless, low-cut in the front and dipping to the waist in the back. The baby pink silk fabric was beaded with white pearls all over. It fit as if it were made for me; it only needed taking in slightly at the waist. I had found the perfect dress that would make Alex proud to say I was his bride. When I told Alex about my new find, he acted a little weird when he said, "Baby, I thought we agreed this was going to be a simple wedding without all the fuss."
"It will be, I just want to look pretty for you."
"You always look pretty to me without all the extras," he said.

It was apparent the wedding day plans were not going according to Alex's expectations and his way of thinking. But I tried to put that out of my mind and hoped he would be happy with my plans; I found out I was wrong. I was beginning to think he honestly did want to elope (as he had stated previously) instead of having a wedding ceremony with our friends.

427

It wasn't long before my house closed, and Alex moved back aboard *Lady in Blue.* Windy and I temporarily moved into the guestroom at Nathan's and "Bride-number-two-hot-to-trot-n-hot-snot's" home.

Alex and I continued to make our home building plans. It was amazing how Alex and I were of like mind on decisions like finding a lot and choosing a suitable house plan. We agreed on the subdivision because we had friends living there and we liked the location. I would have been happy with a less expensive house, but Alex kicked it up a notch. He said we might as well get what we wanted, because it may be our last home. It made sense, so we agreed to build a larger home than what was needed. All of this was happening so fast, I couldn't believe my life was so happy. I did not feel that I deserved it, but there I was. . . with the man of my dreams, that I had yearned for and dreamed of---for years.

Windy went to work with me every day. She loved the customers, and they loved her. One of my best customers loved Windy; she made wedding cakes professionally. When she found out I was getting married, she insisted that she make our wedding cake. Any cake in her book that I wanted, she would make at no charge, just because she liked my dog and me. I was overwhelmed at her kindness; therefore, I did not take advantage of her generosity. I chose a simple three-tier vanilla and buttercream cake. She made it look gorgeous by adorning it with fresh pink roses. That was one more item off my list.

Leda and Sam lived in an upscale, gated subdivision with an elegant clubhouse over-looking the bay. The residents of the neighborhood could reserve the clubhouse for special occasions like weddings or parties. Leda booked their clubhouse for our wedding, and the clubhouse staff catered the food; that took a load off me.

There could not have been a more beautiful venue for our wedding day. The clubhouse had rustic cathedral ceilings, while the back of the clubhouse was all glass, facing the bay toward the setting sun. Tall double doors opened onto a pebbled-stone pavement that surrounded the crystal-clear oval swimming pool. A wrought iron fence surrounded the pool area and deck. Stepping down from the deck, was a long plank boardwalk which led to the pier and bay. The plan was for Alex to dock *Lady in Blue* at the end of the pier on our big day. *Lady Blue* was to be our escape to our honeymoon after the wedding.

Alex and I agreed we would only invite fifty of our closest friends and their spouses. When it came time to order our invitations, we found we had more invitees on our list than what we had initially agreed. Over two hundred to be exact. The list grew because our friends heard the good news that we were getting married and they wanted to come help us celebrate. How could I say no? Alex told me how I could---"Just say, 'No.'" He was irritated, I could tell.

One night after dinner aboard *Lady in Blue,* I was excitedly discussing what I had planned for the wedding/party, i.e., the clubhouse, the band, the food, the cake, the silver-free-flowing-champagne-fountain, etc.

All the intricate details were more than he was willing to accept. It was overwhelmingly boring to him.

"You have to remember; this is my third marriage and your second! You are making a spectacle of you and me, especially knowing our history. What will my parents think?"

Suddenly it dawned on me. *Yeah! It's all about his blue-blooded-high-society-family and keeping up their image in public!*

Not knowing what to say, I said nothing more. I realized that I had greatly displeased the man whom I loved and adored more than anything in this world! I wondered *if this was how my life would be as a married couple? Would he be finding fault with me in the future? He had never openly stated his disapproval of anything I had done in the past. Why now? Could this be his way of backing out of marriage? Maybe he really wasn't ready for marriage and Tina embarrassed him into signing the date on the calendar that night in front of our friends. Would I ever really be accepted into his socially elite family?*

The air was heavy between us, with neither of us speaking. I started getting ready to leave the boat and go back to Nathan's home, where I was living at that time. Windy wanted to stay with her daddy, but I made her go with me. As I was leaving his boat, I softly said, "I love you with all my heart, and I would never do anything that would embarrass you or your family. I'm sorry. We can alter the plans." He remorsefully said, "I love you too."

Chapter 69 Stephanotis (Madagascar Jasmine)

The stephanotis flower means happiness in marriage.

Windy and I left his boat and slowly walked down the dark pier, toward my car as I was silently crying, trying to hold back my tears. While lying in my little single bed that night, I cried myself to sleep, as I had done so many times in the past. Once again, I was totally unsure of my future with Mr. Wonderful.

The next day Windy and I heavyheartedly made it to my workplace. He did not call all day; I knew something was wrong! By days end, I was almost out of my mind, wondering what was going on in his head! I just couldn't force myself to call him. It was one of those things that I figured:

"A man's gotta do—what a man's gotta do."

I had to give Alex the space to do whatever it was that he had to do, for the good or for worse. I had to be patient and wait him out. Those thorns were unbearably painful!

The next day there was still no communication between us. I could not get out of bed, much less go to work. There was no need to call in sick, my partner was my son, so he let me have my privacy. Staying home all day, I was suffering from extreme heartache and extreme headache. My head was throbbing, and every time I tried to get up, I would get dizzy and nearly faint. I realized I was weak because I had not eaten in almost two days.

Sitting up in my bed, I had to once again regain my Warrior Princess attitude; it was easier said than done.

The first thing I had to do was eat, whether I wanted to or not. Getting out of bed slowly and carefully, I walked to the kitchen and opened a can of chicken noodle soup. It tasted good, although I could only eat half a bowl; it was a start. Getting a coke out of the fridge, I took two aspirin and shuffled back to bed. Windy faithfully followed by my side, she never left me during my sorrow.

The Warrior Princess within me rose up and began making plans for a brand-new future once again, with or without Mr. Wonderful. As I was lying there in my bed, I was thinking back over what went wrong between Alex and me. I couldn't help but know that we both deeply cared for and loved one another or we would not have made it thus far. Deep thinking and contemplating went on for the rest of that day. It was becoming crystal clear to me that I was more concerned with throwing a big party---and not listening to what Alex wanted. Not once did I listen to Alex when he hinted about the ring, or the dress, or the number of guests. After all, it was his wedding party also.

I decided I would halt all plans and say nothing to anyone about what had happened until I heard from Alex. I had no idea what he was thinking, but the ball was in his court. He knew from times past when things got testy between us, I would never call him; he had to be the one to call me. (Remember that little-deer-running-thing?) I would have to be patient and wait to see if his call would come through before the wedding date. I had done all I could do, so I slept and rested for the rest of the day.

The next day was day three of no communication with Alex; I was getting increasingly anxious to hear from him. But in my heart-of-hearts, I knew it wasn't the end. We had gone through much worse arguments in the past, and every time things worked out for the best. Windy and I went to work so I could pass the time and try not to think of him, try not to worry, and try not to cry. It didn't work, I did all three.

Around noon, what do you suppose happened? The front door of my store opened and,

"Here he comes again, lookin' better than a body has a right to. . ." (so the song goes)

I was mad; I was sad, and my heart was filled with joy. I ran to Alex, and we hugged and kissed. Windy was jumping up on him and yapping with glee to see her daddy. We were all three back in one another's arms, and I knew that whatever-it-was would be worked out satisfactory for all.

Taking the rest of that day off, we went sailing on *Lady in Blue.* It was a brisk and windy April day and a perfect day to be on the bay. The only sounds were the wind rushing through the mighty sails of our vessel and the seagulls as they flew by bidding us hello. Occasionally, a pelican would splash-land on the water as he caught his dinner. The westward afternoon sun was getting ready to set as we were dropping anchor at our favorite little island.

Alex and I enjoyed our afternoon libations in the cockpit as he grilled our steaks, and we discussed our situation. I said nothing about him not calling me, I did not have to. He brought it up in his explanation. I did not ask for an explanation, his guilty conscience offered it freely. I sat and listened attentively, careful to catch any lies. Not that he would tell me a lie, just that I am no fool, and I know a lie when I hear one.

Alex told me that after our last night together, he felt compelled to talk with his father. When he got to his family home, his father suggested that they go to their family's fishing camp for a few days, just to get-away. Alex agreed that he needed a few days to get his thoughts together and to receive counseling from his father.

Alex said it was the first time he and his father had a father-son talk in many years without his mother around to interrupt with her opinions. The father-son team fished a little, then cooked the fish for dinner each night. Of most importance, Alex was able to discuss his fears and concerns with his father. Alex was worried about what people would say and think of the family because of his third marriage.

By the end of their father-son-fishing-counseling-trip, Alex was feeling much better. His father wisely advised him that he had to "live your life for yourself." It did not matter what other people thought. Other people also have secrets in their lives that they are covering up, and they do not want other people to know!

His father said, "If you love that little girl and she makes you happy, go and make her happy. You'll never regret it."

Alex then said, "So, I'm here asking you to forgive me for hurting you and avoiding calling you. You can have whatever party you want Baby if you will just be my bride!"

I leaned in closer to him and kissed his lips softly and tenderly with all the love in my heart and soul. The party was no longer critical. It was all about us and making one another happy for the rest of our lives.

That night, we made love, long and tenderly in the stateroom of his beautiful boat, as the gentle sea breeze was blowing through the front hatch and Windy snoozed on the floor beside our bed. The stars were twinkling high above in the silent, black sky. When we finally kissed good night, the only sound, was that of the halyards swinging back and forth, tinkling against the mast, as the boat was rocking on the waves. I closed my eyes and was grateful to be back in the arms of Mr. Wonderful, the man of my dreams.

The Wedding Day

No further extravagant plans were made for the wedding day party. We went forward with the plans that were already in place and no more.

The only thing Alex had to do on the wedding day was to bring *Lady in Blue* around to the clubhouse pier and dock her, get himself dressed, pick up Windy from the groomer and get to the wedding venue on time.

I was getting dressed at Sam and Leda's lovely two-story home. My best friend and bookend from the Glee Girls, Barbie, was putting my hair up in a French-braid and helping with my makeup. Leda, Barbie and I were dressing, laughing, and sipping champagne. It was getting time to start the ceremony.

Sam was keeping a check on the guests at the clubhouse, making sure they received a glass of champagne or beer upon arrival. We told the guests that the dress was casual. I did not know how relaxed Alex told his friends to dress!

Barbie looked out the window as Alex drove up wearing a Hawaiian shirt and khaki pants. *What the fuss?* She opened the window and yelled down to him, "You'd better take it off!" I peeked to see his response. He just smiled and walked toward the clubhouse. Six others were standing outside waiting for him, wearing different colored Hawaiian shirts!

That was okay with me. . . I wasn't going to let that spoil my day! Just because I had on a gorgeous pink-silk-pearl-beaded gown and he wore a Hawaiian shirt! Who really gives a damn? It's a party! I asked Leda if she had a Hawaiian/Caribbean blouse that I could borrow. She said she did, and I put it on over my gown.

Nathan came for me when it was time to begin the ceremony. He was to escort me in and around the pool area, up to Alex and the clergyman. Nathan was not 'giving me away,' just accompanying me. There we went, me in my pink-silk-pearl-beaded-gown and Hawaiian blouse over it, with my son in his distinguished black suit walking around the pool. As we walked in, everyone laughed because they caught on to what was going on. As I was approaching Alex, I slipped out of the blouse, exposing that gorgeous gown.

The ceremony began. Alex and I had written our own private vows that we were to say to one another. The clergyman asks for Alex's first. It was so sincere and sweet, then I accepted his ring. Okay, my turn. I was so nervous I couldn't remember one damn thing that we had written. All I could say to him was, (in front of everyone who could not hear what I was saying) "You remember all that stuff we wrote down that I promised you I would do for the rest of my life? Well, I really did mean it, and I promise I will do it, but I can't remember what all it was, at this moment." He said, "Okay." We both laughed.

It was my turn to give him his wedding ring. What do you suppose happened? You guessed it! I dropped it! Not only did I drop it, but it rolled and rolled and rolled! And I chased it and chased it and chased it---in my gorgeous-pink-silk-pearl-beaded-gown-with-pink-dyed-stilettos! It was about to fall into the pool drain gutter when I finally was able to grab it. I thought I was going to have to make a crash-landing, or slide into first base to catch it, but I didn't.

Whew! I made it, and everyone laughed again as I embarrassingly tucked my head and walked back to my groom. Alex said, "You did that on purpose, didn't you?" "No!" I exclaimed!

After the ring debacle, the clergyman said a few words of blessings and a closing prayer. We kissed and were officially Mr. and Mrs. Alex (Wonderful) Rosenberg. It felt great! I was grinning from ear to ear for the rest of the evening. My cheeks were getting cramps in them from smiling so much!

It was a good thing I was ecstatic about the day. It may not have been a pretty scene, had there been a confrontation between "Bride-number-two-hot-to-trot-n-hot-snot" and me for her spilling red wine down the front of my wedding dress. The dress was so pretty; I wanted to wear it for the duration of the party. It was a disappointment to come out of it before our boat departure. Shortly after the ceremony, "Bride-number-two-hot-to-trot-n-hot-snot" stumbled and dumped a full glass of wine onto the front of my dress. A friend saw what happened and whisked me away quickly. My friend told me to take off the gown immediately so she could put it in cold saltwater; that would take out the wine stain. Doing as she insisted and changing into my going-away-outfit, my friend was right, the stain came out.

"Bride-number-two-hot-to-trot-n-hot-snot" apologized and all was well.

It was the happiest day of my life. The day I had dreamed of for years. Absolutely nothing could have spoiled it.

So many times, we prepare for the big wedding day and the party seems to be *the most important thing*. You know, it's not about the dress, the ring, or the party. It's all about the love between the bride and the groom.

When all the celebrating, dancing, hugging, and kissing our friends was over; it was our time to begin the first day of the rest of our lives together as husband and wife. After throwing my bouquet, Alex took Windy by her fresh-pink-rose-clad leash in one hand and me on his other arm. We smiled and waved good-bye to the most loyal friends in the world, who had stuck by us through thick and thin for fourteen-years. We then turned and walked down the pier to *Lady in Blue,* where she was waiting in the sunset to sail us away to our happily-ever-after-life-together as Mr. and Mrs. Alex (Wonderful) Rosenberg.

Dreams do come true; just follow your heart, and never give up!

Epilogue

After twenty years of marital bliss, Alex and I moved into another new home in lovely, warm southern Alabama. I was anxious to make new friends in this unique neighborhood. Although we had lived in New Fort for many years, this was on the northern side of town.

The property owner's association newsletter stated they were starting a garden club for the ladies which would meet monthly. That sounded like something I would be interested in because I was good at gardening and had a little knowledge on the subject. It would also be an excellent way for me to get to know the ladies in the new neighborhood.

The first meeting was, to put it mildly, not organized at all. I found myself in a room full of beautiful ladies of mixed ages, but mostly young. Each one was all-decked-out in her pretty fashionable summer attire. It reminded me of a younger me. I could see a little of me in every one of them. I watched each of them from a distance as they interacted with one another. None of them were listening to the other. Most of them only wanted to tell the other ladies "how-wonderful-she-was" and "how-wonderful-her-children-were." I could tell most of their stories were slight exaggerations. These ladies were married to successful, powerful men. They also were movers and shakers; they knew how to get things done in the community.

After the meet and greet, it was time to get down to the business part of the meeting. Everyone kept their champagne flutes and took their seats. I sat on the front row as I had always done in my younger years while in college because I was an excellent student. That day I sat on the front row because I was hard-of-hearing.

After a short time, it became apparent they did not know what direction to take to get this garden club organized. No one wanted the responsibility of presidency, because, at each meeting, this person would have to plan the program on gardening. It appeared no one knew a bloomin' thing about that subject. It was also evident to me that no one was really interested in knowing a bloomin' thing about gardening. These pretty ladies were not interested in a "Garden Club," they wanted a "Garden Party." It would be a great excuse to dress up, get together, sip champagne, and try to impress one another. They were off to a great start at that first meeting.

When it was apparent that no one was going to be nominated for president (being the shy little thing that I have always been), I decided to volunteer. I stood up and introduced myself. Being new in the neighborhood and one of the few older ladies in the group, I was well accepted and voted in as president. I was no threat to these lovely, rich younger ladies. They were glad to have me as their pseudo-leader; no one wanted the position anyway. Being simply their vehicle to keep the club going, I was happy to help. I thought, *Surely, some of them would turn into gardeners before the year was over.*

The meetings were set for the third Friday of each month, 10 o'clock at the subdivision clubhouse. A light cocktail brunch was the central interest, and extravagant free-flowing cocktails were of most importance.

At our first meeting, I wanted everyone to have an input as to what they expected and wanted from their club. So, I asked for ideas from the group. No one had any suggestions. Again, I concluded these girls only wanted to gather for the social event and have the opportunity to bloviate about themselves. Their conversations were like empty, tinkling champagne crystals. I was determined to break through all that and get to the "meat" of their conversations and find more depth.

Taking charge of the garden club/ garden party, I told the group I would begin each meeting by introducing a new flower, (since I had some experience in a variety of flowers and knew a little about each.) That idea sounded acceptable to the ladies. At least now they legitimately had a topic on gardening, a good excuse to party.

That short first meeting was adjourned, a few girls lingered and continued to sip champagne and talk about their love life and other private affairs, which was mostly bashing their husbands, (never a good idea!)

Listening quietly, I realized that this club was the perfect setting where I could collect data for my next book.

These young movers and shakers were successful at getting things done in the community. They appeared respected in the public's eye, but there were secrets as to *how they went about getting those things done* so successfully. Dirty little secrets they enjoyed while working behind the scenes on their volunteer projects. I would find out their secrets, which were all different.

Then I will share those dirty little secrets with you in my next book, *The Garden Club.*

After my term of service in the garden club had ended, looking back, I was wrong about *some of those girls* learning to be gardeners. But I do think some of those girls may have learned a little something about their "Garden of Paradise" that year.

Stay tuned for *The Garden Club.*

Appendix

References

https://www.hgtv.com/outdoors/flowers-and-plants/birth-month-flowers-pictures

https://www.flowermeaning.com

https://www.weheartit.com/articles/316249910-meanings-of-the-love-yourself-flowers

https://www.pinterest.com

https://www.goodhousekeeping.com/home/gardening/2503/surprise-flower-meanings

https://www.classicalwisdom.com/culture/quotes/

https://www.en.wikipedia.org/wiki/catbirdseat

https://www.blog.igmatrix.com/law-of-cause-effect

https://www.everydayhealth.com/columns/lauren-streicher-midlife-menopause-and-be

https://www.everydayhealth.com/sexual-health/sexual-dysfunction/testosterone-and

https://www.healthline.com/health/lowtestosterone/testosterone-levels-by-age

https://www.drtami.com.2014/04/04/the-untold-testosterone-story-for-women/

https://www.lyrics.com/

The Holy Bible, King James Version